Amy in the Attic

Michael Raine

To my Mother and Father.

1 MOVING

Toby Burrows was five years old when his Mum and Dad died.

He didn't know much about what had happened to them, but he knew they'd been driving and another car had hit theirs and killed them. It was a man who'd hit them. Toby sometimes wondered why the man had decided to drive into Mum and Dad's car but then he remembered that he couldn't ask him because he was dead too. You're supposed to feel sad when people die because it shows that you miss them, but Toby didn't feel sad when he heard that man had died. This was for two reasons. The first reason was that Toby had never met the man and didn't even know what he looked like, so he didn't have anything about him to miss. The second reason was that, because of that man, Mum and Dad were dead now. That was the only thing he was sad about; he didn't care about the man.

1

Toby didn't like getting in cars much anymore. He'd used to when he was younger, but after what had happened to Mum and Dad he'd never wanted to get in one again. They'd been dead for a while now. Toby didn't know exactly how long. It wasn't quite a year because he was still only five, but he still knew that it had been a long time. Even so, Toby still got scared being in cars, scared that someone would hit and kill him, but he was in one now and he didn't mind it too much. He was in the back of the car, sitting on a booster seat and looking out of the window. It was raining outside and water slid down the glass as he watched. Toby watched as little drops ran all the way down from the top of the window to the bottom. He liked doing that when he was in the car. He would find two drops that were close to each other and see which one would reach the bottom first, like a race. After looking for a while, he found two at the very top of the glass. One drop slid straight down in a long line, not turning at all, whilst the other one twisted and bumped its way to the part of the window where the glass hit the frame. Toby looked at the one going straight and watched it slide down to the very bottom and break up as it hit the frame. That drop had won. Toby tried to find the other drop again, the one that was going off to the side, but he couldn't see it. It was like it had vanished or maybe he'd just lost it.

After getting bored with that game, Toby decided to have a look at his reflection in the window. There was nothing else to do. He couldn't see himself very well because of the rain, but could a little bit. He had a round face, which was weird because the rest of his body was skinny, and big cheeks that were very red because of how cold the car was. His hair was brown and shaped like a bowl on top of his head. Toby knew that it looked silly but he liked how it looked. Apart from that there wasn't much else to see. His mouth was normal, his nose was normal and the little tops of his ears that poked out from underneath his hair looked very normal indeed. Toby sighed and looked away from the window.

There was music playing in the car. It was a strange music that Toby didn't like very much, but he wasn't really listening to it. He knew it was playing but he didn't really care. Even so, Toby did notice when a big strong hand reached across the car and pressed a button that turned the music off completely. The person in the front of the car, the one driving it, was called Daniel. Daniel was Toby's brother and was much bigger than him. Mum and Dad had been quite old when they'd had Toby but they weren't old when they'd had Daniel. Daniel was much older than Toby. In fact, Daniel was fifteen years older than Toby. Toby began to watch his big brother. Daniel and Toby were very different. Toby was small, skinny and quiet. Daniel wasn't any of those things. He had short hair, really short, that was really scratchy and prickly to touch. His body was different too. Daniel had really big muscles, much bigger than Toby's. Sometimes it made Toby feel sad because Daniel was big and strong and he wasn't which wasn't fair. Even though Daniel was big and strong and looked like a giant, he was never mean to Toby. In fact, Daniel was nicer to Toby than a lot of people were. Mum and Dad had used to make him do stupid things like make his bed and pick up his stuffed animals which he didn't want to do, but Daniel had never made him do anything like that. He was always nice and happy and had a big smiling face, even when things were bad. Now that Mum and Dad were dead they couldn't look after Toby so that meant that he had to live with Daniel which Toby didn't mind. He was used to spending time with Daniel and he liked it a lot. He couldn't remember spending much time with Daniel when he was younger because Daniel had lived in the city and had a big important job that meant he didn't have much time for anyone. But, after Toby turned four, he got to spend more time with Daniel. Daniel said that he didn't have to work as much which was brilliant. Sometimes, Toby had even been able to stay over at Daniel's flat in the city and Daniel had even decorated a room especially for him to sleep in. Toby had liked that room, a lot.

There was a sneeze in the seat next to Daniel's. It made Toby jump because it was so loud and he hadn't expected it. Toby thought Karen had been asleep and he didn't think that people could sneeze when they were asleep but Karen just had. Karen was Daniel's girlfriend and she was going to be living with them because she and Daniel were going to get married. Daniel had told him they'd met in a bookshop but Toby wasn't sure if that was true because Daniel didn't read much. Toby liked Karen. She had a long pointy nose, like a bird, that stuck out in front of her. She also dressed differently to everyone else. She usually wore blue jackets and white t-shirts that made her look like a rock star. Not only that, but she would always have loads and loads of bracelets and rings that jangled as she walked and sounded awesome. She was also the only person that Toby knew with blue hair. He'd never known that people could have hair that colour and when he'd first met Karen his mouth had dropped wide open because of how cool it looked. It wasn't very long, it only came down to her shoulders, but it was still the best hair that Toby had ever seen.

But, even though he thought Karen looked cool, he still wasn't sure if he liked her that much. She always used to play with him and Toby loved how fun she could be, but it felt different playing with her. Daniel was Toby's brother but he didn't know Karen that well and, even though he still liked her, he wasn't sure how much. Not sure at all.

Still, he'd had a lot of really good times with her. After Mum and Dad had died, Toby had gone to live with Daniel and Karen in Daniel's flat. Daniel's job meant that he wasn't around during the day and, because Toby didn't have to go to school after what had happened, someone had to look after him. This meant that Karen, who didn't have a proper job, had stayed at home with him. Toby hadn't minded that, but he hadn't really cared either. After Mum and Dad had died, he'd stopped caring about a lot of things and just spent most of his time in his room. He'd think lots of thoughts about Mum and Dad when he was there, bad thoughts that he couldn't push out of his brain. They were always bad when he stayed in his room but he still never wanted to leave it. The inside of his head had become like what happens to a light bulb when you turn off the switch. Everything had gone dark.

The only person who tried to help him when he

thought those thoughts was Karen. She'd knock on the door and ask if she could come in. She had a nice voice, a sweet one. If Toby said yes then she would push the door open slowly and poke her head around the edge, her eyes wide and bits of blue hair falling in front of her face. She looked funny when she was like that, but Toby never laughed. Then she'd come in and smile at him. Her smile was a big one and she had big teeth. Sometimes Toby would try and smile back, but it was never a proper smile.

She'd always ask him to do something when she came in. Toby could tell that she didn't want him to stay in his room all the time. He never really wanted to do anything but Karen was always so nice to him, so he usually did what she said.

'Want to play a game?'

'Want to help me cook lunch?'

'Want to help me paint?'

That was his favourite. Even though Karen didn't have a real job, she still said that her job was being a painter. She didn't paint very much, but when she did she always asked Toby to help and, unless the bad thoughts in his head were really bad, he would always say yes. In the flat there was one big long window that always had loads of light coming through it. This was where Karen did her painting. There was a big stand called an easel with a comfy brown armchair sitting in front of it. The easel, a word that Karen had taught him, was where she put the painting. She was always stuck on the same painting and it stayed that way for a long time. At first the painting wasn't really anything, just a big white square of nothing. Karen said this square was called a canvas and that was what you had to do the painting on.

'What's it going to be?' Toby had asked as the two of them sat in the armchair. He'd liked that armchair, it had been nice and comfy but a bit small which meant that he always had to sit on Karen's lap. They didn't have that armchair anymore;

Daniel had sold it.

'A bridge,' she'd told him. 'A big stone bridge over a little stream of water. It'll be cute.'

'That's boring,' he'd mumbled.

That had made Karen laugh.

'It won't be boring!' she'd said. 'It'll be the best bridge in the whole world and we'll have made it. All we've got to do is paint.'

And they did. It had taken them a long time but, when they'd finally finished it, Toby knew that he'd been wrong. It wasn't a boring bridge; it was a brilliant bridge, the best bridge in the world even. It had big grey bricks that looked even better than real ones and the whole thing went up in a curve over a stream. The stream was filled with water that looked just as good as real water. It was the best bridge in the world and, even though Toby never really felt happy anymore, when he saw that bridge and how brilliant it looked, he felt a little better inside. Karen still had that painting and it was going to come to the new house with them but not in the car. It had been put in a box and was going to be dropped off with all the other stuff tomorrow.

It was raining hard now. Toby could hear it against the car windows. It was getting louder and Toby could only just make out the sound of the windscreen wipers over it. That's how loud it was. Even the swish-swoosh of the windscreen wipers was quiet compare to that. Toby looked out at the road in front of them. It was long and wet and grey and there were lots of cars driving down it. Sometimes a car would get close to theirs and spray water up across the windows which made it even harder to see. It was a horrible day.

'Are you okay there, Toby?'

Daniel was talking to him from the front seat. He sounded happy but that's because he was trying to sound happy. Grown-ups do that sometimes. Toby didn't really want to talk so he just nodded. He didn't know if Daniel had seen him because he was looking out at the road but he didn't say anything else so Toby thought he must have done. The car stayed quiet for a while after that so Toby laid his head against the window and went back to playing the rain game. It wasn't until a long time later that something happened. After ages and ages of driving down the same long straight road, Toby heard Daniel flick something attached to the steering wheel which made a tick-tock sound like a clock. As Toby listened to the tick-tock sound he felt the car moving to the side, just a little bit at first but then more and more until they weren't on the big road anymore. Instead, they were on another road, a smaller one that was going up like they were driving up a hill. Toby felt a pain in his tummy. He was nervous and wasn't quite sure where they were going. Then, as the road stopped going up and started to go flat, he felt the car turn.

Toby pulled his head away from the window. As he looked out at the road, he saw how different it was to the one they'd just been on. This road was still long but not as long as the other one and it wasn't as grey either. In fact, Toby could see loads of big fields all around him, filled with the greenest grass he'd ever seen in his life. He could even see a few big black and white cows lying down on their bellies. This was a much more interesting road than the other one had been. He should have felt excited, and he almost did for a little bit, but then he noticed the rain again and that stopped him.

'Toby.'

He turned his head towards the sound of his name. Looking at him in the little mirror that hung above the windscreen, Daniel was staring at him, smiling and pointing out at the road in front. Toby sat up in his seat and stretched his neck to try and get a better view. Finally, after a lot of fidgeting and squirming about, he managed to get a good look out at the road and what he saw made his eyes go wide.

Down in front of them was a place. Toby didn't know what to call it. It was too small to be a city, like where Daniel had lived, but he could still see lots of little houses. They were far away and looked much smaller than they should have done and they were all built around the long road. This particular road ran right through the middle of the place and, from what Toby could see, it looked like the biggest houses were built closest to it. He could just make them out. They were much bigger than the others and were all attached to one another, sharing the same brown roof. Toby looked around, trying to see if there were any other places nearby, but there weren't. The only things he could see were fields and this place. It was completely alone.

'Here we are,' said Daniel, his voice happy and excited. 'Lawton. Our new home.'

That last part sounded weird to Toby. It was strange thinking about how they were a family now and even stranger to think that Mum and Dad weren't going to be part of it. The only people that Toby had in his life were Daniel and Karen, and Karen wasn't even part of the family. She would be soon though, when she and Daniel got married. Daniel had asked her just before Mum and Dad had died but they still hadn't had a wedding yet.

It wasn't long before they reached the first houses. As he stared out of the window, Toby saw a brown sign standing next to the road. It was a new sign, one that looked very shiny, and it had some words printed on it that Toby couldn't read. Behind the sign stood the houses. They were all old fashioned and were all very small. They were all joined together in one long line so that it looked as though they were all one house but Toby knew that they couldn't be. Nobody had a house that big and there were lots of doors. That meant that they were lots of smaller houses instead of one big one.

Toby spent a long while thinking about the houses and by the time he'd gotten bored of that, the car was in a completely new part of Lawton. Now they were in the middle of that long road he'd seen when they'd been looking down at Lawton. It was a wide road and it looked even wider because there weren't any cars on it except theirs. On both sides of the road there were shops. They weren't big ones like supermarkets, instead they were little ones that didn't look like they had much in them. Most of them had their curtains closed too, whilst the others had big metal sliding things pulled down in front of them. Toby didn't know what any of these shops sold but he knew that it wouldn't be anything interesting. He didn't like Lawton so far. It was ugly and wet and empty. The place scared him and he didn't like that.

Because of the rain there were a lot of puddles on the ground. Some of them were little but some of them were big like lakes. As Daniel drove, the car went through a huge puddle that splashed water all up the front of them, so much water that Daniel had to slow the car down. It was a loud splash and it was so loud that it woke Karen up from her sleep.

'Where are we?' Toby heard her ask. She sounded very tired.

'Nearly at the house,' Daniel replied, his voice starting to sound tired too. 'I've just got to find the turning.'

'Is that it? The one up ahead?'

'Ah yes. Right there.'

Toby felt the car slow down and start to turn. The car journey had been long, very long, but it was almost over now and Toby was finally going to see the new house. He didn't know what it looked like. Daniel had wanted to show him pictures on the computer but Toby hadn't wanted to see.

The road they were driving down now was smaller than the last one. As he looked out both sides of the car, Toby saw tall brown fences stacked on top of long stone blocks that continued all the way down the road. Above them, past the tops of the fences, Toby could see the tops of other houses, ones that weren't on this road and faced away from the car. Toby felt the car start to bump up and down. There were lots of holes in this road, holes that were filled with water.

They weren't driving down the road for very long before Daniel spoke again. He lifted one hand off the wheel and pointed out the windscreen at something Toby couldn't quite see. When he spoke he sounded happy, like he'd seen something very exciting.

'There it is!' he said. 'Our new home!'

Toby stretched his neck as he tried to get a look at the house but he still couldn't see anything. The rain didn't help either, there was too much of it and that made it even harder to see. But, just as Toby was about to give up looking, he finally saw what Daniel had been pointing at.

Near the end of the road, off to the side, was another little road. This wasn't really a road, it wasn't long enough, but it was almost one. As the car began to slow down, the not-road got closer until the car was right next to it. What Toby saw next was very strange.

The shape of the not-road was something that he hadn't ever seen before. It was like a half circle and in the half circle there were three houses, one on the left, one on the right and one in the middle. They were weird houses. They were white with black tops but none of them looked like they had an upstairs. Toby had seen houses like these before and Daniel had told him that they were called bungalows. The one in the middle had a very tidy front garden with a gnome standing out in it and, even though the curtains were shut, Toby could still see some light coming though from the inside. The house on the right was basically the same. The only house that was different was the one on the left, the one closest to the car. The house on the left didn't have any lights on and the front garden was covered in grass that was much too long. As Toby looked, he saw that the house had one big window right next to the front door but, unlike the others, this window didn't have the curtains shut. Toby found it hard to see in because the rain was so bad but he could just make out an empty room with a little kitchen at the back of it that had lots of cabinets. Toby looked at the house in the middle, then he looked at the house on the right. Then, with a deep breath, he turned his head and looked again at the house on the left. He knew which one was theirs.

'Here we are!' cheered Daniel, as he turned the car into the not-road. The house on the left had a little driveway next to the garden that was filled with gravel and, as the car turned once more, Toby heard little stones crunching underneath the wheels.

'Our new home! Shame about the weather though, isn't it, Toby?'

Daniel had turned off the engine and was looking over his shoulder. He was trying to get Toby to talk, he did that a lot, but Toby didn't want to talk. Instead, Toby just gave a kind of half-smile that wasn't really a smile but showed Daniel that he wasn't ignoring him. Daniel sighed and opened the car door. With the door open, the rain sounded even heavier and Daniel got soaked the second he stepped out onto the drive. Toby watched through the window as his brother ran along a little stone path towards the front door of the house. As Daniel struggled with the lock, Karen, who'd been watching with Toby, began to speak.

'He is funny, isn't he?' she laughed. Toby didn't say anything, he just kept on watching. By the time he'd finally got the door open, Daniel was drenched with water and Toby could hear his shoes squelching as he made his way across the path and back to the car.

'Come on!' he yelled from outside, just loudly enough for Toby and Karen to hear him. Un-buckling her seat-belt and taking a deep breath, Karen opened the door and stepped out into the rain. Then, covering her head with her hand so as to keep the rain off, she ran around to Toby's door and opened it for him.

'Come on, Toby!' she shouted over the noise of the rain. 'Let's get you inside!'

Toby knew he should be moving. The open door was letting cold air into the car and he knew that he'd feel so much warmer when he was inside the house, but for some reason he stayed still. Maybe it was because he was scared or maybe it was because getting out now would make it all real. If Toby got out, everything would change and that made him very nervous. He could feel his face starting to scrunch up sadly. He tried to stop it, to make his face look normal again, but it was too late. Karen had seen it and knew instantly that he was upset. With a little smile that only came across half of her mouth, Karen un-buckled Toby's seatbelt and picked him up in her arms. As she closed the car door and carried him across the stone path towards the new house, Toby nuzzled his face in close to her shoulder. For a second, he stopped thinking about everything and just held on tight as Karen took him closer and closer to his new home.

Toby heard the sound of a door closing. He was inside now, inside the new house. He wasn't quite sure if he wanted to look, to lift his head away from Karen's jacket, but he guessed he had to at some point, so he decided to get it over with quickly. He lifted his head, rubbed his eyes and took a look around.

They were in a room, a room that was almost completely empty. Apart from the kitchen at the back which Toby had seen through the window, there was nothing at all. The room was in two parts. The first part was the living room, or at least Toby guessed it was a living room. This part had dirty green carpet on the floor which had lots of brown and red stains splattered over it. This part of the room was empty. The second part of the room was the kitchen part. This part had green cabinets that were old and wooden and had bits of paint peeling off. Between the first part and kitchen part, there was a long counter with a dirty white top that looked like it was for putting food on. The whole room was old, dirty and, most importantly, empty.

'The movers will be here tomorrow,' Daniel told Karen, pulling two dirty green curtains across the front window, 'In the meantime we'll just have to get on with it.'

The room looked darker now that Daniel had closed

the curtains, but there was still some light coming from above them. Toby looked up. Hanging from the ceiling by a short piece of white cord was a light bulb. It was completely still and flickered every few seconds which made Toby's eyes ache. He didn't like that it did that, so he looked away.

'Is it okay if I put you down now?' Karen whispered into Toby's ear. Toby nodded and she placed him carefully onto the carpet.

'Shoes off, Toby,' Daniel told him, pointing at his wet red trainers. Toby looked up at Karen. She bent down onto one knee and undid his laces, taking his shoes off and putting them down beside a box that was sitting by the front door. That box was the only thing, apart from clothes and a few other things, that they'd brought with them in the car. Toby didn't know what was in it but he didn't really care enough to look at the moment. He scrunched his toes into the carpet. It was hard, not soft like the one Mum and Dad used to have.

'Let's have a look at your room!' Daniel said happily, grabbing his little brother's hand tightly and pulling him across the room. As Daniel dragged him, Toby noticed something that he hadn't noticed before. Between the kitchen and the living room there was an open door that lead into a hallway. It was a dark hallway and Toby wasn't sure whether or not he wanted to go down it but by the time he'd thought this he was already right in front of it. Toby looked up at Daniel. His brother was feeling along the wall, trying to find a light switch. When he finally found it after a long time of looking, Toby heard a click and all of a sudden the hallway lit up.

As he looked down it, Toby realized that the hallway wasn't very long. Even Toby, who wasn't very tall and didn't have very long legs, could probably have walked to the very end and back whilst holding his breath without it being too hard. There were four doors attached to the hallway, two on each side. They were big doors made of wood with big round doorknobs and they all looked very old. Toby could see dents and scratches and holes that made him wonder who could have lived in this house before them. Toby looked up at Daniel, who smiled and pointed to the closest door on their left.

'This is your room,' he told him. 'Would you like to have a look?'

Toby didn't really know if he did want to look. The whole house made him feel weird. Toby didn't know what had happened here but he knew it must have been something bad. Still, even though he wasn't sure, he still looked at Daniel and nodded.

'Great! Come on then.'

Daniel went first. He walked over to the bedroom door and, after struggling for a few seconds, pushed it open and walked inside.

'Come on!' he told Toby, waving him forward with his hand. Toby looked down at the floor. The floor in the living room had been carpet, except for the kitchen bit, but the hallway had something different on the floor. Instead of an old stained green carpet, this part of the house just had long pieces of wood covering the floor. It looked very cold and, as Toby was only wearing his socks, he wasn't quite sure if he wanted to step onto it. After taking a deep breath, Toby placed a foot onto the wood. It was cold, but not as cold as he'd thought it would be, so he took another step and then another until he was almost inside the bedroom. Then, out of the corner of his eye, he saw it. He hadn't meant to see it and, if he hadn't been so slow getting across the floorboards, maybe he wouldn't have seen it until much later. Still, that wasn't what had happened and he could see it now.

In the middle of the ceiling there was a little wooden square. Toby didn't know what to call it. It was like a trapdoor, except he was looking up at the bottom of it. He'd seen something like that before, in Mum and Dad's house. In Mum and Dad's house, it had been the way up to the loft, at least that's what he thought it had been called. Dad had always called it the loft but Mum never did. Mum had always called it the attic. The square was just sitting there. It wasn't open and looked like it was closed pretty tightly. Toby turned his head to get a better look, but then he realized there wasn't much else to see. It was just a wooden square in the ceiling that went up into the loft or attic or whatever it was called. There were only two other things that Toby thought were interesting about it. One was the piece of string. Hanging from the square and dangling just a little too high for Toby to reach was a piece of white string. There wasn't much interesting about the string, it was just something that was probably used to open the attic, but there was one thing about it that Toby found odd. As he watched the piece of string carefully, he saw that it seemed to be moving, swaying back and forth like it was being pushed by the wind. Toby found that very odd. There wasn't any wind in the house, not any he could feel, but it was still moving. To a lot of people this might have been the strangest thing about the square but not to Toby. As he looked longer and harder at the square trapdoor, Toby noticed some little marks on it. They were black marks, marks that Toby could see all over the white wood, but he wasn't quite sure what they were. He'd seen marks like this before; he knew he had. They looked like smudges, big black smudges. They reminded him of the time a policeman had come into school and put black ink on everyone's fingers to show them how they catch people who do bad things by checking their finger...

'Hurry up, Toby!' Daniel's voice called from inside the bedroom. Toby looked away; the marks were probably nothing.

As he stepped into the bedroom, Toby's first thought was that it was very dark. In fact, the room was so dark that Toby couldn't actually see Daniel at all. Well, that wasn't really true. He could see him a little bit, like a shadow, but not really. There were two bits of light in the room. One bit of light came from the hallway through the open door. The other bit came in through a big window on the far side of the room. It was a huge window and, even though it was covered, glowing light was still coming through. This was because,

15

instead of curtains, the window had two pieces of thin cloth covering it, cloth that was so thin that Toby could actually see through it. There wasn't much out there, in the garden behind the window. All Toby could see was a gigantic black hedge. Toby watched it for a second, staring at it through the thin cloth, but then he decided he didn't really like it, so he turned away. The rest of the room was pretty empty, like the rest of the house was, but there were a few things in it. There was an old bedframe made out of wood with a yellow mattress lying on top of it. Across the room from the bed there was a wardrobe but it wasn't like any other wardrobe Toby had ever seen before. In Toby's head, wardrobes were big and tall and made of wood and had little legs that they stood on so that they didn't fall over. This wardrobe was big and tall and made out of wood but it didn't have any legs. Instead, the wardrobe filled the entire side of the room, like a wall, which Toby thought was very weird. Like everything else in the house, the wardrobe was very old and, even though it was dark, Toby could see parts where the white paint had started to peel away from it. The doors of the wardrobe were strange too. They weren't like normal wardrobe doors because these ones had long slits in them. As he stared, Toby realised that if he looked at it just right he could actually see inside the wardrobe. Toby strained his eyes, trying his hardest to see what was inside, but he couldn't see anything except for the back of the wardrobe.

Apart from that, there wasn't much else in the room. There was no toy-chest, no book-shelves, nothing. Just a bed and a wardrobe and nothing else. Toby sighed. He didn't like this room. Maybe there was another one he could have. Maybe Daniel and Karen would swap with him. Toby liked that idea but he knew it would never happen. This was his room now and he couldn't change that.

'The lights don't seem to be working here,' Daniel muttered as he flicked the light-switch on and off. 'I'll fix that soon.'

Toby tried to smile but failed.

'You feeling okay, Toby?'

'Uh-Huh.'

'You sure?'

'Yep.'

Toby heard a shuffling noise. Turning around so that he was facing the open door, he saw Daniel walking over to him, his brother's big feet making a weird sound as they dragged across the carpet.

'It will be okay, Toby,' Daniel whispered, crouching down so that he and Toby were the same height. Toby liked it when he did that, it didn't make Daniel look so gigantic. He still couldn't really see his brother, it was too dark, but a little bit of the light from outside now shone across him.

'We will make this work, Toby. It might not feel like it now but I'll make things better for us. I'll do my best, I promise.'

Even though Toby still couldn't see him properly, he could tell that Daniel was smiling. More than that, Toby could even tell what kind of smile it was. It wasn't a happy smile, the kind of smile that you make when something really good happens, it was the sort of smile that you make when someone is hurting. The smile you make to let them know that things will be okay. That was the smile Daniel was smiling and it made Toby feel just a little bit better.

Daniel's head turned left and right as he looked around the dark room.

'Are you going to be okay sleeping in the dark tonight?' he asked.

Toby froze up a little. He didn't want to be in the room at all, let alone in the dark. He felt his teeth chattering inside his head. He couldn't stay in here, not in the dark.

Toby wasn't sure how he did it. Maybe his brother

was just psychic or something, but he knew that Daniel had figured it out. He could tell how Toby was feeling. With a little sigh, he rubbed his shadowy face with a thick hand and turned his head over his shoulder to face the door.

'Karen?' he shouted, his voice croaky and tired. 'Do you have the nightlight?'

Toby had a hard time sleeping that first night. It hadn't taken Karen long to find the nightlight but even with it's white glow the room still felt much too dark. He hadn't had dinner until late so that meant he'd had to go to bed when it was much darker than he was used to. As he lay there in his new bed, on top of some old sheets Karen had brought with them and with only a thin blanket to keep him warm, Toby began to feel colder than he'd ever felt before. Holding on tight to his spaceman pyjamas, he curled up in a little ball and tried his best to stay warm.

'The heating will kick in at some time after ten.' Daniel had told him. Well, Toby knew it was well past ten now because Daniel and Karen had gone to bed a long time ago and the heating still hadn't come on. Toby's nose was starting to go red from the cold. He sniffed. He didn't like how this old house smelled. It smelled like old people and old things and Toby didn't like that one bit. It wasn't the same as his old house, the one he'd lived in with Mum and Dad. He missed that house, missed how warm it was even in the winter. That house hadn't smelt like old people; it had smelt like Mum and Dad. Still, even though he missed his old house so much, that wasn't what he missed most about how things had been before. He shut his eyes tight and saw them there, standing right in front of him. Mum was with him, her round face smiling and her arms stretched out towards him. Dad was there too. Toby could see him there right next to Mum, his bald head shining and his old wrinkled face smiling at him just like Mum. They were both there, smiling at him like nothing had happened at all and Toby never wanted them to go. He didn't want to open his eyes; he just wanted to stay with them.

Toby heard a sound and opened his eyes. Sitting up with his back against the bedframe, he saw that, even though the room was dark, it wasn't as dark as he'd thought. Even though it was very late at night, he could still see a little bit of light coming through the cloth and into the room. He looked at the window, to see where the light was coming from, but there wasn't anything outside except the hedge. It must have been the moon, that was probably it, just the moon shining in. Toby should have felt safer but he didn't, not one bit. He kept on looking, looking out the window at what was outside. But this time he wasn't looking for where the light was coming from. He was looking at the hedge.

He watched the hedge, the big black hedge that filled up the whole window frame except for a little line of night sky above it. Toby didn't like this hedge. As he looked into it, between the leaves and the branches, he thought he could just make out two big eyes, red and angry like monster's eyes, staring back at him. Maybe they weren't real or maybe they were, but Toby could still see them looking at him, waiting for him to fall asleep. First, the monster would climb out of the hedge, then it would slide through the window and stand by his bed, looking over him like how you look at food before you eat it. The monster would swallow him whole and spit out his bones. That was how they did it.

Toby looked away; he didn't want to think about being gobbled up. If he didn't think about it, maybe it wouldn't happen. Maybe the monster would go away. He stared straight ahead, trying his best not to look back at the hedge, and focused on the long wardrobe on the other side of the room. Toby hadn't realized how big it really was. He'd known it was big but looking at it now he realized that not many people had a wardrobe that filled up a whole side of their room. For a second, he forgot about the monster in the hedge. He forgot all about how it might come into his room late at night and gobble him up and spit out his bones and instead, he just looked at the wardrobe and thought how nobody else had a wardrobe quite like it.

19

Then he saw it, staring at him through the slits in the door. It was a pair of eyes, exactly like the ones in the hedge and they were watching him. It was another monster, a monster actually in his room. Toby felt his hands start to shake. There were monsters, monsters everywhere and there wasn't anything he could do about it. He slid down under the sheets and hid, closing his eyes tight to keep the monsters out. They weren't real. They weren't real. Or were they? Toby didn't know. He just didn't know.

Toby tossed and turned a lot that night. It took a long time for him to finally fall asleep and in that time he'd thought about so many scary things. He thought about the monsters, the one in the hedge and the one in the wardrobe who would eat him as soon as he fell asleep. Then he thought about what had happened to Mum and Dad and how they were gone and were never coming back. Those things were scary, there was no doubt about that, but the thing that scared Toby the most was what he heard just before he fell asleep. Maybe he'd imagined it or maybe it had really happened, but he knew what he'd heard and it had made his whole body go cold.

He'd heard a woman crying in the attic.

2 GOING UP TO THE ATTIC

Toby lay awake for a long time before getting out of bed. It was early, too early for him to be up. Little rays of light flew through the cloth that covered the window and coated the room with a yellow glow. Now that Toby could see his room better he noticed that, like much of the house, the walls were a dirty white colour. The light bounced off the white, keeping the room much lighter than it should have been at this time. Toby wondered what the time actually was. After waking up he looked over at the wardrobe. Peering through the slits, he saw that the inside looked brighter now. The blackness had faded slightly. The eyes that Toby knew had been watching him were gone now. They wouldn't be back until later that night.

Toby knew he had to get up. It took a few tries because the bed had become so comfy but he finally managed to pull himself out from under the covers. He sat on the edge of the bed for a while, his feet dangling over the edge. If it had been night-time, Toby wouldn't have done this. He would have been afraid that a monster's hand would grab hold of his ankles and pull him under the bed. But, because it was morning, Toby knew that wouldn't happen. With a great heave he pulled himself off the mattress and plopped his heels onto the carpet. The carpet in his room was strange because it

21

wasn't like the carpet in the living room. This carpet was white like the walls but felt scratchy on his feet. He slunk across the room towards the door and clasped a hand around the doorknob. Before he left, Toby took a quick look around the room. It wasn't as scary as it had been last night, but it still wasn't home. He twisted and the door creaked open.

Toby was surprised. Peering out from behind his bedroom door he saw light coming from the living room. Toby thought this was very weird. It wasn't dark so a light didn't need to be on. What was it? Slowly, he crept out into the hallway and tip-toed towards the kitchen. Looking out from behind the doorframe into the living room, he saw two long legs stretched out on the carpet. Toby craned his neck for a better view but he couldn't quite see who it was. He could hear sniffing noises and short shaky breaths that sounded painful. His mouth went dry and his hands began to shake. What was this person doing here? Who was it?

Toby felt something warm in his pyjamas. He looked down. He'd wet himself. He started to cry. It started off silently, his tears dripping onto his cheek and burning as they fell, but soon his crying turned into a loud sobbing that filled the house. Toby shut his eyes tight, to keep the tears in but also to keep the scary person sat in his living room away. He put his hands over his ears. His cries were so loud that he couldn't hear the long legs stand up and rush over towards him. In fact, he couldn't hear the second pair of legs, thicker and stronger ones, hurrying along side them.

'Toby!' yelled Karen as she grabbed his shoulders tight. He recognised her voice, her sweet voice, and opened his eyes. He saw Karen staring at him wide-eyed and with smudged makeup on her cheeks. She was wearing a big t-shirt that looked more like a dress and her blue hair poked out in weird tufts. But it was Karen's eyes that Toby noticed most. The white parts had turned red and little lines were criss-crossed all over them. Toby was relieved that the legs in the living room belonged to Karen. He grabbed her and pulled himself into her arms, the wet from his pyjamas soaking her baggy shirt.

'What happened?'

A voice came from behind Karen. It was a deep, scratchy voice that was quiet and cold. Toby didn't want to look at Daniel; he just wanted to keep hugging Karen. Despite this, he pulled his head away from Karen's chest and peered through tear-filled eyes at his brother. Daniel looked very strong as he stood in the hallway, with his arms folded across his chest and his muscles bulging. He looked like a superhero. Toby had never seen anyone else who had muscles like his brother. He looked at his own body. He was very different to his brother. Daniel was strong and Toby was skinny. How were they even related? Toby sniffed and wiped his runny nose with his sleeve. His brother was so big but he was so small. He was nothing compared to Daniel.

'Legs,' Toby cried. 'I saw the legs and they scared me.'

Karen and Daniel looked at each other for a second, then turned back to Toby.

'Could you let go please?' Toby asked Karen sadly. She was still holding his shoulders and her nails were starting to hurt. She pulled them back and put his little hand in hers.

'Toby,' she whispered, her teary eyes looking into Toby's, 'I am so sorry. We didn't mean to frighten you.' Her voice was soft and made Toby feel better.

'Its okay, Toby,' Daniel told him, coming closer to the two of them. As he put his hands on Karen's shoulders, Toby's brother looked down and saw the wet patch.

'Um...Karen?' he muttered nervously, nudging her gently and pointing to Toby's pyjamas.

'I noticed,' she replied, not looking away from Toby. She ran her hand up the little boy's arm and smiled.

'How about we find you some new pyjamas?'

Toby sat forward in his bed as Karen carefully fluffed his pillows. Sunlight was pouring through his bedroom window but she'd thought it would be a good idea for him to get a little bit more rest. He wasn't tired anymore, not even a little bit, but he did what he was told.

'There we go!' smiled Karen, makeup still smudged across her face. 'Pillows have been fluffed.'

Toby fell back and hit the mattress with a thud. He threw his arms out across the bed and a small smile appeared across his face. The sun was warm and the worries of the night before were a long way away. All except one. Toby's smile shrunk, something that Karen noticed instantly.

'What's up?' she asked.

Toby felt his head fill with fog. It blocked out any clear memories he had of last night, but through the mist he could hear a quiet noise that echoed in his brain. He opened his mouth to speak but his lips were too dry and he felt a lump in his throat. Karen began to look worried.

'Are you okay?' she asked, her voice shaky and nervous. Toby took a deep breath and ran his tongue across his lips.

'Last night,' he whispered, 'I heard crying. A woman was crying.'

Karen stared at her hands, her head pointing down towards the floor. As she looked back up at Toby, he could see that her happy face was now very sad. Her smile had vanished and the smudged makeup made her eyes look darker than before. Maybe it was just the room, maybe it just made everything darker.

'That was nothing,' she mumbled. 'Try and get some rest.'

She slunk across the room and placed a hand on the door. Then she looked up at Toby, only really seeing him through the corner of her eye.

'It wasn't anything to worry about,' she told him. 'There is no need to be scared.' And with that she left, shutting the door gently behind her.

Now Toby was alone again. As he looked around at his room, he noticed how little colour there was in it. The whole room was all a boring shade of dull white that made Toby feel empty. There was nothing. Toby turned onto his side and shut his eyes tight, his head pressed deep into the pillow.

He crinkled his toes. The sunlight was heating up the room a lot so he stuck his feet out from under the blanket to cool them down. Karen had done a good job of tucking him in and Toby felt bad for messing it up with his fidgeting, but it didn't matter too much. He thought back to what Karen had said after he'd told her about the crying. He was confused. Why hadn't it scared her as much as it had scared him? Then, through the ear that was not pushed into the pillow, he began to hear footsteps trudging down the hallway. They were heavy, so heavy that they made the wooden floorboards creak.

'Shhh!' came Karen's voice from just outside Toby's room. The footsteps became quieter. There, right behind Toby's bedroom door, the footsteps stopped dead and Daniel began to talk.

'Is he okay?' he heard Daniel whisper. Toby thought he sounded worried. Karen let out a long sigh.

'He's better but he's still shaken,' she told him, her voice shaking as the words came out. 'He told me that he heard someone crying last night.'

Toby heard Daniel pull Karen into his arms. She started to cry. Toby thought her crying was an awful noise, not because of how broken it was, but because Toby could tell just from hearing it that she was trying to stop herself. She would try and hold everything in before it would all get too much and escape. Toby listened to the noise for what seemed like ages. It stabbed at his brain and made his head hurt.

He listened as Karen's cries become softer and fainter until they went away completely. Well, not completely, but close enough.

'I just feel so awful,' she whispered through shaky breaths. 'It's all my fault.'

'No.' Daniel told her very seriously. When he spoke again, his voice became softer and quieter.

'Does he know that it was you?'

'I don't think so. All that he said was that he heard a woman crying.'

'Do you think we should talk to him?'

The hallway went quiet for a long time after that question. Toby held his breath, waiting for one of them to say something. Finally, after a long time, Karen spoke.

'No,' she whispered. 'We shouldn't do that.'

'But what if it happens again?'

'It won't.' Karen told him, and that was the last thing that was said. The two of them made their way into the kitchen and left Toby all alone.

Even though he was alone, he felt calm again. That had explained everything. It had been Karen. He knew that the thought of Karen crying should have made him sad but it explained a lot. Her crying had kept him awake, just hers. His body relaxed, sinking deep into his mattress. With all his worries put in place he drifted into sleep, all his fears now wiped from his mind. That is, at least, for now.

It was just after lunchtime when Toby woke up. Despite only having slept for a few hours, he felt better than before. He propped his pillows up against the wooden headrest of his bedframe and sat up. His brown hair fell in front of his eyes and, as he pushed it away, he began to smile. The sun was pouring heavily into the room, turning the walls a bright yellow, and warming Toby's cold skin. He yawned and stretched out his skinny little arms as far as they could reach. Then, he slid out of bed and onto the scratchy carpet. He opened the door and walked through the hallway and into the kitchen. Karen was standing there, a glass of tap water in her hand. She didn't notice him at first. Her eyes were unfocused and stared out into space. Her blue hair was tied back in a ponytail and she was dressed in faded black jeans and a baggy white t-shirt that fell almost to her knees. Toby looked at her wrists. She wasn't wearing any bangles today. As Toby's feet landed on the green living room carpet, she noticed him and put her glass down. Then, she dropped to his height, her hands cupping over her bony kneecaps, and smiled.

'Hey, Toby,' she said happily. 'Did you sleep okay?'

Toby nodded, his smile widening so that his teeth showed and his tongue flicked out. He threw his arms around Karen's thin waist in a big bear-hug that took her by surprised. She fell backwards onto the floor - Toby falling with her - and let out a snort of laughter as the two of them lay back on the tiles. He giggled loudly at her laugh which only caused her to laugh even more as the two rolled around together happily. The two giggled and chuckled and laughed together for some time before they stopped to catch their breath. They lay with their backs pressed against the freezing cold tiled floor of the kitchen, their heads gazing up at the ceiling. They looked to each other and Toby grabbed Karen's hand tight. Her grin faded a little but a small smile stayed in its place.

Toby heard the front door creak open and both he and Karen listened from their spot on the floor as Daniel made his way into the living room. He was carrying something that crinkled and crackled as he moved but Toby couldn't quite figure out what it was. Karen pushed herself off the floor and pulled herself up with the other hand which held onto the kitchen counter. Once up, she reached out a hand and pulled Toby to his feet. Toby could only just see over the kitchen counter, even on his tip-toes, but could just make out his brother standing in the middle of the living room with two heavy plastic bags filled to the top with food.

'Hey, Toby!' smiled Daniel as he noticed his brother's thick brown hair poking out from behind the counter. Immediately Toby flattened his little feet on the floor and bounced around the side of the counter towards his brother. He ran up to Daniel and hugged his brother's leg tightly. Daniel grinned a big grin and placed a hand on top of Toby's thick head of hair. Toby watched as Daniel and Karen looked at each other. He could tell that they loved each other and he loved them too. Both of them.

Toby heard a thick crunching noise from outside the house. Hearing the same noise, Daniel rushed over to the window and stared outside. As they watched, a gigantic white truck pulled up by the side of the house. It had a wide white bonnet that was covered with a picture and a stumpy black antenna poked out from just above the driver's seat. Daniel opened the front door and walked out. After a short talk with someone that Toby couldn't see, he came back, his smile even wider than it had been before.

'Is it the movers?' Karen asked him. Daniel nodded happily and the two of them followed him out into the sun.

Pretty soon, the house was filled with boxes. There were boxes of books and films and pots and pans and a whole mess of other stuff. Toby's toys had been flung across his bedroom floor but he wasn't allowed to play with them until all the boxes were unpacked. After most of the boxes had been emptied, Toby went to sit in the living room. A white sofa had been brought from Daniel's old flat and Toby lay back comfortably on it like a king. There was a cartoon show playing on a small flat television. The living room looked very different to how it had yesterday. The television and sofa made the place feel more like home.

Toby wasn't really watching the cartoon. His eyes were staring at the wall above the television as he sat not really thinking about anything. The work had made him tired. All the furniture had been moved in by the removal men, who were all big with no hair and square chins, but carrying the boxes had still made Toby feel exhausted. Suddenly, he heard heavy footsteps stomping down the hallway. Toby turned to look. As he watched, his brother made his way into the living room and smiled at him.

'What are you watching?' Daniel asked. He'd been in Toby's room fixing the light switch and looked very tired. Toby didn't answer. Daniel sighed and rubbed his forehead.

'I need some help,' he told him in a quiet voice. 'I've just found one of the boxes. It's full of Christmas decorations. Will you help me put them up in the attic?'

Toby's eyes went as wide as teacups. The attic, that was where the bad thing had happened. Toby was frightened, something his brother could easily see. However, Daniel was having none of it.

'There's nothing to be worried about,' he told him, forcing a smile. 'You'll have to go up there some time and it's better that I'm with you. That way you'll have me there to protect you.'

Toby looked up at his brother and gulped. Daniel cared about him, Toby knew that, so maybe it would be a good idea to go up with him. His bedroom had been scary at first, so maybe if he went up to the attic he wouldn't be as afraid. Toby nodded silently and Daniel clapped his big hands together.

'Brilliant!' he shouted happily. 'Let's go.'

Toby slid off the sofa and the two of them walked into the hallway, leaving the TV buzzing behind them.

Toby stared up at the attic. It was still as scary as Toby remembered it but he didn't look away. Daniel grasped the end of the string and pulled it down slowly. As he did, the hatch began to open and a large folding ladder began to slide down. It was a steel ladder. Once it was fully open and the legs were flat on the floor, Toby saw that one of the rungs was missing.

'Do you want to go first?' Daniel asked him. Toby nodded nervously. Daniel slid his hands under Toby's armpits and lifted him up through the hatch and into the attic, setting him down on the edge so that his legs dangled in the air. Toby tried looking around him but the attic was pitch black. He couldn't see a thing. He stared down at his brother and smiled anxiously. He was starting to feel dizzy. His brain was swirling around in his head like a ship caught in a whirlpool. The dark was spinning around him, about to swallow him whole.

'There's a light switch next to your head,' Daniel told him, pointing with his finger. Toby turned his head sharply to see a wooden beam with an old switch slapped onto it at a weird angle, wires poking out from the side of the casing. Toby flicked the switch and a light flickered but then went out with a flash. It was dark again. Toby stared back down at his brother who looked back at him with with a disappointed expression.

'I'll have to get us some torches,' he yelled up at Toby, before he strode out of view in the direction of the kitchen. He returned with a large silver torch in his fist. He threw it up to his little brother. Toby caught it in both hands but dropped it onto the wooden floor. He went to pick it up and grabbed it in his little hands. He turned it on and a beam of light shot out the end of it into Toby's eyes. Toby pointed the light away and looked around as best he could slowly. His eyes became adjusted to the light quickly but he still couldn't see much at all.

'I'm going to look for another one,' his brother told him from down in the hallway. Toby heard his brother's heavy footsteps stomp into his and Karen's bedroom to look for another torch. Toby's face went white. The attic had gotten very cold all of a sudden. It was already colder than the rest of the house but it seemed even colder now. Toby tried to calm himself and placed a hand on the old wooden floor. He felt a pain and pulled his hand away sharply. He turned the torch's light onto his hand. A thin bit of floorboard had lodged itself in his pale skin. Placing the torch under his chin and balancing it so that it's light stayed pointing at his palm, Toby used his other hand to pull the splinter out. It was a big splinter and hurt a lot as Toby pulled it out, but he never cried out. After pulling it out Toby looked back at his hand. A small bit of blood was running down his hand towards his wrist. He rubbed the blood off on his leg and put the torch back in his stinging hand.

Toby looked around the attic. The floor was all wooden floorboards and the triangle roof was covered in wood too. Beams poked out from the floor at odd angles and went to the ceiling. Apart from the beams, there was nothing in the attic. Toby guessed that everything had been removed by the last owner of the house, whoever that may have been, and didn't think much of it. That would be the normal thing to do if you moved house.

The cold air prickled against Toby's skin and sent a shiver up his spine. He stopped dead. Something was watching him, he knew it. What could it be? Was it the monster from the wardrobe? Had it followed him up the ladder? Was it waiting to gobble him up? Or could it be the one from the bush outside his bedroom? Maybe there was some way into the attic from the outside. Maybe the monster had climbed up and was watching Toby right now. With all the courage he had in his little body, Toby lifted a shaking hand and pointed the torch into the furthest corner of the attic. He looked around in the darkness for a sign but couldn't find anything. There was no sign of the monsters.

Everything would have been fine for Toby if he'd shut off the torch then and just left the attic. But the light stayed on and Toby kept looking. He searched every inch of that dark and dingy corner before finally stopping. He felt himself turned to stone; his body seizing up as his wide eyes stared into the distance. His brain froze and every single hair on his body stood up on end as he dropped the heavy torch with a clang on the floor. The light went out and everything went dark. Toby would have scrambled to get the torch if he hadn't been so scared. What he'd seen terrified him. At the end of the attic, sticking out from behind a large wooden beam, he'd seen a set of bruised legs, poking out in front of him.

3 AMY

Toby was terrified. He hadn't imagined it. He knew what he'd seen. A set of girl's legs were poking out from behind one of the beams. He hadn't dreamt it. They were real. The attic was completely black now that the torch had gone out. Toby couldn't see anything but still he kept his eyes glued to that spot. He might be able to see them again if he kept looking. His whole body had gone stiff and he could feel a chill running up his neck. It made the hairs on his arms stand up and sent a sick feeling down into his tummy. Where was Daniel? He should have been back by now. Toby could feel his tummy getting tighter and knew he was going to pee himself again. He was more scared than he had ever been in his life and, no matter how hard he tried, he couldn't get himself to keep breathing. He was going to faint. Toby closed his eyes. His body felt weak and he could tell that he was going to fall over any second now. He was so scared. He was so scared.

He couldn't be scared, not now. Toby thought about his brother. He thought about Daniel's strong arms and big chest. He thought about how tall his brother was and how tough he was too. Daniel wouldn't be scared. Daniel never got scared. Toby knew his brother wouldn't be frightened. His brother wouldn't be scared of a pair of legs! Why should he be? Toby's felt a warmness fill his body. He opened his eyes and took a deep breath. He reached down to grab the torch. Then, after turning it on, he pointed the torch toward the corner. He started to walk. Toby heard his footsteps echo all around him as he crept slowly across the floorboards. As he got closer, he began to hear quiet rustling noises from behind the beam. He changed his direction, walking out to the side a bit so that he could get a better look at the legs. Then, when he was only a few steps away, he saw them. They were skinny legs, very skinny legs, and were covered with big black and purple bruises. There were lots of red cuts on them too. Toby rubbed his eyes and stared at them. The bruises made the legs look lumpy and bumpy but if Toby looked hard enough he could see that the skin around them was very smooth. They were nice legs, just a bit broken.

But the legs weren't the only things hidden behind the beam. As he walked further around the beam, he realised that the legs were attached to a person. They were attached to a girl.

The girl wasn't very tall, he could tell that even though she was sitting, but she wasn't short either. She had long hair, very long hair that dropped down to her chest. The hair was dirty and frizzy and Toby thought it looked a bit like straw. The girl was very skinny and wore a pretty white dress that had a big red stain in the middle, right over her tummy. She was a girl that Toby thought looked very unwell and she was looking up at him with a pair of quiet eyes. The two stared at each other in silence for a long time. After a while, Toby decided to speak.

'Are you sick?' he asked, worried that the girl wasn't okay.

The girl's eyes became very wide which made Toby shudder. She looked behind her and then back at Toby. She opened her mouth.

'You can see me?' she asked him, as if she almost didn't believe him. The girl had a strange look on her face that

Toby couldn't figure out.

'Uh-huh,' he told her, pointing at her with his finger. The girl's eyes lit up and she smiled the biggest smile Toby had ever seen.

'Really?' she asked happily, not realising that the question was stupid.

'Yes,' he told her and her smile grew. She had a nice smile; it made Toby feel happy and warm. He wouldn't smile back though. He didn't know this girl and she didn't know him. Toby also didn't like that fact that she wasn't moving. She was too still and it made Toby nervous.

'Who are you?' he asked her. As he watched, he saw tears start to come up in the corners of her eyes, even though she was still smiling. He thought that was very strange.

'I'm Amy,' she replied. The tears in her eyes were getting bigger and one even started to run down her cheek.

'I'm Toby,' he told her seriously. 'What are you doing in my attic?'

The girl called Amy looked down at her lap and began to cry. Toby felt bad; he hadn't meant to upset her.

'Don't be sad,' he said to her, his voice a little nicer now. He looked down at Amy's lap and saw something that he thought was very strange. Wrapped around the lower part of her tummy was a thick grey chain that tied her too the beam. It was wrapped tight and looked like it was hurting her.

Toby watched as Amy's crying got quieter. Finally, she stopped and wiped the tears away. Then she stared at him looking very surprised.

'What did you say?' she asked him, her hands shaking as she spoke.

'What?'

'Before,' she continued, her voice louder than before. 'You said that this was your attic.'

Amy's hands were trembling. He reached out to touch them but she snatched them away. That scared Toby and he shuffled back a few steps.

'Please!' Amy yelled, sounding very scared. 'What did you mean by that?'

Toby looked at her, confused.

'Daniel bought the house,' he told her. 'We live here now.'

Amy looked like she didn't understand what he was saying. She tried to move closer to Toby but the chain pulled her back. Then a noise came from downstairs.

'Toby?' Daniel called, yelling up at him from by the bottom of the ladder. 'I found the torch!'

'Okay.'

'I'm coming up!'

'Okay.'

Toby heard his brother climbing. He turned his head to look. Suddenly, a torch flickered on and Toby felt a bright light shine in his eyes. It hurt a lot, so much that he had to look away.

'Sorry, Toby!' said Daniel as he pointed the light away from his brother's face. Toby looked at Daniel. He could see his brother's body bending as Daniel tried to fit inside the cramped attic. The bending made Daniel look very weird. Toby didn't like it. He looked back at Amy. Her mouth was moving but her voice had gone very quiet, which meant that Toby couldn't figure out what she was saying.

'What's that, Amy?' he asked her innocently. She

stared at him angrily.

'Don't let him know you can see me,' she told him, her voice only a little bit louder. Toby nodded and looked back at his brother.

'Who's Amy?' Daniel asked in a confused voice.

'The girl in our attic,' Toby replied. He turned his head and watched Amy roll her eyes.

'What on earth are you talking about?' Daniel asked as he clambered over to where Toby was stood. Toby heard Amy whisper loudly by his side.

'Don't tell him!' she told Toby, but he didn't listen.

'Amy,' he said, getting a little annoyed at Daniel for not understanding. 'She's right here.'

He pointed at the wooden beam. Daniel was stood right next to Toby now. He'd left the Christmas decorations by the side of the hatch and was looking at Toby very strangely. He looked straight at Amy and she looked back. Daniel didn't seem surprised to see a girl tied up in the attic. Toby had found it very strange but Daniel didn't seem to feel the same way. He'd known that Daniel wouldn't have been scared of her but he might have at least been a little bit surprised. But he wasn't. He looked back at Toby and spoke, his voice low and heavy.

'What girl?'

Toby was confused. He pointed at Amy again.

'Her,' he told his brother firmly. Daniel looked again but shook his head. Toby looked at Amy. She had a strange look on her face. She seemed disappointed.

'You can't see me!' she yelled loudly, so loudly in fact that it made Toby jump. Daniel didn't move. He couldn't see or hear Amy. This made Amy sad and she started crying again. Toby didn't like that. He didn't want her to be sad. So his five-year-old mind came up with an idea.

'Touch the beam,' he told Daniel, speaking in a very serious voice.

'No,' his brother replied stubbornly.

'Why not?'

'Because its silly,' Daniel told him. 'There's no one here and that's that.'

Toby was angry. His brother was being very stupid and he hated that. He put his lips together and stuck out his tongue. That made Daniel mad and he grabbed Toby by the arm.

'Now you listen here,' he said firmly. 'This has been hard on you, I know that, but you can't say stuff like this.'

'Why not?'

Daniel's face turned red.

'Because its not going to change our minds! We aren't moving back home. This is our home now Toby and you aren't going to make up stories to scare us away.'

Toby started to cry. His eyes were shut, so he didn't see him do it, but he felt Daniel's arms hug him tight. His brother dried the tears away and Toby opened his eyes again. He stared at Amy and saw that she was crying too. Toby wanted to tell Daniel that Amy was crying but he knew he wouldn't believe him.

'We're going back down,' Daniel told him. 'This was a stupid idea.'

He grabbed Toby's hand and pulled him towards the hatch. Daniel was the first to climb down the ladder. When he got to the bottom, he held out a hand for Toby to grab onto.

Toby looked at Daniel, then looked at the beam. He couldn't see Amy anymore but he could hear her. She was crying behind the beam.

Toby thought about Amy a lot that night. She'd looked very scared and lonely. It made Toby feel sad when he thought of her. She seemed so nice and he didn't want her to be upset. As he lay in bed, thinking about her, he rolled over and stared out of his bedroom window. It was very dark outside. It was nearly bedtime for grown ups but Daniel and Karen were still in the living room watching TV. Toby could hear them from his bed as they talked to each other. He listened carefully, not daring to make a sound.

'Work will be a killer on Monday. I'll have to sort myself out tomorrow evening.'

That was Daniel's voice. Toby had heard him talk about his job before. Daniel had worked in an office when Mum and Dad were alive but he hadn't like it. He'd talked to some people and had gotten a job somewhere near where they lived now. He had it sorted before they all moved in. It was another job in an office. Toby listened as Karen started to speak.

'I thought that I might look for a job soon.' she told Daniel, her voice very quiet. Toby heard someone shuffle on the sofa.

'Could you wait a bit? Just until Toby's settled in at school?' Daniel asked her, his voice getting softer, 'Just give him this week to settle into the house. He'll be at school soon enough.'

Toby heard a quiet grunt from Karen.

'I think he needs it,' Daniel told her. 'Something creepy happened when we were up in the attic.'

Toby heard someone sit up. It was probably Karen because she started talking.

'What?' she asked. Her voice sounded worried.

'He said that he saw a girl up there.'

'That's really creepy,' Karen replied after a long silence. Toby heard Daniel fidget in his seat.

'It was just him acting out so he could get us to move back,' he told her. 'Either that or he's got a very wild imagination.'

Karen went quiet.

'But you have to admit that's creepy,' she finally whispered, her voice so quiet that Toby almost couldn't hear her. 'It's like something out of a horror film.'

'I know and I think that's where he's got it from. I mean, I'm not pointing fingers but I remember someone thinking it was a good idea to show him all those classic monster movies.'

Toby heard a thud followed by an ouch.

'Sorry!' Daniel told her, his voice higher than usual, 'but do you see what I mean? Toby's seen this stuff somewhere and is using it to freak us out so that we'll move back. I know Toby and that's how his mind works. He wouldn't actually talk to us about how he's feeling,'

The two of them were quiet for a while. Then, after what seemed like ages, Toby heard the sound on the TV change. He listened carefully and heard somebody stand up.

'Are you coming to bed?' Karen asked Daniel.

'Sure, why not?' he replied. Daniel's voice sounded happy. Toby heard him get up and stand with Karen. For a moment, there was no sound at all. Then, as Toby listened, he heard the sound of kissing. After a long time, the kissing stopped and Toby heard the two of them walk out of the living room and across the hall. They stopped for a second and opened Toby's bedroom door a bit to check on him. He stayed very still and pretended to be asleep. After a little while, they closed the door and went to bed. Then there was no sound. Everything went quiet.

As he stared up at the ceiling, Toby heard a noise. Someone was talking. It was a girl, a girl with a nice voice. The talking came from straight above him. It was coming from the attic.

'Toby,' the voice called. 'Are you there?'

'Yes," he replied, quite loudly so he could be heard

'Toby be quiet!' the voice yelled. Toby didn't say anything.

'You need to do me a big favour,' the voice continued. 'Cough if you understand.'

Toby coughed.

'Good,' the voice replied. 'I need you to do something for me. Come back up to the attic. Please.'

He slid out of bed and crept across his bedroom, shutting the door very quietly behind him as he left. Then, as he stood in the cold hallway, he noticed something very strange. The attic was open and the ladder was down. Toby gulped. Daniel had left it open; he hadn't realised that. He was sure it had been closed. Maybe Daniel had put some more stuff up there after Toby had gone to bed. Maybe that was it. Toby heard a voice call out to him.

'Toby?'

'Yes?' he whispered.

'You need to listen to me. I need you to come up here

and help me out, but be quiet.'

Toby's legs turned to jelly. He couldn't go back up there. It was scary and dark and there was a girl that he didn't know up there. It would be a bad idea to go back up there so he stayed quiet.

'Please, Toby,' the voice begged, sounding very desperate. 'I need your help.'

Toby didn't know what to do. He didn't want to go back up to the attic. It was scary and he didn't have Daniel with him, but the voice needed his help. He thought about what to do, his thumb on his chin and his tongue sticking out as he did so. Finally, Toby decided.

'Okay,' he whispered. He lifted his little feet onto the first step and grabbed the sides of the ladder. Then, he started to climb. By the time he'd gotten halfway he realised how high up he was. It was scary but he wanted to be brave like Daniel so he kept on going until he reached the top. He pulled himself up and sat on the side of the hatch. He dangled his feet in the air for a bit and smiled. He'd been very brave and he was proud of himself. Then he heard a noise and his heart dropped.

'Toby! Come over here!' Amy told him loudly. Toby turned and saw her skinny legs pointing out from behind the beam. He got up and crept over to her. When he got there, Amy looked at him and smiled.

'We might not have long so I need you to be fast. Look behind you.'

Toby did as he was told and looked over his shoulder.

'Do you see that red toolbox over there?' Amy asked him. Toby squinted his eyes. It was dark, very dark, but he kept looking. Then he saw it, a red box in the far corner of the attic.

'Yes,' he whispered, trying his best to stay quiet. He listened carefully as Amy spoke again.

'I need you to bring it to me,' she told him, her voice very serious. 'Can you do that?'

Toby thought for a moment and looked back at the toolbox. It looked heavy and he wasn't sure if he'd be able to lift it. Even so, he had to try.

'Uh-huh,' he replied and with that he placed one small foot out in front of him and began to creep towards the toolbox.

As he got closer, he realised that there was a big black handle on the top of the toolbox. Toby grabbed onto it and tried to lift the toolbox, but it was too heavy to carry. So, instead of lifting it, he decided to drag the box along the floor. It was hard work bringing it over to Amy. Finally, he made it over to her.

'Now, open it,' she told him.

Toby did as he was told. He had trouble opening the lid but when he finally managed it he saw that there were lots of tools inside.

'Now, pick up that saw,' Amy said to him. Toby stared into the box and saw a big square saw that looked very dangerous. All of a sudden Toby stared to feel very nervous.

'Daniel says that I shouldn't touch sharp things,' he told her. Amy started to sound angry.

'I don't care what Daniel says, just grab the saw!'

Toby reached out his hand and picked up the saw. He didn't want to get in trouble so he was extra careful with it. He looked back at Amy.

'Good. Do you see the chain?'

Toby looked at the chain that tied Amy to the beam. It was big and thick. He nodded. He wasn't sure if Amy could see him nodding as it was so dark in the attic, but it seemed like she could because she spoke as soon as he'd done it. What she said made Toby feel even more anxious.

'I need you to cut through it.'

Toby looked at the saw and then back at the chain. The saw was big and sharp but the chain was big too. He scooted over to the chain and placed the saw on top of it. He was about to start cutting when a very strange thing happened. As soon as he put the saw against the chain the blade slid straight through it. It didn't make a cut or anything like that at all. It just slid straight through and came out the other side, almost like the chain hadn't been there at all. Toby didn't know what had happened. He looked back at Amy. Even though it was dark, he could still tell that she was crying. Toby put the saw back in the box.

'It didn't work,' he told her. Amy didn't say anything which made Toby feel bad. Then, all of a sudden, he heard a thud and the sound of a light switching on. Amy spoke again, this time sounding very frightened.

'Toby,' she said to him nervously, 'Grab another saw.'

Toby looked in the box again. Then, he looked back at Amy.

'There aren't any more,' he told her, shaking his head. Toby heard heavy footsteps stomping along the hallway downstairs. They sounded close.

'Please look again. Please, Toby.'

Amy was very scared now. Toby looked again but he couldn't see anything.

Then, after searching the whole toolbox, he noticed

44

something. In the top of the box there was a red pocket and inside the red pocket was a knife. It was a big knife and it was a sharp knife. It was the kind of knife that Toby's mother had used to cut up bread. He looked closer at the knife and saw that the blade was covered in something red. The knife did not belong in the attic. It was the sort of knife he shouldn't be anywhere near and he knew that Daniel would be very upset if he found out that Toby had gotten hold of it. Toby looked back at Amy. Even in the dark he could tell how scared she was. He knew what he had to do. He reached into the pocket and picked up the knife. Toby heard the footsteps getting even closer. Daniel was coming. Toby heard as his brother lifted himself onto the ladder. Then, as he listened, he heard Daniel start to climb.

Toby held the knife over the chain and pushed down. The knife touched. It didn't go through the chain like the other one had. Toby didn't have time to think about how strange this was because just as the knife touched the chain a light came on. It was Daniel; he was there. Toby threw the knife away and heard it landed with a thud. He saw Daniel crouching by a beam, staring at him with angry eyes. His big brother did not look happy.

'What the bloody hell are you doing up here?' Daniel yelled.

Toby stared at him.

'Nothing,' he lied. 'What are you doing up here?'

Daniel's face turned red.

'Get over here now!' he said angrily, pointing at the space in front of him.

Toby did as he was told. When he reached him, Daniel grabbed Toby's arm and looked behind him at the toolbox, which was not too far from where Amy was.

'What were you doing with those tools?'

Toby wanted to tell him. He wanted to tell Daniel that Amy had told him to get them. She needed them. She had asked him to come up and help her. He wanted to tell him all those things but he didn't. Toby didn't say anything and that made Daniel angrier.

'You aren't to come up here again. Do you understand me?' Daniel told him. Toby nodded, his hands shaking at his sides. Daniel saw the shaking and started to calm down.

'Right. Let's get you back to bed.'

He grabbed Toby's hand and pulled him down the ladder. Toby watched the attic start to disappear. He felt awful. He couldn't help Amy and that would make her very sad. Sad people cry but he didn't want her to cry because then he would feel bad and then he would cry. Daniel lifted the ladder back up into the attic and closed the hatch. He led Toby back to bed and tucked him in. Then, he shut the door and went back to bed.

Toby felt so bad that he was nearly crying. Amy would be sad now. He couldn't help her. It was all his fault. He'd messed it all up. He pulled the blanket up over his face and closed his eyes. Then, as he lay there, sad and alone, he heard a voice talking to him from inside the attic.

'Thank you, Toby,' the voice whispered.

Toby felt better after that.

Toby didn't see any monsters that night. He fell straight asleep and had nice dreams but when he woke up he couldn't remember what they were. He got out of bed and went into the kitchen. Karen was there. She was cooking something in a frying pan. It was bacon. Toby didn't like bacon.

'I want cereal.'

Karen looked tired. She was hot and sweaty and her face was red like a big tomato.

'I'll get you some cereal in a minute,' she told him as she ran to the fridge to get a carton of orange juice. 'Just one thing at a time.'

Toby heard the heavy footsteps in the hall. Daniel walked into the kitchen. He was wearing a big blue suit and had a black case in his hand. He had a white shirt on underneath the suit with a collar that was too tight for him. It made his neck look big and fat. Toby giggled. It made him look like a frog, a big silly frog.

'I have to go now,' he told Karen. 'I'll get something to eat from the vending machine.'

'Damn it,' said Karen, who never usually swore in front of Toby. 'I thought I had more time.'

Daniel went over to Karen and kissed her on the cheek. Then, he rushed out the door and Karen smiled as she watched him leave.

'Cereal!' yelled Toby loudly. Karen stared down at him.

'Toby,' she whispered. 'Don't.'

She was very angry. Why was she mad at Toby? He hadn't done anything wrong! She was just being stupid. There was a loud beeping noise, so loud that Toby had to cover his ears. Karen jumped and looked around. He watched as she stared up at the ceiling. There was a white circle stuck to it with a red light flashing on and off. That was where the sound was coming from. Karen looked at the bacon. There was smoke coming from it. She jumped towards the grill and fiddled with the knobs. The smoke stopped but the beeping kept going.

'Make it stop!' Toby screamed, his hands still over his ears. Karen jumped to try and reach the circle thing but she was too short. She had to get on the counter to reach it. Finally, she pressed a button and the beeping stopped. She got down and looked at the bacon. It was black. She looked at Toby and Toby looked back at her.

'Cereal.'

Karen put the bacon in the bin. Then she slammed a bowl onto the counter and poured out some Extra Crunch Coco-Bites. She shoved it into Toby's hands and went away to her bedroom without even giving him a spoon. Toby stomped over to the sofa, turned on the TV and watched a cartoon whilst he ate the cereal with his fingers.

When he'd finished, he went back into the kitchen and put his bowl on the counter. He walked out from behind that counter and stopped dead. Standing right in front of him, between the sofa and the TV, was a girl with bruised legs and a white dress that had a big red stain on it. She had smooth skin, frizzy blonde hair and big eyes that were looking right at him.

Amy was out of the attic.

4 A NEW FRIEND

Toby didn't know what to do. He didn't know what to say. Amy, the girl Toby had found tied up in the attic and the girl that his brother couldn't see, was standing right in front of him.

'Hey, Toby.'

Amy had a big smile on her face. Toby looked into her eyes. They were brighter than before. Amy looked much better than she had done last night. She still looked unwell but she was definitely better. Toby's jaw dropped. He was shocked, so shocked that his whole body had gone stiff. He wanted to go over to her but he couldn't move his feet. He was completely stuck. Amy walked towards Toby. As she came closer, he noticed that her steps didn't make a sound. Everyone made a sound when they walked, especially Daniel with his big heavy feet, but Amy didn't. She was different. She lay down on the floor and spread her arms and legs out like a starfish. Then, she closed her eyes and took a deep breath.

'You have no idea how good it feels to be out of there,' she smiled, waving her arms and legs about as if she was making a snow angel.

Toby watched as she sat up. He felt a warm, fuzzy feeling rise up inside of him. Amy was a funny girl. His body loosened up and he smiled. All of a sudden, he decided that he wanted to hug her. He wanted to squeeze her tight and show her that he was very happy to see her again. He leapt forward and jumped, throwing his body into her arms. That was what he tried to do but it didn't happen like that. Something strange happened to Toby. He thought that he'd end up hugging Amy but instead he found himself face down on the floor behind her.

Toby stood up quickly and looked back at Amy. She was staring at him, her eyes wide and looking very worried. Toby felt a sharp pain in his nose and touched it with his little fingers. He wished he hadn't done that because touching it made it hurt even more. He started to cry. Tears ran down his cheeks and burned his eyes but he didn't make a sound. Seeing that he was hurt, Amy ran over to him.

'Are you alright?' she asked anxiously. 'What did you do that for?'

'I...wanted...a...hug,' he whispered, his voice quiet and upset. He kept on crying and Amy began to panic.

'I'm so sorry,' she told him. 'Oh fuck, I'm so sorry!'

Toby's tears began to dry. He looked into Amy's eyes and spoke to her in a serious voice.

'You shouldn't say bad words.'

Amy started to laugh. She had a good laugh. It wasn't too loud but it wasn't too quiet either. It sounded very nice and it made Toby feel better. Then, after listening to her laugh for a long long time, he finally realised what had happened.

'Why did I fall on the floor?' he asked her.

Amy looked at him with a strange face. Toby knew that face, it was the face that grown-ups made when they didn't want to tell you something. She thought hard for a while. Then, Toby saw her face change. It looked happier, like she had just figured something out.

'What a silly question!' she told him. Toby became very confused.

'I'm imaginary,' she said to him, as if it were obvious. 'That's why you fell through me!'

Toby looked at her. It wasn't a silly question. Toby had fallen straight through a person and he didn't find that silly at all! Actually, he found it a little bit spooky, but then it all made sense. He'd fallen through her because she wasn't real, that was why. But, even though it made sense in his head, somehow he still wasn't convinced.

'Prove it,' he told her, arms folded over his chest. Amy smiled.

'Well,' she said, 'if I was real you would be able to touch me, wouldn't you.' Toby nodded, that would make sense. He knew a table was real because he could touch it. Toby guessed that a real person would have to be like a table. He would have to be able to touch the person, or else they couldn't be real. Toby put his hand out and placed it on Amy's bruised leg. As if by magic, it went straight through and came out the other side. Toby stared as he pushed his whole arm through Amy's leg and then pulled it back out again. His eyes went wide and he smiled. Amy wasn't real; she was imaginary! He looked at Amy and she looked at him.

'You're not real!' he told her happily. 'You're imaginary!'

Suddenly, a noise came from Daniel and Karen's bedroom. Amy turned her head sharply to look. As she did, her hair flew in front of her face which made Toby laugh loudly. Amy stared at him.

'Toby, be quiet,' she whispered softly. Toby shook

his head and bounced up and down.

'No!' he told her, smiling and laughing manically. 'Why should I listen to you? You're not even real!'

The noise came again. Amy's hands started to shake.

'You need to be quiet,' she told him, but Toby wouldn't listen.

'I don't want to be quiet!' he shouted. 'You can't tell me what to do because you're my imaginary friend and you're not the boss of me!'

There were footsteps in the hallway. They were getting closer and closer. Louder and louder. But Toby didn't care.

'Not real, not real, not real!'

'Who's not real?'

Karen was standing in the hallway door. She was wearing a fluffy pink dressing gown over her clothes and Toby thought that she looked very tired. Her eyes were nearly shut and her skin was white, nearly as white as Amy's. In fact, Karen was stood right next to Amy. She didn't seem to notice her though, but that wasn't a surprise because Amy wasn't real. Toby looked at Amy. She was completely still.

'Amy's not real,' Toby told Karen, pointing at his imaginary friend. Karen looked at where Toby was pointing. After a little while, she looked back at him, an angry look on her face.

'Is this that silly girl your brother told me about?' she asked him in a very serious voice. Toby looked at Amy. She was shaking. Toby could tell that she was scared. He could see it in her eyes. Toby didn't want Amy to be scared so he got rid of his smile and looked at Karen, a blank expression on his face.

'Amy's my imaginary friend,' he told her, looking at Amy as he spoke. Both Karen and Amy looked happy when he said this.

'Christ, Toby. Don't do that to me,' Karen told him, the seriousness gone from her voice.

'Sorry,' he replied. Karen turned and went into the kitchen, walking straight through Amy and towards the fridge.

'Toby, I'm not feeling great,' she said to him, grabbing a cold bottle of water as she spoke. 'I think I need a lie down. Are you going to be okay to play with…'

She giggled.

'…your imaginary friend?'

Toby nodded. Karen smiled and walked into the hallway. She closed the door behind her but opened it again quickly.

'If you need anything come and get me.' she told him.

'I will,' he said.

'I love you, Toby.'

'I love you too.'

Karen closed the door and went to bed. Toby and Amy were alone again.

'Do you want to watch TV?' he asked Amy, smiling politely as he spoke. Amy was still looking at where Karen had just been. Her eyes had tears in them.

'Why are you sad?' he asked, worried that there was a problem.

Amy didn't look at Toby.

'I'm okay,' she told him. 'Let's see what's on TV.'

Toby sat on the sofa. Amy stood up next to him. Toby wondered what she was doing but the realised that she would probably fall through the sofa if she tried sitting down. He grabbed the remote and turned on the TV. The first channel was playing a cartoon so Toby put the remote down and they watched as a squirrel and a fish tried to take over the world.

'This is so lame,' said Amy, rolling her eyes as she spoke. 'Cartoons were better when I was a kid.'

'How old are you?' Toby asked her innocently. Amy looked at him with a smile.

'You're not supposed to ask girls how old they are,' she told him. 'Didn't your mum ever tell you that.'

Amy pointed at the door that Karen had walked through a few seconds ago. Toby could tell what she was thinking and shook his head.

'She's not my mum,' he told her, saying it like it was obvious. 'That's Karen. Mum is dead.'

Amy looked shocked. She let out a long breath and stared down at her feet.

'I'm sorry,' she whispered. Toby didn't look at her.

'Why are you sorry?' he asked. When Amy spoke next her voice was very quiet.

'I didn't know your mum had died,' she told him, sounding very sad. Toby kept on watching the TV.

'Dad died too,' he told her. Amy let out another long breath.

'Are these your new parents?' she asked him, sounding very unsure of what to say. Toby shook his head.

'Nuh-uh' he said, still not looking at her. 'Daniel is my brother. He's going to marry Karen soon.'

'Oh,' Amy replied.

They watched TV in silence for a while. All that could be heard was the buzzing of the TV. Finally, after what felt like ages, Toby turned his head and spoke.

'But how old are you?'

Amy laughed loudly.

'Well,' she asked, 'what year is it?'

'You don't know what year it is?' Toby laughed. Amy shook her head.

'No. Do you?'

Toby thought. No, he didn't know what the year was. Why didn't he know? That was very strange. Then, Toby remembered something. There was a button, a button on the remote. If you pressed it, it showed the time. If it showed the time, then maybe it showed the year. Toby looked over the remote. There were too many buttons on this remote. They should get a new one. Toby mashed the buttons and a lot of things happened. The screen went black, then turned on again, then the people on the TV started to speak funny and then, after pressing all the other buttons, the time came up in the corner of the screen. Toby was only five so he couldn't actually read the time, but he knew what time looked like. He looked up at Amy.

'Is this right?' he asked her. Amy looked scared. She was staring at the TV, her mouth wide open. Toby looked at the screen. Underneath the time was a load of numbers. Toby didn't understand what they were, but they made sense to Amy.

'Um…' she whispered, her voice low and afraid. 'I

55

thought that I was seventeen, but I'm not.'

Toby watched her as she spoke, her eyes staring straight at the glowing TV.

'I'm twenty-two,' she told him. Toby laughed.

'You're old!' he told her, pointing at Amy as she watched the TV. Amy didn't look at him, so he stopped.

'What's wrong?' he asked. Amy turned her head. She looked down at Toby and smiled.

'Nothing,' she said, smiling softly. 'I just didn't realise how old I was.'

Toby looked Amy up and down, confused by what she was telling him.

'How can you not know how old you are?' he asked, genuinely not understanding. 'I know how old I am. I'm five!'

Amy didn't say anything.

They were quiet for a while after that. Toby, beginning to get bored, picked up the remote and started to flick through the channels. There was nothing on at all so, after searching for a long time, he turned the TV off. Then, he looked at Amy and asked her a question that had been on his mind ever since the first time he'd seen her.

'Why were you in our attic?'

Amy scratched her chin as she thought about what to say. As she scratched, Toby saw for the first time that her some of her fingernails were broken. In fact, as Toby scrunched up his face and stared, he noticed that on a few of her fingers almost half the nail was missing. The rest of the space was just skin. Red angry skin.

'Well,' she began, bending down so that she and Toby were the same height. 'I was left there. Some bad people took me up to the attic but forgot to bring me back down. So, that's why I was in the attic.'

'Our attic,' he reminded her.

'Yes,' she replied. 'Your attic.'

'Why were you tied up?' he asked innocently. As he spoke he noticed that Amy's eyes had turned very dark all of a sudden.

'Because they didn't want me to leave,' she told him, her voice barely a whisper. Toby frowned.

'They sound mean,' he told her. Amy nodded. Her face was very serious.

'Yes, they were. They were very mean. Very mean indeed.'

The room felt colder. Toby shivered and Amy reached out to warm him. Her pale hand went straight through his shoulder and made her lose her balance. She fell forward and went through the sofa, landing on the floor underneath so that her body was completely hidden. For a second, Toby wondered where she'd gone but then Amy crawled out into the living room, laughing loudly as she came out of the sofa. Her laughing made Toby laugh too. They laughed and laughed and laughed until the laughs turned into giggles and the giggles turned into smiles. Then, they looked at each other and Toby felt the room turn warm again.

Toby and Amy talked for a long time that morning. Toby liked talking to Amy. She was very funny and he liked listening to her tell jokes. Once she told Toby a joke that he didn't understand but she told it in a funny way so he laughed anyway. They talked about a lot of things. They talked about Toby's parents and Daniel and Karen and what Toby liked and what he didn't like. Toby talked a lot that morning. He didn't mind. He kept on talking and talking and talking until his mouth felt dry and his voice went croaky. By that time, Toby noticed that the room had gotten much brighter. He hadn't been paying much attention to the room but now he saw that the walls had more colour because of the sun coming through the front window. Toby looked at his hands and saw that the sun had turned them yellow. He looked at Amy. Her skin hadn't gone yellow; it was still white. He stared at her. Amy wasn't looking at Toby. She had her eyes fixed on the hallway door. Toby was confused. There wasn't anything special about the door; it was just the same as it always was.

'What are you doing?' he asked her, looking up at her from his spot on the sofa.

Amy looked down at him

'Listen,' she whispered, placing one of her fingers over her mouth. Toby nodded and stayed quiet. He listened and waited patiently for a sound to come. He didn't hear much at first. For a while there was nothing but silence and Toby began to think that Amy was just being silly. Maybe she was just playing a joke on him. Then, Toby heard it. It was the sound of a door opening,

'Karen,' he said quietly. Amy nodded.

'Remember, Toby,' she told him. 'I'm not real. I'm imaginary. Do you understand?'

Toby nodded. At that very moment, Karen walked into the room. Toby stared at her. She was looking better than she had done at breakfast. Her skin looked brighter, like she was glowing. She looked happier than she had done and Toby was glad that she seemed to be feeling better.

'Hi,' she yawned.

'Hi,' he replied.

Karen went into the kitchen and got a loaf of bread out from one of the cabinets. It was the bread in the blue plastic. Toby liked that one; it was the only one he'd eat.

'Sandwich?' Karen asked him, her eyes still half closed.

'Uh-huh,' he told her. He heard a cough and looked back at Amy. She was shaking her head.

'Yes please,' she said firmly. 'I'm sure you weren't dragged up.'

'Okay,' he replied, whispering so that Karen wouldn't hear him. He cleared his throat and tried again.

'Yes please,' he said to Karen, who looked at him from out of the corner of her eye. She didn't say anything, but Toby could tell that she was glad he'd been polite.

Toby watched as Karen opened the fridge. He looked at her bony hand and frowned. She wasn't wearing any bangles today.

'Cucumber?' she asked him. Toby shook his head.

'No, I don't like that,' he told her. Karen sighed.

'Well, what would you like then?' she asked, sounding a little annoyed. Toby didn't even have to think about it.

'Chocolate spread please,' he told her happily. He pointed at one of the cabinets.

Karen rolled her eyes. She walked over to the cabinet and picked up the pot of spread. She made the sandwich and brought it over to Toby. He took the sandwich. It was on an old plate that had flowers on it. The sandwich looked good.

'Thank you,' he said to her, but Karen didn't reply. She sat down on the sofa and sighed. They two of them were silent for a while. Finally, after a very long time, Karen spoke.

'Toby?'

'Yeah?'

'Sorry.'

'Why you sorry?' he asked her, not sure why she was apologising. He didn't think she'd done anything wrong.

'Because I'm not good at this,' she told him, her voice croaky and tired. 'I'm sorry I've been in bed. I just needed a break.'

Toby ate his sandwich, smearing chocolate spread on his chin as he took a bite.

'Why?' he asked.

He looked up at Amy. She was watching Karen.

'It's been stressful these last few days,' Karen told him. 'I've never had to be a mum before.'

'Oh,' Toby replied. He kept on eating.

'Toby!'

Amy was looking at him angrily. She had her teeth pushed tight against each other and was staring Toby right in the eyes. She pointed firmly towards Karen.

'Say something,' she told him. 'She's upset.'

Toby put the sandwich down on the plate and looked at Karen. She didn't look upset. She wasn't crying. Amy was being silly. Karen looked down at her feet. She was holding her hands tight together and her leg was bouncing up and down.

'Are you sad?' he asked her, not sure what her answer would be.

Karen looked at Toby.

'A little.'

Toby looked back at Amy. She pointed at Karen again.

'Hug her,' she told him. Toby nodded and did as he was told.

Toby grabbed Karen tight with both arms and gave her a big bear-hug that almost knocked her over. He held onto her soft dressing gown and lay his head against her chest. Even though it wasn't a very cold day, Toby noticed that she wasn't very warm. He rubbed his hands up and down her arms to try make her feel warm and snug. He always felt better when he was warm and snug. He looked up at Karen and he saw that she was smiling. That made Toby happy. He knew that she was okay now. He moved himself so that he was sat on Karen's lap and snuggled into her chest. He closed his eyes. Then, as if it were coming from a million miles away, Toby heard a quiet whisper float into his ear.

'Good job, Toby. Good job.'

After Toby had finished his lunch, Karen decided that it would be fun if they went shopping together. Toby needed clothes because his ones were old and had holes in them, so he could do with some new ones. She told him she'd seen a little shop in the high street and she thought that Toby might like to go there. He thought it was a very good idea.

Toby went to his room and took off his pyjamas, which he'd been wearing all morning, and put on some proper clothes. Once dressed, he sat down on the side of his bed. Then, just as he was about to put on his trainers, he heard a voice coming from the hallway.

'Toby?' Amy asked softly. 'Can I come in?'

'Yep,' he replied, placing the first shoe over his foot.

He thought that Amy would open the door and walk into the room. This was a silly thing to think as Amy wasn't real so she couldn't open the door. Instead, as Toby watched, she walked straight through the big wooden door and appeared in his room. He jumped and fell off the bed, landing on his knee as he hit the floor. Amy ran over to him and knelt on the floor next to him.

'Sorry!' she said nervously. 'I didn't mean to scare you. I keep forgetting what that must look like, but it is cool isn't it?' She laughed and Toby forgot about the pain in his knee.

'It's awesome,' she told him. 'Hey, watch this.' Amy ran back through the door so that Toby couldn't see her anymore. He stared carefully and watched as Amy's head poked through the solid wood and into the room. She stuck her front teeth out and pointed her eyes towards her nose. It was a silly face and it made Toby laugh until his belly hurt.

'Hey, Toby,' she giggled. 'Why couldn't the skeleton go to the party?'

'Why?' he asked.

'Because he didn't have any body to go with!'

Amy fell through the door and onto the floor, laughing as she hit the carpet. Her laugh was so funny and Toby couldn't help but laugh too. Together they laughed and laughed until they couldn't laugh anymore. Then, they sat up on the floor and looked at each other. Toby liked Amy. She was fun. But, as Toby watched, he saw that Amy didn't look funny anymore. She looked very serious

'I don't think I'll be here when you get back, Toby,' she whispered, looking him dead in the eye.

Toby was confused.

'Why?' he asked angrily, his bottom lip sticking out

and his arms folded over his chest. Amy thought for a second before replying.

'You know when you have friends over? How when it gets to a certain time they have to go back home to their family?'

'Uh-huh.'

'Well, I guess this is a little like that. I have to go home Toby.'

'No!' Toby shouted, standing up and looking down angrily at his imaginary friend.

'Don't be angry Toby,' Amy told him. 'I've had so much fun today but I have to go home.'

'You can't go home.' he told her. Amy raised her eyebrows.

'And why is that?' she asked.

Toby stared at her, his eyes red and watery.

'Because you're not real!'

The room went quiet after that. It was like someone had turned the sound off. The room was silent. Amy stared at Toby but didn't say a word. She just looked at him with a face that showed just how hurt she really was.

Toby stomped out of the room and into the living room. Karen was leaning against a kitchen counter, doing up the buttons on a bright blue jacket that matched her hair. Toby snatched his coat off the sofa and stared at her.

'What's wrong?' she asked him, walking over to him and putting her hand on his shoulder.

'Amy is being mean,' he told her, his bottom lip still sticking out.

Karen rolled her eyes. She gave Toby a little hug. When she let go, she grabbed Toby's hand in hers and walked him to the door.

'Oh well,' she told him, her hand on the doorknob. 'She's not real. You don't need to worry about someone who isn't real.'

Karen opened the door. Toby felt the warm sun hit him as the two of them stepped outside. He looked back into the living room. In the centre of the room, he could see a girl with long blonde hair, dark eyes and white skin watching him and Karen leave. He looked up at Karen and nodded.

'Yes,' he told her. 'Not real.'

With a push of air, the door slammed shut.

It didn't take Toby long to forget about Amy. He and Karen were having too much fun for him to worry about what had happened. The clothes shop in the high street was very small, but it was good because it only had a few people in it. Toby didn't like places where there were lots of people. After they'd bought some clothes, Karen and Toby went to a little café that was next door to the shop. Karen bought Toby a strawberry ice cream in a pot because he didn't like eating ice cream out of a cone. Karen got a bubble-gum flavour ice-lolly that was the same colour as her hair.

As they stood outside the shop, Karen licking her ice-lolly and Toby scooping up bits of his ice cream with a ittle plastic spoon, he had a look through the café window. At a table right by the window and sitting on a wooden chair, was an old man having a drink. He wasn't really old but he was still a lot older than Mum and Dad had been when they died. He was wearing a big red woolly jumper that made Toby's skin itch just looking at it and a big brown beanie that came down almost over his eyes. The man's face was strange to Toby. His nose was big and red and his eyes were just really small slits that Toby couldn't really see. Still, even though he looked strange, Toby thought he looked nice. He had a fuzzy white beard that Toby thought looked funny. After a while, the man saw that Toby was watching him and didn't look very happy about it. Toby didn't look away. The old man ignored him and took a sip of his drink. He didn't look at Toby again.

It didn't take them long to walk back to the house. They walked side-by-side, Karen carrying a plastic shopping bag that swung with every step. She looked happier than she had done that morning. Toby thought that was very good because he didn't want Karen to be upset. He looked at the very end of the road and saw their house far away in the distance. He looked up at Karen.

'Going to run back,' he told her, pointing at the house.

Karen smiled and pat him on the shoulder.

'Go on then,' she said with a wink and Toby started to run along the pavement. He watched the sun above begin to turn orange and felt his feet hit the ground as they pushed him further and further forward. He watched as the house got closer and closer. He smiled, his mouth open wide, and felt the wind flying through his thick brown hair as he ran.

He saw the side of his house come into view. He sped up to reach it and put his cold hand on the brick wall. For a second, he stopped to catch his breath. He looked back down the pavement and saw Karen far away from him, the bag in her hand still swinging. As he watched her, she waved at Toby. Toby, still smiling, waved back. He hadn't felt this happy in ages. He couldn't even remember the last time he'd felt like this. He felt fantastic, he felt super, he felt....

Toby heard a cough. It was a wet cough, like when you swallow water in a swimming pool. Toby turned around to see if anyone was near him. There was no one. He heard the cough again. It was coming from outside their house. Toby felt a sick feeling in his stomach. He looked back at Karen and saw that she was still far away. Toby looked down at the floor and took a deep breath. He was going to have to be a very brave boy. He grabbed onto the corner of the brick wall of the house and looked around at the front lawn. Toby nearly screamed. Lying on her side, her head on their doorstep, was Amy. She wasn't breathing much and when she did breathe she took long, wheezing breaths that made Toby feel ill. She wasn't white anymore either. Her skin had turned green and Toby could see that there was a lot of sick around her mouth. The sick was on the doorstep too. But, what scared Toby most was what he saw in the sick. It was blood. As Toby stared at Amy, he saw her lips begin to move. She whispered to Toby in a frightened, croaky voice that sent tears running down his cheek.

'Help me,' she pleaded.

Toby felt the world collapse around him.

5 THINGS START TO GO WRONG

Toby stared at Amy's shaking body. The world had become darker all of a sudden and, apart from the noise his friend was making, Toby couldn't hear anything at all. It had all gone quiet except for Amy. She was still coughing. She wouldn't stop. Toby wanted to put his fingers in his ears and pretend that it wasn't happening but he couldn't lift his arms. They were too heavy. He wanted to run but he couldn't feel his legs. He wanted to close his eyes and make the tears stop, but he couldn't. All that Toby could do was stare at his imaginary friend, her face pale and covered with sick and blood.

'Help,' Amy whispered, her voice weak and unsteady.

Toby screamed. He screamed and screamed until his throat burned. He screamed louder than he'd ever screamed before and his screaming was so loud that Karen heard him from all the way back down the road.

'Toby!' he heard her yell.

Toby didn't answer. Instead, he ran towards the front door and tried to help his friend.

Amy was very sick. Toby tried to grab her skinny arm but his hand just went straight through. It hit the stone step below with a painful thud. He pulled his hand back and rubbed his fingers. They hurt a lot but he didn't care. He tried to pick her up but his arms just slid through her. The tears in his eyes were stinging. He kept on screaming louder and louder but he still couldn't help his friend. He couldn't save her. She was going to die. Mum and Dad had died and now he was going to let Amy die because he was little and stupid and wasn't good enough. He fell down next to Amy and began to sob. He was so upset and crying so much that he didn't hear Karen's footsteps racing towards him.

'What's wrong?' she yelled, her voice only just loud enough to be heard over his crying. Toby pointed at Amy.

'She's sick!' he told her, screaming at the top of his lungs.

Karen looked at Amy. As she stared, Amy threw up all over the doorstep, covering it in sick and blood. Toby wanted to run over to her but Karen grabbed his shoulders tight. He looked at him with horrified eyes.

'Who the hell are you talking about?' she asked in a frightened voice. Toby pointed at Amy again.

'Amy!' he said, tears running down his face. 'She's not well.'

Karen's grip on his shoulders became tighter, her fingernails stabbing sharply at the skin underneath his shirt.

'Is this your imaginary friend?' she asked him.

Toby nodded. Karen was mad, very mad, but it wasn't just that. Her voice was afraid and Toby could tell that she was almost as scared as he was.

'Toby,' she whispered. 'You need to stop this now. Do you understand me?'

Toby shook his head and stomped his feet.

'No!'

'Why not?'

'Because!'

'Because what?'

Toby threw his arms up and down. He didn't know what else to do. Everything was going bad and he couldn't fix any of it. His face went red as he got angrier and angrier until he let out one gigantic scream that was so loud it made Karen cover her ears. Toby didn't stop screaming. He didn't know what else to do. His screaming was so loud that people from the other houses had walked out into the road. They were all looking at him but he didn't care. Finally, Karen decided enough was enough. She wrapped her fingers around Toby's wrist so tightly that he thought his hand was going to fall off.

'Ouch!' he cried, trying to pull his arm away. 'You're hurting me!'

Karen didn't listen to him. She dragged him over to the door and pulled the keys out from her pocket. Toby heard them clink together in her hand as she searched for the right one. Then, he looked down and saw that they were standing inside Amy.

Toby let out another gigantic scream and a person from one of the other houses ran over to them. The person was a woman, an old woman.

'Are you alright?' the woman asked Karen politely, her voice raised so that she could be heard over Toby's screaming. Karen glared at her with furious eyes.

'No, I'm not alright!' she yelled, causing the woman to take a few steps back. 'Go away and mind your own business.'

The door opened with a bang and Karen shoved Toby inside, slamming the front door shut and dropping her bag onto the floor. She ran to the middle of the living room and put her hands on the back of her head, before starting to walk manically in a circle. She was taking very deep breaths but Toby could hardly hear them. His screaming was too loud.

Then, he saw something out of the corner of his eye. He looked back at the front door and jumped. As he watched, Toby saw a shaking hand slide through the wooden door and land silently on the carpet. The hand was green and parts of the fingernails were missing. Toby realised what was happening. Amy was trying to get back inside.

She came in head-first, her long hair dragging across the floor as she pulled herself through the door. Toby wanted to see her face but she wasn't strong enough to lift it off the carpet. It took a while, but the rest of her body soon started to follow her through. Toby watched, amazed by what he was seeing. Finally, after what had seemed like forever, her feet entered the room. Then, as soon as she was completely inside, Amy stopped moving. She went very still and, for a moment, Toby thought that she might have died. Then, as if by magic, he watched Amy's skin turned from green to the pale white it had been before. His imaginary friend looked up at him, blood still smeared all over her lips, and let out a long sigh of relief.

'Thank you, Toby,' she whispered, the words barely making it out of her lips. Then, he watched as Amy closed her eyes and passed out on the living room floor.

Karen didn't speak to Toby for the rest of the day. One of the few times he saw her was when she called him out of his room for dinner. Toby tried talking to her and gave her a big smile to let her know that everything was okay, but she just stared at him and handed him a bowl of spaghetti. She went to her room after that and that was the last he saw of her for a while. Toby sat down on the living room sofa and scooped up a big pile of pasta. He shoved it into his mouth and chewed. The spaghetti was cold. He wanted to throw it away but he was really hungry, so he swallowed what he had in his mouth and scooped up some more.

Karen had left the TV on and it was still on the same channel that she'd been watching. It wasn't a channel that Toby recognised and he knew instantly that it was a channel for grown-ups. There was a very important looking man on the screen. He was sitting behind a big white desk and talking about something that Toby didn't understand. The man had a very square face and was wearing a posh black suit with a bright red tie that was clipped down with a piece of silver. He had greasy black hair that was slicked back so far that Toby could see his forehead bulging out over his eyebrows. Daniel had taken Toby to a museum once. He'd seen a painting there of a mammoth stuck in a pit of black tar. Toby thought about how much the man's hair looked like the tar in that painting, all oily and dark, but then he decided to have some more spaghetti.

He scraped another forkful and looked at Amy, who was still lying down by the front door. Her eyes were open a little and Toby could hear her soft breathing, even above the noise of the TV. She looked much better now. Her skin was white again and all the green had gone from her body. She hadn't thrown up again since she'd been inside either. Now, Amy was still and was watching the TV with Toby.

Toby stared at the screen. He ate another forkful of pasta and listened as the important man continued to talk. Toby didn't understand what he was saying but he knew that it was important. He watched as pictures of places he'd never been to flashed up on the screen. Some of the places looked nice but some of them didn't. Still, he kept on watching, eating his dinner quietly as the important man continued to talk.

After a while, Toby finished the bowl of spaghetti. As he used his finger to scoop up the remaining sauce from the sides of the bowl, he heard a noise coming from by the front door. It was a quiet, frightened noise that made Toby's whole body go cold. He crawled across the sofa and stared over the armrest, his eyes fixed firmly on the pale body of his friend Amy.

'Are you okay?' he asked her.

Amy didn't say anything. She just stared at the TV like a zombie, her eyes heavy and unfocused. Toby looked back at the screen. The important man was talking about something. Toby didn't understand what it was he was talking about and the man was speaking so fast that Toby didn't have any time to figure it out. Toby didn't know many big words but, as he listened to the man on the TV, he tried his best to find any shorter ones that he could understand.

Two

Boys

Knife

Killed

Fire

Burned

Those were a few of the words. He didn't know many more and still couldn't quite figure out what the man was talking about. As he tried to arrange the words in his head so that he could figure out what was going on, the important man on the TV disappeared and something else came on in his place. Something very different.

There was another man on the TV now. He wasn't like the very important man at all. The man before had been wearing a suit but this man looked very scruffy. He was dressed in a grey jumper and baggy trousers that looked very big on him, so big that they hung loosely around his ankles. The man before was also quite square and strong but this new man looked very skinny. He didn't look very well at all and

Toby thought that he might fall over at any second. He watched the man walk, shuffling his feet as he went. Every step looked like it hurt. There were two policemen walking with him, their big muscly arms hooked under the man's bony little shoulders. They were almost carrying him as the man could barely move. The man and the two policemen were leaving a big brown building. As Toby watched, they hurried down a row of big grey steps and made their way towards a black car. As they got closer to the car, people began to crowd around them, taking pictures and flashing lights as they shouted questions at the man. Questions that he didn't answer. Then, as the policemen pushed through the crowd, Toby heard a voice. It was louder than all the other voices but was calmer, as if it didn't have to shout to be heard. Toby didn't know what the voice was talking about but he still managed to understand a few of the words that were spoken.

Life

Death

Amelia

Amelia. Toby knew that word. It was a name. He'd heard it once before but he couldn't quite remember when. The policemen pulled the man into the car. As soon as they were inside, it began to drive off. The woman stopped speaking and Toby watched in silence as the black car disappeared. Then, the important man came back onto the screen. He had a very serious look on his face. Toby listened as he spoke, the man's voice quiet and heavy as if the words were weighing him down.

Never

Forget

Amelia

The man vanished. For a second, the screen went black. Then, something new appeared on the TV. It was a

73

picture, a picture of a girl. She wasn't very tall but she wasn't small either and she had long frizzy hair that fell down by her shoulders. Her cheeks were rosy red and her bright eyes shone like stars. Toby stared at the girl's mouth. She was smiling. He smiled back at her even though he knew she couldn't see him. Still, as he looked into the girl's eyes, he could tell that she was happy. Then, just like that, she disappeared.

As Toby watched, the important man came back onto the screen. The man was talking about something, he knew that much, but Toby wasn't listening. He crawled across the sofa and peered over the armrest. Amy didn't look at him. He could tell that the programme had done something to her. Toby knew that she was upset. Her face was blank, as if she didn't feel anything, but her dull eyes were filled with tears. Something on the TV had upset her. Maybe it was the skinny man, who'd been so weak that he could barely walk. Maybe it was the man in the suit, whose slimy hair reminded Toby so much of the tar in that painting he'd seen long ago. Somehow Toby knew it wasn't either of those things. He knew why she was upset. She was upset about the girl, Amelia.

'Did she die?' Toby asked her, staring down at her with wide-eyes. Amy didn't say anything, but she didn't have to. Toby had gotten his answer. The girl called Amelia was dead and Amy was very upset about it.

Amy didn't get up that night, at least not before Toby's bedtime. By the time Karen came to get him, it had become very dark outside and the only light that Toby could see out the window was one lonely street-lamp shining over the pavement. Karen looked exhausted. She was wearing her dressing gown again, with matching blue slippers on her feet that shuffled along the carpet as she made her way into the living room.

'Right,' she mumbled, running a hand through her hair. 'Bedtime.'

'When's Daniel getting back?' Toby asked, looking up at her from his spot on the sofa. Karen shook her head.

'I don't know. He's working late.'

'Why?'

Karen glared at him. She edged closer to the sofa and leant on the armrest, her fingers wrapping around it like the claws of a lion.

'Toby,' she whispered firmly. 'I've had a very long day. I don't need anything more to go wrong. Just go and get ready for bed.'

Toby looked over his shoulder and pointed down at the spot where Amy was.

'What about Amy?' he asked Karen, his voice quiet and innocent.

That was the wrong thing to ask. Karen stormed over to Toby and grabbed him by the wrist. She pulled him off the sofa and dragged him out of the room, mumbling under her breath angrily as they went. Toby didn't struggle. Karen's grip was very strong so he couldn't have escaped even if he'd wanted to. He knew he had upset Karen. He hadn't meant to, but he hadn't known what else to do. Amy was still lying there all alone and he didn't want her to be sick again. He was afraid, afraid that it would happen again. Karen pulled him into his room and slammed the door shut. She grabbed a pair of pyjama bottoms and shoved them into Toby's hands.

'I want you in bed by the time I get back. Do I make myself clear?'

Toby nodded and Karen left the room. As he pulled the pyjamas over his legs, tears started to burn in his eyes. He didn't know what to do anymore; he didn't even know what was real. Amy wasn't real, he thought he'd known that, but things that aren't real don't cough up blood. Only real things did that, so Amy must be real. She must be.

Toby crawled into bed and pulled the blanket up to

his chin. He waited for Karen to come back. He waited a while for her but, when she finally did come back, she didn't say goodnight. She just stared at Toby from behind the half open door and then left him without saying a word.

Toby closed his eyes and slid into an uneasy sleep, one filled with nightmares. They were nightmares filled with blood, sick and the name of that girl on the TV.

Amelia.

As Toby slept restlessly, his imaginary friend continued to lie on the living room carpet. The sickness in Amy's stomach was finally gone and she could feel her exhausted body starting to recover. It hadn't been what she'd expected, but her journey outside had revealed one key thing about her condition. She couldn't leave the house. The idea filled Amy with a sense of dread. She'd been trapped in the house for five years and she wasn't going to be getting out anytime soon. She would have to stay; that was her only option. As she lay there, alone on the floor and covered in sick and blood, Amy began to think of her friend, Toby.

'He shouldn't have seen that,' she thought, remembering the terrified look on his face. 'They already think he's losing it.'

Toby didn't need this. Amy had never wanted him to think that she was real. Never. It would have been dangerous for him, being the only one who could see her. Ever since that first time he'd asked, she'd told him that she was imaginary. That had been a good lie and it had worked, at least for a while. Life had been hard enough on Toby already. First his parents had died, then he'd had to move into a new house. That was enough to deal with. He didn't need a girl throwing up blood on his doorstep.

Amy wasn't the same as she had once been. She had seen that picture on the news and it was scary how she could hardly recognise herself. She'd looked so alive in that picture but she didn't look like that now. Her hair was dirty, her face was thin, and her skin was almost completely white, except for the bruises of course. That photo was old though. It hadn't shown what she'd looked like that summer, the summer that seemed so far away from where she was now.

The front door opened and Daniel's black leather shoes stepped through Amy's body. She didn't feel anything when that sort of stuff happened. She hadn't felt anything when Toby had fallen through her chest and she didn't feel anything now either. Still, it wasn't an experience that she was used to. Not yet. As Daniel slipped off his shoes and slumped into the sofa, Amy's view of him became blocked. All that she could see of him were his legs, which stretched out across the carpet in front of him. Amy wondered what Daniel was like as a person. She'd only seen him those times in the attic and they hadn't painted the best picture of him. Then again, who wouldn't have been scared after what Toby had told him. Daniel yawned and picked up the TV remote. As the screen flickered on, Amy heard the familiar voice of the news reporter. She tried to cover her ears but she didn't have the strength to lift her hands. She didn't want to hear him talk about it again. She didn't want to have to listen to what a tragedy it was and how she would be missed. All that she wanted was for him to go away. Then, all of a sudden, Amy heard the hallway door open.

'We need to talk.'

It was Karen, her voice seeming to echo in the room as she spoke. Turning off the TV, Daniel pulled his legs back.

'What's the matter?' he asked in a worried voice. Amy heard Karen sit down on the sofa next to her fiancé.

'What do you think?' she said angrily. Daniel voice became confused.

'I really don't know,' he told her. 'Is there a problem with the house?'

Karen let out a sarcastic laugh.

'No,' she replied. 'There's nothing wrong with the house. It's Toby.'

The room went silent. Amy could hear her heart beating heavily in her chest.

'Do you remember when you found him up in the attic?' Karen asked Daniel, her voice more concerned than angry now.

'Yes,' Daniel replied, 'Why? Has something happened?'

'Toby and I went shopping today,' she told him, her voice trembling slightly. 'We were walking back to the house when he ran off. Not long after that, I heart him screaming so I ran after him. Do you know why he was screaming? It was because his imaginary friend wasn't well.'

No one spoke a word. Amy could tell that Daniel didn't know what to say. She could tell that he was trying speak but he was so shocked that he seemed to be lost for words.

'Is...'

'Is he okay?' Karen yelled at him. 'He's fine now, but he wasn't when she was about to roll over dead! This is getting scary Daniel. Do you know how terrifying that was?'

'Karen, children have imaginary friends!' Daniel told her, his patience wearing thin, 'Didn't you have an imaginary friend when you were his age?'

'Not like this, Dan! Never like this!'

Karen started to cry. Amy felt sorry for her. It wasn't her fault; she was bound to be worried. It was Amy's fault, not Karen's. Amy had caused all this. If Toby hadn't found her then maybe things wouldn't have gotten to this stage. As she listened, Amy heard Daniel take Karen into his arms.

'I'm a horrible person,' Karen sobbed as Daniel held her tight. 'I hate it.'

'Don't be silly,' Daniel told her. 'You're not a horrible person at all.'

'Yes I am!' she cried. 'I'm never usually like this with Toby, or you either. I just don't know what to do.'

Amy listened as Daniel ran his fingers through Karen's hair. Her crying began to get quieter, but when she spoke the hurt in her voice was unmistakable.

'I'm so bad at this,' she mumbled quietly. Daniel shook his head.

'No,' he told her firmly. 'You're not bad. You're just new to this.'

'What about Toby?' Karen asked.

Amy heard Daniel scratch his stubbly chin. He was clearly thinking hard about how to answer the question.

'If it's getting as bad as you say, then I guess we have to look at our options. Like you've said, this is sounding a lot different to a simple imaginary friend.'

'What can we do?' Karen whispered nervously.

'I'm not sure at the moment,' he told her. 'I think that our best course of action is to just see how things go. It could be a sign that he's still not coping with what happened. He might need some help.'

'What, like professional help?'

'If this carries on, then I think we'd better at least look into it.'

That was all that Daniel said on the matter, but it was enough to ease Karen's mind.

'Thank you, Dan,' she whispered, the words faint in her mouth. 'I'm sorry.'

'What are you sorry about?' he asked. Karen's voice was stronger now, but she still had things to get off her chest.

'I'm sorry for being like this. I didn't think that I would be looking after a family when I was this young. It wasn't what I thought would happen but I'll do my best to make things work out.'

'I know,' Daniel replied, his voice calm and soothing. 'Hopefully not too long until the wedding either.'

Karen laughed quietly to herself.

'I think we'd better get this year out of the way first,' she told him.

'I agree,' Daniel replied. 'This has not been our year.'

And with that final summation, the voices of Daniel and Karen went silent. The two fell asleep on the sofa, wrapped in each others arms. Their night had ended well; it had ended with a plan. They knew what they were going to do and they were going to stick to that. They knew what to do but Amy didn't. As Daniel and Karen slept comfortably on the sofa, Amy lay awake, thinking about what they had said. They were going to send Toby to a therapist. Toby was going to have to go to a trained professional and tell him about his imaginary friend, the imaginary friend that he'd found tied up in chains in his attic. She was the friend who had a bloodstain in the middle of her dress, the friend who'd told him to pick up a kitchen knife, the friend who'd vomited blood on his doorstep. He was going to have to tell a therapist about everything. They'd probably prescribe him something to make her go away, except she wouldn't go away because she couldn't leave. Toby would still see her and then something much worse could happen. He could get committed. He could get sent away to a place that he'd never get out of, especially when they found out that his imaginary friend was none other than Amelia Moore, the girl who'd died almost five years ago.

6 THE LAST STRAW

Toby was the first one to wake up the next morning. Propping himself against his pillows so that he was more or less sitting up, he rubbed his bleary eyes and turned his head towards the window. As he looked through the thin piece of cloth that covered the glass, he saw that the morning sun had turned the leaves on the hedge outside orange. Toby yawned. It was early, too early for him to be up. He should have rolled over and tried to get some more sleep but, all of a sudden, he became very thirsty. He slid out of bed and went into the kitchen to get himself a glass of water. After picking up a plastic cup that had been sitting on the side, he made his way over to the sink and turned on the tap. Once he'd filled the cup to the brim, he brought it to his lips and drank happily. The water tasted very good. Toby finished drinking and put the empty cup back on the side. He was just about to go back to bed when he heard something. It was a noise, a quiet noise. Someone had whispered his name. Nervously, he peered out from behind the kitchen counter and stared into the living room

Amy was standing there, just like she'd done a few days ago. She was in the same space she'd stood when Toby had first seen her out of the attic, only this time she looked very different. She'd been smiling that time but she wasn't smiling now. Her eyes looked down at Toby very seriously. It was as if she was mad at him, as if he'd done something wrong. Toby was worried; he knew he hadn't done anything wrong. Or had he? Toby thought hard and tried to figure out what he could have done to upset his friend. Was she mad at him for not sharing his spaghetti last night? No, she couldn't have eaten it anyway. It would probably have just fallen through her body and landed on the floor. Was she mad that he hadn't been able to help her when she'd been throwing up? That wasn't his fault! He'd tried to help her but he hadn't been able to because she wasn't real. But maybe she was real. Toby wasn't sure he knew anymore. Then, out of nowhere, he remembered something that had upset Amy, something that could have be the reason she was mad at him.

'Are you mad at me because of Amelia?' he asked, looking up into Amy's serious eyes. 'Is that why you're mad at me?'

Amy looked surprised. She walked over to him and knelt down so that she and Toby were the same height.

'No, Toby,' she whispered. 'Of course not.'

'Then why are you mad at me?'

'I'm not!' she told him. 'I'm not mad; I'm worried.'

Toby felt his stomach sink. Grown-ups were only worried when things were really bad.

'What's wrong?' he asked, his voice nervous and unsteady. Amy didn't look at him. Instead, she looked to the side of him, almost as if he wasn't there at all. She was silent for a while, her lips moving quietly as she tried to force the words out. When she finally managed it, they came out croaky and broken, like they were hurting her.

'You can't tell Daniel and Karen about me. If you keep telling them that you can see me, we won't be able to be friends anymore.'

Toby didn't know what she was saying. His palms became sweaty and the room started to spin.

'Not friends anymore?' he asked her, tears welling up in his eyes. Amy sighed sadly.

'Not if you keep doing this,' she told him. 'Not if you keep telling Daniel and Karen that you can see me.'

Toby started to cry. He curled his hands tightly into fists and glared at Amy through teary eyes as his face began to turn red.

'Toby?' she whispered nervously. 'Are you alright?'

There was no response. Toby's face got redder.

'What's wrong?'

He didn't say anything. A vein started to appear in Toby's forehead.

'Stop it.'

Toby was starting to feel dizzy.

'Stop it!'

He was surprised by what Amy did next. He hadn't expected it and, once it had happened, he found it very hard to believe that it had actually happened. Just as Toby's face had started to turn purple, his imaginary friend, who wasn't really there, had grabbed hold of his shoulders and shaken his whole body. Air was forced into his lungs and Toby felt the dizziness disappear sharply. Startled, he fell backwards, landing on his bottom far away from his friend. Then, once his crying had stopped and the room had gone silent, it all hit him. Amy had just touched him. His imaginary friend who nobody else could see had put her hands on his shoulders. It was right then that Toby knew exactly what Amy was. Amy was real.

He jumped to his feet and ran towards Amy. She

looked almost as surprised as Toby. Amy stared at her hands with wide eyes and looked at Toby, her mouth open wide with shock.

'You're real,' Toby whispered.

Amy shook her head.

'No, Toby,' she told him. 'I'm imaginary, remember?'

Toby wasn't convinced.

'You touched me,' he said. 'Imaginary friends can't touch because they're not real, but you can touch so you are real.'

Amy turned her head sharply towards the open hallway door. Toby looked into her bright eyes. They looked afraid. He followed her gaze and saw instantly what she was staring at. A light had been turned on in Daniel and Karen's room. Toby looked back at Amy. She was shaking.

'Don't tell them anything,' she begged. 'Please don't let them know that you can still see me. You'll get in trouble.'

Toby froze. Trouble? Toby didn't want to get in trouble. Would Daniel and Karen really think he'd done something wrong? He hadn't done anything wrong! He didn't want to get in trouble.

The bedroom door opened and Daniel, wearing just a pair of black pants, walked into the hallway. Both Toby and Amy stared at him. They watched him yawn and both of them remained silent as he began to walk down the hallway. Quick as a flash, Toby slammed the hallway door shut and ran into the kitchen, Amy following close behind him.

'Toby,' she said, her breathing heavy and fast. 'I love you. Whatever happens I want you to know that I love you.'

Toby nodded.

'I love you too,' he told her. He wanted to hug her, to squeeze her tight and never let her go. But he knew he couldn't.

Boom.

The hallway door flew open. Toby watched as Daniel slunk into the room, rubbing his eyes hard with his knuckles. He turned his head and saw Toby standing in the kitchen, looking up at him with big nervous eyes.

'What's going on?' Daniel asked him, creeping slowly closer towards his brother. Toby stayed quiet. He didn't know what to say. He wanted to tell Daniel that his imaginary friend had somehow turned real and that she wasn't imaginary anymore, but then he thought about what Amy had said.

You'll get in trouble.

'Come on,' Daniel said impatiently. 'What have you been doing out here?'

Toby didn't know what to do. His brain was melting inside his head and he didn't know how to stop it. What could he do? Tell the truth and get in trouble, or lie.

He knew what he had to do. He couldn't lie to Daniel because lying was a bad thing that only bad people did. It didn't matter if he was going to get in trouble, because if he told the truth then he'd still be a good boy. He stared up at Daniel. His lips parted and his mouth opened, ready to tell his brother about everything that had happened. He was going to do it. He was going to tell him that Amy was real.

Toby stopped. His mouth was wide open but, for some reason, no words were coming out. He was just standing there silently, looking up into Daniel's tired eyes. But he wasn't looking into Daniel's eyes anymore. Somehow, without even realising it, Toby's eyes had stopped looking at his big brother and were now focused just to the side of him, looking at someone else completely. His eyes were looking at Amy. She was crouching by the edge of the kitchen counter now. Her skinny arms were wrapped around her shoulders and her head was hanging down towards the floor. He could only see a little bit of her face from where he was standing. As Toby watched his imaginary friend, he saw a tear roll down her cheek and land quietly onto the floor. Toby didn't say anything. Amy was crying. That meant that Amy was sad. Why was Amy sad? Then he realised. He'd made Amy sad.

'Well?'

Toby looked once again into the tired eyes of his big brother. He took a deep breath and finally spoke.

'Water.'

The room went silent.

'Water?'

'Yes.'

'You wanted water?'

'Yes.'

Daniel stared down at his little brother. Toby didn't dare breathe. He looked from Daniel to Amy and then back. They were both like statues. For a long time, nobody spoke. Then, after what felt like forever, Daniel broke the silence.

'Try not to be so loud next time,' he told Toby. 'I've got work in a couple of hours.'

Toby nodded. He'd done it! His lie had worked! As Daniel left the living room and shut the hallway door behind him, Toby looked over at Amy and smiled. Amy looked back at him. She was smiling too, but it wasn't a big smile like Toby's.

'What's wrong?' he asked her.

'Nothing,' she told him. 'I just got myself a bit worried. Thank you for lying Toby.'

Toby puffed out his chest and put his hands on his hips.

'I lied. I lied and got away with it.' he smiled. Amy nodded. She still didn't look very happy but she didn't look sad either, so that was good. She got up and stood in front of the hallway door.

'I need a lie down,' she whispered, just loudly enough for him to hear.

'You can use my bed,' Toby told her happily. 'I'm not going back to bed. I'm awake now.'

Amy let out a little laugh. It wasn't really a laugh, more like a little sniff of air that came out of her nose.

'I'd fall through, remember?'

Toby nodded. He'd forgotten that.

'But you touched me,' he told her.

'I don't even know how I did that,' she replied, looking down at her feet. 'I don't think I could do it again.'

Then, out of nowhere, the hallway door flew open and passed straight through Amy's body. Daniel's head poked around the the edge and glared at Toby, who was trying not to laugh at how funny it had looked.

'I said quiet!' his brother told him, looking very cross. Toby nodded again, scrunching his lips together to stop himself laughing. As Daniel pulled the door closed, Toby couldn't help letting out a little giggle as he saw Amy smiling at him. When it finally closed and the both of them were sure that Daniel wasn't coming back, they burst into silent laughter. Then as the laughs died down into smiles, Toby realised that Amy was probably right about what she'd said. She wouldn't be able to do that again.

Toby didn't say a word about Amy for the rest of the day. After Daniel had left for work, he and Karen went to the supermarket to do some shopping. Daniel had driven the car to work, so they had to get the bus there instead. The bus stop was right in the middle of Lawton and to get there they had to walk past the café they'd been to the day before. As Karen pulled Toby along the pavement and past the big window at the front of the café, Toby looked inside and saw something that he hadn't expected to see. The old man, the one with the fuzzy white beard that Toby had seen there the other day, was sat in the very same spot all by himself. Toby didn't get a very good look at him, but he did get a little glimpse. Toby wondered why the old man was all alone on such a nice day.

After the shopping was done, Karen asked Toby if he wanted to have lunch in the supermarket café. As she dropped the heavy bags onto the floor and sat down at one of the little metal tables, she let out a big sigh that Toby heard easily, even over all the other noise in the café. It was a very noisy café. Toby could hear knives and forks clinking together and people chewing with their mouths open and little babies screaming loudly for food. It wasn't what he'd thought the café would be like, but he hoped that the food would still be nice.

'What would you like?' Karen asked him, pointing up at a menu above the counter where all the food was. Toby couldn't read very well so he didn't know what all the words meant, but that didn't matter. He knew what he wanted.

'Sausages and beans, please,' he told her, smiling as he thought of the food.

Karen nodded.

'Right,' she said. 'I'll go get the food. Can you look after the bags please?'

'Yep,' Toby replied.

'Good boy,' she said, smiling as she spoke. She got up from her chair and went to get the food.

It didn't take long for what they'd ordered to come and when it did Toby ate it all very fast. It tasted so nice that he gobbled it all up before Karen had even finished half of her meal.

'Enjoy that?' she asked, a little smile creeping across her face. Toby nodded.

'I did,' he replied, smiling back at her as he spoke. 'Thank you, Karen.'

Karen put her knife and fork down. Toby became worried. He looked at Karen. Her eyes were a little teary but her smile had gotten bigger somehow. Toby was very confused.

'Are you okay?' he asked her. Karen looked at him and nodded.

'Just happy,' she told him. 'I love you, Toby.'

'I love you too, Karen.'

Toby felt very happy after that.

The day had been a good one for Toby and when he got home it got even better. That evening, Karen and Daniel watched a film in the living room whilst Toby and Amy played games in his bedroom. Then, a little later than usual, Karen came in and told Toby that it was time for bed. As he snuggled under the covers, he watched his imaginary friend walk through the bedroom wall, turning back to look at him before she disappeared.

'Goodnight, Toby,' she whispered. 'See you in the

morning.'

And then she was gone. Toby whispered goodnight to Karen and watched as she left too, closing the door behind her as she went. As he closed his eyes, Toby thought about how good the day had been. It had been one of the best days Toby had ever had and he'd loved every second of it. However, Toby wasn't to know that the next day wasn't going to be a good day. In fact, it was going to be a very bad day indeed.

It was all fine in the beginning. When Toby woke up that morning, happiness still swirling around his body from the day before, he jumped out of bed and bounced out into the living room. There, he saw Karen helping Daniel get ready for work. Daniel was having trouble with his tie so Karen was trying to sort it for him.

'Morning, Toby!' Karen said happily.

'Morning,' Toby replied, smiling back at her. Toby looked at his brother.

'Morning, Champ.' said Daniel, not really paying attention to him.

Toby wanted to reply, but by the time he'd opened his mouth Daniel had left. Toby sighed sadly and looked down at his feet.

'Would you like any breakfast?' Karen asked him, as Toby sat down on the sofa. He looked at Karen. She was wearing her dressing gown again.

'Yes please,' he said to her. Karen smiled at him.

'What would you like?'

Toby thought hard. He wasn't quite sure what he wanted.

'Toast?' Karen suggested. Toby shook his head.

'How about cereal?'

Toby grinned. He liked that idea.

'Yes please,' he told her. With a little bounce, Karen went back into the kitchen to get him a bowl.

They didn't say much for a while. Toby stared blankly at the TV as Karen sorted out his breakfast. They didn't look at each other for a while. That is, at least, until Karen asked Toby a question.

'How's Amy?'

Toby froze. It was all over. She knew he'd lied to Daniel. He tore his eyes away from the TV and stared at Karen.

But her face was strange. She didn't look angry; she looked happy. That huge smile was still on her face. Toby didn't know what to say. Was she trying to trick him? Was she playing a game? He couldn't tell, but he knew one thing for sure. He couldn't let her know that he was still friends with Amy.

'Don't know,' he mumbled, biting his nails as he spoke. 'Not seen her.'

Karen looked surprised when she heard Toby say that. He didn't know why that had surprised her, but it didn't matter too much. Very soon after, her surprise faded away and a happy, carefree expression took its place. As Karen went over to the sink to do some washing up, Toby suddenly heard someone whispering his name. He turned his head and saw Amy standing next to him. She was smiling just like Karen. Toby could tell that Amy had seen him lie to Karen and knew that she was glad that he'd done it. She pointed at Karen and gave Toby a thumbs-up. Toby smiled and looked back at the TV. Things weren't as difficult as they had been before. Everyone was happy and he liked that. Everything was going great.

Karen and Toby didn't go out that day like they usually did. Karen said that the house needed to be cleaned so she asked Toby to help her out. Toby had never cleaned before, Mum had always done that, but he said he'd help Karen because he didn't want her to have to do it all by herself. They were going to start off with Daniel and Karen's room. Then, just as he was about to follow Karen through the door to the bedroom, he looked over his shoulder and saw Amy standing in the hallway behind him.

'Do you want to help?' he asked her, whispering so that Karen couldn't hear him. Amy shook her head.

'I can't,' she told him. 'Go have fun with Karen. I'll find something else to do.'

Toby wanted to ask her again. He liked spending time with Amy and he thought that having her there would make the cleaning even more fun. But, instead of doing what he wanted, he just nodded and followed Karen into the room. Having Amy's help would have been nice, but he was happy to be spending the day with Karen.

They spent the whole day cleaning the house. It shouldn't have taken them very long because it wasn't very big, not compared to Mum and Dad's, but it took Toby and Karen ages because they were laughing so much. Karen would do this thing where she'd poke the corners of her bottom lip up over the top one so that she looked like a vampire. That made Toby laugh and she spent a long time chasing him, pretending that she was going to get him. It was good fun and Toby loved every minute of it.

It was nearly dark by the time they'd finished cleaning. The last room they tidied up was Toby's room and that took ages to do. They were both tired by that point, so they were pretty slow, but they didn't stop until the room was clean. When it was finally done and every room in the house had been tidied, Karen gave Toby a big hug and kissed him on the forehead.

'You did a good job, Toby,' she told him, her arms pulling him close.

Toby looked at Karen. She looked very happy. There was a little quiet smile on her face and her thin cheeks looked rounder and softer than they usually did. As they'd been cleaning, her blue hair had fallen out of the bun that she'd tied on the top of her head so that the front bit was now dangling in front of her. Toby smiled and pushed his head closer to her, feeling as though it would be impossible for him to be any happier than he was at that moment.

Karen got a call from Daniel just before dinner. She and Toby had been in the living room when the phone had started ringing. Daniel told her that he was going to have to stay late because of how much work there was to do, so he wouldn't be having dinner with them that night. He was going to get a takeaway instead. As Karen put the phone down, Toby looked up at her from his spot on the sofa. She looked disappointed.

'I love you.' he said to her, giving her a big happy grin that showed off all his teeth. Karen looked at him and smiled. It wasn't a very big smile. As Karen went back to making dinner, baked beans on toast, Toby noticed something moving out of the corner of his eye. Turning his head, he saw the skinny body of Amy sitting on the floor in front of him, looking up into his eyes. She could see that Toby was feeling sorry for Karen. Amy smiled kindly at him and somehow Toby felt a little better.

Toby and Amy watched the TV, neither one of them saying anything. They didn't need to talk to each other, they didn't need to say anything, they were just happy watching. When the programme ended and the adverts came on, Karen placed a hot plate on Toby's lap. On the plate staring back at him, was a piece of burnt toast with a heap of baked beans splatted on top of it. As he watched the red sauce run off the crusts and onto the plate beneath, the adverts disappeared from the screen. He didn't notice when the important man came back on the TV, just like he had done two days before. He wasn't really listening to the TV as he poked at the pinkish beans with his fork and swirled them around on his plate. It took him a while to look up from his dinner. He was having a lot of fun playing with the beans, and it wasn't until he heard one very frightening word that he finally stopped to listen.

Amelia.

He'd heard that word again. Amelia. That word. The word that had made Amy so upset. The important man was talking about Amelia again. Toby started to worry. He looked down at Amy, who was still sitting on the floor below him. She was sitting with her legs crossed, her back to him and her body completely still. Toby couldn't see anything past her. She was blocking most of the TV from his view. She'd moved closer to it at some point and now Toby could hardly see any of the screen in front of them. Stretching his neck to the side, Toby stared at the tiny bit of the TV he could see and waited for the face of Amelia to appear on the screen.

But it didn't. Amelia wasn't on the TV this time. Some other people were.

As Toby watched the screen, he saw two people walking towards a car. The car was parked on the side of a road next to a big grey building that Toby thought he'd seen before. As the two people got closer, Toby saw that they were old and were holding hands, as if they would float away if they let go of each other. They were a man and a woman, both with grey hair and wrinkled faces. They were walking slowly and both of them looked sad, especially the woman. She looked very sad.

When they finally reached the car, Toby noticed that there were people around them taking pictures. It reminded him of when he'd seen the skinny man on TV, except there weren't as many people as there had been then. As the car drove away and the people stopped taking pictures, Toby heard the important man start to speak. Toby only knew a few words of what he was saying.

Parents

Never

Coming

Back

The car faded away into nothing and the TV went black.

The important man returned. He was sitting behind a desk and frowning. He looked sad but Toby wasn't sure if he really was sad. The man's frown was too stiff and wooden and it made him look like a puppet. After a while the man's face changed and became more normal looking. Then he started to talk about something else so Toby didn't bother listening to the rest. He stopped watching the TV and looked at Amy.

She still had her back to Toby so that he still couldn't see her, but Toby could still tell that something was wrong. It started with her hands. Toby could see Amy's fingers start to shake and watched as she pushed the tips against her legs so that the broken nails almost cut her skin. As Toby stared, her whole hand began to twitch.

Toby was getting scared. He didn't know what was wrong. Then, suddenly, Amy started breathing weird. They weren't normal breaths; they were dry and scratchy and fast. They sounded like they hurt.

'Amy?' Toby whispered, his voice nervous and afraid.

Amy didn't answer.

Toby looked desperately around the room, desperately trying to find Karen. His eyes darted from the kitchen to the living room and then back to the kitchen. She wasn't anywhere. She'd gone.

'Amy?'

He spoke a little louder this time but Amy still didn't say anything. She kept on breathing weird. The breaths got drier, they scratchier and, after a while, it sounded as though she was going to be sick.

Toby climbed off the sofa and crept over to his friend. Amy was really scaring him now, but he kept on walking. When he finally reached Amy's side, he looked at her face and felt as though he was going to faint.

Her eyes were fixed on the TV. The white light lit up her face but not in a good way. It made her look sick, as if she was going to die at any moment. As Toby stared at her, horrified by what he was seeing, he saw silver tears fall down Amy's cheek and land in her lap like rain.

Then it happened. Her eyelid began to twitch. As Toby watched, Amy started to make wet choking sounds. It sounded like she was drowning.

In that moment, Toby forgot that Amy was imaginary. He hadn't been sure for the last few days if she was real or not, but seeing her choking and spluttering and crying and twitching made him know for sure. He knew that she was real and he knew that he had to help her. Toby ran out of the living room and down the hallway. He threw the door to Karen and Daniel's room open and saw Karen perched on the edge of the bed. She was wrapped up in her dressing gown.

'What's wrong?' she asked, noticing Toby's horrified expression instantly.

Toby couldn't speak. He wanted to tell her. He wanted to open his lips and scream for Karen's help but his jaw stayed shut. He couldn't make a sound. Toby stared at her, his eyes wide with fear and his hands shaking madly.

'You're scaring me,' Karen told him, getting to her feet. 'What's the matter?'

Using all the strength he could muster, Toby raised his arm. Then, turning his whole body so that he was facing the door, he pointed into the hallway. Toby didn't see Karen's face as she ran past him, he didn't even follow her. His whole body had frozen solid. He couldn't walk, he couldn't run, he couldn't even put his arm down. It just stayed there, pointing at nothing. He couldn't pull it back down.

But that didn't last long. After a few seconds, Toby heard a noise that brought back his movement all at once. It was the scariest noise Toby had ever heard. It was a noise that shot through his brain like an arrow and made the hairs on the back of his neck stand up. The noise was so painful to hear that Toby clasped his hands over his ears. He had to try and stop the sound getting into his brain. But the sound wouldn't stop, it just wouldn't.

It was the sound of Karen screaming.

7 KAREN GETS ANGRY

Toby didn't know what was going on. His brain was full to bursting with so many bad feelings. He was sad, scared, anxious and afraid. There were so many feelings racing around inside his head that it felt as though they were pushing against his skull. Toby had a headache. He wanted the feelings to go away, to jump out of his mouth or climb out of his nose or even scramble out through his ears, but they wouldn't. They just kept on cramming themselves into his brain, filling every nook and cranny until there was no room left at all.

If those feelings hadn't been the only things in Toby's terrified brain, he might have been puzzled. If these feelings hadn't been there, he might have been able to think properly and ask himself a question that really needed answering. Deep down, Toby knew that Karen couldn't see Amy because Amy was imaginary and Karen was real. Real people couldn't see imaginary people so Karen definitely wouldn't be able to see Amy. So why had Karen screamed? Normally, Toby would have figured out the answer to that question, but not now.

He heard something. It was quiet and muffled and Toby couldn't quite figure out what it was. It sounded far away, as if it was coming from outer space. Toby's head twitched. He heard it again. It was the same noise, only now it sounded just a little bit clearer. It was getting closer. Toby's palms began to sweat. His fingers were shaking so much that his hands bounced up and down by his sides. No matter how hard he tried, he couldn't stop them. It was like his hands were being controlled by someone else. Toby wanted his hands to stop shaking but they wouldn't.

Then he heard it again. It was a voice. It was still quiet and muffled and Toby couldn't tell who it was or what they were saying, but he did know one thing for sure. The voice was coming from inside Karen and Daniel's room, the room that he was in right now. He felt a pair of hands wrap tight around his shoulders and flinched as two sets of sharp fingernails dug deep into his skin. He knew those fingers, he'd felt them before.

'Toby!'

Toby didn't even realise that his eyes had been shut. The lids had just closed at some point without him noticing. Maybe the bad feelings could have got out that way. Maybe they could have climbed down from his brain and crawled out through his pupils. Maybe that would have made them go away. It didn't matter anymore anyway. All that mattered now was that he had to open his eyes. He had to see where the voice was coming from. He opened his eyes slowly and stared nervously at what was standing in front of him.

Karen looked angry, very angry. She was staring down at him, her eyes wide and furious like a ferocious lion.

'What did you do?'

Toby didn't say anything. He didn't know what to do. Karen was angry but he didn't know why and he couldn't figure out how to make her happy because his brain was full to bursting with bad feelings that he couldn't get rid of.

'Answer me!' she shouted, her teeth bared like the

fangs of a tiger. Toby stared straight into Karen's eyes. They were filled with tears and the white parts had turned a painful red colour. Her eyes looked like they were hurting. Hurting bad.

Toby didn't answer. He couldn't answer. But, unfortunately for him, his silence only made Karen angrier. Her fingernails pushed deeper into his skin. They felt like knives, long sharp knives that hurt Toby so much that he wanted to cry. Karen's eyes bulged and her nostrils flared. She looked like an animal. As Toby watched, he saw Karen's face turn a dark red colour and stared in horror as a thick vein appeared on her forehead. She wrapped her bony fingers around his skinny little wrist and dragged him out of the room. As she pulled him along the hallway floor, Toby began to scream. He wanted to escape but Karen's grip was too strong. He just slid along the floor, desperately trying to pull his arm out of her tight grasp. The hallway, which had never been very long, had suddenly grown massively. It looked as though it went on for miles and miles. It was the longest hallway in the world and with every step that Karen took the door to the living room got closer. Toby stared at the door. It had never looked this big before. It was gigantic. It glared down at Toby like a giant ten times his size. The door grew and grew until it was the only thing that Toby could see. It filled the hallway now. It was about to swallow him whole. Then, just when Toby thought there was no escape from the enormous size of what was in front of him, the door stopped. Karen and Toby stared up at the massive piece of wood that separated the hallway from the living room. With one final angry glare, Karen placed her hand on the doorknob and shoved. The door flew open and crashed against the wall on the other side. Karen dragged Toby into the living room, her hand curling even tighter around his wrist as she did so. She raised her bony hand slowly into the air and pointed a long finger towards the middle of the room.

Toby didn't want to look. He didn't know what had made Karen so angry and he wasn't sure if he actually wanted to find out. But, after getting another look at Karen's furious face, Toby decided that he had to do it. Slowly and nervously, he turned his head and stared at the space she was pointing at. What Toby saw made his jaw drop. His eyes bulged, the way they do when a person has seen something so strange that they can't make sense of it. Still, even though what he saw confused him, at least he now knew what had made Karen so angry.

Usually in the living room, the sofa was pressed up against the back wall. The TV normally stood on a wooden stand on the other side of the room directly opposite the sofa, a stretch of green carpet separating the two. What Toby found strange about the living room was that one of the two things wasn't in its regular place. Instead of being on top of the stand like it usually was, the TV had moved to somewhere else in the room. Now, it was in the middle of the room, face down on the dirty green carpet. Toby tried to walk forward. He wanted to get a better look at the television but he felt a sharp tug pull him back. He looked up and saw Karen staring down at him, shaking her head firmly. He looked back at the TV and saw why she didn't want him to go near it. All around the TV and in between the strands of green carpet, Toby could see tiny shards of glass, shining in front of him like a field of diamonds. He stared around the room, trying to count how many shards there were, but he couldn't get them all. There were so many of them. For a second, Toby wondered where the glass had come from. His mind was slow at that moment and the bad feelings in his brain were making it hard for him to think, but after a while he got it. The bigger pieces of glass were the closest to the TV. He finally figured it out. Someone had shattered the TV, broken the screen into a million pieces. Toby didn't know who'd done it. Who would want to move the TV? They couldn't have been very good at carrying things if they'd dropped it. They couldn't have been very strong.

Then he saw her. Hidden away in shadow in the far corner of the living room, Toby noticed Amy sitting on the floor. He could tell that it was Amy because of her white dress. He couldn't tell from her face because her head was in her hands. She was crying too. Toby could hear her crying and he didn't like it. It was a quiet cry that made Amy sound weak and hurt. It was the sort of cry that a very old dog would make if it had hurt its leg. It was quiet, it was slow and it told Toby that Amy was hurting very badly on the inside. He wanted to go over to her, to wrap his little arms around her and hug her tight. He wanted to help her but, as he tried taking a couple of nervous steps towards his imaginary friend, he felt a sharp tug at his wrist. Karen pulled him back to her side. Nervously, he stared into Karen's angry red eyes and whispered, barely opening his lips as he told her what had happened.

'Amy did this.'

As Toby waited for Karen to reply, he noticed something strange happen. As he watched, Karen's red eyes filled with tears that slid down her cheeks and flowed all the way to her chin. They were big, thick tears, but she didn't wipe them away. Instead, Karen let go of Toby's wrist, covered her face and began to sob loudly into her hands. Karen's crying was very different to Amy's. Amy's crying had sounded like an old dog that had been hurt. Karen's crying was more like a dying dog, a dog that was dying in horrible pain. Toby had never heard crying like that. It sounded like it hurt more than he could ever imagine. As he listened to Karen's sobbing, he felt his whole body freeze over. All he could do was watch as Karen cried. There was nothing that he could do about it. He just had to stand there and watch as the person he loved so much filled the house with her painful sobbing.

It was a long while before Karen said anything. Toby wanted her to speak but, when her hands finally came away from her face, he wished that they'd stayed put. As he stared up at Karen, feeling more afraid than he'd ever felt in his entire life, he noticed long angry lines of dark red zigzagging across the white parts of her eyeballs. It was like her eyes were on fire, burning her in the most painful way. Karen finally opened her mouth to speak. Toby felt the hairs on the back of his neck stand up. He shuddered as the words floated out of her mouth.

'Amy?' she whispered, teeth clenched tightly together. 'Amy did this?'

Toby nodded and pointed at his imaginary friend. He watched as Karen's gaze followed his finger. Her eyes fixed firmly on the spot where Amy was. Karen laughed, but it wasn't a happy laugh.

'Your imaginary friend did this?' she asked, her head jolting back sharply to face him.

Toby nodded again. Karen ran her hands through her hair and let out one long shaky breath that made Toby shudder. Clenching both her hands tightly into fists, Karen got down onto one knee and looked Toby straight in the eye.

'Stop this,' she told him firmly, her voice blunt and strong like a stone wall.

Toby knew that she was mad at him, but what she'd said confused him. He couldn't stop because he hadn't done anything. Amy was the one who'd broken the TV, not him, and he wasn't going to pretend that any of it was his fault.

'I've not done anything,' he told her. 'It was…'

Suddenly, Karen's arms shot out towards him. She grasped his shoulders tightly, squeezing hard as if she didn't want him to escape. Her red eyes were closer to him now. Toby could see all the red lines in her eyes. It was like someone had scribbled a red pen across her eyeballs. Toby didn't like it one bit. He tried to turn his head away but he felt Karen pull him back, shaking him by the shoulders as she did.

'Look at me, Toby,' she told him, tears running down her face. 'Don't you dare look away.'

Toby was getting scared again. Fear was filling his brain, taking up all the space it could. It was giving him an awful headache and it hurt. It hurt a lot.

'Your imaginary friend isn't real,' Karen told him, her voice desperate and pleading. Toby was confused. Everything was upside down and he didn't like it.

'She's not real, Toby,' she continued, almost begging him to believe her. 'You can't blame stuff that you've done on your imaginary friend.'

The fear was pushing harder now.

'You need to stop this, Toby. You can't keep pretending that this friend is…'

'Amy!'

Toby didn't know why he'd shouted that. He didn't know what had made him do it. All he knew for sure was that as soon as he said that word, the fear inside his brain didn't seem to matter as much. For one second, it seemed to disappear completely and Toby almost felt like a normal boy again. But, as that one second ended, the fear came flying back into his brain, exploding in his mind like a bomb. He'd seen the look on Karen's face. It was a furious look.

'I don't care what her name is!' she screamed. It was a gigantic scream that made the windows rattle and the walls shake with fear.

'I don't care,' she told him. 'I couldn't care less if she's called Amy or Mary or anything else! All I care about is you and you can't behave like this, Toby, you can't! How could someone imaginary do something like this?'

She raised a hand from Toby's shoulder and pointed a shaking finger at the broken TV that lay face down in the middle of the room. Toby knew it was true. Only a real person could have lifted that TV, not an imaginary one. It had to be a real person, a person who could actually hold onto things instead of just floating through them. Amy couldn't do that, she couldn't even touch things without her hand sliding through.

But there was that one time. Toby remembered it. He remembered what had happened a few days ago. He remembered what Amy had done. She'd touched him. If Amy had been able to touch his shoulder, then maybe that meant she could touch other things. Maybe, just maybe, she could even have lifted the TV. Toby knew that he shouldn't have told Karen what he said next, but the words flew out of his mouth anyway without a shred of doubt.

'She's not imaginary!' he yelled.

The world seemed to stop. Karen, who's grip on Toby's shoulders had started to get much too tight, suddenly let go of him. She stared at him with wide eyes. Karen was more than angry or mad now. In fact, as Toby looked deep into her eyes, he thought how unhinged she looked and how much he really wanted her to go away.

'What did you just say?' she asked him.

Her voice was quieter now. She was almost daring him to say it again. Bullying him. Taunting him. She was trying to see if Toby would say it again, but he knew that he wouldn't. It was just something that he knew. He knew that he couldn't get those words out again. As Karen waited for an answer, Toby felt his throat begin to close up. He felt his body start to turn off. He was switching off from the world, like when you turn a light off. He knew that he wouldn't be able to say anything for a while. As Karen watched, Toby's lips opened one last time before closing once again without saying a word.

Toby didn't know that Amy had been listening to everything. Honestly, he probably hadn't thought too much about if she could hear him or not. However, there were two things that he did know. He knew that the TV had been broken and that Amy had been the one who'd broken it. As a sobbing Karen led Toby out of the living room and back into the hallway, a horrified Amy pulled her hands down from in front of her face and held them close to her aching stomach. She watched sadly as the two of them disappeared from view.

'What have I done?' she wondered to herself, grabbing large handfuls of her blonde hair.

She didn't know what had come over her. She'd been fine all day but, when she'd seen them on the television, something had happened inside her. She'd felt an anger that she'd never known before. It hadn't been his fault. Toby shouldn't have gotten the blame for that. It had been an accident.

BOOM!

The hallway door slammed shut. Karen stomped into the room, her shaking hands trembling by her sides. As Amy watched the young woman frantically pace back and forth along the green carpet, she couldn't help but feeling sorry for her. Amy had only seen Karen a few times but she had still noticed a change in her. As the family had grown more and more settled in their new home, Amy had noticed that Karen's bright, youthful face had begun to look different. It had become beaten and worn down. She wore the same deflated expression whenever Amy saw her now and it made Amy feel very sorry for her. Karen didn't need this amount of stress and neither did Toby.

Then, as Amy's teary eyes watched Karen pacing back and forth, she realised something that sent a jolt of pain down to her stomach. It was an awful realisation and Amy wished that she'd never recognized it. It was a realisation of what had to be done.

She had to disappear.

That was the only option. What Karen had said to Daniel just a few days ago had left a lasting impact on Amy. Karen had been right. It wasn't normal for a child to react so aggressively over their imaginary friend and Amy knew that. Even so, perhaps Amy hadn't done the right thing. She hadn't meant Toby any harm, she'd just been so happy to finally have a friend after all those years alone. Still, that didn't matter. All that Karen wanted was for Toby to be well and from how he'd been behaving, it was obvious to her that he needed some help. Imaginary friends were one thing, but imaginary friends that broke things around the house were something completely different. Amy didn't want to think about what she'd done. All she knew was that, as long as she was around, Toby couldn't live a normal life. As sad as that was, it was the truth. As the realisation entered Amy's brain, she felt a numbness fill her emaciated body. It was the same numbness that she'd felt for all those years in that attic. A numbness brought on by the sudden realisation of complete hopelessness. Whilst the numbness spread into her chest and along her arms, Amy noticed Karen out of the corner of her eye. She was slumped in the soft cushions of the sofa, painfully crying her heart out.

8 GOODBYE

Toby didn't leave his room again that night. He would have waited at the front door for Daniel to come home from work, but Toby knew that his brother probably wouldn't be back until way past his bedtime. Toby didn't want to leave his room anyway. He didn't want to leave because of what had happened with Karen. He'd never seen her that angry before. There had been times when she'd been angry in the past, but never like this. As Toby lay in bed, the blanket pulled up close to his chin, he began to cry. His crying wasn't loud like Karen's. It wasn't quiet like Amy's had been either. As the tears ran down Toby's freezing cold cheeks, not a single sound left his lips. He just lay motionless as the tears flowed down to the corners of his lips, sliding slowly into his mouth and onto his tongue. The tears tasted awful. As he stared up at the ceiling, a thought marched into his head. Toby hadn't been thinking about her, but somehow she'd found her way in. He began to think about Amy, his one and only imaginary friend.

Toby shook his head. He couldn't call her that anymore. Before, Toby hadn't known if Amy was real or not, but tonight had shown him the truth. An imaginary person couldn't lift up a TV. It sounded strange, even to Toby, but there wasn't a doubt in his mind. He knew that she was real, he just knew it.

Toby's room felt strange to him that night. He wasn't sure why it felt that way but he knew that it didn't feel quite right. Even though the ceiling light was still glowing above him, Toby thought that the room looked very dark. As he looked around, he realised that the room didn't feel like it was his. It was like he was sleeping in a hotel. Nothing felt right. He sat up and stared at the wardrobe on the other side of the room. There was no darkness inside it anymore. He looked in between the slits in the doors but all that he could see were his clothes. Toby clenched his teeth together. He knew that the monster would wake up soon. He turned onto his side and looked towards the window. Karen had covered it with a new pair of curtains, which were pulled shut so that he couldn't look out, but Toby still didn't feel very safe. There were two reasons for this. The first reason was that it was raining. Toby could hear heavy drops of water hitting the glass from outside and he didn't like it one bit. From where he was lying, it sounded as though there was someone standing on the other side, tapping loudly on the glass.

The other reason was a bit different. As he stared at the closed curtains, Toby thought about the hedge on the other side. He thought about the dark leaves that covered its branches. He thought about what was inside it. The monster. It was still there, hiding amongst the leaves. Toby knew it. The monster was waiting, waiting for him to fall asleep. It was just like the monster in the wardrobe. Just because Toby couldn't see it, didn't mean that it wasn't there. The monster was watching him through the curtains.

It was a long time before Karen finally came to say goodnight. After waiting for what had seemed like forever, Toby heard his bedroom door creak open. A pair of feet stepped onto the carpet. Toby didn't see the door open. He was still facing the window, staring at the thick curtains that hung in front of it. He didn't dare turn around. He'd known it was her the second the door had opened. A horrible feeling filled the room. It wasn't nervousness. It wasn't fear either. It was something in between, some sort of strange feeling that Toby couldn't quite explain.

'Toby?'

Karen's voice sounded broken. Toby didn't know what to do. He'd been wanting her to come and say goodnight to him for ages, but now that she was actually in the room his feelings had changed. He wanted her to go away. He wanted her to leave, but he didn't want to say anything that might make her angry.

'Toby?'

He tried to keep still. If he didn't move, then maybe she'd think he'd gone to sleep. Maybe then she'd leave him alone. Toby tried hard to keep himself from moving. He held his breath and focused all his energy on staying as still as possible. He wanted to make Karen go away.

'I know you're awake,' she whispered.

Toby had been caught. He took one deep, silent breath and turned over.

Karen looked awful. Toby was shocked by how tired and worn out she seemed to be. It was like she'd just been back from a run. There were dark bags under her eyes and he could see lots of red lines zigzagging across the white parts of her eyes as well. Karen was very upset. She pulled her dressing gown tight and sat on the edge of Toby's bed.

'Do you have anything to say?' she asked him.

She spoke very quietly, so quietly that Toby almost didn't hear her. He thought for a moment. Did he have anything to say? He couldn't think of anything that would make things better. He decided that he didn't have anything to say so he stayed silent. Instead, he sat up in bed and stared into Karen's eyes, his lips shut tight. After a long time in which neither of them said a word, Karen decided to speak again.

'Why are you doing this?'

Toby heard her voice crack a little as she spoke. It made him feel awful inside because he knew it was his fault. He knew that he was the reason Karen was upset and he hated it. He hated that he'd made her feel like this and he wanted to make things better. But, as a tear slid slowly down Karen's cheek, he realised that he didn't know how. It took a long time for Toby to finally respond to Karen's question and, when he finally did open his mouth, he gave an answer that didn't help things in the slightest.

'Sorry,' he whispered.

'Sorry!' Karen yelled. Her voice was stronger now. It had been a sharp yell and it made Toby jump. He didn't like people shouting.

'I don't care if you're sorry, Toby,' she continued angrily. 'All I need to know is how I can get you to stop this. Don't you see what you're doing to me?'

Toby couldn't look away. Karen's eyes were big and wild. No matter how hard Toby tried, he couldn't pull away from her gaze. It was like he was being hypnotised.

'I'm going to ask you one last time,' she told him. 'Why are you acting like this? Is it because of your Mum and Dad? There are people you can talk to. They'll be able to make you feel better. They'll be able to make that imaginary friend go away.'

That was when Toby started to worry. Make Amy go away? He didn't want Amy to go away! He wanted Amy to be his friend forever and he definitely didn't want her to go away because of Karen. He wanted to yell at Karen. He wanted to open his mouth and scream at the top of his lungs. He wanted to tell Karen that she was being mean and horrible. He wanted Karen to go away. He didn't even like her anyway. She was just jealous. He had a friend and she didn't have any friends. He had Amy and she didn't have anyone. She was all alone and that was why she didn't want him to see Amy. He wanted to tell her all of these things, but he couldn't. His mouth wouldn't open, his body wouldn't move and he couldn't do anything to show her how angry he was. So, instead of responding to Karen, he just stared at her in silence.

Karen waited for a long time. Every second that Toby stayed silent seemed to make her even sadder. Even so, Toby didn't care. He thought that she was being horrible and that she deserved to be sad. Finally, Karen gave up. Toby could tell that she'd given up. He could see it in her eyes. They were still red and tearful but all of a sudden they had begun to turn grey. It was like how the sky could change on a bad day. One moment it could be sunny and the next clouds could roll in. That was what had happened in Karen's eyes. With one last look at him, she climbed off the bed. Then, she walked out of the room, closing the door behind her and turning off the light with a quiet click.

Toby lay awake for a long time after Karen left. Instead of closing his eyes, he stared up at the dirty white ceiling and thought. He hated feeling like this. He hated that he'd made Karen feel so upset. He didn't like making people upset but sometimes he did make them upset. A lot of time passed but Toby kept his gaze fixed on the ceiling above him. He didn't need to look around his empty room to feel alone, just staring up at the ceiling was enough. It filled him with a sense of loneliness that he couldn't shake off, no matter how hard he tried. He was all alone and that wasn't going to change any time soon.

'Toby?'

He didn't know where the voice had come from. Toby sat up in bed and squinted into the darkness. He couldn't see a thing but he knew that someone was there.

'Toby?'

He knew that voice. It was soft and sweet but there was something strange about it. It sounded worried and urgent, as though the person speaking had something very important to say.

113

'Toby!'

It was a girl's voice, one that Toby knew very well by now.

'Amy?' he whispered, not sure where he was supposed to look. The voice came back a little quieter.

'Hey, Toby,' Amy replied. 'Sorry if I woke you.'

'It's okay,' he told her. 'You didn't.'

His words came out a little louder than he'd expected them to, something that Amy noticed almost instantly.

'Please be quiet,' she told him. 'I don't want Karen to wake up.'

Toby nodded, even though he knew that Amy couldn't see him. Even so, his silence told her that he understood.

'Thank you Toby,' she whispered. 'Where's Daniel?'

Toby still didn't know where Amy was in the room. It was so dark that he couldn't even see the end of the bed and not being able to see her was making him very nervous. He tried to follow her voice, to figure out where in the room she was standing, but he wasn't very good at it. Really, he didn't have a clue where she was.

'Work,' he replied, his eyes darting around the room. 'He's still at work.'

'Oh.'

Amy sounded strange. Toby didn't like it. He tried to figure out in his mind why her voice was so different. He replayed the words she'd spoken to him. They'd sounded happy, but not a real kind of happy. It was the kind of voice grown-ups used before they told you bad news. It was never just bad news either, not when they spoke like that. It was always the worst kind of news.

'I need to talk to you,' Amy told him.

Toby felt the hairs on the back of his neck stand up. That was how it started, most of the time anyway. Grown-ups always pretended that they wanted to talk to you about the bad thing. It was never true. They didn't want to talk to you about the bad thing, they had to. There was a short silence after Amy said that. It was like she was waiting for Toby to say something, but he wouldn't. He didn't want to say anything. Maybe she wouldn't tell him about the bad thing if he stayed quiet. At least, that's how he saw it in his mind. However, just as he was starting to get hopeful, he heard a short whisper echo in the dark.

'I have to go, Toby.'

That was good news to Toby. She was going to go and that was good. He could could get some sleep and then, when everyone was feeling better, he could talk to Amy in the morning. Maybe they would even play together! He'd like that a lot.

'Okay,' he replied. 'See you in morning.'

'No, Toby,' Amy told him, her voice heavy and firm. 'No.'

Toby didn't understand. What did she mean? She had to go! He wouldn't be able to sleep if he knew she was watching him. They would have to see each other in the morning. He thought she would have known that. But did she mean what he thought she meant? Maybe she meant something else. The way she'd said it made him worry. It had been something in her voice. It was almost like the words were hurting her.

'What do you mean?' he asked, staring blankly into the dark.

'I won't see you in the morning,' Amy told him. 'Not in the morning. Not ever. I can't see you again, Toby. I have to go away, for good.'

Toby didn't know what she was saying. Why did she have to go? Why? His mind became cloudy and he couldn't figure out what she meant. She was confusing him.

'You're leaving?' he asked her, hoping that it wasn't true.

There was a long silence before Amy answered.

'Yes, Toby.'

Toby didn't understand. Why was she was leaving him? Had he done something wrong? He hadn't meant to do anything wrong! It wasn't his fault Amy had dropped the TV on the floor! She shouldn't be leaving! It wasn't fair!

'Why?' he asked her in a shaky voice. Toby wanted an answer. He didn't understand one bit of what was going on. Everything was upside-down and backwards and he wanted to know why.

'I just have to,' Amy told him. 'I can't stay here.'

She was being stupid! Why couldn't she stay? Why? Toby wanted to shout. He wanted to scream and yell and call Amy the rudest names he knew. She was being horrible and he hated it.

'No!' he shouted, not caring if he woke up Karen. No one had been nice to him today so he didn't want to be nice either. He was angry, very angry. Toby threw the blanket off his bed, jumped down onto the floor and stomped across the room towards the light switch.

'Please don't yell Toby,' Amy whispered, her voice sounding very worried. 'Stay in bed. We can talk about this.'

Toby didn't care. Amy was leaving him all alone in a

house filled with people who hated him. He reached up the wall and felt the light switch under his finger. He was so angry. All he wanted to do was scream. With a flick of his finger, light filled the room, bouncing off the walls and landing on Amy, who was standing in the middle of the room.

Toby had really wanted to yell at her. In fact, he hadn't just wanted to yell at her; he'd wanted to get angrier than he'd ever been in his entire life. But, as soon as he saw Amy standing there, all the fight went out of him. Amy was crying. Her white cheeks were covered in tears and her eyes had turned red. They looked like they hurt. Toby began to feel very sorry for her. He was still angry, he knew that, but he couldn't help feeling bad for his friend.

'Sorry,' he whispered, looking down at his feet. Toby felt awful. He shouldn't have turned the light on, he knew that Amy didn't want him to see her upset. Sometimes grown-ups were like that, they didn't want to be seen when they cried.

'It's alright,' she told him as she wiped away the tears. 'You don't need to be sorry. I just couldn't leave you without saying goodbye.'

Toby ran towards her. He wanted to hug Amy. He tried wrapping his arms around her skinny legs, as though he could somehow stop her from going, but it didn't work. He fell through her and came out on the other side, landing on the floor with a quiet thud.

'I'm so sorry, Toby,' Amy whispered, turning her body so that she was facing him once again, 'but I have to do this.'

Suddenly, Toby felt something sliding down his cheek. It was wet and cold and it made his eyes sting. It took him a few seconds to figure out that he was crying.

'You can't go!' he yelled as he picked himself up from the floor. 'You have to stay here with me!'

'Don't shout, Toby,' Amy told him. 'You'll wake Karen up.'

'I don't care!' he shouted, stomping his feet on the carpet. He didn't care, not one bit.

'Stop it now!' she yelled, loosing her patience with him.

Toby had never heard Amy speak to him like that before. It was strange hearing such a big, angry voice come out of her mouth. It was strange and he didn't like it.

'Now you listen to me!' she told him, her voice firm and strong. 'I love you Toby. You've been the best friend I've ever had and I wish that I didn't have to do this, but I do. I have to go.'

Toby shook his head. She couldn't leave him. He didn't want her to go, but there was something in her eyes that told him she wasn't going to back down.

'Where you going?' he asked her desperately. 'I'll come with you.'

'You can't come, Toby,' Amy told him. 'You have to stay here.'

All of a sudden, Amy's voice had changed. It wasn't loud anymore and Toby could tell that she wasn't as angry as she had been. She mainly sounded hurt now. She crouched down and stared straight into Toby's eyes.

'You have to look after Daniel and Karen,' she told him. 'They need you to help them make the house nice and happy. They love you, Toby, and you can't leave them.'

Toby thought for a second. What Amy was saying made sense, even in his five-year-old mind. Even though he was angry at Karen, he knew that he loved her. He loved Karen and Daniel and he knew in his heart that he didn't want to lose either of them. But, despite all that, Toby loved Amy too and he knew that he couldn't lose her.

'No!' he yelled, his voice so loud that it burnt the back of his throat.

He couldn't let Amy go. He didn't care about anything else. Toby just wanted them to stay together and that couldn't happen if Amy left. He started to cry. It was a mad, angry cry but he didn't care. He didn't understand how she could be doing this to him. Amy reached out to hold him but her hands just floated through his body as if they were nothing. Toby didn't hear the noise coming from the other room, but Amy did. It was the sound of a bed creaking. Someone in Karen and Daniel's room had gotten out of bed.

'Toby!' Amy shouted, firmly enough to make him go quiet. He was still crying, but she'd gotten his attention and that was the important part.

Toby didn't know that Amy was about to lie to him. He was only little and he trusted her so much that he never thought she'd do something like that. Even so, Amy had to make things better for him. She knew that she couldn't risk him finding her again. She had to go away, for good, and there was only one way of doing that.

'You need to listen to me,' she told him as she looked into his innocent eyes. 'I have to tell you about the attic.'

Toby didn't understand. Why had she brought up the attic? It didn't have anything to do with what they were talking about. Still, despite Toby's puzzled expression, Amy kept on talking.

'It's the monsters,' she continued, 'the ones in this house. The attic is where they live.'

Toby froze. How did she know about the monsters? He didn't think anyone knew about the monsters, anyone for except him. He'd seen two of them, or at least knew where

119

they were. They watched him as he slept, one in the wardrobe and one in the hedge outside. But did they live in the attic? Maybe his room wasn't the only place they could go. Was Amy telling the truth? She couldn't be. There hadn't been any monsters when he'd gone up to the attic. But maybe they'd been hiding.

'I've seen them, Toby,' Amy continued, her gaze fixed on him, 'I've seen the monsters. They're big and evil. They have gigantic teeth. They eat little boys. Sometimes they don't even have to use their teeth. Sometimes they don't even chew. Sometimes they just swallow them whole. You can't go back up to the attic, Toby. Grown-ups can go up there, but not little boys like you. You wouldn't stand a chance.'

Toby didn't know what to say. He'd always known that there were monsters in the house but he never thought that they'd be living in the attic. Toby stared at Amy, waiting for her to speak. She looked upset and he didn't like it. He wanted her to talk to him, but she didn't say a word. Then Toby heard it, the sound of a door creaking open. It was clear that Amy had heard it too as she broke the silence soon after.

'I need you to promise me something,' she said, her voice nervous and afraid. 'Promise me that you'll never go up to the attic. Never again.'

There were footsteps in the hallway. Someone was coming for them. Toby stared at Amy, not sure how to respond.

'Please, Toby!' she yelled, her hands beginning to shake. 'Swear on your life that you won't go up there.'

The doorknob started to rattle.

'Please!' she begged him, eyes filled with tears.

Toby knew what he had to do.

'I swear,' he told her, his voice barely a whisper. As

soon as the words left his lips, the bedroom door opened.

'What's going on?'

Karen was only half awake but she could still tell that there was something strange occurring. She looked down at Toby, the bedroom door wide open behind her. She did not look happy. Her eyes were tired and there were black bags hanging beneath them. Toby could tell that she hadn't been asleep for very long.

'What going on?' she asked him again, repeating the question firmly.

Toby turned to look at Amy, to get one last look at his imaginary friend before she went away, but she wasn't there. It was as if she'd disappeared. He'd wanted her to stay a little longer, so that he could say a proper goodbye, but she'd gone now. That was the end of it. He looked back at Karen and stared into her tired eyes. Then, out of nowhere, he began to cry. It was a long, silent cry. He didn't dare make a sound in case it made Karen angry again. He tried his best to keep the sadness from showing on his face. However, despite his best efforts, Karen could tell that he was upset.

'What's the matter?' she asked, sounding quite concerned. She closed the bedroom door and hurried over to him, crouching down in front of Toby just as Amy had done before.

'Amy's gone,' he told her, whispering as tears flowed down his face. 'She's gone away and it's because of me.'

Karen didn't usually like Toby talking about Amy. She would normally get angry at Toby for it, but she didn't look angry when he mentioned Amy this time. In fact, she seemed almost happy about it.

'Well that's good, Toby,' she told him, placing a hand on his shoulder. 'Amy wasn't good for you. Hopefully things will get better now that she's gone.'

'It's not good,' Toby replied. 'Amy left because of me, just like Mum and Dad.'

He knew that he didn't have to be quiet. Karen was up now, so he didn't have to worry about waking her, but, for some reason, the words would only come out in a faint, almost inaudible whisper. Karen looked at him with sad eyes. For a moment, he thought she was going to shout at him again. But she didn't. Instead, Karen grabbed hold of Toby, her soft dressing gown rubbing against his face as she pulled him in for a tight hug. As Toby felt the fluffy fabric stroking against his tear-stained cheek, he realised that he could hear Karen sniffling. Pulling away so that he could see her face, he gazed into her eyes and checked to see if she was crying. There weren't any tears but she still didn't look right and Toby couldn't understand why.

'What wrong?' he asked her. 'Are you sick?'

That made Karen laugh for some reason. He wasn't quite sure why.

'No, Toby. I'm not sick, but I need to tell you something.'

Karen grabbed his shoulders and stared at him with a very serious face.

'You need to know something, Toby,' she told him, her voice strong as steel. 'What happened to your Mum and Dad wasn't your fault. Never think that Toby. I promise you that they didn't go away because of you. I never want you to think that any of this has been your fault.'

Toby was surprised. He hadn't expected Karen to act like this. She'd been mean to him all afternoon but now she was being nice. It was very strange but it made him feel happy. It filled him up, like a cosy fire warming him from the inside. Toby smiled at Karen and she smiled back. Then, she pulled him in close and held him tight, a few strands of blue hair falling down in front of her face and tickling Toby's nose.

'I love you, Karen,' he whispered in her ear.

'I love you too, Toby.'

They were like that for a long time. It was a nice hug, a really nice one. It was so nice that neither of them wanted to let go, but when they finally did, none of the happiness faded away. Karen kissed him on the forehead and put him back to bed, tucking him in tight so that he was as comfortable as he could be. She kissed him on the cheek and smiled at him. Toby smiled back. He loved Karen so much. Even though they sometimes fell out, he knew that she was always there for him. He rolled over and closed his eyes as Karen made her way towards the door. Even though Amy was gone, even she wouldn't be coming back, he knew that everything would be alright. He just knew it.

'Toby?'

He didn't know where the voice came from. It was a voice he'd heard before and one that sounded beautifully calm and soft. Toby didn't know if he was dreaming or not but he felt as though it didn't really matter either way. He listened as the voice continued on.

'Don't say anything,' the voice whispered. 'I need you to do something for me. Tell Karen to go into the back room. Do it quickly, before she leaves.'

Toby felt very tired. He still wasn't sure whether he'd really heard the voice or not, but he didn't think too much about it. As the sound of Karen's footsteps grew fainter, he decided that he knew what to do.

'Karen?'

'Yes?'

'Can you go in the back room, please?'

'Why?'

'Please?'

'Okay. Night, Toby.'

'Night, Karen.'

The bedroom door closed softly. Toby was all alone once again, but this time it didn't feel as bad. He still had the warm feeling inside him. It had filled him up to the very top with happiness. The fears that had been packed into his brain were all gone. They weren't gone for good, he knew that, but at least they were gone for now. That was something. As he drifted into a comfortable sleep, Toby thought about Karen and how much he loved her. Then, he thought of Daniel. Even though he hadn't seen a lot of his brother recently, he still knew that he loved him too. Toby felt very lucky to have two people who loved him as much as Karen and Daniel did. Then, in his last waking moments, he thought of Amy. He thought of all the great times they'd had together. They'd had so much fun and he was sad to see her go. Still, he knew that he'd never forget her, not in a million years.

As Karen left Toby's room, she thought about what he'd asked her. Why did he want her to go into the back room? What did he want her to see? She couldn't work it out but, as she walked down the hallway, she knew that something was up. However, she was unaware that walking just a few steps behind her was a girl, a girl who was following her.

The back room was the only empty room in the house. It was opposite Daniel and Karen's room and had been left almost completely untouched since the day they'd moved in. They'd planned to use it as a sort of storage space for all the clutter they didn't want to throw away, but then they'd discovered the attic which was much better for that sort of thing. As a result, the room had remained empty. Karen had only been in it a few times. Once directly in front of the closed door, she raised a hand to the wood and pushed. The door opened with a slow creak. Stepping inside, Karen discovered that the room was just as empty as it had ever been. A bare wooden floor and dirty cream coloured walls were the only things that Karen could see, apart from a small window that looked out onto the cul-de-sac. There wasn't anything inside the room, nothing except...

It was still there, in the same place she'd left it the day they'd moved in. It was a cardboard box, a medium sized one that had its lid hanging open a little. Karen had meant to take it up to the attic but she'd forgotten. It was just filled with tinsel and fairy lights from what she could remember, but it wasn't doing any good downstairs. She bent down and stared into the box. The tinsel and fairy lights were all tangled up at the bottom, but there was something else there too.

It was a photo frame. It lay face down on top of the decorations. The frame was plain, but had a certain charm to it. It was silver and looked as though it had been bought at some kind of department store. Reaching into the box, Karen picked up the frame with both hands and turned it over.

Inside it was a picture. It was a nice picture of three people who all looked very happy. One was a middle-aged man. He was partly bald and wore a big coat with a collar that almost completely covered his neck. The other was a woman, a friendly looking woman. She had a white scarf wrapped gently around her. The third person was a little boy. He had brown hair that had been cut into a bowl shape and happy eyes that seemed to sparkle with joy. The people looked happy and Karen could tell instantly what she was looking at. The boy in the picture was Toby. The other two people were his Mum and Dad.

Karen knew why Toby had sent her into the back room. He'd wanted her to see the picture. He didn't want the fairy lights or the tinsel; he just wanted a picture of his family. Perhaps it should have made Karen sad, but instead it made her happy. He was finally telling her how he felt. Maybe now that his imaginary friend was gone, he might start telling the truth. With one last look at the picture, she slid the photo frame into the pocket of her dressing gown and let a hopeful smile creep onto her face. Maybe this was the start of something better. Maybe.

Karen thought that Amy had gone but that wasn't true. Amy hadn't gone. In fact, she was standing right behind Karen and her mind was racing.

'What if she doesn't do it?' she thought to herself. 'What if I'm stuck down here?'

Amy had already relied on luck too much that night. She hadn't fully expected Toby to believe her story about the monsters. It was something she'd heard him talk about in his sleep and she knew that it was a fear he wouldn't let go of easily. But he had believed her, so that wasn't the issue now. What Amy needed now was for Karen to make a decision.

Amy held her breath and began to wait. She waited and waited and waited some more, but nothing happened. Karen just stood there, thinking to herself about what to do next. Then Amy saw it, the twinkle in Karen's eyes. It was a sign that she'd made up her mind. Even though it was late and even through it probably could have waited until the morning, Karen decided to do it. With both her hands she raised the cardboard box off the floor and carried it out of the room. She shut the door and left Amy alone. But Amy didn't have any time to waste. She ran through the closed door and out into the hallway. There, she watched as Karen, still holding the box with one hand, pulled on the thin white cord that dangled from the ceiling and opened the attic hatch. She was going to do it. She was going to put the box in the attic. As the ladder came down, Karen began her ascent. Amy followed silently behind her. With one hand, she grabbed onto the ladder and pulled herself up. She didn't know why she was able to touch it but she didn't really care. Even after five years of being dead she still didn't know what rules there were. Still, it didn't really matter to her at that moment. With one last look at the closed door of Toby's room, Amy felt a smile begin to form on her face. It was a sad smile. She continued climbing and followed Karen up into the attic.

Both Toby and Karen slept soundly that night. It seemed to them that things had gotten better somehow and they didn't wake up when Daniel finally walked through the door. He got home in the early hours of the morning and fell asleep on the sofa. He slept well, but then again the whole family slept well that night. The only person in the house who didn't sleep well was Amy. She lay awake for hours, just like she had done on so many other nights, her body resting against the same pillar she'd been tied to for five years. That was how things had to be. As she stared up at the beams above her head and silently sobbed, she promised herself that she would never make a sound, never say a word and never do anything that would make Toby remember she was up there. That was how things had to be and that was how they were going to stay. As time went on, Toby would soon forget about his imaginary friend, but he would always remember one rule. Never go into the attic. That rule would stay with him for years and, in his mind, he had made a promise to himself that he would never go up there again. However, of course, as many people know, promises like that are made to be broken.

Ten Years Later...

9 THE BOX

Toby. What a stupid name.

That was how Toby Burrows saw it. He hated his name with a passion. Fifteen-year-olds weren't called Toby, kids were. It was such a juvenile name. Nobody cool was called Toby. Tobias was a much better name. Sure, it sounded incredibly posh but it was certainly better than the alternative. Toby wanted people to call him Tobias, to use his full first name and grant him some dignity by not calling him something that made him sound like a toddler, but they wouldn't, because everyone already called him Toby.

It was a quarter to four on a cold Friday afternoon. Toby stared idly at the classroom clock, his body hunched over his desk as he watched the minute hand move sluggishly closer towards the twelve. He wasn't paying attention to anything else in the room. All of his brain power was focused on that little piece of plastic moving across the clock face. It had been a boring lesson, so boring that Toby couldn't even remember what they'd been discussing. He'd zoned out about half an hour ago and wasn't going to start paying attention anytime soon. He could feel his heavy eyelids beginning to droop and knew that his body wanted him to sleep. He yawned quietly and began to feel his mind go cloudy. He couldn't fall asleep, not now. It would be embarrassing. People would laugh and point at him. There would be no coming back from that. He rubbed his eyes with his knuckles and shook his head. Why was he so tired? He'd slept fine the night before! He always tried to get eight hours sleep and he hardly ever got less than six, so why was he finding it so hard to stay awake?

'Toby?'

The voice seemed to be coming from miles away. It was a low, gruff voice that echoed in Toby's ears.

'Toby?'

Someone was talking to him, but he couldn't quite figure out who. He didn't know what the voice wanted. It couldn't have been that important. Maybe he could keep his eyes closed for just a little…

'Toby!'

Toby woke with a jolt and sat bolt upright in his seat. Standing over him and staring with big bulging eyes was Toby's English teacher, Mr Morrison. He did not look happy. His nostrils were flared and his lips were pursed together tightly as though he'd eaten something sour.

'Yes, sir?' Toby replied groggily.

'I won't tolerate sleeping in my classroom,' Mr Morrison said sternly, his already low voice deepening considerably. 'Detention. Monday, after school.'

Toby nodded agreeably. It was never a good idea to get Mr Morrison angry. Most of the time he was a boring old sod but he could be evil when he wanted to be. As Mr Morrison marched back across the classroom towards the whiteboard, the heels of his brown shoes clinking on the wooden floor, Toby began to notice an uneasy feeling rise up inside him. He felt as though he was being watched. It was then that he became aware of the rest of the class, all of whom had turned around in their chairs to look at him. Toby shrunk in his seat. They were all staring at him, the girls giggling behind their hands hand the boys smirking arrogantly. He'd never live this down. He wasn't unpopular, but he didn't have many friends and he didn't think he'd be making more any time soon, especially after what had just happened. As Mr Morrison went back to teaching, the heads of Toby's classmates slowly began to turn away. After about a minute or so, there was only one person in the room who was still staring at him. Lily Roberts.

Toby tried his best not to look at her. He made a conscious attempt to keep his eyes fixed on the whiteboard in front of him, but he could still feel her gaze burning into the back of his skull. Glancing out of the corner of his eye, Toby was able to catch a glimpse of Lily. It was the only way he could see her without being too obvious and, even though he couldn't see much of her, it was enough. Lily was a pretty girl. Toby noticed her silky blonde hair and admired how gracefully it flowed down onto her shoulders. Her hair kept falling in front of her face, which meant that she constantly had to brush it away with a pale hand, sometimes knocking her glasses as she did so. Toby thought that she looked wonderful. Then, just as he was about to twist his neck even further in hope that he might get a better look at her, Lily stopped staring and went back to her school work.

The rest of the lesson went by at a snail's pace. Toby could barely keep his eyes open and almost fell asleep on numerous occasions. He tried his best to pay attention to what Mr Morrison was saying, but his heart wasn't in it and he felt incredibly relieved when the classroom clock finally signalled that the lesson was over. As the rest of the class hurried out into the hallway, ready to enjoy the weekend, Toby remained in his seat, staring blankly into space as he realised that he'd just lost a whole hour of his life. He couldn't even remember what the lesson had been about, let alone any of the finer details. After returning to his senses, he got up and slung his backpack over his shoulders. As he made his way towards the open classroom door, he kept his gaze fixed firmly downward. He didn't want to be caught by Mr Morrison.

'Toby.'

Damn.

'Yes, sir?' he replied, reluctantly turning to face his teacher. Mr Morrison did not look happy.

'I want a word with you,' he told Toby firmly. 'Now.'

Toby knew that was bad news. He shuffled over to Mr Morrison's desk and waited with bated breath for his teacher to speak.

'Now,' Mr Morrison began, clearing his throat with a loud cough. 'I don't know what's been the matter with you recently, but I will not tolerate sleeping in class. I don't mind telling you that you are an incredibly intelligent young man, but you have to apply yourself. Do you understand me?'

'Yes, sir,' Toby replied in a polite, emotionless voice. 'I'll try harder.'

'Good,' said Mr Morrison, nodding his head in an authoritative manner. 'Was there any reason for your falling asleep today? Are things okay at home?'

'Yes, sir,' Toby told him. 'I just didn't get much sleep last night.'

Then, as Mr Morrison's grey eyes stared deep into Toby's, the impossible occurred. For a brief moment in time, Mr Morrison smiled. It wasn't a proper smile. In fact, it looked more like someone was pulling the corners of his lips up with fishing hooks, but it was still something positive and something that caught Toby completely off guard.

'Well,' Mr Morrison continued, 'you can tell your

brother that, apart from the aforementioned problem, I believe that you are doing remarkably well.'

Toby nodded and forced a small smile. Mr Morrison was being nice for once and Toby wasn't sure if he liked it. He wanted the conversation to end as soon as possible.

'Will do, sir,' he replied. 'Is it okay if I go now?'

'Of course,' Mr Morrison told him, the smile vanishing from his face. 'I will see you on Monday, Toby.'

'Thank you, sir.'

Toby didn't need to be told twice. Closing the classroom door behind him and politely smiling at Mr Morrison once more as he left, he hurried out into the hallway and breathed a heavy sigh of relief. He was free at last. Toby didn't really care if Mr Morrison thought he was intelligent. He'd humiliated Toby in front of the whole class without so much as a second thought. Still, what he'd said about him had been nice.

As Toby made his way down the long hallway, he thought about how run-down the school looked. Blue paint was peeling from its ancient walls and the floorboards beneath his feet were covered with half a century's worth of dried gum. Toby supposed that he was lucky Lawton could even to accommodate a secondary school. If it hadn't been able to, he'd have been forced to commute to one of the neighbouring towns every day which would have involved a very early bus journey. However, as he looked around at the awful state of the hallway, he couldn't help but think that he'd rather be anywhere else. Lawton Secondary School was falling to pieces and he couldn't wait to get out of there.

The winter air hit him hard as he opened the main doors. As he stepped outside into the school grounds, he was struck by a sudden realisation that everything was much quieter than he'd expected it to be. He'd expected crowds of people to be hanging around outside, given that last period had only ended a few minutes ago, but, apart from a few stragglers, there were hardly any students left. Toby was surprised. He found the lack of students very odd, very odd indeed. Then again, he guessed it wasn't really that strange. There weren't many students at the school, only a few hundred, and none of them hung about for very long after their lessons. As he walked across the tarmac and towards the school gates, Toby felt his phone vibrate in his trouser pocket. As he pulled out his smooth black smartphone and held it in his hand, he stared at the screen and discovered that his brother Daniel was calling him.

Toby pressed the answer button with a cold, shaky thumb and raised it to his ear.

'Hello,' he said, his warm breath creating a cloud of mist in front of him.

'Hey, Toby.'

Daniel's voice was very happy, which surprised Toby. His brother never usually sounded positive when he was at work. He didn't like his job very much, so he never had much reason to be cheerful when he was there.

'What's up?' Toby asked, his voice uncertain.

'I just wanted to let you know,' Daniel told him, 'that Karen and I are going into town. We're going shopping and then heading to a restaurant afterwards, so we won't be back home until late. We've left you a microwaveable curry if you want it.'

Toby rolled his eyes. That was why Daniel sounded so happy; he had a chance to spend money.

'Okay,' Toby replied, his teeth chattering from the cold.

'Brilliant,' Daniel said gleefully. 'Could you also pop into the shop on your way home. We need a pint of milk.'

Toby let out an annoyed sigh. It was freezing that day. It was supposed to be the coldest day that winter and Toby didn't want to be out in it any longer than he had to be. Still, he did have to walk through the high-street to get back, so he didn't really have any excuse.

'What kind?' he asked.

'Semi-skimmed.'

'I can think of nothing better,' Toby told Daniel sarcastically. His brother didn't seem to understand his lack of sincerity, either that or he just wasn't paying attention.

'Okay,' he replied. 'I'll see you later, Toby.'

'See you.'

Toby ended the call with a push of his thumb. As he walked out of the school gates and into the road, he felt the cold wind blast against his frozen face.

'Bet Daniel and Karen won't have this problem,' he thought to himself. 'Bet they'll have a great time, all warm and cosy in some shop.'

Daniel never used to be interested in shopping. It was strange how attached he had become to material possessions recently. He'd changed a lot since they'd moved into Lawton all those years ago, but then again so had Toby. He'd been a little kid when they'd first arrived, but he was a full-fledged teenager now. Toby had grown taller, his voice had deepened and, most importantly, his brown hair, which had once been cut into an uneven bowl shape around his head, was now short, neat and very grown up.

Things were different between Karen and Daniel too. In January, it was going to be a decade since they'd married and Toby had been listening to the two of them go on about it for a very long time. Daniel had booked an expensive restaurant and was making sure that nothing whatsoever could go wrong. It had taken him weeks to get the reservation and, what with all the presents he was buying Karen, it was starting to become obvious that he was getting a little carried away with himself.

It took a while for Toby to reach the high-street but, when he finally got there, he was glad to see that it was mostly empty. Some days, especially on the weekends, it could be packed tight with people. Toby hated it when it was like that for one main reason: he couldn't stand crowds. He hated being surrounded by people and it was a sure fire trigger for his claustrophobia. He'd always been afraid of enclosed spaces, ever since he could remember, and he couldn't bear being in them for even short periods of time. He hated narrow hallways, despised low ceilings and there were even parts of his own house that he wouldn't go into because of it. Actually, it was really only one place.

The attic.

Anytime he'd attempted to go up there, anytime he'd had to bring down Christmas decorations or set up mouse-traps, he'd never been able to. Whenever he saw the attic hatch open, his whole body began to shake. He would break out in a cold sweat and feel so sick to his stomach that he'd have to remain downstairs. The fear would cloud his mind and stay with him for hours afterwards. The claustrophobia had become a part of his life and it made Toby feel uneasy whenever he thought about it.

The shop was located in the middle of the high-street. It was a convenience store, filled with all kinds of household items, and it was the only place Toby was going to find milk without walking to the other end of Lawton. As he walked through the sliding doors, he felt the central heating bathe his cheeks with warmth. It was like heaven after the freezing cold walk he'd just experienced and for a moment he simply stood in the open doorway, letting the heat radiate throughout his body. He stayed that way for almost half a minute before he came to his senses. It was then that he focused his mind and went off to collect what he'd come for. The milk was at the very back of the shop in a refrigerated section. Toby had to search for a while before he found it. After scanning the shelves, he realised that they didn't have any semi-skimmed milk, so he had to settle for full-fat instead.

'Daniel won't mind,' he told himself as he went to go pay.

Toby joined the queue and waited patiently as an old man paid for his shopping in huge amounts of loose change. After a while, Toby began to feel as though he was being watched. Taking a quick glance over his shoulder, he realised that two boys about his age were staring at him. As he slowly turned to get a better view, Toby noticed that they both had black hair and were wearing identical brown jumpers. In fact, they were wearing the very same jumper that he was wearing. They even had the crest of Lawton Secondary School stitched on the front. With one final tentative look, Toby raised his head and focused on the faces of the two students behind him. As he did so, his eyes met the gaze of two people he definitely didn't want to meet.

Charlie Merchant and Andrew Cocks.

Charlie and Andrew were the toughest kids in Toby's year. They spent most of their time at the local park, smoking and drinking cheap cans of beer which they always chucked onto the grass for someone else to pick up. The two of them were always starting fights. They didn't care who they went after. If another student so much as gave them a funny look, they would attack the poor soul without a second thought. In short, they were dangerous and they certainly weren't the sort of people Toby wanted to make angry. But, as he gazed into their sadistic eyes, he shuddered, realising with horror that they'd both been in his English class. They'd watched him fall asleep at his desk.

Toby turned his head back quickly and stared straight ahead. He had to leave, now. He had to get out of there fast, but the old man in front of him was still counting his coins. Toby's fingers began to twitch by his side. He'd just stared dead into the eyes of Lawton's two most dangerous students and he could tell that they would make him regret it. Then, as the cashier handed the old man a receipt, Toby heard a low voice whisper into his ear.

'Hi, sleepy-head.'

Toby darted forward and threw the milk onto the counter. He was dead, there wasn't any doubt about it. Charlie and Andrew didn't let anyone look at them without their say-so. He'd disrespected them and he had to pay for it. As he heard the two boys behind him edging slowly closer, Toby thrust a dirty coin into the cashier's hand and bolted out through the sliding doors.

'Don't look back,' he thought to himself as he hurried along the pavement. 'Keep walking. Eyes forward. Hopefully they aren't following you.'

He could feel his whole body seizing up. It might have just been down to the cold, or maybe it was the fact that Toby could sense two sets of eyes staring at him. Toby knew that they were watching him. Charlie and Andrew had left the shop. They were following him home.

Toby quickened his pace, trying to get as far away from his pursuers as possible without appearing as though he'd noticed them. As he sped up, the pint of milk in his hand began to sway back and forth at his side, the liquid inside the carton sloshing about as his skinny legs took longer, faster strides. Toby could hear Charlie and Andrew close behind him, their heavy boots crashing down onto the pavement as they followed. They were going to catch him; he could feel it. Despite his deep fear of crowds, in that moment, Toby would have given anything to be surrounded by more people. People could separate him from Charlie and Andrew. That was what he wanted; a crowd that he could get lost in.

Then, Toby saw it. Just a little bit in front of him, on the other side of the street, was the mouth of a road. It was the road he lived on. Toby's spirits rose. He was almost there! He was almost back home! All he had to do was make it to the end of that road. If he could do that, then he would be safe. Throwing caution to the wind, he stepped off the edge of the kerb and bolted across the road. His heart was pounding in his chest, beating with such force that he could hardly hear the car horns blaring at him as he ran through the traffic. His palms were sticky with cold sweat, so sticky that the milk almost slipped out of his hand. As he jumped onto the pavement on the other side of the road, he felt a wave of relief crash over his body. He'd made it across in one piece and that was something to be proud of, but he didn't stop running. As his feet propelled him across the pavement, Toby noticed that the mouth of the road was starting to get closer. When he finally reached it, he found that he had to take the turn at a very tight angle in order to maintain his speed. As he ran, he twisted his body to the side and felt the soles of his shoes skid across the concrete. He'd made it. He was almost home. Safety was within his grasp but he wasn't out of danger yet. The road was long and Toby's house was at the very end of it, so he still had a long way to go. He kept running, running as fast as his lanky legs would take him and not daring to look back for even a second. He'd never run this fast before. He could feel the muscles in his legs burning as he forced himself to keep moving. Then, as he stared into the distance, he saw it. It was his house. It was there in front of him. It was still far away, but he could see it. He couldn't believe it! He was actually going to make it! He'd never thought it possible but was actually going to do it! He was going to outrun Charlie Merchant and Andrew Cocks! He was going to be safe! He was going to make it!

THUNK!

Toby's head hit the pavement hard. For a second, he wasn't quite sure what had happened. Had he tripped? Had he fallen over his own feet? He simply didn't know. Then, as he noticed the blurred outline of Charlie's foot pulling away from in-between his legs, he realised what had happened. Raising a hand to his forehead, Toby felt blood and grit coat his sweaty fingers. He'd cut his head when he'd fallen and it stung like hell. The rest of his head was in pain too, throbbing from the force of the fall. Everything ached. Staring up from his spot on the pavement, Toby saw the ugly faces of Charlie and Andrew looking down at him. Charlie had a huge, lumpy nose that had become crooked after a break. Andrew had a long scar running down the bridge of his for the same reason. They were staring at him, their eyes wide and their mouths contorted in laughter. As he looked at them through his blurred vision, Toby noticed their yellow teeth, stained from cigarettes. Then, all of a sudden, Charlie's mouth began to change shape. He stopped laughing and his lips began to move up and down as if he was talking to Toby. Unfortunately, due to the fall, Toby didn't have a clue as to what Charlie was saying. His ears were filled with a high pitched ringing noise that made listening impossible so he was unable to understand what Charlie was going on about. After a few seconds of watching Charlie silently talk, Toby's eyesight started to become clearer. He tried reading Charlie's lips in order to get some idea of what he was saying. Sadly, Toby found that he couldn't read Charlie's lips but, luckily for him, it didn't take long for his hearing to return to normal.

'I'm talking to you!' said Charlie, in a nasal whine. Toby knew well enough not to make fun of Charlie voice, but he couldn't help letting a small smile creep across his face when he heard just how ridiculous his attacker sounded.

'What are you smiling for?' Charlie asked angrily. 'Bet you wouldn't be smiling if you had to fight me like a man, huh?'

Toby shook his head. Best not to aggravate him.

'Are you tired sleepy-head?' Andrew chuckled in the background, running a thick hand through his black hair and spitting on the pavement. The two of them laughed and, for a moment, Toby thought he might be safe. Perhaps if they kept laughing they'd forget why they'd been chasing him. Unfortunately for Toby, this hope faded away the second Charlie opened his mouth to speak.

'So,' he whispered, grabbing hold of Toby's jumper, 'you like giving us dirty looks?'

Toby shook his head in protest. No, of course he didn't. He knew better than to do a thing like that. He wanted to tell them, to let them know that he'd never even dream of doing such a thing. But, even though he wanted to desperately, Toby found that he couldn't because there was no sound coming out of his mouth. He tried to talk, to force the words out, but all he managed to do was flap his lips about so that he resembled some kind of fish.

'Think you're funny?' Charlie snarled, obviously taking offence at Toby's facial movements. 'I should knock you out right now, but I'm not going to. I'm feeling nice.'

Toby knew better than to feel relieved. If Charlie Merchant was being nice to you then you were probably in more trouble than you realised.

'But what can we do?' Charlie wondered, scratching his chin sarcastically. 'How can we teach you a lesson?'

'I know!' said Andrew, an idiotic smile on his face. 'What about that?'

As he spoke, he raised his arm and pointed at something on the other side of the road. With all the strength he could muster, Toby craned his neck over his shoulder and managed to catch a glimpse of the punishment which awaited him.

Separating the pavement from the residential gardens was a tall brown fence. It was set in a long row of concrete, which formed a wall at the base of the wooden planks. It stood thick and strong and provided the fence with much more stability than it actually needed. Pushed up against this concrete base was a plastic box. It was a box that Toby knew very well and one that sent fear straight into his heart. It was a grit box, one filled with salt. The council used the salt to get rid of ice whenever the roads froze over in winter. It was unlocked and Toby knew for a fact that it was never full. Often, the salt only came up about half way to the top, which meant that there was always a small amount of space inside it. Enough space for a person.

Toby felt his throat begin to close up. No, not that. Anything but that. He turned his head back to face Charlie. As he stared into the sadistic eyes of his captor, Toby understood exactly what he was thinking.

'Brilliant idea, Andy,' Charlie whispered, a smile creeping across his lips. 'Brilliant idea.'

Toby tried desperately to shake himself free. He tried to run, to escape from Charlie's grip, but he just wasn't strong enough. Charlie was much bigger than him and it was clear that he had no trouble keeping his grasp on Toby's jumper.

'Grab his legs!' he shouted to Andrew.

Andrew happily obeyed. They lifted Toby into the air so that he was completely horizontal like a wooden board. As they carried him across the road, Toby continued to struggle. He kicked and thrashed about as hard as could, but all in vain. He opened his mouth, ready to scream for help, but one angry look from Charlie was enough to keep him quiet.

'Open it.' Charlie told Andrew as they reached the box.

Leaving Toby in Charlie's grasp, Andrew threw open the plastic lid and grinned. Due to the cold weather, the salt level had depleted considerably, which meant that there was plenty of room for Toby. This was a fact that Toby realised as soon as he saw Andrew's eyes light up with sadistic glee.

'Please,' he begged Charlie, gazing up at his captor. 'Anything but this.'

For a moment, Charlie looked at him. A nicer person might have taken pity on Toby, might have seen the dreadful fear in his eyes and heard the desperation in his voice. A nicer person might have let Toby go, but not Charlie.

'Have fun,' he said, an evil grin forming on his face.

Andrew ran to Charlie's side and grabbed Toby's flailing legs. As they lowered his body into the box, all the fear Toby had felt for Charlie seemed to disappear. The only thing he was afraid of now was the box. No longer fearing his captors, Toby screamed for help, but no one came. As his body hit the cold salt below him, he heard the two boys laughing hysterically above. He watched as they closed the lid on top of him, shutting it with a resolute thud and leaving Toby alone in complete darkness. There was nothing, nothing but a cold inky blackness that surrounded him as though he'd been buried alive. Toby felt the salt rubbing roughly against his skin as he struggled to find a way out. He tried pushing the lid open. He tried slamming his sore hands against the plastic desperately until blood dripped down onto his face. They were sitting on the lid; Toby knew it. They were determined to punish Toby and they weren't going to let him go.

It was very hard to hear what was going on outside the box. Sound didn't seem to travel very well through the plastic and the only sound that Toby could make out was the manic laughter of Charlie and Andrew. He stared blankly around him. The walls were closing in; he could feel it. The space inside was getting tighter and tighter and the air was being sucked out with every passing second. Toby couldn't breathe. He was going to suffocate. He could feel his claustrophobia setting in and he knew that he had to find a way out. He clawed at the lid in desperation but it didn't help. He could feel the top closing in on him. It was dropping down, closer and closer until it was merely inches from his face. Toby kicked and screamed, splashing salt up into his eyes. He couldn't see a thing. He didn't know where he was. The only thing he knew for certain was that he was going to die. He was going to die.

With a loud wretch Toby vomited. Brown liquid exploded all over his jumper and the smell of sick filled the box to the brim. The vomit covered him completely. It stuck to his clothes and ran down onto the salt below him. For a moment, Toby couldn't scream. His throat had seized up and he couldn't force a single sound out of his mouth. All he did was lay there, covered in vomit and shaking in a cold sweat. Then, Toby heard a voice coming from outside the box.

'Think he's had enough?'

'Yeah. I'm bored anyway.'

'Go for a smoke?'

'Yeah.'

They were leaving. Charlie and Andrew were leaving. Listening intently, Toby heard their thick boots land heavily on the pavement as they jumped off the plastic lid. They began to walk away, their footsteps becoming quieter and quieter until the sound faded away into nothing. Everything went silent. Even though Charlie and Andrew were gone, Toby still didn't make an effort to get out. Instead, he just lay there, covered in salt and sick, and began to cry. He'd never been so humiliated in his entire life. He was angry, not at the fact he'd been shoved into a grit box, but because of what he'd done. A normal person wouldn't have acted like he had. A normal person wouldn't have been sick. When he finally found the energy to move, he lifted the lid and pulled himself up into the fresh air. He looked around and noticed that there wasn't a single person in sight. No one could have helped him. No one. As he gazed at the sky above him, he saw the sun fading away behind the horizon. It would be getting dark soon and that meant he needed to get home. Lifting himself out of the box, Toby placed a foot onto the pavement and took a few shaky steps into the empty road. He raised a hand to the cut on his forehead and found that several grains of salt had become lodged inside it. He started to walk home, tears running down his face, and began to think. His claustrophobia, the fear of tight spaces that he'd had for as long as he could remember, had gone on long enough. As he gazed out into the sunset, Toby made up his mind and decided on what had to happen next. He had to face his fears and there was only one way to do that.

He had to go up to the attic.

10 A FRIEND RETURNS

BANG.

The door slammed shut. As the sound echoed throughout the house, Toby felt a pang of loneliness radiate inside his chest. The house was empty and he was all alone.

For a moment he stood in front of the closed door, staring into the living room. It had changed a great deal in all the years he'd been there. The carpet, which had once been dirty green, was now a fluffy cream colour and was immaculately clean. The walls too, which had once been covered in black smudges, were now pristine and matched the carpet so well that the two almost seemed to melt together. Where the old sofa had once stood, another new leather one now sat proudly. It was a slick, refined sofa and it was positioned so that it faced a top of the range fifty-inch flat-screen television, complete with huge box speakers on either side. Toby rolled his eyes. Daniel certainly hadn't been shy about spending money recently. Kicking off his shoes, Toby shuffled into the middle of the room. He looked at the sofa, shiny and immaculate, and wondered if he could lie on it without getting dried vomit between the leather folds. In the end he decided against it; it would be better not to risk such a thing.

146

Then, all of a sudden, something swelled up inside him. For a moment, Toby thought he was going to be sick again but, after a few seconds, he realised what he was feeling. It was determination, a fierce fire in his heart that made his fingers shake with anticipation. He had to go up to the attic; it was the only way to get rid of his claustrophobia. However, just as he began to get used to this new feeling inside him, he started to notice something else. Fear was fighting with determination. He could feel the two punching, kicking, scratching and clawing inside him, each one struggling desperately to become the dominant force. For a moment he waited, listening to the two wage war inside his chest, until there was finally a winner. Determination had won, stuck a spear right through the heart of fear, and Toby knew instantly what he had to do. He stomped across the white carpet and towards the hallway door. He was going to do it. Nothing was going to stop him. With a forceful hand, he twisted the doorknob and made his way into the hallway.

It was just sitting there, waiting for him. The white hatch in the ceiling with the fabric cord hanging down below it. It stared at Toby, watching him calmly. He could see it all, the chipped wood, the peeling paint, the smudges. It was all there. Then, all of a sudden, the fear inside him rose up, ready to fight once again. The fear wanted Toby to run, to go and never again even consider going up to the attic, but Toby couldn't let it win. With a trembling hand, he grasped the fabric cord and pulled.

Everything seemed to fall into place. The attic hatch opened and the ladder came tumbling down in front of him. Toby gulped and stared at the black square above him. It looked down at him menacingly, ready to swallow him whole. Toby wanted to run, to do anything except go up there, but he knew that he didn't have a choice. Grasping the ladder in his hand, he began to climb. Then, taking in one long breath, he poked his head up through the hatch and into the attic.

Toby hadn't gotten this far before. He'd never dreamt that he would actually do it. As he gazed around in the

147

darkness, he felt something strange. It was a memory, a memory that he couldn't quite figure out. It was as though he'd been up there before. Maybe it had been when he was younger, but Toby didn't know. Yet, despite the fact that he couldn't remember ever being up in the attic before, he was still able to find it. The light switch on his left, attached to one of the beams. Without so much as even looking in its general direction, Toby placed a cold finger onto the switch and flicked it upward.

Light flickered above him. A single bulb suddenly lit up and illuminated the whole attic in a white glow. Toby raised a hand to his face. The light stung his eyes and he couldn't see a thing. After a moment or two the stinging stopped and Toby's vision returned to normal. As he lowered his trembling hand, his heart racing inside his chest and his palms sweaty with excitement, he at long last saw the inside of the attic. It was very cramped and it was nowhere near big enough for someone like Daniel to fully stand upright. However, Toby, who was several inches shorter than his brother, would be able to manage. All around him, Toby saw thick wooden beams jutting out at odd angles, supporting the roof in areas that it probably didn't need supporting. There were so many beams, all of them old and splintered and beginning to look rotten. Hidden behind these beams, stacked high like towers, were piles and piles of cardboard boxes. Some of them were Christmas decorations, some souvenirs from Toby's childhood, and there were some that Toby was unable to identify. All of them were sealed with brown masking tape and some of the older boxes were dotted with little teeth shaped holes from where mice had been at them. In short, the attic was in an awful state and was in dire need of repair, but Toby didn't care about that now. All he cared about was doing what he'd set out to do and he knew that he couldn't just call it a day after only poking his head inside. He had to go into the attic, properly.

Toby tightened his grip on the ladder. He was grasping so tightly that he could feel the cold metal almost cutting into his skin. With one deep breath, he gathered all the courage he could muster and pulled himself up into the attic.

The first thing that Toby noticed, once he was fully inside, was the smell. Somehow, he hadn't quite experienced the full extent of it before, but now that his whole body was up in the attic he was almost able to taste the stench. It was the smell of decay and it was putrid. As it wafted down his airways like a toxic airborne chemical, Toby felt the combined aroma of mouse droppings and rotting wood burning up his insides. With one hand cupped over his nose and mouth, Toby sat on the floorboards and closed the hatch with a quiet yet definite thud. He'd done it! He was inside the attic! Did he feel scared? Of course he did, but he'd still done it. If he could just stay here, for a minute or so, without throwing up or going into a panic then he would have won. All he needed to do was keep calm.

ACHOO!

Someone had sneezed. Someone else.

That was when Toby felt it, the kind of feeling you get when you lean too far back in your chair. His stomach seemed to drop out of his body. His throat, still stinging from the smell, seized up and he found himself fighting for every breath. He desperately tried to force air into his lungs as his heart raced faster and faster, beating like a tribal drum. He wasn't alone. There was someone else inside the attic.

Toby thought about running. He could run downstairs and seal up the hatch with a hammer and nail and never go back up to the attic for as long as he lived. He thought about it, but he knew that he couldn't do it. He had to find out who had made that noise. Toby got to his feet and took a tentative step forward. He heard the floorboards creak underneath him, their strength depleted from years of neglect. As he continued onward, he felt the hairs on the back of his neck stand up. Someone was watching him, he knew it.

Then he heard something else, a sort of sniffling noise. It was the sort of noise people make when they feel a sneeze coming on. Toby stopped moving. The person was going to sneeze again. They were trying their best to stop it, to keep the sneeze inside, but they weren't going to manage it. They were going to sneeze again which meant that Toby would be able to find out where they were. Holding his breath so as not to make any noise, he listened carefully, waiting for the sound to come.

ACHOO!!!

The boxes. The boxes behind him; that was where the noise had come from. As soon as the sound reached his ears, Toby spun around. The pile of boxes was big, very big. In fact, it was the only pile of boxes in the attic big enough for someone to hide behind.

Clenching his shaking hand into a pitiful fist, Toby crept across the floorboards and towards the boxes. With every step he took, he felt the wood underneath him groan loudly. In any other situation he would have been worried about falling through, but not now. With one final step, Toby reached the boxes. He didn't know what to do. Should he push them over? Should he look over the top of them? Should he run? Maybe he should do what was best and avoid the problem. Every bone in his body was telling him to leave but he knew he couldn't. Throwing caution to the wind, Toby raised his fist over his shoulder and punched the boxes clean out of the way.

'What are you doing!?'

Toby stood paralysed with shock. A girl, slightly older than him with pale skin, matted blonde hair and dull eyes, was sitting behind the boxes, one hand supporting her body and the other raised in front of her face.

'You didn't have to punch them!' the girl yelled angrily. 'You almost gave me a heart attack!'

Toby stared at her in silence. His brain was still trying to figure out what was going on. There was a girl in his attic. A girl in the attic. As he tried his best to understand the situation, a swarm of questions began to fly around in his mind.

Who was she?

What was she doing there?

What was going on?

They were all relevant questions but, as far as Toby could see, there weren't any answers. He could have talked to the girl, asked her any one of these questions. That would have been the rational thing to do but, unfortunately, Toby wasn't feeling very rational at that moment. Therefore, instead of having a thoughtful, intelligent discussion with the girl in front of him, he decided that the best thing to do was pass out. Turning white as a sheet, he fell backwards onto the floorboards behind him, hitting his head on the wood with a loud *thunk*.

'Are you dead?'

The voice seemed to be coming from a million miles away. It was a nice voice, soft and gentle, like candy floss. Toby forced his eyelids open. His vision was very blurry, so he couldn't quite make out the finer points of his surroundings, but what could tell was that he was staring up at the attic ceiling. The beams above him were wobbly but, apart from the fact that his vision was impaired, everything seemed to be normal. Everything was normal, everything except for the strange girl standing over him.

'Hi, Toby,' she said, smiling happily at him. 'I've missed you.'

Toby jolted upright, but a sharp pain in his neck forced him back down again. As he rubbed his aching body with a splintered hand, he looked up at the smiling girl and began to speak in a croaky, shaken voice.

'How do you...?'

'Know your name?' the girl said, her hands on her hips. 'I'm slightly offended Toby! I thought that you might have remembered me at least a little bit. Then again, I guess it means that my plan worked.'

Toby rubbed his eyes hard with his knuckles. His vision was beginning to return to normal and his focus was becoming clearer, which meant that he could finally see the girl properly. Her skin was much paler than he'd realised. In fact, her skin was almost white and her body was covered in little red scratches that didn't seem to be healing very well. She wore a formal white dress that hung off her emaciated frame and clung to her shoulders by two frayed straps. As he stared up at her gaunt face, he noticed that her smile had begun to fade. She looked serious now, very serious.

'You've probably got questions,' she said, her eyes firmly fixed on Toby's, 'but do you think that I could answer them downstairs? I've been up here for far too long.'

Toby sat on the edge of the bed, trying his best not to look nervous. His face was forced into an expression of calm collection, one that he knew wasn't convincing in the slightest. He should have been asking questions but he didn't really feel like speaking yet. For a long while there was nothing except silence, but then the girl, who was standing at the foot of his bed, decided to get the conversation rolling.

'Your room looks different.'

Toby nodded. His bedroom was different; Daniel had redecorated it only a few months ago. The walls had been painted grey and a new set of curtains had been hung up in front of the window. They kept the light out better than his old ones had. Still, Toby got the sense that the girl wasn't referring to how his room had looked only a few months ago.

'The last time I was in here you couldn't move for stuffed animals and space stuff,' the girl continued. 'Do you still like space?'

Toby shook his head. The girl shrugged.

'I guess you grew out of it,' she said as she began to walk around the room. 'We all have to grow up at some point.'

As Toby stared blankly ahead, his mind still numb from shock, the girl, clearly noticing Toby's anxiety, made her way over to him and sat quietly on the carpet beside his bed. Looking up at him with empathetic eyes, she took a deep breath, rubbed her hands together and started to talk.

'Well,' she began, 'As you clearly can't remember anything about me it's probably best to start from scratch. Ask me anything you want to know.'

Toby remained silent.

'Come on,' the girl told him impatiently. 'We haven't got all day.'

With one deep breath, Toby forced the words out of his mouth and asked the most important question he could think of.

'Who are you?'

The girl sighed.

'Full title? Or will you settle for just my first name?'

'Both,' he whispered. 'Both names, please.'

The girl ran a hand through her knotted hair. She was clearly frustrated but she still answered him.

'Amelia Moore.'

'How old are you?'

'That depends.'

'Depends on what?'

The girl let out another long, exasperated sigh. After rubbing her temple with two pale fingers, she looked up at Toby and spoke in an almost angry tone.

'Is that really what you want to ask me? Wouldn't you rather know what I was doing in your attic?'

Toby began to sweat nervously. She was right; he was being stupid, but did she really have to be so harsh about it? The girl, noticing Toby's obvious discomfort, looked down at the floor.

'I'm sorry,' she told him apologetically. 'That was unfair. It's just that I've been alone for a very long time.'

After a long period of uncomfortable silence, the girl spoke again, this time so that she could point Toby in the right direction.

'You're missing the big one here! Come on, I know you're smarter than this.'

All of a sudden, Toby understood. He knew what she was getting at.

'What were you doing in the attic?' he asked her.

Toby knew that was the right question, he could see it in the girl's eyes. However, despite this, as soon as the words left his lips, the room seemed to get darker.

'Do you want the long or short version?' she asked him, speaking in a very serious tone.

'Short, please,' he whispered, his lips barely moving. He stared at her and waited with bated breath for her to continue.

'I am a ghost,' she told him. 'I've been dead for the last fifteen years.'

Suddenly, all sound seemed to leave the room. There was no rustling from the curtains, no whirring from the radiator and no buzzing from the light bulbs. The room had become well and truly silent. Toby's initial thought was that he'd gone mad. He wasn't dreaming, he knew that, so the only logical conclusion was that he'd lost his mind.

'I've gone insane,' he whispered, as though resigning himself to some horrible fate.

The girl stood up, an expression of anger on her face.

'Don't think that!' she yelled, her voice hoarse but powerful all the same. 'Don't ever think that, not because of me. I didn't go through all this for you to think like that. Don't ever think that I'm not real, because I am.'

Toby shook his head. The girl wasn't real; she couldn't be real. Perhaps he'd swallowed too much grit when Charlie and Andrew had stuffed him into that box. He didn't know why he was seeing things that weren't really there, but he did know one thing. The girl standing in front of him wasn't real.

'I need to call Daniel,' he muttered, getting shakily to his feet. 'I think I might have a problem.'

'A problem?' the girl shouted. 'A problem!'

'Yes,' Toby told her, his voice calm. 'I've gone insane and I need some professional help, maybe medication.'

Medication.

As soon as Toby spoke that word, a change came

over the girl. There wasn't just anger in her face anymore, but fear too. Toby didn't know why she looked like this. Perhaps, because she was a hallucination, she was reluctant to be obliterated from his subconscious, but he didn't really care. The girl wasn't real and he wasn't going to waste time talking to someone who wasn't real. He began moving towards the door, his eyes fixed firmly on the exit.

'Please,' the girl begged, throwing her body in front of him. 'Don't do this.'

The girl's efforts to stop him did nothing. Her body wasn't physically present and Toby was able to walk straight through her. He didn't have time for this.

'Please, Toby,' the girl continued. 'You can't tell them about me. I'm real, I promise!'

But Toby wouldn't listen. He knew that she wasn't real. As he reached the bedroom door and extended a steady hand towards the doorknob, he felt a calm certainty rise up inside him. However, he wasn't expecting to hear what the girl said next.

'Remember the TV,' she told him. 'Remember Amy.'

Toby stopped. He knew that name.

He didn't know what TV she was talking about, but he did know that name. Amy, where did he know that name from? All of a sudden, something inside him clicked. Deep in his brain, a memory that had been long forgotten began to bubble to the surface. It was a memory from a long time ago but Toby could see it in his mind's eye, clear as day. He saw a woman, standing over a broken TV set and shouting at him as a girl sat shaking with fear in a corner of the room.

'Amy?' he whispered, not daring to believe it.

'Amy,' she replied. 'Amy from the attic.'

11 TRYING TO MAKE SENSE

The room was incredibly dark and the blackness seemed to fall heavily on Toby's shoulders. He still wasn't sure how to respond after what had just happened. On paper it would have seemed so insane. He'd been talking to a girl who'd been hiding in his attic, a girl who claimed to have been dead for fifteen years. It was logical to assume that he'd lost his mind and Toby understood that, but he knew this girl. He knew her tangled hair, her faded eyes and, most of all, he knew her name: Amy.

'It's been a long time, Toby,' she whispered. 'I wasn't sure if I was ever going to see you again.'

Toby could feel a lump in his throat. It was impossible. Dead people didn't just come back to life! That wasn't how things worked.

'I know you,' he said, his voice trembling as he spoke. 'I remember you. Why do I remember you?'

'It's okay.' she told him, taking a few tentative steps

157

closer. 'Keep calm, Toby. I'll explain everything.'

'Calm?' he croaked. 'How can I keep calm?'

'Because if you do I'll tell you everything, deal?'

The darkness seemed to intensify. Hardly any light was coming through the curtains but some still managed to sneak its way into the room. The light flickered over Amy's face, dancing like the flames of a fire. Toby remained silent. Nothing made sense anymore. He had to be crazy, he had to be. But, despite knowing in his mind that he'd gone mad, he took a long look into Amy's calming eyes and nodded in agreement.

'Right,' she said firmly, in a tone not unlike a mother trying to calm a hysterical child. 'Sit down on the bed, okay?'

Toby nodded again. He moved away from the door and reassumed his position on the edge of the bed. As he sat, the mattress creaked, echoing in the unnaturally quiet room. He looked up at Amy and saw her stern expression turn thoughtful. She was clearly trying to decided how best to explain the situation. Finally, after several seconds of mental deliberation, she opened her mouth and began to speak.

'When you were five,' she began, 'your parents died. Am I right?'

'Yes,' Toby whispered, not sure how that was relevant.

'After that you moved into this house with your brother and his fiancée. Their names are Daniel and Karen. Am I right again?'

'Yes, but can we get to the point?'

'Be patient,' Amy told him firmly. 'When you moved here, Karen began to think that you needed some therapy. Did you know that?'

'No!' Toby replied, the shock clearly visible on his face.

'Well,' Amy continued, her manner unchanged, 'when you first moved into this house, on the second day I think it was, Daniel asked you to go up to the attic. Do you remember that?'

Toby shook his head.

'Well, he did,' she told him, 'and that was where you found me.'

'Found you?' Toby asked.

'Yes,' Amy replied. 'You found me, tied to a beam by a chain. I'd been there for five years. I asked you to come back that night and help me get out. I couldn't do anything because of the chain, so…'

'Sorry?' Toby interrupted. 'A chain?'

Amy sighed. Toby could see that this wasn't easy for her but, then again it wasn't easy for him either.

'Yes,' she replied, running a pale hand through her hair. As she spoke, Toby stared at the hand and noticed that several of her fingernails were missing. Some were partially there with half of the nail still intact, but on some fingers the whole nail was missing. All that was left on these fingers were spaces of red skin.

'You came up that night,' she continued, 'and tried helping me escape. You used some tools. Most of them didn't work, but one of them did. It was a knife. I didn't know why that knife had worked and the others didn't, but something else happened after you found it. Before I could escape, Daniel found you and put you back to bed. After you were gone, I used that knife to escape and that's how I finally got out of the attic. Are you with me so far?'

Toby nodded. He had his doubts but he didn't raise any of them. Amy continued with her story.

'We became friends,' she whispered. 'Do you remember all the fun we had?'

Toby wanted to remember. He wanted to see these memories in his mind but, no matter how hard he tried, he just couldn't find them. He looked down at the floor below him and shook his head despondently, ashamed at himself for not remembering.

'Anyway,' said Amy, going back to the story, 'it was all going well, until a couple of things went wrong. They were all my fault and Karen started to get worried. I used to mess up so badly and it used to make you cry which upset her. She was scared Toby, scared about what was happening to you. I knew it was getting bad, that me being around was only making things worse, but I still stayed. It was selfish but that's what I did and things only got worse after that.'

At this moment, Amy began to cry. The tears welled up around her eyeballs like watery spheres. Then, all of a sudden, they began to fall, streaming down her cheeks like rivers.

'We were watching TV,' she told him, her voice barely a whisper. 'That's when I saw it.'

'Saw what?' Toby asked, not sure if he wanted to know the answer. Amy looked at him, her eyes red and bloodshot.

'My Mum and Dad,' she said. 'I saw them there, on that TV. It was the first time in years that I'd seen them. I wanted to hug them, to squeeze them tight and say sorry for leaving, but I couldn't.'

She paused for a moment, searching her body for the energy to speak. As Toby waited, he watched her take a few steps towards his bedroom window. The steps were silent and didn't leave any imprint in the carpet below, but somehow her walk seemed to be heavy. It was as if she were dragging a heavy load behind her, a load that she couldn't shake off.

'You went to get Karen,' she told him. 'I wasn't moving and you were scared. You thought that something was wrong. You wanted to help me. I shouldn't have done what I did, but I was so angry. I had to do something.'

She turned to him, tears flowing down her face, and bared her teeth as she spoke.

'I smashed it,' she said furiously. 'I grabbed that television with both hands and threw it onto the floor. I don't know how I did it, but I did. The screen shattered into a million pieces and for a moment everything seemed just a little bit better. But then Karen came back into the room. She screamed at you and, after that, I knew that something had to be done. That's when I came up with the plan.'

'What plan?' Toby asked.

'I came into your room one night,' said Amy, 'and I told you that I had to go away. I said that I had to leave and that I could never come back.' Her voice sounded broken and Toby could feel her pain with each word she spoke.

'You were upset,' she continued, 'and so was I. You cried and you yelled and I thought you were going to wake up Karen. That's when I told you the story, the story about the monsters.'

All of a sudden, Toby remembered. The monsters, he remembered them. There had been a monster in his wardrobe, the long one at the end of his room. There had been a monster in the hedge, the hedge outside his room that Daniel had cut back but never fully removed. There had been other monsters too, monsters in the attic.

'Never go up to the attic,' he whispered to himself. 'Monsters in the attic.'

'I've been living up there,' Amy told him, 'for the past ten years. I've been as quiet as I could. I never spoke, never laughed, never cried. I've barely moved for an entire decade, just so that you wouldn't have to deal with me. So please Toby, don't tell anyone because, if you do, it will have all been for nothing.'

The air in the room seemed to become heavier. It pressed down on Toby, like strong arms on his shoulders forcing him down. He could feel himself collapsing underneath the weight of the world around him. He remembered everything, the attic, the monsters, the TV set, everything, but he still didn't know what to do. He opened his mouth to speak but, at that exact moment, the front door of the house flew open.

'We're back!' yelled Daniel. 'Can you help us with these bags?'

Toby didn't know what to do. He could act normal, pretend that everything was the same, but was that the best thing to do? He got to his feet and looked at Amy. He stared deep into her eyes and smiled. Perhaps he was crazy, but there was always the chance that he wasn't.

'Coming!' he told his brother, yelling loudly so that he could be heard. With his gazed still fixed on the girl in front of him, Toby silently mouthed four words that put her mind at rest.

I won't say anything.

As he opened the hallway door and made his way into the living room, Toby could feel a nervous knot twisting inside his stomach. His teenage mind was still attempting to process what had happened and it was failing miserably. As he entered the room, he tried his best to look normal. He straightened his back and kept his heavy breathing under control as best he could. Toby had to make Daniel and Karen

162

believe that there was nothing wrong, he had to.

His brother was stood by the front door, handfuls of plastic shopping bags stuffed into his fists. Dressed in a white collared shirt and wearing an expensive brown coat, Daniel looked slightly overdressed. He might have been out for a meal, but that didn't really warrant such a lavish outfit. Even so, Daniel's dress sense wasn't the most important thing on Toby's mind.

'Hello,' Daniel smiled, running a thick hand through his bristly hair. Daniel was taking after their Dad in certain aspects and premature baldness was one of them. His hair had always been short but it was looking thinner and thinner every day, a fact that he was ignoring as much as he possibly could. With a little nod, Toby reached out his hand and pointed at the bags.

'Did you do a little shopping before dinner?' he asked sarcastically. All of a sudden, Daniel's eyes widened. He raised a finger and pointed at Toby's vomit-stained school jumper, the jumper that he'd forgotten to take off.

'What's happened here?' his brother asked, demanding an explanation. Toby turned away, desperately trying to rub away the stain with his hand, but Daniel, who was infinitely stronger than him, placed a firm hand on his shoulder and turned him back around.

'What's going on?' called a loud voice from outside the house. The voice was shrill and rang in Toby's ears uncomfortably. From just her tone, he could tell that Karen had been drinking.

'Have a look at this!' Daniel replied, his voice firm and serious. After only a few seconds, Toby heard the front door slam shut and watched out of the corner of his eye as Karen entered the living room.

His sister-in-law had changed a great deal in ten years. For Toby the change had been gradual, quietly taking place over a long period of time, but whenever they would go to visit family, distant relatives who they only saw once or twice a year, comments would always be made. They were always shocked at how different she looked. Her denim jackets, which had once been her favourite item of clothing, had been thrown from her wardrobe and replaced by designer tops, respectable trousers and even dresses! She was wearing one of these dresses now. It was a long black dress that clung tightly to her thin body and on her face she wore large circular sun-glasses that she didn't need as it was now late evening. She looked strange but there was more to come. As Toby turned to face her, he caught sight of something perched on top of her head. It was a large black sun-hat, no doubt chosen by Daniel. It sat uncomfortably on top of her flat hair, hair that had been stripped of its blue colour and dyed an unremarkable shade of black.

'What's happened?' she asked, her voice concerned.

Toby shrugged nervously, fully aware that he had to come up with an explanation quickly.

'I felt sick,' he muttered under his breath. 'I got home and started throwing up. Didn't realise I got some on my jumper.'

Daniel and Karen stared nervously at each other. They did look anxious and appeared to be very sympathetic, but Toby wasn't buying it. Karen might have been concerned about him but he knew that Daniel was more worried about something else.

'Don't worry,' Toby told his brother. 'I didn't get it anywhere. I got to the toilet in time.'

Daniel breathed a heavy sigh of relief.

'Thank you, Toby,' he said in a much calmer voice. 'I assume you didn't eat the curry then?'

Oh yeah, the microwave curry. Toby had forgotten

about that.

'No,' he replied. 'I wasn't hungry.'

'Oh well,' said Daniel. 'Would you like something else?'

Toby shook his head.

'No thanks,' he said. 'I might just go to bed.'

'Oh,' Daniel replied. 'Okay then. Karen and I were going to watch a film. Wouldn't you like to join us?'

'No, thank you,' Toby told him, eager to leave the conversation. There was a short silence in which both Daniel and Karen smiled at him awkwardly. Then, just as Toby was about to turn away, he saw Karen's eyes light up.

'Wait here,' she told him. Karen hurried past him and went into the hallway. She was gone for only a moment but, when she returned, she was clutching one of Toby's t-shirts in her hand.

'I've got a clean one for you,' she smiled, handing it over to him. 'Have a good sleep, Toby.'

Karen wrapped her arms around Toby's shoulders and hugged him tight. For a second, Toby forgot about everything: the ghost, the attic, all of it. He was able to forget about it all, even if only for just a little while. Karen was good at making him forget about his worries. She gave the best hugs and Toby felt very sad when she finally let him go. As Toby muttered a quiet goodnight to both her and Daniel, the sense of contentment that Karen's hug had pumped into his body began to drain away. He made his way into the hallway and closed the door behind him.

He was facing it now, the door to his bedroom and the place where Amy was waiting for him. Toby sighed heavily. He'd kept up his end of the bargain. He hadn't told

Daniel and Karen about what he'd seen. He'd done what she'd asked, now she had to repay him. Toby had questions, questions that needed answering. With a deep breath, he placed a cold hand onto the doorknob and twisted. The door creaked opened and he made his way into the room.

What Toby saw caught him by surprise. He'd assumed that Amy would have been sat there, waiting for him to return, but that wasn't the case. Amy was nowhere to be seen and that confused Toby a great deal. Where had she gone? He walked slowly towards the wardrobe at the end of the room and pulled the doors open. He searched inside, pushing rows of t-shirts and jackets out of the way as he did so, but without any luck. Amy wasn't there.

Then, all of a sudden, a thought came into Toby's mind. Maybe he was mad. Maybe he'd imagined it. It would make sense. Perhaps none of it had been real. Perhaps there was no girl after all.

A thought like this wouldn't have worried him earlier. He'd been certain of his madness, ever since Amy first told him about everything that had happened, so such a thought shouldn't have concerned him. He should have been happy, it explained everything. But he wasn't happy. He was sad because he remembered her. The words she'd spoken had brought memories back, forced them into the front of his mind and hung them up for him to see. The memories were real and he knew that he hadn't imagined them, but none of it made sense. The room began to spin and Toby could feel his heart racing inside his chest. Suddenly, the whole world went quiet. The only sounds he could make out were his heavy breathing and the beating of his heart. It pounded away inside him. Toby didn't know what to do. His palms were sweaty and he couldn't see properly. Nothing made sense and he couldn't figure out how to fix it. He was going to faint. He was going to pass out. He couldn't stand. He couldn't move.

'You're not okay, are you?'

All of a sudden, the room returned to normal. The

voice seemed to ground Toby and, as soon as he heard it, his anxiety began to disappear. His heartbeat slowed, his breathing became calmer and the only thing that remained was an empty feeling inside his stomach. As his vision became clearer, Toby turned to the side and faced the source of the voice that had saved him.

Amy was standing by the door. She was looking at him, eyes wide with concern, and Toby breathed a heavy sigh of relief. He hadn't imagined her! She was right there in front of him, her eyes staring deep into his as if she were looking into his soul.

'What?' Toby replied, wiping the cold sweat from his forehead.

Amy sighed.

'I thought that things might be easier now, but I guess not. It's a big thing to have to come to terms with, I know that really. I shouldn't have thought that you'd instantly believe me.'

Toby didn't say a word. He knew that what she was telling him was completely rational. Anyone would have been scared if they'd found someone in their attic but, even so, he couldn't help feeling a little guilty. It was like he was wrong for feeling that way.

'I'll give you some time,' Amy told him, her voice calm and steady. 'I'll go back up there for a bit. That might help you think it through. I'll come back down when you're ready. We don't have to rush things but please, Toby, try not to worry.'

Toby nodded in agreement, even though he knew full well that he would worry. Amy smiled at him and Toby could tell that she was scared.

'Could you do something for me?' she asked, her voice croaky and nervous.

'Of course,' he told her. 'What is it?'

'Daniel and Karen,' she told him. 'When they put the film on, could you…'

She paused for a second, clearly finding it hard to get the words out.

'Could you open up the attic? I can't get up there unless you open it.'

Toby felt sorry for Amy. Perhaps she was a hallucination but, even so, he could tell that she didn't want to go up to the attic. She was doing it for him and he appreciated that.

There was a knock at the door. It was a quiet knock and sounded as though the person making it wanted to be a discrete as possible. Toby's eyes darted to the door, then back to Amy.

'Go on,' she said. 'Tell them to come in.'

Toby nodded and took a deep breath.

'Come in,' he called loudly.

The doorknob twisted, first one way, then the other. On the third twist, the door opened and Karen made her way into the room, the muffled sound of the television following with her.

'Hey, Toby,' she whispered, clearly still concerned about him.

'Hey,' he mumbled.

Suddenly, Toby's eyes widened in shock. He couldn't believe what he was seeing. Amy was standing no more than a foot away from Karen, yet Karen, who was never one to ignore people, didn't even seem to notice. Toby looked at Amy. Out of the corner of his eye, he saw Karen follow his gaze in an attempt to figure out what he was looking at. For a moment, she stood there silently, eyes staring directly at Amy, yet not saying a single solitary word. Finally, after what seemed like an eternity, Karen asked Toby a question.

'What are you looking at?' she asked, her eyebrow raised. Toby snapped out of his trance and stared at Karen, his mouth hanging wide open like a fish.

'Nothing,' he told her unconvincingly.

On another night Karen might have questioned him, given how he clearly wasn't telling her the whole story, but she was under the impression that Toby was ill and that was all the explanation she needed. Whilst Karen's mind was clearly at rest, Toby's was working rapidly as he tried to figure out what was going on. After a few seconds, rational thought returned to him. He guessed that it did make sense, Karen not being able to see Amy. Whether she was a ghost or a delusion, Amy would still be invisible to anyone that wasn't him.

'Well,' Karen told him, 'I just came to bring you this.'

As Toby watched, Karen raised a hand up to her head and grasped the rim of her sun-hat. With a flourish, she raised it off her head to reveal a single bar of chocolate sitting on top of her hair. With a cheeky smile, she picked up the chocolate and motioned for Toby to hold out his hand. As he did so, she placed the treat in his open palm and gave him a hug.

'Have a good sleep, Toby,' she whispered in his ear. 'Love you.'

With a sigh of contentment, Karen let go of Toby and made her way quietly out of the room, gently closing the door behind her. As he watched her go, Toby could feel himself smiling.

'Love you too,' he whispered.

'That was nice.'

For a moment, Toby was surprised. He'd almost forgotten that Amy was in the room.

'Yeah,' he mumbled, staring at the floor.

'Hey, look at me,' she told him.

As Toby met Amy's gaze, he once again saw her sad eyes looking back at him, fighting back tears with all the power she had. She looked scared, but she was still smiling.

'Whenever you're ready,' she whispered.

As Amy walked towards the bedroom door, her feet dragging along the carpet as though she'd been sentenced to death, Toby caught a glimpse of something red on her dress.

'Wait,' he said in a confused voice. Amy stopped and turned around, which meant that he was able to see it much clearer. How had he not noticed it before? Perhaps he'd been too preoccupied with his own thoughts, but he could see it now. Just below Amy's stomach was a large red wound. It was a deep cut in her flesh that had sliced through the fabric above it. The wound wasn't bleeding, but it looked painful.

'What happened?' he asked, his eyes filled with morbid curiosity. Amy, puzzled for a second, looked down at her dress and sighed when she realised what had caught Toby's eye.

'Some other time,' she told him, and with that, she turned around and walked out of the room.

12 SOMEONE ELSE

The weekend that followed that fateful Friday evening was, in Toby's mind, one of the most uncertain times he'd ever experienced. Throughout both Saturday and Sunday not a single sound came from the attic above him and, after a while, he almost began to suspect that he'd dreamt everything. He continued to suspect this until the final few hours of Sunday afternoon.

The day had been pleasant enough. The weather had been cold but not freezing and the sun had stayed out for longer than had been expected. Normally on winter days in Lawton the sun stayed firmly hidden behind the clouds, but on this day it had been different, so Daniel had suggested that they take advantage of it. He, Karen and Toby had all piled into the car and set off, driving out of Lawton to one of the nearby villages for some lunch. After arriving at a riverside gastro-pub, they'd all ordered Sunday roasts, beef for Daniel and Toby and a nut-roast for Karen. Once well and truly full, they'd drifted back to the car and driven home, where Karen and Daniel both promptly fell asleep on the sofa. As a result, Toby was left on his own for most of the afternoon and he couldn't have been happier. After all the intense emotions he'd felt that Friday, he welcomed the chance to get some peace and quiet and was more than happy to spend the time reading in his room. After making his way through two chapters of a big leather-bound book, he rose groggily to his feet and walked toward the back room, in order to get his jumper for school the next day. Karen had washed it the day before, using their new high-tech washing machine, and had left it to dry on the clothes rack overnight. However, for some

171

reason, Karen had forgotten all about it and, as she clearly wasn't getting up anytime soon, Toby figured that he might as well go and get it.

Upon entering the room, Toby sighed. The room looked incredibly bare. Despite the rest of the house being filled with all manner of items, the back-room had been left mostly empty. The once white walls were turning yellow with age and the cream carpet looked patchy, which was strange as the room generally got little use. The only time anyone went in it was when they needed to sort out washing and, aside from that, none of the family had much cause to go into it. The room was old, empty and pointless. It depressed Toby, which was why he generally avoided it whenever he could.

As Toby made his way towards the metal clothes rack that was set up in the corner of the room, he heard a single, quiet cough above his head. For a moment he froze, not quite sure where it had come from. He looked up and stared at the dirty ceiling above him. It glared down at him menacingly. All of a sudden, he realised where the sound had come from and it all came back to him.

He remembered the girl in the attic, the girl who was hiding away so that he could come to terms with the fact that only he could see her. When he remembered this, he didn't feel deeply anxious - that came later - but he did feel a sense of annoyance. He was irritated, both by the situation and the fact that he'd almost been convinced that he'd dreamt it all. As he made his way back into his bedroom, Toby hung the jumper up in his wardrobe and slid into bed. As he lay there, staring up at the ceiling, a sense of anxiety flooded over him. Amy had gone up there to give him some time. That time was supposed to help him come to terms with the situation, but he hadn't done that. All that he'd done was stick his fingers in his ears and tried to forget all about it. It had been almost two days since she'd gone up to the attic and he still couldn't figure out what to do. Was he insane? Had he really spoken to a ghost? He just didn't know.

For most people, surprises come in small amounts,

one here, one there, but not usually clumped together like sardines in a tin. For most people, the discovery of a ghost in their attic would be a solitary surprise. Another one wouldn't follow it, at least not for a while. Toby, however, was not one of those people. His second surprise came when he was eating breakfast the next morning.

Sitting on the leather sofa in the living room, Toby stared blankly at the TV. He was watching the morning news and happily eating a slice of buttered brown toast. It was then that his sister-in-law came into the room. Karen, who was dressed in a tight grey skirt and an immaculately clean black blazer, was on her way to the office of a local law firm, where she worked part time as a receptionist. She'd been working there for some years now and seemed to enjoy it reasonably well. However, it left her little time to focus on her paintings.

'I've got something to ask you,' she proclaimed, waltzing into the room. Toby, whose mind had been clouded with nervous thoughts about Amy, only faintly heard her and responded with a disinterested grunt. Even though she was clearly aware that he wasn't listening, Karen continued to talk.

'How would you like a little brother?' she asked him happily.

Toby nearly choked on his breakfast.

'What?' he spluttered, crumbs falling from his lips. Karen laughed.

'Well,' she said, 'I guess it might not be a boy. It could be a girl.'

'Are you? I mean are you really...?'

Karen shook her head.

'No,' she told him. 'Not yet anyway. I just wanted to

get your opinion on the idea. What do you think?'

Toby was stunned. He knew that he had to say something, but there were already a lot of things going on in his mind and he wasn't quite sure if he could deal with another one. Karen stared at him, waiting patiently for his response.

'Great,' Toby finally croaked. 'Fantastic idea.'

Karen beamed, her smile lighting up the room.

'I knew you'd like it,' she said, her face filled with joy. 'I've loved taking care of you all these years, Toby. You've been like my own child and its been so much fun watching you grown up into the strong, handsome man you are today.'

Toby snorted. He certainly wasn't either of those things.

'But that's the thing,' Karen continued. 'You're growing up and I think, after taking care of you all these years, that I'd make a good mum and Daniel thinks that he'd make a good dad.'

'He does?' Toby asked, a hint of suspicion in his voice.

'Of course,' she replied. 'It was his idea in the first place but, if he says anything to you, don't tell him that I've told you. We're supposed to be keeping it secret.'

'What's going on here?' came a loud voice that echoed from the other side of the house.

Toby heard Daniel's heavy footsteps creaking on the floorboards as he made his way along the hallway and into the living room. As he appeared, Toby saw that, like Karen, he was dressed for work. He was wearing a brand new navy suit that he'd bought recently from a high-end tailor. He and Karen both had jobs, but his was management level, which meant that he had to be at work a half-hour earlier than her. Therefore, given that they only had one car, it meant that both of them had to leave at the same time.

'Nothing,' Karen told him, a sly smile stretching across her face. 'Toby got crumbs on the carpet and I was telling him to clean them up.'

Daniel raised an eyebrow and looked at Toby.

'Make sure they're gone,' he told him, a playful smile on his lips.

Toby smiled and nodded obediently. Daniel walked over to him and tussled Toby's hair.

'Come on,' he told Karen. 'We had better head off.'

Smiling like idiots, the two of them left, closing the front door behind them with a loud bang. They had left Toby alone in the living room to contemplate not only the thought of a ghost in the attic, but also the idea of a new addition to the family.

As Toby entered his English class that morning, frozen stiff from the winter weather outside, his first instinct was to make his way over to his desk, where he promptly slumped over in his chair and buried his head in his hands. This wasn't going to be an easy day to get through, not while he was still thinking about her. Still, he had all day to convince himself that Amy was real. It was strange because, even though Amy had given him so much evidence and even though her words had awakened memories inside him that were so clear they could have been made the day before, he still wasn't sure whether or not it was all one big trick. Deep down, he knew that she was real, he just couldn't accept it, not until he could be sure.

Despite Toby's attempts to ignore them, he was

distracted by the fact that his classmates were making an ungodly racket. It was strange because Mr Morrison would have normally been there by that point but, for some reason, the class was still without its teacher. It didn't surprise Toby that the class were making the most of their lack of supervision. With his face still buried in his freezing cold hands, Toby wasn't able to see exactly who was making the noise, but he could make some fair assumptions. He was sure that he could hear the voices of Charlie and Andrew high above the rest, informing everyone of how they'd made him throw up in the grit box. In a desperate attempt to block them out, Toby tried searching for the voice of Lily Roberts. Her voice was softer than anyone else's, he could remember it. It had a silky quality to it that sounded smooth and comforting. It was a voice he knew well but, no matter how hard he tried, he couldn't find it in the classroom. He sighed quietly; she probably wasn't talking. Lily could be quiet sometimes and she was more than likely copying down some notes or flicking through old ones in order to keep herself caught up.

BANG!

The classroom door slammed shut. As Toby listened, he heard a quiet hush fall over the room. A pair of feet began to make their way softly across the floorboards. Someone had definitely entered the room, but those light footsteps couldn't belong to Mr Morrison. They had to be coming from another teacher, a different one all together. A new one. Toby lowered his hands from his face and stared out in front of him.

Standing by the whiteboard was a man that Toby felt he recognised. He was an old man, maybe sixty or seventy, and looked like someone who was perpetually tired. His eyes were little more than thin slits, the lower-lids dragged down by heavy black bags and had a fuzzy white beard, one that clung to his wrinkled face. He wore a red jumper, a tatty one with holes in it that hung limply off his shoulders. The man was old, the man was tired, but somehow his presence seemed to make Toby feel warm inside. It was like he was just meeting a distant relative, one that he'd only seen a few times, but had fond memories of all the same.

The classroom was silent. That is to say, no one was talking, but Toby could hear the other noises they were making. He could hear the eyes rolling in their sockets, the impatient grinding of teeth and, most of all, the quiet uncertain breaths every student was making as they waited for the man in front of them to speak.

'Mr Morrison is unwell,' the man told them in a raspy voice. 'I will be teaching you today.'

Toby heard a few muffled whispers from his classmates. They never took substitute teachers seriously and Toby doubted whether any of them would pay much attention to this one. As the man surveyed the class with his beady little eyes, the corners of his mouth began to turn upward into a polite smile. He turned to face the whiteboard and picked up a black marker. It was then that he began to write. The man wrote slowly and shakily, but in an elegant cursive that put all other handwriting to shame. Then, once he had finished, he faced the class, smiled once again and pointed at what he'd written...

Mr Thornhill

'Now,' he told them, gazing out over the rows of desks. 'Would someone please tell me where you left off.'

The rest of the lesson went reasonably well. As it turned out, Mr Thornhill, despite his age, was a very engaging teacher and Toby was fascinated by him. He watched in awe as the old man described all manner of complex literary concepts with an obvious passion and zeal that made the hairs on the back of his neck stand up. The old man was a great teacher and it was a great lesson, much better than any of the ones they'd had with Mr Morrison. In fact, when the lesson finally reached its end, Toby felt quite disappointed that it hadn't gone on longer.

'Well,' Mr Thornhill said, after noticing the time. 'Class dismissed.'

Nobody needed telling twice. As soon as the words left Mr Thornhill's mouth, all of the students darted out of the classroom, leaving an almost completely empty room behind them. Only two people remained: Mr Thornhill and Toby. Cramming a book of notes into his backpack, Toby had a quick look at the teacher. Mr Thornhill was standing by the whiteboard, his eyes catching the light so that they shone bright as diamonds. The old man looked around happily and smiled. Somehow, from just this one action, Toby could tell that Mr Thornhill hadn't set foot in a classroom for a very long time.

Knock. Knock.

The sound of knuckles tapping on wood echoed throughout the room. On hearing the noise, both Toby and Mr Thornhill turned their heads. There, standing by the open door, was none other than Mr Hinkley, the head-teacher. He was a bald man, very bald indeed. A lot of people go bald in their lifetime, but some more than others. That being said, Mr Harold Hinkley, to use his full name, was the baldest man Toby had ever seen in his entire life. The top of his head glistened under the bright ceiling light and the shine that came off it was so great that Toby found it difficult to look at him. His skull was unnervingly smooth and completely free of any stubble. Aside from his baldness, there was very little about Mr Hinkley worth mentioning. He wore a cheap suit and had a long crooked nose that turned upward at the tip, but that was all that could be said about him.

'Hello, Thomas,' he leered, staring at the old man.

Mr Thornhill nodded nervously. His eyes were wide

and frightened, as if he were staring down the barrel of a gun. Mr Hinkley's slimy grin broadened, revealing two rows of pointed yellow teeth. He turned and looked at Toby.

'Would you give us some privacy?' he asked him. Toby knew better than to refuse.

'Yes, sir.' he replied.

With a polite smile, Toby slung his backpack over his shoulder and hurried out of the room. Mr Hinkley slammed the door shut. For a moment, Toby stood there in the busy hallway, staring at the closed door and wondering what the two of them were talking about. Normally, Toby wasn't the curious type. He'd spent most of his life sticking to the safe paths and rarely ventured down dangerous ones. However, despite this, he could feel something inside him. It was like a bubble rising to the surface of a boiling pot of water. That bubble was curiosity. It was a curiosity that he'd not felt for a long time and only now was it coming into the forefront of his mind. He knew that he shouldn't act on this feeling. There was a private conversation going on in that classroom and it had nothing to do with him. They could be discussing personal things that shouldn't fall onto the ears of a student. However, despite knowing that he shouldn't do it, the curiosity inside him became too much. Toby had to know what they were talking about.

The classrooms in Lawton Secondary School were large and, in order to save space, they had been built close together, separated only by uncommonly thin walls. It was this structural flaw that Toby knew he could exploit. In the classroom next door there was a hole in the wall. It was only a small hole and one of the more obsessive teachers had covered it with a poster. However, if that poster was pulled back it would be quite easy to listen in on the conversation next door. Turning to face the other classroom, Toby noticed with delight that it was empty and that the light inside had been turned off. As a result, the whole room was in almost complete darkness. It would provide the perfect amount of cover.

Toby knew that he didn't have long to decide. The conversation had already begun and he could tell that it wasn't going to be a long one. He closed his eyes and thought. He could either stand in the corridor, grappling pointlessly with his own conscience, or he could do something. After thinking for only a moment, he made up his mind. Quick as a flash, he darted through the door and entered the classroom. As he closed the door behind him, Toby realised that his palms were sweating. He was very nervous. He'd never done anything like this before and he could feel his heart racing inside his chest. Toby crept silently across the mottled blue carpet and ducked behind the teacher's desk, which was at the very front of the room. The desk provided even greater cover for him and, as he arched his back downward, he knew that he would be virtually undetectable. Placing a hand on the side of the desk, he turned to face the wall and found what he was looking for. It was the poster, the one with the hole behind it. It was a new poster, an orange one with a cartoon divide symbol printed onto it. The cartoon had wide eyes that seemed to glare back at Toby, almost as if it were warning him, trying to dissuade him from going any further.

'Big Brother is watching,' Toby thought and, with a flash, he ripped the poster from the wall.

The hole wasn't very big. In fact, it would be a struggle to even call it a hole as it wasn't completely open. Little shreds of plaster had blocked it up and only a few specks of light could be seen through it. Even so, it still let sound through and that was all that Toby needed.

'Well,' came Mr Hinkley's voice through the hole. 'It's good to hear that you're getting back on your feet, Thomas.'

The sound carried well through the tiny hole. Toby smiled slyly. His plan was working and he couldn't help feeling a rush of excitement flow through his body as he continued to listen.

'Thank you,' Mr Thornhill replied, his voice quiet

and nervous.

Mr Hinkley let out a quiet *hmm* sound.

'It's great to have you back,' he told Mr Thornhill. 'Though I must say it has been a while hasn't it.'

Mr Thornhill didn't say a word.

'It must be almost twenty years now,' Mr Hinkley continued. 'Is that right? Has it been that long?'

'Yes,' Mr Thornhill confirmed, in a weak voice.

'I thought so,' Mr Hinkley said snidely. 'I hadn't been working here for that long when the incident occurred.'

The room went dead silent. Toby, whose ear was pressed hard against the hole, could tell that Mr Thornhill didn't know what to say. The mood of the conversation had changed, all because of that last sentence. Toby's mind began to race. What were they talking about? Had Mr Thornhill done something? What could he have done? All of a sudden Toby wished that he hadn't decided to eavesdrop. He'd known that it was a bad idea and now he was going to overhear something that could get him into a lot of trouble. Big trouble.

'How is your wife, Tom?' Mr Hinkley asked, his voice thick and slimy. Toby listened intently for Mr Thornhill's reply. The old man's breathing had become heavy and laboured and, when he spoke next, it sounded as though he was holding the weight of the whole world on his shoulders.

'I haven't seen her,' he told Mr Hinkley, 'but I know that she's well. Thank you for asking, Harold, but I should be going.'

'So soon?' Mr Hinkley replied. 'Break doesn't finish for another ten minutes. Don't you want to chat with an old friend?'

Mr Thornhill was beginning to panic. His heavy breaths had turned into thick wheezes that sounded painful. Toby winced as he heard each breath, a harsh knot twisting inside his stomach as he listened.

'It's just...' Mr Thornhill began, but Mr Hinkley cut him short.

'I hope that you know what a risk I'm taking with you, Tom,' he told the old man. 'Not a lot of people would hire someone like you. I'm doing you a favour. It wouldn't do for you to forget that, would it?'

The room remained silent but Toby could almost sense Mr Thornhill's head nodding fearfully in agreement.

'Good,' Mr Hinkley replied. 'Glad we're on the same page.'

Toby heard Mr Hinkley's shoes clinking on the wooden floorboards. The sound was unmistakable. Then, as Toby held his breath nervously, the footsteps came to an abrupt halt.

'If I were you, Tom, I'd keep to myself,' Mr Hinkley told the old man, his voice cold and inhuman. 'I wouldn't want anyone knowing that I'd seen dead people, especially if that dead person happened to be my wife. It might present the wrong image, if you get my drift.'

The classroom door closed softly and the room fell silent. Toby pulled his ear away from the hole. He'd thought that eavesdropping on the conversation would have been a huge mistake. It could have landed him in trouble, much more trouble than he needed right now, but it hadn't been a mistake. In fact, it had been the best decision he'd made all day. If what Mr Hinkley had said was true, then Toby might have discovered the key to finding out if he was insane or not. He'd never stopped to think if there were others, other people who could see what Toby could. Mr Thornhill could see ghosts and, if that really was the case, then maybe he would be able to see the one that Toby had in his attic.

'What are you doing in here?!'

All of a sudden, the classroom lights came on above him, blinding Toby with their brightness. For a moment, he was so dazed that he couldn't see where the voice had come from. However, Toby could tell instantly who had spoken. Something gave it away, the Welsh accent. As his vision slowly returned, Toby peered over the edge of the desk and shuddered with horror as he saw the angry red face of Mr Jones, the Maths teacher.

13 A SECOND OPINION

'Get up!' snarled Mr Jones, his eyes bulging out of their sockets. 'Get up now!'

Toby didn't waste any time. Quick as a flash, he jumped to his feet and stared nervously at his captor. Mr Jones was a beast of a man. He wasn't muscular, but he was strong. He was a man that you definitely didn't want to be caught on the wrong side of. His strength often showed itself on sports day, when he could be seen trying to throw the shot-put over the fences that surrounded the school playing field and into the neighbouring gardens.

'What are you doing?' the Welshman repeated, his thick brown moustache crinkling up in anger.

'Nothing, sir,' Toby lied. Mr Jones wasn't convinced.

'Do you take me for a fool, boy? Do you think that I'm stupid?'

'No, sir,' Toby muttered.

'What was that?'

'No, sir,' Toby told him. 'I don't think that you're stupid.'

For a moment, Mr Jones just looked at him, the way a boxer sizes up an opponent before a fight. After realising that Toby was a scrawny kid with no real body strength, the corners of his lips curled upwards into an evil smile.

'Come on,' he barked, raising a thick finger towards the door. 'Follow me, now.'

Toby gulped and nodded. Most of the teachers knew never to touch a pupil except in only the most extreme circumstances, but not Mr Jones. With his strong hand, he grasped Toby's arm, his grip so tight that it felt as though he might snap it in two. As he was pulled into the hallway, Toby noticed that the crowds had dispersed. Not many people stayed in the hallways during break time, so it wasn't a surprise to him. Even so, break would be over soon. There were still a few people in the corridor, keen students already lining up for lessons that they didn't have to be at yet and, even though they stared as Mr Jones pulled him into the classroom next door, Toby realised that he didn't care that much about what they must have thought of him. It wasn't the people watching that concerned him, it was what was going to happen next. He could see it in his mind: Mr Jones screaming at him, telling him that he should have known better, Toby being hauled to Mr Hinkley's office, where his leering smile would tell him that there was no other option than to expel him. That was what was going to happen and Toby wasn't ready to face it. Even so, he knew that he had to be strong. Pushing the fear deep down inside him, he kept his face straight and emotionless as the burly hands of Mr Jones threw him through the doors of the English classroom and right at the feet of a very confused looking Mr Thornhill.

'Caught him!' boomed Mr Jones, his voice thick and

jovial. 'Found him spying on you in the other room.'

Toby gazed up at Mr Thornhill. Even though he'd gathered that the old man wasn't a very loud or particularly mean person, Toby had still expected him to be at least a little bit angry. However, this was not the case. There was no anger in Mr Thornhill's eyes, only sadness. His tired face looked defeated and his lips were pursed tightly together in a vain attempt to keep himself composed. He didn't want to show how deeply hurt he really was. As Toby watched the old man, he couldn't help feeling guilty for what he'd done.

'Thank you, Mr Jones,' Mr Thornhill said to the Maths teacher. 'I'll deal with him now. Would you give us a minute?'

Mr Jones's face dropped. He'd clearly wanted to see justice come to Toby but, unfortunately for him, that would not be the case. He left the room with a disappointed grunt, slamming the door behind him loudly like a sulking child. It was just the two of them now: Toby and Mr Thornhill. For a while neither of them spoke, allowing the uncomfortable nature of the problem to sink in. Finally, after a minute or so, Mr Thornhill's lips parted and he began to speak.

'Well,' he asked in a broken voice. 'What was your name?'

'Toby, sir.'

'Ah.'

Again there was silence. Toby could tell that Mr Thornhill was trying to talk. He could hear the old man's tongue moving about inside his mouth, but not a single word came out. The situation was difficult for the poor man and it made Toby feel even worse about what he'd done.

'Well, Toby,' the old man finally said. 'What did you hear?'

'Nothing, sir.'

Mr Thornhill coughed. Toby stared at the floor, his head lowered in shame.

'Look at me,' the old man said to him. 'Please.'

Toby did as he was told. The sadness which had filled the old man's eyes had been replaced by an intense seriousness.

'Now, I will ask you again. What did you hear?'

'About your wife, sir.' Toby told him.

'What about her?'

Toby wanted to tell him. He wanted to tell Mr Thornhill that he could see ghosts, just like he could. He wanted to yell it. He wanted to scream it at the top of his lungs, but he couldn't. This was his only chance and he had to make sure that he did everything right.

'That you could see her, even though she's dead.'

Toby wasn't quite sure what reaction he'd expected from Mr Thornhill, but it wasn't the one he got. Maybe he'd thought that Mr Thornhill would be upset or angry, but he certainly hadn't expected what happened next. The old man stared at Toby with an emotionless face. Even so, Toby could tell that there was a lot more going on under the surface.

'And what do you think of that?' Mr Thornhill asked, his eyes fixed on Toby.

The room suddenly felt colder.

'I won't say anything, sir.' Toby told him.

'You won't?'

'No.'

'How can I be sure of that?' the old man asked.

Toby wasn't sure of what to say. He was being honest. He would keep quiet about what he'd heard, but he needed answers. He needed someone to show him the truth and if anyone was going to be able to see Amy, it was going to be Mr Thornhill. Suddenly, out of nowhere, a poster caught Toby's eye. It was a small poster that had been in the classroom for as long as he could remember. It was pink with frayed edges and written on it in black marker, was the following word...

Tutoring

Toby continued reading. Although he was barely able to make out the words, he still managed to figure out what the poster was advertising and read each line without much trouble.

Having trouble understanding fractions?

Think that Shakespeare is a bunch of boring words?

Just don't get it?

Why not ask about tutoring?

Teachers at Lawton are participating in a scheme which involves coming to your home and tutoring you on any subject you're having trouble with.

If it's Maths, English, Science or anything at all, you can be sure that a teacher will help!

Ask your subject leader now for information and prices.

A thought came into Toby's brain. He had a plan. It could work! It might work but, then again, it might not. Either way, Toby was out of options and he knew that this was the only way to get what he wanted.

'Well, sir,' he began, adopting a humble demeanour. 'It's just that I've been needing some help with English. I'm finding it a bit hard and I need someone to explain it to me. My brother and his wife keep telling me that I need to sort it out. I didn't know what to do about it, but then I found out that teachers can do tutoring and I thought it might be good for me. I was going to ask about it, but I thought that paying for it might be a bit difficult. I need a lot of sessions because I'm finding English very hard, that's why I didn't ask Mr Morrison. If it was possible, could I get some tutoring that I didn't have to pay for. It would really help me and it would help you be sure that I won't tell anyone, because I'm not going to, sir, honest.'

The room was still. The long silence that followed was one of the most nervous times in Toby's whole life. As he waited patiently, his hands behind his back and an anxious smile forced onto his face, Mr Thornhill did nothing but stare at him. The old man looked puzzled, almost afraid, but there was something else there as well. Despite the oddness of Toby's request, Mr Thornhill looked interested.

'Deal,' he said, nodding cautiously.

As Toby looked at Mr Thornhill, he felt certain that the old man could tell he was planning something. Even so, it was clear that he was relieved and, as he reached out a wrinkled hand for Toby to shake, it was obvious that the agreement had lifted a mighty weight from his shoulders.

They had arranged for the first tutoring session to take place the next day at 5pm. As Mr Thornhill would have to come to his house to tutor him, Toby decided that five o'clock on a Tuesday afternoon was the best time to do it as both Daniel and Karen would still be at work. That would give him plenty of freedom to make sure that the plan went smoothly. As soon as he got in from school, he would open up the attic and explain to Amy how things were going to work. He'd tell her on the day and not before. It would be less stressful that way.

The plan was as follows. Amy was to come down from the attic and, when Mr Thornhill arrived, she would pretend to be Toby's cousin from one village over, who was waiting at the house until Karen got back so that she could be driven home. That way, if Mr Thornhill could see her, they would be able to prove Amy's existence without having the old man feel as though he were being mocked. Also, Karen wouldn't be back until after Mr Thornhill was due to leave, so there wouldn't be any awkward incidents regarding the fake story. Mr Thornhill would be long gone before he could talk to Karen about the girl who was waiting to be driven home. The plan was fool-proof and it would go down without any problems if everything just went as it was supposed to. Toby truly believed that the whole thing was sorted but, as he should have known by this point, nothing in life ever goes completely according to the plan.

The sad thing was that everything started off so smoothly. After running the whole way home after school, Toby arrived at his house. He was there by a quarter-past four. Slamming the front door behind him, he sprinted through the living room and into the hallway. Then, all of a sudden, he stopped. He hadn't spoken to Amy in days and the prospect of seeing her made him feel anxious. He felt a chill crawl up his spine, tingling as it went and making his whole body turn cold. He stared up at the attic hatch and spoke.

'Amy?' he whispered, the words barely coming out.

There was nothing but silence.

Toby took a deep breath. She wouldn't be able to hear a whisper; he had to be louder. He tried pushing the words out faster so that they might gain a little more volume but, when he finally spoke again, they came out in a sort of inhuman squawk.

'Amy!'

'Toby?'

She'd heard him! Whether she was real or not, she'd heard him! The plan was going well so far.

'I have a plan.' he told her, shouting up through the ceiling.

'What plan?' she yelled back.

'There's a man,' he told her. 'A teacher, at my school.'

'Uh-Huh.'

'He can see ghosts.'

There was a moment of silence before Amy spoke again.

'Open the hatch,' she said loudly.

Toby did as he was told.

As he pulled on the fabric cord, his hand shaking with adrenaline, he began to feel uncertain, even afraid. Was the plan going to work? He wasn't sure now. What if Mr Thornhill couldn't see her? What if Toby was insane?

The hatch opened and there, standing by the top of the ladder, her pale white face staring down at him, was Amy. She looked as real as she always did, except now, as she made her way slowly down the rungs of the cold metal ladder, she seemed to emit a bright warm glow. She was like an angel

191

coming down from heaven.

'What's the plan?' she asked him.

There was no need for small talk.

'He's coming at five,' Toby told her, his mind focused and ready. 'He doesn't know about you, so we can't tell him that you're a ghost. We're going to tell him that you're my cousin from Botchling, the next village…'

'I know where Botchling is,' Amy replied impatiently. 'What if he tries to shake my hand? He won't be able to touch me. Did you think of that?'

Toby paused. No, he hadn't thought of that.

'I don't know,' he replied. 'We'll make something up. That's not important right now. What we've got to do now is wait for him. We'll figure the rest out when he's here.'

'What about my finger-nails?' Amy continued. 'Or my bruises? Or the three-inch stab wound in my stomach? Did you think this through at all, Toby? Why didn't you tell me this sooner? We could have figured something out!'

'I don't know,' said Toby. 'I was nervous. I…'

All of a sudden, the room went quiet. It took Amy a while to figure out why Toby had stopped talking but, after a moment or so, she realised what she'd done.

'Stab wound?' he asked.

Toby's voice wasn't angry. The only thing he felt was sadness. He was sad that such a thing had happened to Amy and he was sad that she'd hidden it from him.

'It's not important right now,' she told him. 'I'll hide in your bedroom. Then, when he's here, I'll poke my head into the living room and say hello. If he can see me, I'll go back into the room. If not, then we'll see what happens.'

Toby thought about it. She was right; he hadn't thought this through. He'd been so caught up in creating the plan that he'd forgotten one crucial fact. Amy was dead and she looked like someone who was dead. The plan was crumbling, turning to dust in front of his very eyes, but this was his only shot and he had to take it.

'Deal?' Amy asked him, her voice nervous yet firm.

'Deal,' he replied.

For a while they waited, just sitting in the living room, Toby on the sofa and Amy on the floor. They sat in silence like soldiers waiting for battle, their full attention devoted to the door in front of them. They stared at it, neither one of them daring to look away. They were waiting, waiting for the knock to come.

Toby pulled out his phone and checked the time. It was ten minutes past five.

He began to sweat anxiously. Mr Thornhill was late. Perhaps the old man was stuck in traffic, or maybe there was something else keeping him. Maybe he wasn't coming. Maybe he'd decided not to tutor Toby. Maybe he was filing a formal complaint with Mr Hinkley about some nosey boy who'd been spying on him. Maybe Toby was going to be expelled.

No, Mr Thornhill wouldn't do that. Toby had seen the look in his eyes. The old man was terrified of Mr Hinkley, but even more terrified of people finding out his secret. Toby knew that Mr Thornhill wouldn't let him down, he just knew it.

Then it came, the sound of tyres on tarmac. Just outside the house, a car was pulling into the cul-de-sac. It sounded like an old car and from the god-awful crunching noise that it made as it moved, Toby could tell that it was falling apart.

'An old car for an old man,' he thought.

The car stopped and, as Toby and Amy held their breaths, one of its doors opened with a rusty creak.

Someone was coming. Their footsteps were light on the gravel driveway, but still very audible. The sound echoed throughout the living room, each step louder than the last. Then it came, the knock at the door.

Toby and Amy looked at each other.

'You do it.'

'How can I? I'm dead!'

'Right, sorry.'

As Toby rose from his seat, he watched Amy slink away into the hallway, her body floating through the closed door. He was alone now, alone for a few last seconds before the plan finally went into action. Toby sighed heavily and the knock came again. It was louder this time. With a few tentative steps, Toby reached the door. Placing a shaking hand on the door-knob, he took a deep breath and twisted.

The door flew open and a blast of cold air hit Toby's face. It wasn't windy outside, but the freezing temperatures had taken on a force of their own that almost knocked Toby backward. Forcing his eyes open, he looked out onto the doorstep and saw Mr Thornhill standing in front of him, bundled up in a thick moth-eaten coat.

'Hello, sir,' Toby smiled, stepping aside to let him through. 'Please, come in.'

Mr Thornhill smiled back, but with a smile much less sincere. He clearly didn't want to be doing this at all, let alone when it meant travelling in such awful conditions. As the old man made his way into the house, Toby noticed that the cold had been particularly harsh on Mr Thornhill. His wrinkled face was red raw and his nose was almost scarlet. Not only that but, to cap it all off, the old teacher's hands had seized up into rough gnarled claws. Toby began to feel a little bad for dragging him out in such cold weather but, then again, there was work to be done.

'Well, Toby,' said Mr Thornhill, as he surveyed the living room with mild curiosity. 'Where should I sit?'

'Just on the sofa,' Toby replied. 'There's isn't really anywhere else.'

'As you wish,' said the old man, his voice sending a shiver up Toby's spine. Mr Thornhill lowered his frail body into the sofa and slumped back against the cushions. He looked up at Toby and motioned for him to sit.

Then, just as Toby was about to take his place next to the old man, he stopped and looked to the hallway door. It was shut. How could Amy poke her head into the living room if the door was shut? Well, actually, Toby knew exactly how she could do it. However, the sight of a teenage girl poking her head through solid wood might have given Mr Thornhill a heart-attack.

'One second,' he said as he hurried over to the door. He opened it wide and turned back to his guest who looked very confused at Toby's actions.

'It'll get some air through,' he told the old man. 'The house needs it.'

Mr Thornhill nodded. Toby breathed a sigh of relief and sat down next to him. The plan was still going well.

'So,' Mr Thornhill asked, 'what do you want to get out of these sessions?'

'Well,' Toby lied, 'I guess it's the textual analysis part that I don't understand. It just doesn't make sense to me.'

Mr Thornhill gave a bored nod, his eyes fixed on Toby as he thought.

'Well,' the old man said with a smile, 'that sounds like something we can fix.'

And so they began. Mr Thornhill, in his relaxed manner, carefully explained all the key points of textual analysis. With his forefinger and thumb, he presented how much of a paragraph should be devoted to textual analysis and Toby nodded along politely. He'd had this explained to him before and he was very much aware of how to analyse texts, due to Mr Morrison's overly-excessive focus on it during lessons. However, he kept up the charade for as long as he could, smiling at Mr Thornhill and asking as many questions as possible in order to keep the conversation flowing.

'Where's Amy?' he thought to himself as Mr Thornhill explained the proper way to structure a compound sentence. There was no reason for her to be late. Her only job was to stick her head around the side of the door. Why was she taking so long?

Toby stared out of the corner of his eye. He could see the open door, but there was nothing else. Nothing, not a single movement. He could excuse himself, that might help. He could go and find Amy and figure out what was going on.

He looked again and still there was nothing. Where was she? Amy didn't have to be anywhere else! Didn't she want to help him?

Still there was nothing.

Mr Thornhill was coming to the end of his sentence. There wasn't much more to explain and Toby was running out of questions to ask him.

Nothing.

It was over. Mr Thornhill was finishing up. He was

talking to Toby but Toby didn't know what he was saying. The whole room had gone silent. There was nothing, nothing at all. Mr Thornhill looked worried. He was mouthing something but Toby couldn't tell what. Mr Thornhill knew that something was wrong. The plan had failed.

'Hello.'

The voice was quiet and soft. Toby turned and saw her. It was Amy. Her head was poking around the side of the door. Her pale face shone and her eyes seemed to light up the whole room, twinkling brightly in their sockets. She'd come. Finally, the plan was back on track.

'Sorry, I didn't realise that we had company,' she said, making sure that her body was well and truly covered by the door. 'You must be Toby's tutor.'

Toby turned to face Mr Thornhill. The old man was staring at Amy, his mouth hanging open and his eyes wide like dinner plates.

'Pleased to meet you,' Amy continued, smiling at Mr Thornhill. 'I'm Amy, Toby's cousin.'

For a moment, Toby had thought they'd done it. For one beautiful second, the nervous air that had filled the room vanished and for the first time since seeing Amy that Friday, Toby felt completely and utterly sane. However, if Toby's life had told him anything, it was that good things never last. With a loud, wheezy breath, Mr Thornhill rose from the sofa. The old man raised a shaking hand to his face and placed it carefully over his mouth in shock. Then, as he moved the hand down to his chest, a quiet whisper left his lips.

'I know you,' he said, staring directly at Amy.

14 THE MURDER OF AMELIA MOORE

The world had become very dark since they'd started talking. Toby could tell from the lack of light coming through the closed curtains that clouds had rolled in. The change could have been attributed to the temperamental nature of English weather. However, it could also have been due to the time of year. Winter tends to be a darker season. Sunlight is often hard to find and the temperature outside frequently plummets without warning. Whatever the reason, it had set the stage better than anything else could have in preparation for what Toby was about to learn.

It was a long while before anything else was said. After Mr Thornhill's shocking revelation, it was hard for any of them to figure out how to respond. For a while they were still, motionless in the half light. Then the old man spoke again, his voice quiet and broken.

'Did you know about this?'

Toby knew that the old man was talking to him. Mr Thornhill's head hadn't even twitched in Toby's direction, but he could still tell. There were so many emotions in that one sentence, all of them present in Mr Thornhill's voice. Fear, anxiety, anger: they were all there. They dripped from the words he spoke.

'Yes,' Toby told him. 'I did.'

'Ah.'

Silence fell once again. As the room remained still, the silence intensified. Toby could hear his heart beating heavily inside his chest. He should have felt bad for deceiving Mr Thornhill, but he didn't. He didn't have time to feel sorry for himself.

'I know you,' said Mr Thornhill.

He wasn't speaking to Toby anymore. As the old man stared at Amy, Toby followed his gaze and looked at her. He noticed that the shine in her eyes had faded away. They were now no more than dull spheres of cold iron.

'How do I know you?' the old man questioned.

'I don't know,' Amy told him, the smile that she'd worn on her face now gone.

'What was your name?' he asked.

'Amy,' she replied, but the old man wasn't happy with that answer.

'Your full name.'

Amy paused for a moment. No one had expected this to happen, least of all her, but Toby knew that things had to be settled today.

'Amelia Moore,' she told him, her voice barely a whisper.

All of a sudden, something clicked inside Mr Thornhill's mind.

'Amelia Moore,' he said. 'You were that girl.'

'Was I?' Amy replied, her voice drenched in dry sarcasm. 'I didn't have a clue.'

Mr Thornhill didn't even smile. He clearly didn't think that the situation was amusing.

'You're the girl who died,' he told her.

'How does he know that?' Toby asked, not understanding in the slightest.

'It was on the news,' said Mr Thornhill, 'a long time ago. She was the girl that was murdered.'

'Murdered?'

'Yes, Toby. Murdered.'

Mr Thornhill ran a hand through his beard and sighed heavily.

'I remember when it happened,' he said solemnly. 'It was years ago but I never forget a face, especially in circumstances like those.'

Both of them looked at Amy. Whilst Toby and Mr Thornhill had been discussing the murder of Amelia Moore, she herself had kept silent. She was quiet as a church mouse and was looking down at the floor as if trying to avoid attention. As they stared at her, waiting for an explanation, she raised her head and met their gaze. That was when Toby saw them again, her eyes. They weren't dull anymore. Instead, they looked like little frozen puddles that twinkled like stars.

'Okay,' she began, rubbing her hands together. 'You win. I'll tell you.'

Toby was surprised. He'd expected a bigger reaction from her. Amy clearly wasn't comfortable, not at all, but after how she'd acted on Friday he'd almost expected her to break down on the spot. Then again, Amy was strong; he knew that somehow. She wasn't hidden behind the door anymore. Her whole body was inside the living room and, with a quiet gasp, Mr Thornhill noticed the wound in her stomach.

'I was seventeen when I died,' she began, no longer able to meet their gaze. 'Have you ever heard of The Lawton Bonfire?'

Toby shook his head. Lawton did tend to have a lot of carnivals and fetes but The Lawton Bonfire wasn't something he'd ever heard of. They did have a firework night, but there were never any bonfires.

'I remember,' said Mr Thornhill.

As Toby looked at the old man, he noticed that his face was contorted into a pained expression, as if he'd stepped on something sharp.

'How old are you, Toby?' the old man asked him.

'I'm fifteen,' he replied.

'Well,' Mr Thornhill explained. 'Fifteen years ago was when the last Lawton Bonfire was held. Nobody talks about it anymore. Not many people remember it. Most people left soon after it happened and the rest of us, we got old.'

Mr Thornhill fell backwards into the sofa, his eyes gazing blankly into space.

'They used to do it after the fireworks,' Amy said, continuing the old man's story. 'It was always on November the fifth. I was there that last year. That was when it happened. Everyone in Lawton went to the bonfire: kids, grown-ups, everyone. The bonfire was for everybody and everybody went, so I was going too.'

Amy took a deep breath.

'It was a formal event, the bonfire, which was strange. You'd spend all this money on a nice shirt or a pretty dress and it would always come back smelling of wood smoke.'

She stopped again, this time to catch her breath.

'Mum and Dad were going to meet me there. I was taking a long time to get ready, so they told me to follow on later. We lived off the high-street, down by the school. The bonfire was the other side of the village.'

'They used to do it in the big field at the bottom,' Mr Thornhill interrupted. 'The last one before the road out.'

'Yes, they did,' Amy continued. 'The fireworks were almost over, but nobody really cared about them. All anyone cared about was the bonfire. It was dark by the time I was ready. Mum and Dad wouldn't have let me go on my own if they'd known how dark it was going to be, but I still went anyway.'

'That's when they got me,' she said, the pain in her voice all too real. 'I didn't know who they were at first, but I know now. I know one of them, the one that got away. Brian Shepard, he was the one who killed me. He was scrawny, only a little bit bigger than me, but he was strong. I don't know who the other guy was.'

A memory appeared in Toby's mind, a mental picture that he'd forgotten long ago. In his mind he could see himself, sitting on a sofa and staring at a television screen. There was a man on the TV, a skinny man, with a baggy jumper and loose trousers that were barely keeping themselves up. His head was shaved and his face looked thin and cold.

'They came up to me,' Amy whispered. 'One of them held a tea-towel to my face. It was soaked in something, something that smelled. After that, I woke up in the attic.'

'They brought you here?' asked Mr Thornhill.

Amy nodded.

'They chained me to that wooden beam. They used a long, rough chain and it cut into me as I tried to escape.'

Toby wondered why Amy wasn't crying. What she was describing was one of the most awful things he'd ever heard in his life. So why wasn't she upset? For a brief moment, she paused once again, clutching her chest as if the words were weighing heavy on her heart.

'They weren't making any sense,' she said. 'They were talking about sacrifice. They had to perform a sacrifice in order to make the voices stop, Brian told me that. He was the furthest gone out of the two of them. Brian was the one who did it. He picked up the knife, the one that you found, Toby, and stabbed me once in the stomach. It didn't hurt at first but, when I finally realised what he'd done, I screamed. I screamed for so long that I though I was going to pass out, but it didn't matter. Everybody was at the bonfire, so there was no one to help me. They left me there for a long time. Then, after a while, Brian did something. He stared right into my eyes and smiled. I haven't forgotten his face, not even after all these years. I don't think I'll ever really forget it. His face was the last thing I saw before I died.'

Amy stopped talking. She hadn't anything else to say. Instead of speaking, she simply stared at the two them, waiting for them to respond so that she wouldn't have to say anything else. Neither Toby or Mr Thornhill said anything. There was nothing they could say really, and there was a long silence in which time seemed to stand still. Then, after what seemed like forever, Amy realised that she had to speak again.

'Any questions?' she asked.

'How did you figure it out?'

It was Mr Thornhill who spoke.

'How did I figure what out?' Amy replied.

'That you'd died,' the old man asked, his voice blunt.

Amy stared at him, surprised.

'I watched them drag my body away,' she told him. 'I woke up, still tied to the beam, and saw them crouching in the middle of the attic. They wrapped my body up and carried it down the ladder. I didn't see them again after that.'

'Ah,' Mr Thornhill replied, no emotion in his voice.

'Oh for God's sake!'

It was Toby's turn to speak. He was angry, angry that both of them were behaving so calmly. It wasn't normal for people to be murdered but they didn't seem to realise that. Neither of them were acting like they cared. Mr Thornhill turned and looked at Toby, his eyebrow raised.

'I can't believe you!' Toby yelled, much louder than he'd intended. 'She's just told you that she was murdered. She's told you all these things and you want to know more? Don't either of you think that this is awful?'

Mr Thornhill continued to stare at him. After a few seconds, the old man pursed his lips together. Then, he gave one almighty sigh and spoke in a plain, unflinching voice.

'My wife didn't know that she was dead when it happened. She didn't understand what was going on. I first saw her when they came to take away the body. She was standing in the doorway, staring blankly at all the people around her. They raised her tiny corpse onto a stretcher. They pulled a sheet over her face, so that nobody had to see it. She couldn't tell who was under the sheet. I didn't know that I was looking at a ghost. I stared at her, not believing what I was seeing. She was alive in one part of the room and dead in the other. My wife came up to me, glanced at the body on the stretcher and asked me a question. Do you know what she asked me?'

Toby didn't answer, but that didn't bother Mr Thornhill. The old man leant in close to Toby, so that their faces were almost touching, and whispered.

'She asked me, who died?'

That was when Toby understood. Amy and Mr Thornhill didn't look upset to him because they'd been through all of this already. This world, the world of ghosts, murders and people living after they'd died was all new to Toby, but it wasn't to them. They'd lived in this world for a long time and they knew that there was no use crying about it.

'Sorry,' he mumbled, feeling very guilty, but Mr Thornhill didn't mind. He gave Toby a smile and pat him on the shoulder comfortingly.

'I'm assuming that this is why you asked me to come over,' the old man said to him, his voice warm and reassuring. Toby nodded and smiled back at his teacher.

'Well,' Mr Thornhill continued, rising from his place on the sofa. 'In that case, I'd best be off.'

'Thank you,' Toby said to him, helping the old man to his feet. 'Thank you so much.'

'Don't worry about it,' the old man replied. 'You know that she's real now.'

'Thank you so much,' Amy said to him, smiling as she spoke. 'You've no idea how much you've helped.'

'I think I have some idea,' Mr Thornhill said back. 'I know all too well what its like to feel alone, and I know even better how it feels to question your sanity.'

As the three of them stood there, staring at each other with smiles stuck stupidly on their faces, Toby opened his mouth and breathed a heavy sigh of relief. Despite everything, the plan had worked.

CRUNCH.

A car pulled up outside. Toby's eyes widened with fear. Someone had come home.

He held his breath and listened as a set of high-heeled shoes tapped across the ground, hurrying ever closer towards the front door.

Karen, she was home early.

'Toby?' her voice called through the closed door. 'Are you home?'

'Yes,' he replied.

'Who's car is that on the drive?'

None of them spoke. All they did was stare at each other in confusion as Toby tried his best to figure out how to respond.

'Tutor,' he yelled, deciding that it was best to tell the truth.

A key turned inside the lock. As the front door creaked open, Toby saw Karen, dressed in her work clothes and staring at him with a puzzled expression on her face.

'You're home early,' he said, his gaze firmly fixed on his sister-in-law. 'I thought that you said you'd be working late.'

'We finished early,' she told him. 'Daniel and I are going to get dinner but he's left his wallet here. What's going on?'

It was at that moment that Mr Thornhill came to Toby's rescue.

'Sorry, Miss,' he said. 'I thought that Toby had told you. I'm Mr Thornhill. I'm a substitute teacher at Toby's school and I'm also part of its tutoring scheme. Toby told me that he was having some trouble with his English work and he asked if I could help him out. He should have given you a form to sign but I'm assuming that he didn't. Why didn't you hand over the form, Toby?'

'I forgot,' Toby lied, looking down at the floor. 'Do you have another one?'

'I do at home, but you'll have to make sure this one gets signed. Anyway, it doesn't appear that you need much help with English, so I don't think that we'll need another session.'

'Maybe you're right, sir,' Toby said to the old man.

'Perhaps I am,' he responded.

For a moment, Karen just stared at them. However, soon after Mr Thornhill had finished speaking, a car horn sounded outside and a voice followed Karen through the open door.

'Come on!' Daniel shouted. 'We have to make sure that we get a table.'

'Coming!' Karen yelled back at him. She looked at Mr Thornhill and smiled politely.

'If you could,' she asked him, 'would you be able to recommend somebody else?'

Toby was confused. He'd not expected that to come out of Karen's mouth. He looked to Mr Thornhill, who was nodding in agreement.

'Yes,' he told her, his voice warm and friendly. 'Of course I can. That shouldn't be any trouble.'

'Its just that English isn't really an issue,' she

continued. 'He does well in it. The only thing that he needs help with is his Maths.'

All of a sudden, Mr Thornhill's eyes lit up excitedly.

'Well,' he said, 'I'm not just an English teacher. I also fill in when the Maths teachers become ill. I'm actually quite adept and I know the syllabus very well. In fact, I'm on the list as a potential Maths tutor.'

Karen stared at the old man uncertainly, her head tilted to the side so that a strand of black hair fell in front of her face. Something was going through her mind that she wasn't going to say out loud, but Mr Thornhill seemed to understand.

'The school puts us all through intensive examinations,' he told her. 'Just to make sure that no bad eggs get through. All records are available at the school if you'd like to check. Your child's safety is their main priority. They usually charge a fee but, given Toby's excellent performance in English, I would be more than happy to waive it.'

'Fantastic!' Karen squealed, obviously convinced. 'If you know the syllabus then I think that it's a perfect idea. It saves us a lot of time.'

She smiled happily at Toby, who was quietly staring at his feet.

'Do you like that idea?' she asked.

For a moment, Toby was taken by surprise. He hadn't expected his opinion to be taken into account. For as long as he could remember, Daniel had always made decisions like this for him and he hadn't thought that this would be any different. However, as Karen looked at him with her kind eyes, he felt a warm fuzzy feeling rise up inside of him. He was glad that she'd asked him.

'Yes,' he told her. 'I like that idea.'

'Then it's settled,' she said gleefully. 'I'll leave you two to sort the logistics out.'

The car horn sounded again. Karen bit her lip awkwardly.

'I'd better be off,' she smiled. 'Time waits for no one! There's a meal in the fridge if you'd like it, Toby.'

'Okay,' he replied, a little grin creeping onto his face. 'Have a nice time.'

'It was nice to meet you,' Mr Thornhill told her as she rushed towards the door.

'Nice to meet you as well!' Karen said happily.

She blew Toby a kiss and and shut the front door with a bang.

Toby let out a sigh of relief. Not only did he now know for certain that he was sane, but he also now had a tutor who could see ghosts as well as him. With his mind now much clearer, he turned to Mr Thornhill. The old man looked at Amy and then back at Toby. There was a sly smile on his wrinkly face.

'Well,' he said happily, a chuckle escaping his lips. 'What do you think, Toby? Same time next week?'

15 REVELATIONS

Mr Thornhill was as good as his word. Every Tuesday after school, without fail, he would drive to Toby's home for tutoring sessions. However, these didn't always involve a lot of tutoring. Mostly, they would do what was needed. Mr Thornhill would teach his young student and Toby's mathematical skill improved as a result. Yet, on other occasions, they would simply sit and talk, with Amy joining in as they discussed all manner of subjects.

After finding out once and for all that he was sane, Toby decided it was time for Amy to come and live downstairs. There wasn't anywhere for her to sleep, as she couldn't lie down on any furniture, but anything was better than being up in the attic. She took to sleeping in the corner of Toby's room, in a spot where the built-in wardrobe met the wall next to it. Living with a ghost was incredibly different to how Toby had pictured it, but it wasn't as hard as he'd thought it would be. Most of the time, the two of them ignored each other, out of fear that Daniel or Karen might catch Toby talking to thin air. However, when it came time for bed, they would often have conversations that lasted long into the night. They would talk about Toby's life, they would talk about

Amy's life but, most of the time, they would simply talk about how the world had moved on since she'd died all those years ago.

As the air outside got colder and the freezing winds got stronger, Toby became much more aware that Christmas was coming. He loved Christmas, as most people do, and he was starting to focus more and more on what presents he could buy for those he loved. In the summer, he'd gotten a job delivering papers which had paid very well. As a result, he now had ample funds to spend on gifts. During a trip to the local shopping centre with Daniel and Karen, Toby was able to find a set of designer ties for his brother. They were silky and new and were very much in his style, so Toby had bought them without much deliberation. That was Daniel's present sorted. Toby also found a pair of expensive sunglasses that he knew Karen would like. They were thin and sleek and would go well with a number of her outfits. That was Karen's present sorted. As he carried the gifts through the shopping centre, Toby realised something. Even though the presents hadn't been cheap, his wallet still wasn't empty. There was still a decent amount of money at his disposal. So, as he wandered through the rows of jazzy outlet shops, he thought about who else he could get gifts for. It didn't take long for him to decide.

After the trip to the shopping centre, Karen and Daniel went out again. Karen had a doctor's appointment and Daniel was going with her. They wouldn't tell Toby exactly what the problem was, but he had his suspicions. A long time had passed since that fateful morning when Karen had told him of their plans to have a child.

They didn't get back until late that night. Toby had begun to worry around dinner time when they still hadn't returned, but a quick text from Daniel reassured him that everything was fine. Eventually, both Toby and Amy went to bed. Toby had school the next day, so they didn't stay up for very long. By ten o'clock, both of them were in his room, Amy on the floor and Toby in bed. They talked for a little bit but not about anything in particular. However, their idle conversation was cut short when they finally heard a car pulling into the driveway.

The front door shut with a heavy slam. They were back. Toby wanted to go and see them, but somehow he knew that they wouldn't be in the mood to talk. The door had slammed shut very loudly and it told him that something was wrong. As they lay in their beds, both Toby and Amy became silent. A conversation had started in the living room.

'It will be okay.'

'How?'

'It will, I promise.'

'You've always wanted this, ever since the beginning. You won't have changed your mind, not just because of what we've heard.'

'There are ways around it.'

'Would you do any of them?'

'Maybe. I mean yes, I would. This doesn't have to be the end of it.'

'I just can't believe it. I can't believe that it's my fault.'

'No, Karen. It isn't your fault.'

'Yes it is! There's nothing wrong with you!'

'There's nothing wrong with you, either!'

For a moment, there was silence. As Toby listened, he began to hear the sound of Karen crying. It was a painful sound and it sent a raw aching sensation into the pit of his stomach. He wanted to look at Amy, to see her face and have her tell him that everything was okay. She was good at that, reassuring Toby. He wanted to look at her, but he didn't dare move.

'It will be okay,' Daniel told his crying wife. 'I'll fix this, I promise.'

'You can't,' Karen replied. 'You can't fix everything, Daniel. There are some things in life that can't be fixed.'

'But, we can try.'

Toby stared up at the ceiling. Karen's voice was fainter now, so faint that he had to focus all of his energy on listening to her. After a while, she spoke again for the final time. Her voice was almost a whisper and the words trembled as she forced them out of her mouth.

'I love you, Daniel,' she told her husband.

'I love you too,' he replied.

'So if A^2 equals 36 and B^2 equals 81, what is C^2?'

Toby wasn't listening to Mr Thornhill. He hadn't had a very good week. Karen and Daniel were pretty upset about what the doctor had told them, so they weren't speaking much. When they did talk, it was usually Daniel who spoke. Karen was often much too distant to reply and any words that she did speak weren't any longer than a couple of syllables. Toby thought about how happy she'd been before it all and how sad she was now. It made him feel awful.

'Are you listening?' the old man asked him impatiently.

'Sorry, sir.'

Mr Thornhill got up from the sofa and placed the exercise book that they'd been working from to one side.

'If you aren't going to pay attention,' he said to Toby, 'then I won't waste my time teaching you. Are you going to listen or not?'

'Yes, sir.'

'Thank you,' the old man sighed, retaking his seat. 'Now, what would C^2 be?'

'One hundred and seventeen, sir.'

'Very good, and how would you find C?'

'Find the square root.'

'The square root of what?'

'One hundred and seventeen.'

'Well done Toby!' the old man told him happily. 'Quite the improvement.'

Toby didn't reply; he wasn't in the mood to talk. Not many other teachers would have been bothered by this, but Mr Thornhill could see that there was something wrong. He placed a hand on Toby's shoulder and smiled.

'Where's Amy?' he asked.

'In my room,' Toby replied. 'She's asleep. Doesn't want to come out today.'

'How come?'

'I think she feels bad for me,' Toby said.

Mr Thornhill looked concerned.

'Is something wrong, Toby?'

Toby stared at the old man.

'Just family problems,' he told him. 'Things will get better.'

The room went quiet. As Toby looked at Mr Thornhill, he could almost see the old man's brain working inside his skull. Mr Thornhill wanted to help, but it had clearly been a long time since he'd reassured anyone about anything. At least, anything that wasn't ghost related.

'It will be okay,' the old man finally said to him. 'Things tend to have a way of working themselves out.'

Toby nodded and smiled back at him. It wasn't Shakespeare, but it was something. Toby appreciated it a lot.

'Well,' the old man said, patting Toby's shoulder, 'I'd best be going.'

As Mr Thornhill rose from his seat, Toby decided to get up as well. It would be rude not to show the old man out after all the hard work he'd put into helping him. The two of them looked at each other and Mr Thornhill held out an open hand. However, Toby didn't take it. Instead, he asked a question that had been playing on his mind for a while.

'Can you touch a ghost?' he asked the old man.

Mr Thornhill looked puzzled.

'Sometimes,' he told Toby. 'Why do you ask?'

'I remember something,' Toby replied, his voice unsteady, 'about when I was younger.'

The old man looked at him, both intrigued and uncertain as to what Toby was about to tell him. He leaned in closer and wait for Toby to speak. Toby took a deep breath. He'd told Mr Thornhill that he'd always been able to see Amy, ever since they'd moved into the house. Not only that, but he'd also told him about the brief amount of time he and Amy had spent together when he was five years old. However,

215

most importantly, he'd also told the old man about why she'd gone away for so long. Mr Thornhill knew the whole story and had been sympathetic. He'd understood completely why Amy had done what she did and he knew that she'd probably acted in Toby's best interests. However, there was one thing that Toby hadn't told him.

'One time,' Toby began, looking down at the floor, 'I got upset, really upset. I think that Amy said I was going purple. She reached out her arms and she shook me by my shoulders to calm me down. I didn't think that she could do that. Why did that happen? Why was she able to touch me?'

Toby looked up at Mr Thornhill. The old man was nodding his head. He seemed to understand.

'That can happen sometimes,' he said to him reassuringly. 'Didn't you tell me something about a television?'

'Yes!' Toby exclaimed. 'That was why she went away, because she broke the TV! I didn't actually see it happen, but she told me about it!'

'When did she tell you that?'

'The day that she came back down from the attic,' Toby replied.

Mr Thornhill put his hand back on Toby's shoulder.

'There's no exact science to this,' the old man whispered. 'It's not something reliable. It hardly ever works, even in the best circumstances. Even so, sometimes, when emotions flare, the living and the dead can interact. It doesn't always have to involve people either. Sometimes, ghosts can touch objects, things in the world that they normally wouldn't be able to. A lot of the time there will be things that a ghost can always touch. From what you've told me, there are a few things that Amy can touch whenever she wants: the ladder to the attic, the knife, but that's usually it. However, occasionally, when you least expect it, things can be different.'

All of a sudden, the old man began to cry. His tears were slow-moving and silent, but the sadness was still there.

'What's wrong?' Toby asked him, unsure as to what had set him off.

Mr Thornhill wiped away the tears with the sleeve of his jumper.

'It's nothing,' he told him, but Toby wasn't convinced.

'No,' he said to the old man. 'Go on. Tell me.'

Mr Thornhill's eyes were red, flecked with little bloodshot lines that looked like rivers. Even so, despite all the pain he was going through, Mr Thornhill found the strength to talk. He spoke to Toby in a voice rigid and unmoving.

'What you said,' he whispered. 'It reminded me of her.'

'Who?' Toby asked.

'My wife.'

The silence that followed was deafening. Toby searched his brain for a response but couldn't find one. There was just no way for him to respond to such an admission.

'It was the same with us,' Mr Thornhill continued. 'Have you ever lost someone close to you?'

'Yes.' Toby replied.

It had happened long ago and their faces were beginning to blur in his mind, but he could still remember them. It had been over a decade since his parents had died and yet he still thought about them. He thought about his Mum. He remembered her smiling face and short brown hair. He thought about his Dad too, looking at him with eyes as blue as his. He remembered both of them and he missed them every day.

'Try to imagine what it was like,' Mr Thornhill told him. 'Could you imagine seeing that person every day, even after they'd died. You could watch them and they could watch you. You could talk to each other, as if nothing had ever happened. But then you'd realise what you couldn't do. My wife would get so sad and, no matter how hard I tried, I could never help. I couldn't hold her.'

Toby placed a hand on Mr Thornhill's shoulder.

'It's okay,' he smiled, rubbing the old man's jumper comfortingly. 'You did all you that could.'

Toby held the old man as he cried.

'Her name was Jane,' he told Toby in a heartbroken voice, 'and I loved her.'

All of a sudden, something clicked inside Toby's mind. He pulled himself away and stared at Mr Thornhill, who looked incredibly confused.

'All this time,' he said to the old man, 'you've been saying that you could see your wife, but you didn't say that you still could.'

'No,' Mr Thornhill replied. 'I can't see her anymore.'

'Why?' Toby asked.

Mr Thornhill took a deep breath. After a moment or so, he was able to stop the crying. When he began to talk again, a little tremble was clearly audible in his voice, one that seemed to echo in the living room.

'She went away,' he said.

Toby didn't understand.

'What do you mean?' he asked the old man.

'Ghosts can go away, Toby,' Mr Thornhill explained. 'They can pass on.'

'Pass on to where?'

'The other side,' the old man replied. 'To where the dead are supposed to go.'

Toby didn't know what to say. Mr Thornhill had dumped a huge piece of information on him and he couldn't quite figure out how to respond. Amy had been up in the attic for all this time. Fifteen years she'd been up there and, all the while, there had been a way out.

'I'm sorry,' Mr Thornhill told him sincerely. 'I honestly thought that you knew.'

'How could I have known?' Toby replied angrily, raising a nervous hand to his forehead. 'How could I have ever found this out?'

'Again, I'm sorry,' the old man apologised. 'I should have told you. It never came into my mind, though I don't know why.'

'How?'

Mr Thornhill stopped. He stared at Toby, his thin eyes uncertain and confused. The room went silent. The only sound came from outside. It was the violent howl of a winter gale. It bashed harshly against the windows as if trying to break in, getting louder with each heavy thud.

'What do you mean?' the old man whispered.

Toby brought his hand back down to his side, his movement forceful and deliberate.

'How do they pass on?'

For a brief moment, Mr Thornhill didn't say anything. For some reason, Toby got the impression that the old man wasn't really looking at him. Instead, it felt as though he was far away from the conversation in a place completely different to where they were at that moment. The crashing wind outside got louder, this time battering the front door with all the force of a hurricane. But, Toby wasn't listening to the wind. He stood silently on the spot, waiting patiently for Mr Thornhill to answer his question.

'I can only speak from experience,' the old man explained, rubbing his hands together nervously.

'Go on then,' Toby told him. 'I'm waiting.'

'Jane,' Mr Thornhill began, 'despised being a ghost. I've told you how I hated not being able to touch her and she hated it even more than me, but there was more than that. I think it was the whole concept, the idea of not being present in the world. It tore her up inside. After a while, we began to think about things. Why was she still there? Why weren't there any more ghosts? What was it that made her so special? I didn't want her to go, but I knew that she wasn't happy. She'd been tired of this world, even when she was alive. We thought about it a lot, but neither of us could figure it out, at least, not for a while.'

Mr Thornhill made a croaking sound, as if his throat were about to seize up.

'She came into our room one night,' he continued, 'and told me what she needed to. She woke me up with her voice, her soft voice, and explained everything. She knew what was keeping her tied to this world. Jane leaned in close to my ear and told me the whole story. She told me about a man, one that she'd been seeing for so many years. They used to meet in a hotel. Then she told me how it had all ended and that she hadn't seen him in so many years. She told me about how guilty she felt every second of every day, but that it didn't matter anymore because there was nothing that she could do to change what had happened. She'd told me what she had to and that was all she needed to pass on. I didn't have any time to be upset, not even angry like I should have been. She finished what she had to say and then vanished without a trace. There wasn't a flash or a bang or any noise at all. One moment she was there and the next she was gone. I never saw her again. Now she only lives in the pictures I have of her, as well as in my memory.'

Toby stood in stunned silence as Mr Thornhill finished his story. The whole situation had changed and he wasn't sure how to respond to it. Toby felt sorry for the old man. Not only had his professional life come under attack, but every part of his existence had been radically altered. All because his wife hadn't passed on.

'After that,' the old man continued, 'people found out that I'd been seeing her. I lost my job and was admitted to a hospital. I stayed there for a long time before coming back to Lawton.'

'I'm sorry,' Toby told Mr Thornhill, trying to make the old man feel at least a tiny bit better. Mr Thornhill nodded and smiled sadly.

'It's okay,' he said. 'I know that you are.'

That night, after everyone had gone to sleep, Toby told Amy about what Mr Thornhill had said. Needless to say, she was very surprised.

'What?' she yelled, much louder than she'd intended. 'Why didn't he tell us before?'

'I don't know,' Toby whispered, carefully keeping his voice under control so that he didn't wake up Daniel or Karen. 'I don't think he knew himself. Even so, there's not a lot we can do about that now.'

'Can we trust him?' Amy asked, propping herself up with her elbows.

Toby nodded.

'I think so,' he told her, staring up at the ceiling. 'He's been good to us so far. We shouldn't forget about all that he's done for us.'

Amy didn't reply to that. The wind outside that had been howling earlier in the day was now quiet. The night was calm and still.

'What do you think?'

'What do you mean?'

Toby got out of bed. He walked over to Amy and sat down next to her on the floor, his pyjamas rustling against his ankles as he moved.

'Do you want to do it?' he asked her.

'Yes,' she told him, not an ounce of doubt in her voice.

'Then we'll do it.'

Amy looked down at her hands. Her fingers were twitching.

'It's not because of you, Toby,' she said. 'It's not that I don't like being here. Its just…'

'I get it,' he told her, a half smile forming on his face. 'I think that, if I was in your shoes, I would want to go too.'

Toby picked himself up and went back to bed.

'Do you know what could be keeping you here?' he asked her, settling under the covers. Amy shook her head.

'No,' she told him sadly.

'That's okay,' he replied. 'We'll figure it out.'

16 PRESENTS

Despite thinking long and hard about what could be keeping Amy in the world of the living, Toby and his ghostly friend weren't able to get anywhere. However, they did have some ideas.

They thought of people that Amy might have wanted to meet, places she might have wanted to go. Even so, they knew that none of their ideas were right. There was one specific thing keeping Amy trapped in the world of the living and it was going to take them a long time to figure out what that was. As the days passed and the winds got colder, they both continued to think. They searched their minds for ideas but without success. Toby in particular thought very hard about the problem. In fact, he'd been thinking so hard about it that he didn't even realise until Wednesday that Friday was his last day of school before the Christmas break.

That final Friday started off as an unexpectedly warm one. The sun shone down on Toby as he made his way to school and its warm rays managed to raise his spirits considerably. The heat hadn't quite been able to melt the snow on the ground, but the air was certainly warmer than it had been. Toby exhaled a long contented breath and smiled. He wasn't going to worry about Amy today. However, despite his contentment, he began to feel a tight nervous knot twisting inside of his stomach. He began to feel anxious, not out of worry for Amy, but because today was the day that he was going to give Lily Roberts her present.

He could feel it by his side as he marched down the road. It was in a plastic bag that swung next to him like a pendulum. Toby had thought for a long time about what to get Lily. It couldn't have been something too expensive as he didn't know her that well. Getting her something expensive might have seemed creepy and he didn't want to scare her off. Toby felt his fingers begin to twitch nervously. Was this a bad idea? Maybe it was! Maybe Lily was going to laugh at him.

As it was the last day of term, the school would be shutting at lunchtime. This meant that Toby only had two lessons: Maths and English. He sighed as he thought of them. Maths would only be bearable. He'd been doing well in the subject since starting his tutoring sessions with Mr Thornhill and his abilities had definitely improved since the beginning of the year. However, having the Maths lesson first meant that he'd have to wait even longer before giving Lily her present. They didn't have that lesson together so he'd have to wait until English before seeing her.

Even so, apart from the prospect of giving Lily her present, Toby wasn't really looking forward to the English lesson either. Mr Morrison, who'd been suffering from an illness, hadn't been able to teach them for a while which meant Mr Thornhill had stepped in to teach more than a few of his lessons. Toby loved being taught by Mr Thornhill; the old man made English come alive in a way that Mr Morrison never could and his voice never failed to send chills up Toby's neck. Even so, Mr Morrison's illness hadn't lasted long. He was now in perfect health and back teaching the class. As a result, Toby only saw Mr Thornhill during their tutoring sessions, which meant that he was unlikely to see the old man again until after the new year. Even so, Toby had brought the present he'd bought Mr Thornhill along anyway, just in case.

Maths didn't drag as much as it usually did. Toby was beginning to find the subject almost enjoyable, now that he could understand what was going on. At the start of the year, he would have never dared to raise his hand but now he'd put it up at least five times a lesson. Even so, despite not being as bored with the subject as he had once been, Toby still felt himself smile when he saw on the classroom clock that the lesson would be ending in less than five minutes.

Toby's Maths teacher was a round woman. She had greasy black hair and a face like a bulldog. Her name was Mrs

Hunter. Mrs Hunter usually spoke in a bored, dismissive tone that made it sound as if she had better things to be doing with her time. However, as soon as she noticed the time on the clock, her demeanour changed. As she spoke, she no longer sounded bored. In fact, she sounded excited.

'Well class,' she began, her nasal voice ringing in Toby's ears as she spoke. 'As this is your last year at Lawton, I wanted to take this time to talk to you about sixth-form colleges. You should begin submitting applications for places this January. Therefore, the Christmas break would provide a prime opportunity to find out which of the local colleges are right for you.'

Toby's eyes widened. He'd forgotten that he had to start looking at colleges. All this time thinking about ghosts and the afterlife and he hadn't even stopped to realise that he'd be leaving school in a few months.

'I see from the looks on some of your faces that many of you had forgotten about this,' Mrs Hunter continued, staring directly at Toby. 'You need not worry. Most of you will get into at least one of the local sixth forms whatever your exam results. However, I did want to take this time to inform you about another opportunity that might excite some of you.'

Mrs Hunter reached a hand into her trouser pocket and pulled out a leaflet. It was a small leaflet and it was a little crumpled from the time spent inside the pocket. Even so, it seemed to radiate an excellence and importance that immediately took Toby's eye. With a smug smile, Mrs Hunter opened up the leaflet and began to read aloud from it.

'Pine Mount Sixth Form College' she proclaimed, her chapped lips cracking as her grin widened, 'is offering scholarships to students whose academic ability far outshines their economic situation. This privately run institution of learning, located in the north of England, prides itself on the success of its former students and knows that the standard of teaching it offers is some of the best in the country.'

Mrs Hunter paused and looked out at the class, no doubt waiting for some sort of ecstatic reaction to what she had just said. Her students stared back at her with blank faces. Hardly any of them cared about getting into a place like Pine Mount and they were showing it all too well. Then again, there was one student who did seem interested.

All of a sudden, the bell rang loudly and all the students hurried towards the classroom door. In the mad rush to get out, Toby was pushed to the back of the crowd. As he tried valiantly to force his way forward, he felt his eyes drawn back to the leaflet in Mrs Hunter's hand.

Pine Mount Sixth Form College - he would remember that name.

With the Maths lesson finally over, Toby spent his break-time mentally preparing for what he was about to do. After a few funny looks from some of the students, he decided to try and fit the gift into his backpack. After a lot of trying, he finally managed to cram it inside and threw the plastic bag into a nearby litter bin. After that, he sat on a bench outside. The world was much colder than it had been earlier. As he sat on the bench, he began to stare through a misty window and into one of the empty classrooms. There was a clock in the classroom and he spent the rest of his break watching it nervously as the minute-hand ticked onward.

When lesson time finally came, Toby felt himself beginning to sweat nervously. He couldn't believe that he was doing it. He was going to give Lily Roberts a present, even though the two of them had barely ever spoken. Why was he doing it? He was going to be laughed at, he knew it. She was going to laugh at him and then everyone else would laugh at him. No. There was no need to worry. It was all going to be fine. As he marched through the doors and into the classroom, he saw her standing by her desk. Lily Roberts.

She looked good. Very good. Toby couldn't quite

find the words to describe how incredible she looked. He noticed that she'd tied her hair up at the back. The hairstyle made her look beautiful. It showed off the sides of her face, which were normally hidden from view.

Toby gulped. He was determined. He was going to do it and he had to do it now. Toby marched across the classroom towards Lily, his eyes focused and a nervous smile fixed onto his face. He couldn't believe it! He was doing it! He was actually doing it! Then, all of a sudden, he found himself stood in front of her, his blue eyes staring into her brown ones.

'Hey.'

'Hey.'

'What's up?'

Toby took in a deep breath.

3.

2.

1.

He pulled the gift out of his backpack. It was a jar and it was filled with sweets. There were loads of different sweets inside: chewy sweets, crunchy sweets, soft sweets, hard sweets. They were all there and they created a sort of swirl shape that made it look like he'd caught a rainbow in a jar.

'Merry Christmas,' he told her.

'Aw, Toby!' Lily squealed, taking the present from him. 'This is so sweet! Thank you so much!'

'That's okay,' he said. 'I'm glad that you like them.'

Toby's nerves were starting to get the better of him. With a sheepish smile he turned away from Lily and went to go and sit down at his desk. However, before he could even take a single step, he felt a soft tap on his shoulder. He turned back to face her and saw that Lily was smiling.

'This is so cute, Toby,' she told him. 'I love it.'

'Good!' he replied, his voice shaky and nervous. Lily giggled sweetly.

'You know,' she began, staring awkwardly at her feet, 'I was wondering if you'd like to meet up sometime, just the two of us. Maybe after Christmas?'

Toby was certain that he was dreaming. Lily Roberts was asking him to meet up. Lily Roberts. He could barely breathe. The shock hit him hard and he stood for a moment in silence, unable to say a word.

'Say something!' he thought to himself.

'Of course,' he finally croaked. 'I'd like that.'

'Great,' she replied, smiling happily at him.

'Quiet down everyone, please!'

A new voice carried through the classroom. Toby knew the voice. It was a quiet, husky voice that was only just audible above the noise of the loud classroom. The voice made the hairs on the back of Toby's neck stand on end. Toby turned his head to the front and felt his smile widen when he saw the hunched form of Mr Thornhill standing by the whiteboard.

'Everyone take their seats,' he told the class.

The class did as they were told and Mr Thornhill thanked them for it. It was then that the old man noticed Toby, who was still standing in the middle of the room. They looked at each other and smiled. After that, Toby took his seat and Mr Thornhill began to teach.

The lesson which followed was one of the best that

Toby had ever experienced. Mr Thornhill's relaxed delivery made his explanations of the subject matter much more engaging than Toby had ever thought possible. The old man was able to make anything sound interesting. Finally, when it came time for the lesson to end, the majority of the class began to pack their things away. As they did this, Toby turned around and faced the desk behind him. Lily looked at him and smiled.

'Have a great Christmas, Toby,' she said to him.

Then, out of nowhere, something unexpected happened to Toby. Lily flung her backpack over her shoulders and made her way towards his chair. She stretched out her arms and pulled Toby into a soft hug. The hug was only a few seconds long, but Toby knew that he would always remember it. The smell of her perfume, the softness of her cheek and the touch of her silky hair against his face. He smiled contentedly. It was a perfect moment.

As she let go of him, Lily smiled once again at Toby. She then turned and followed the rest of the students out of the classroom.

'A friend of yours?' came Mr Thornhill's voice.

Toby almost didn't hear him. To him, the world had stopped as soon as Lily had hugged him and, as a result, he was still trying to catch up with everything that had happened since.

'What?' he replied.

Mr Thornhill laughed. He and Toby were the only two people left in the otherwise empty room.

'You two make a very cute couple,' the old man said as he walked slowly over to Toby. Toby watched Mr Thornhill's leg as he moved. It looked very stiff.

'Are you okay?' he asked.

Mr Thornhill nodded unconvincingly.

'Just the cold,' he replied. 'I'll be okay.'

Toby smiled slightly. Then, all of a sudden, he remembered it.

'Present!' he exclaimed, his eyes widening and his mouth falling wide open.

Mr Thornhill stared at him, confused.

'I got you a present,' Toby continued, reaching into his backpack. 'It's nothing much, but it's just something to say thank you for all your help. All your help with everything.'

Then, with a flourish, Toby pulled the present from his bag. There, in his hand, he held a thick woollen bobble-hat. It was completely black in colour, except for a thin white stripe that ran around the middle of it. Two twisted tassels hung down limply on either side of the hat and the bobble on the top was slightly frayed, but not too badly. As soon as Mr Thornhill caught sight of his present, his whole face began to beam with joy.

'I know that it's not much,' Toby continued, 'but I just thought that where it's been cold you might need something to keep you warm. If you don't like it, I can take it back. I kept the receipt.'

'It's wonderful,' the old man told him, smiling as he spoke. 'Thank you so very much, Toby. I wish that I'd bought you something.'

'Oh no, it's fine, sir,' Toby replied. He looked into Mr Thornhill's eyes. They were glowing with a happiness that Toby rarely saw in the old man.

'Merry Christmas,' he said to Mr Thornhill.

'Merry Christmas, Toby,' the old man replied.

All of a sudden, something wonderful happened. Toby looked out of the classroom window and saw that it was snowing outside. The snowflakes weren't small either. They weren't the kind that melted as soon as they landed. These snowflakes were thick and strong and almost indestructible. They fell heavily to the ground and lay densely on the tarmac. Toby looked at Mr Thornhill, who smiled and placed his present on his head.

'Follow me,' he said to Toby, motioning towards the door. 'I want to show you something.'

With that, Mr Thornhill left the classroom and marched out into the corridor. Once there, he stopped and waited for Toby to follow him, which he did.

The two of them walked together, pushing their way through the crowds of students. Toby could tell that Mr Thornhill was taking him somewhere that he'd never been before. The building that they were currently in was where Toby had the majority of his lessons, so he'd never really had any reason to visit the more remote parts of the school. As he strode across the worn linoleum floor, he realised that they had come to the end of a hallway. In front of them stood a rectangular green door. In places, its green paint had been scraped off, revealing patches of harsh metal underneath. Mr Thornhill reached out and opened the door. He stood beside it and held it open for Toby. Toby nodded at the old man and stepped through the door.

Once outside, the two of them continued to walk. They went on for a little while, neither of them speaking to each other. The world was silent except for the soft crunch of their footsteps on the snow underneath. They began to walk towards a wooded area, one that backed onto the school's neglected playing field. The wooded area clearly hadn't been used in a number of years. As the two of them entered inside of it, Toby saw trees towering above him that were old and rotten. Beneath his feet were thick roots that had become hidden underneath the snow. Overgrown bushes crept out over the dirty footpath that Mr Thornhill and he were trudging down. The thorny branches of unknown plants began to slice at Toby's ankles, never quite penetrating his skin, but tearing at his trousers nonetheless.

It was then that they came to a clearing. It was a strange sort of place. It looked as though it had been created for a reason. A reason that had been forgotten a long time ago. It was a circular clearing and it had two wooden benches positioned opposite each other in the centre of it. Toby wanted to sit down on them, as his legs ached from the cold, but there was a great deal of snow on top of them. Even so, it didn't look like the benches could have supported him anyway. They were rotten and unstable. Toby drew his eyes away from the benches and looked at Mr Thornhill. The old man, who was clearly in pain due to the cold, stared back at him with an emotionless face. He raised his hand and pointed at something between the two benches. Toby turned his head and looked.

Between the two benches, there was a plaque. It was covered with snow, which meant that Toby couldn't see what was written on it. The plaque was attached to a rusty metal pedestal, one that had suffered badly from neglect. Toby crept slowly towards it. He raised his hand and, in one smooth motion, brushed away the snow.

In Loving Memory of Amelia Moore

Gone but Not Forgotten

Forever in our Hearts and Minds

And Always with Us

Toby looked back at Mr Thornhill. The old man walked slowly towards him, his limp even more pronounced in the cold. Once he was by Toby's side, he put his arm around him. The two of them knew that nothing had to be said. To be truthful, they didn't know what they could say. As a result, they kept their mouths shut and stood together, feeling the cold sink into their bodies as they paid their respects to the memory of Amelia Moore.

The snow didn't let up at all that winter and neither did Toby's desire to figure out what was keeping Amy from passing over to the other side. As Christmas day drew closer, he thought as hard as he could about what could be keeping her, but still he came to nothing. Then, after many days of pensive thought, he realised that he would never know the answer unless Amy was able to figure it out first.

The house had been decorated tastefully that Christmas. Subtle silver tinsel had been draped over all of the furniture without exception. It had been Karen who'd wanted to put the Christmas decorations up. In fact, she was the one who'd suggested decorating the house in the first place. However, it was Daniel who'd decided what she could choose. The two of them had been very distant recently. They seemed to talk to each other less and less. Toby had almost became used to the silence that now filled their house. Despite their silence, the rest of their relationship didn't change. They didn't stop going out for fancy meals together, but neither of them seemed to enjoy them very much. They would put on their finest clothes and go out to posh places and eat expensive food, all the while barely talking to each other. For the two of them, going out had become a chore.

It was five minutes to midnight on Christmas Eve. Daniel and Karen were both asleep in their bedroom and the whole house was silent. That is to say, except for Toby's bedroom. As the two of them lay there in the dark, firing whispers at each other excitedly, Toby and Amy waited impatiently for midnight to come.

'Five minutes,' said Toby, checking his phone. Amy

nodded. Toby knew that she had nodded, even though he couldn't exactly see her from his bed.

'What do you reckon you've got?' she asked him, her voice a little louder than Toby's as she didn't have to worry about being heard. Toby shrugged.

'I don't know,' he told her. 'I didn't make a list this year.'

'Why not?'

'There wasn't anything that I wanted,' he replied. 'Karen said that they'd try and surprise me.'

'That's nice of them,' said Amy. Toby sighed.

'Yeah,' he said quietly.

They lay there in silence for a moment. The house was cold and Toby could feel himself shivering. After a while, Amy spoke again.

'I had a thought,' she told him, her voice barely a whisper.

Toby rolled over onto his side, so that he was almost facing her. Amy didn't look at him, she just stared up at the ceiling.

'What about?' he asked her, curiously.

Amy took a deep breath.

'About what could be keeping me here. You know? About what could be stopping me from moving on.'

Toby stared at his friend, his eyes wide and intrigued.

'What is it?' he asked her.

Amy turned her head. Toby could see her now. She

was looking at him, her hair falling gracefully in front of her face. Even though she was staring in his direction, Toby noticed that her eyes weren't really focused on him. It was as if she were remembering something, something that she'd forgotten about a long time ago.

'Have you ever heard of Yardley Bay?' she asked him.

Toby shook his head.

'No,' he replied. 'Never.'

Amy smiled slightly, but not in a happy way.

'It's a beach,' she told him, 'about an hour away from here. It's nice, really nice. I only went there once. Me and a few of my friends, we all went there. We spent the whole day there, lying in the sand and watching the water. It was a great day. The sun was high in the sky and it was so warm. It was like paradise.'

As she finished speaking, she rolled over onto her side, so that she was facing away from Toby.

'Go on,' he said to her, but Amy didn't reply.

'Please,' he asked again. 'Go on.'

As he waited for Amy to reply, he listened to the sound of her breathing. It was heavier, thicker than usual. Talking to him about this was hard for her, but if it meant that she could pass on, she had to tell him.

'I never wanted that day to end,' she finally said to him, 'and I think that, if I could go back there one last time, then I could be at peace.'

'Well, let's go there,' Toby replied. 'We have to try.'

Amy didn't reply. Instead, she just lay there in silence, staring blankly up at the ceiling. Toby was confused.

Amy had always seemed as though she'd wanted to move on. She hated being a ghost and she'd always wondered why it had happened to her. However, for some reason she was being very quiet and Toby didn't understand why.

'You do want to pass on, don't you?' he asked her, nervously. Amy didn't look at him. She just kept on staring up at the ceiling. After a minute or so, Toby gave up. He turned over on his other side and threw his head back down into his pillow. Then, after a long silence, he heard a faint whisper leave Amy's lips.

'Of course I want to move on,' she told him. 'To be honest, I've never wanted anything more. All those years I spent up in the attic, I wanted to move on. I don't want to be here anymore. All that I've wanted since the day that they killed me was to die, but that changed when I met you, Toby. You're the only friend I've got and I don't want to lose you.'

'So, what are you saying?' Toby asked her. Amy sighed.

'I guess that,' she began, 'I just wanted to let you know that, even though I want to move on, it makes me sad to think that I'll never see you again. I do want to move on, but I'll miss you.'

'I'll miss you too,' he whispered softly. 'You don't have to do it. You don't have to pass on. You could always stay here with me?'

'No,' Amy told him in a firm voice. 'I couldn't do that to you. Anyway, what would happen after you'd died? I need to move on, Toby. It's the right thing to do.'

'Are you sure?' he asked her, his voice barely audible.

'Yes,' said Amy, 'but it doesn't matter anyway.'

'What do you mean?' Toby asked her, rolling onto

his back.

'I can't leave this house, remember?' Amy told him. 'Not without getting sick.'

'How sick?' he responded.

Amy let out a quiet snort of laughter.

'Very sick,' she said. 'Don't you remember?'

Then, all of a sudden, Toby remembered. He was there again, in the front garden. He was only a little kid. He was watching Amy's skin turn green. Vomit and blood coated the doorstep.

He remembered now.

'Yes,' he told Amy solemnly. 'I do,'

Toby picked up his phone. The harsh white light blinded him. His eyes stung and he had to look away for a second. After a moment or so, once his eyes had adjusted, he stared back at the screen of his phone and looked at the time.

'Merry Christmas, Amy,' he whispered, his eyes becoming heavy and tired.

'Merry Christmas, Toby,' she replied.

When Toby awoke the next morning, he hurried out of his bedroom and into the living room. He gazed through the large window next to the front door and smiled. He was please to see that the snowy weather of the past few weeks hadn't vanished overnight. The world outside was covered in a thick wintery blanket. Snow had fallen over everything. He felt as though he was in a Christmas card. Toby felt overwhelmed with joy. It was the perfect start to a perfect day.

Daniel and Karen, who still weren't on the best of

terms, managed to push aside their negative feelings for the day. All three of them came together in a day that was one of the best Christmases of Toby's life. There was no tree, owing to the fact that Daniel didn't like pine needles shedding onto the carpet, so all the presents were all spread about in front of the television. They were covered in festive wrapping paper and tied elegantly with tight little bows. There weren't many presents as it was only the three of them this Christmas. Occasionally, they would spend Christmas with distant relatives on Karen's side of the family, but this time it was just them. The celebrations began with the opening of these presents. They sat down on the floor and handed out the gifts in an orderly, yet somehow still joyous manner.

'Fantastic!' Daniel exclaimed, as he opened his present from Toby. 'Thanks, Toby. I needed more ties.'

His overly excited reaction seemed a little forced to Toby but, even so, Daniel did seem genuinely happy to receive his gift. Karen was much the same, although her reaction was a little more subdued.

'Brilliant!' she said, putting the sunglasses he'd bought her over her eyes. 'Very chic. I love them.'

'Good,' Toby replied happily. 'I'm glad.'

'Thank you, Toby,' she said, beaming as she spoke. She pulled Toby in close for a tight hug and Toby smiled as his face became buried in her shoulder.

Toby's presents were mostly unremarkable. He received a couple of pairs of socks, a notebook and a few other assorted items that weren't much to mention. Even so, they made him feel happy.

After that, it was time for Christmas dinner. It was a dinner that surprised Toby. Daniel, who was usually obsessed with making everything perfect, did something that Toby hadn't expected. After disappearing into the back room for a moment or so, he re-entered the living room. Daniel carried an old metal table under one arm and three fold-up chairs under the other.

'They're a little informal,' he told them, 'but who cares?'

Then they sat together, all three of them, eating a roast dinner made of chicken and potatoes and gravy and carrots and peas and pigs-in-blankets. Karen had spent the whole of the day before making sure that everything would be ready for Christmas. As they all tucked into their delicious feast, Toby felt himself smiling. He loved Daniel and Karen.

As the day came to a close, Daniel and Karen fell asleep on the sofa. Whilst they slept, Toby snuck away to see Amy. The two of them sat on the floor of his bedroom. They both laughed sleepily as they talked. They were both very tired. Then, all of a sudden, Toby remembered something.

'I've got you a present,' he whispered to Amy, careful not to wake Daniel or Karen.

Amy looked surprised.

'It's under here,' Toby told her, reaching under his bed. After a brief search, he found it. He pulled the gift out from under his bed and held it out in front of him.

In his open palm was a toy Santa. It was a mechanical one that wore big black sunglasses. It had a straw hula dress tied around its waist and a bare chest above it. As Toby turned a key that poked out of the figure's back, he placed it onto the carpet. The two of them watched as it danced. After a while, it came to a sluggish halt. Then, without worrying about who would hear them, they burst out laughing. They laughed for a long, long time. They laughed until their sides hurt. They laughed until they couldn't laugh anymore. Finally, Amy calmed herself and smiled at Toby gratefully.

'Thank you, Toby,' she said to him, her voice both happy and sad at the same time.

'That's okay,' he told her. 'Merry Christmas.'

17 SAND AND PEBBLES

The days rolled into weeks and the weeks rolled into months. After a while, the members of the Burrows family began to revert back to their normal routines. Daniel and Karen went back to being distant with each other whilst Toby, who was very conscious of his upcoming exams, immersed himself in his schoolwork. After giving it a lot of thought over the winter break, he'd decided that he wanted to send off an application to Pine Mount, the college up north. Initially, he'd been sceptical, not sure as to whether or not he would cope with being so far away from his family. Eventually, his final decision came from one late night conversation that he'd had with Amy.

'Do you want to do it?' she had asked him.

'I don't know,' he'd replied. 'I can't make up my mind.'

'Is it a nice place?'

'Yeah it is,' Toby had told her. 'I've looked it up. It's an old manor house that they've renovated.'

'Fancy,' Amy had said, quietly.

'I don't know if I'll get in,' he'd said to her.

Amy had gotten up from her bed at that point. She'd crawled across the floor and sat down by the side of Toby's bed.

'I think that you should go,' Amy had told him.

'I might not cope,' Toby had replied. 'It's very far away and...'

'Toby,' Amy had interrupted, 'you need to do this. You can't throw away an opportunity like this. Take it from a dead girl, you'll regret it.'

Toby had nodded in agreement. He knew that Amy was right.

'Okay,' he'd said to her. 'I'll sort out the application when I go back to school.'

'Good,' she'd replied.

After that, the two of them went to sleep. Neither one of them said a word until the next morning.

The application to Pine Mount wasn't the only thing that Toby had to focus on. In fact, he'd even managed to sort out a date with Lily Roberts. It was strange to him, that he still called her by her full name, but he couldn't help it. The two of them were going to get the bus into town together and watch a film at the new cinema that had just opened up. Lily was going to choose the film, but Toby didn't mind. The two of them had been messaging back and forth constantly since school had ended back in December. However, despite her eagerness,

Lily was apparently quite busy at that point in time, so neither of them could be sure when the date was actually going to be. Either way, it didn't matter to Toby. There was something else that he needed to do in the meantime.

This other thing actually happened on a Saturday. Daniel and Karen weren't around during the day and had told Toby that they wouldn't be back until later on that evening. The two of them were going to the birthday party of Daniel's boss. As a result, Toby was to be left at home for the day, unless he had anything else planned. Fortunately, Toby did have something else planned.

He'd spoken to Mr Thornhill about this plan during one of their tutoring sessions. It had been an uncertain conversation to say the least.

'Can this work?'

'There's always a chance. What did you tell Daniel?'

'I told him that you were taking me on a field trip to the coast.'

'Didn't he find that suspicious?'

'No, he didn't.'

'I just hope that we can get there.'

'You said that it worked with your wife?'

'Once or twice. Not always.'

'Damn.'

'Don't swear, Toby.'

'Sorry, sir.'

'Do you still want to do this?'

'Yes.'

'Then we have to try.'

Toby opened the door to his bedroom. He saw Amy, sitting cross-legged on the floor.

'What's up?' she asked him, noticing the very serious look on his face.

'We're trying something,' he told her, 'and we need your help.'

'What are you talking about?' she asked him.

'We're going to Yardley Bay.'

Amy rolled her eyes.

'Yardley Bay?' she replied in an unconvinced voice.

Toby didn't even crack a smile. He nodded once in agreement.

'Oh, come on!' Amy exclaimed. 'Have you already forgotten?'

'Do you think that you could hold out?' he asked her, 'for a couple of hours or so? If we could get you there and back, could you hold out?'

'No!' she replied angrily. 'We can't walk to Yardley Bay! We wouldn't be able to do that even if I didn't get sick every time I left the house!'

'What about in a car?'

Amy looked at him, her eyes wide, as if she were concerned about Toby's mental state.

'I can't get in a car,' she told him, speaking in a simple, slow tone. 'I'd fall through. I always fall through things.'

Just as Amy finished informing Toby of why his plan wouldn't work, she noticed something.

Toby was hiding something behind his back. It was something tall that he could barely keep hidden behind his thin frame. It was thick too, and Toby was obviously finding it hard to keep it upright.

'What's that?' she asked him. 'What are you hiding behind your back?'

All of a sudden, Toby did something very strange. As he stared at Amy, he contorted his mouth into a sly smile and pulled out three planks of rotting wood from behind his back. The planks were splintered and wet and looked as if they might fall apart at any second. Amy recognised those planks of wood.

'Those are from the attic.' she whispered nervously.

Toby nodded.

'I got them out last night,' he said, 'whilst you were asleep. I didn't make much noise, at least I don't think that I did.'

'What are you doing?' Amy yelled at him as she got to her feet. 'Have you lost the plot?'

Toby shook his head defiantly.

'No,' he replied. 'Mr Thornhill told me something, about a mattress.'

'What mattress?'

'The mattress that his wife died on. He told me that he'd cut it up and fit it into his car. Sometimes, she used to be able to lie down on it, so that they could drive to places. That way she didn't fall through the car.'

'How does that work?' Amy asked, disbelievingly.

'I don't know,' he told her, 'but it did work, at least, sometimes it did. Not all the time. I'm learning more and more that there isn't a specific science to all this.'

'But this is different,' she replied. 'That was a mattress! It wasn't a couple of chunks of floorboard!'

For a moment, Toby looked at her, his eyes focused and determined. Then, after a moment of silence, he spoke again.

'If you don't want to do this,' he told her, 'then you don't have to. But, if you want to do this, now is our chance.'

The two of them stared at each other. Amy's eyes were watery and confused. Then, as Toby watched her pupils dart nervously back and forth, he saw it bubble to the surface. It was passion, the desire to pass on.

'Okay,' she whispered, her hands shaking by her sides.

Toby smiled.

'Okay,' he said softly, and the two of them left the room.

When they reached the open front door, Mr Thornhill was there to greet them. He was stood by the side of his car, which had one of the doors open. It was ready for Toby to lay down the pieces of floorboard onto the backseats. The world was cloudy and grey with a forceful breeze brushing through the air.

'Wait here,' Toby told Amy, whose nerves were

clearly starting to get the better of her.

Amy's hands, which had already been shaking, were now trembling fiercely and her breathing was loud and heavy. As Toby carried the planks of wood to Mr Thornhill's car, he shot the old man a thankful yet uncertain smile. Mr Thornhill smiled back at him. Toby laid the floorboards across the dirty back seats and turned to face the front door. Amy was standing there, her feet teetering on the edge of the threshold.

'Are you ready?' he asked her.

'Yes,' she replied.

'You're going to have to run,' he told her.

Amy looked at him. The fear on her face had melted away and was replaced with a fierce determination. Toby began the countdown.

'Three…two…one…go!'

Amy ran out into the world. Immediately after she'd stepped over the threshold, Toby saw that she was struggling. The sickness hit her like a ton of bricks, but it wasn't going to stop her. She bolted across the front lawn as fast as her thin legs would carry her.

She was almost there. She was nearly at the car, but her skin was starting to turn green. Toby could see it. Her face began to contort with pain. Amy was starting to slow down. There was only a little bit further to go, but Toby wasn't sure if she could make it.

But she was so close. If she could just force her legs to go faster, then she'd make it. Toby held his breath. Amy was struggling. She spat out a globule of red salvia onto the road.

But then, she finally made it. With a pained grunt, she threw herself into the car and landed on top of the wooden planks. Somehow it had worked. The floorboards were supporting her. Amy had made it to the car, but it had been hard for her. As she lay on top of the planks, Toby saw a stream of vomit shoot out of her mouth. He wanted to help her, to call the whole thing off and bring her back inside, but he knew that he couldn't do that. Amy would be in pain, a lot of pain for a long time, but they had to do this.

Toby shut the car door and stared at Mr Thornhill. The two of them looked at each other in silence until Mr Thornhill finally spoke.

'Are you sure about this?' he asked Toby. Toby took a deep breath and nodded.

'Yes,' he told the old man.

Mr Thornhill put a firm hand on Toby's shoulder. Then, the two of them got into the car.

'Amy.'

The whisper came from a long way away.

At least, that's how Amy heard it. The whisper was a faint sound that seemed to echo in her head, bouncing off the inside of her skull and crashing softly onto her brain. She was awake, but her eyes weren't open. All that Amy could see was darkness. It was a black so empty that it was almost as if she weren't anywhere at all.

But then she heard it again.

'Amy.'

It was a little louder this time. Still soft, but louder. Amy was tired, very tired. She tasted vomit in her mouth and the smell of it clogged up her nose. Amy knew that she had to get up, even though she didn't want to. All she wanted to do was sleep, but that voice had called to her.

Amy's eyelids flickered open. The light which they let in was so dazzling that Amy had to shut them almost immediately. It was a struggle to force them open again.

A young man was leaning over her. He was handsome, and he had a nice face that smiled down at her. The young man reminded Amy of a boy that she'd known a long time ago. A boy named Toby.

'Toby,' Amy whispered, her voice faint and weak. The young man nodded.

'I'm here, Amy,' he told her. 'It's okay.'

His voice was soft and comforting. As Amy turned her head, she caught a glance of Mr Thornhill, who was sitting patiently in the driver's seat. His old eyes looked at her through the rear-view mirror. Amy gagged and spluttered before spitting out blood onto the floor of the car. As she looked around her, she saw that the car was mostly clean which was odd. She could remember throwing up a lot. Amy noticed Toby leaning closer in towards her.

'Look,' he told her, pointing out of the windscreen. 'Have a look.'

With a painful heave, Amy managed to raise herself up, not very far but just far enough to see what Toby was pointing at. When she saw what lay out in front of her, she raised a shaking hand to her mouth and began to cry.

Stretched out in front of them was a fine ribbon of white sand. The previously dreary weather had changed completely. A clear blue sky filled the horizon and a warm sun beat down onto the beach with a golden glow. A crystal-clear ocean lapped calmly at the shore, little crested waves rising and falling as they made their way to the sand. Above them, a seagull glided through the air. The beach was empty, but that made it even more beautiful. As Amy turned her head, she saw two gigantic cliff-faces guarding either side of the beach. They were huge. With a wide smile, Amy took in a deep breath of fresh sea air and spoke in a trembling whisper.

'Yardley Bay.'

She looked at Toby, whose eyes had become watery and tear-filled. He wasn't crying like she was, at least not quite.

Then, all of a sudden, Toby's eyes became concerned. He turned to Mr Thornhill.

'What's going on?' he asked the old man. 'Why isn't it working?'

Then, Amy saw it. The look on Mr Thornhill's face told her that it wasn't going to happen. The old man didn't speak, he didn't even make a sound.

'What if we take her off the boards?' Toby asked desperately. 'Maybe if she touches the sand. That could work! Go on, Amy, try and get up!'

The tired Amy tried. With a heave she attempted to pull herself up, but the exertion was too much for her. She vomited a tidal wave of blood and collapsed into a heap on the floorboards. Toby reached out to her, but Mr Thornhill shot him a stern look. As Toby watched Amy, he felt tears begin to creep out of his eyes. If it hadn't been for Mr Thornhill, who pulled him into a reassuring hug, he might have burst into a fit of sobbing. Instead, he just cried quietly into the old man's jumper. It was a long time before the crying stopped.

Then, as the two of them stared at the crumpled form of Amelia Moore lying on the floorboards, Toby decided that it was time to speak.

'Shall we go?' he asked.

Nobody spoke for a moment or so.

'No,' Amy whispered, her voice almost inaudible.

Toby didn't understand. What was the point in staying? Then he saw it. As he followed Amy's gaze out through the windshield, he saw the beach and it brought a smile to his face. He looked at Amy and saw that she was smiling too. There may not have been a reason for staying, but if it meant that he got to see Amy happy then it was worth it. Finally, in a voice that was so quiet that Toby could only just make it out, Amy spoke to them.

'Five more minutes, please.'

18 A DATE

After their unsuccessful trip to Yardley Bay, both Toby and Amy seemed to give up on trying to find out why she couldn't pass on. Whilst neither of them would talk about it, it was clear to see that they couldn't think of any more ideas. Spring had well and truly swept over Lawton in the weeks that followed the trip and the weather was becoming much warmer. The sun was now a dominant presence in the sky and the warmth that it beat down on a daily basis became common-place. The leaves on the trees shone and the gardens of Lawton were fresh with gleeful bloom. However, there was one garden that wasn't. That garden belonged to The Burrows family. Daniel and Karen had been neglecting the garden recently, as they had been with all their household chores. They weren't talking much either. However, despite the negative feelings between them, Toby could still detect the worry in Karen's voice when she would inform him that Daniel was working late again.

Whilst the weather outside had perked up, Toby's disposition had remained low. He wasn't particularly happy. Not only were Daniel and Karen not getting along, but he was also upset at his inability to help Amy. In boredom, he wandered the house, not quite sure how to rise out of his depressive slump. Even so, he knew that he did still have a few positive things in his life. Mr Thornhill was one of them. His weekly tutoring sessions were fast becoming one of Toby's favourite parts of life. Now quite adept at mathematics, at least enough to pass the exam, Toby still made sure to work with the old man, honing his abilities until the calculations almost became second nature to him. The tutoring sessions were definitely paying off and it was all down to Mr Thornhill. Toby liked the old man and he would be sad to stop the sessions once the exams were out of the way. Still, that wouldn't be for a while.

The other positive thing that Toby had in his life was Amy. The fact that he had someone to turn to at all hours of the day, apart from when he was at school, was a blessing. The two of them talked and joked and laughed and were together whenever they could be. The moments that they spent together made Toby forget about everything else that was going wrong in his life.

Both Mr Thornhill and Amy made Toby's life better and he was very glad that he could call them his friends. However, they still weren't the only things keeping Toby happy. There was a third thing. He and Lily had finally organised a date.

They'd decided against seeing a film. There was never much on at the cinema and Lily couldn't choose what to watch in the end. As a result, they decided to go out for a meal instead. They'd eventually chosen to meet in Lawton's high street, at a restaurant called The Olive Branch. The Olive Branch was Lawton's only major restaurant. It served good Italian food at a low price, which was why it was so popular. Toby was excited at the prospect of meeting Lily for the first time outside of school, even if it was just for lunch. However, he was also very nervous as this would be his first ever date.

'Which shirt?' he asked Amy as he held up one in each hand.

Amy, who was sitting on Toby's bedroom floor, pointed to the one in his left hand.

'Are you sure?' he said, still not convinced. 'It is nice, but I think that it's a little too old. Then again, I've only had the other one for a few weeks. She might think that I've bought it just to impress her, which might make her think that I'm trying too hard.'

'She might think that it's sweet,' Amy replied calmly.

Toby shook his head nervously.

'No, she'll think that it's weird. Then she'll think that I'm weird and it will all be over before its even started.'

He dropped both shirts onto the floor in frustration and began to pace up and down. As she watched him with a concerned eye, Amy rose from her spot on the floor and walked over to him

'It's okay,' she said, her voice smooth and silky. 'It will be okay.'

'No, it won't!' Toby said loudly, almost yelling but managing to control the volume of his voice. He didn't want to be loud as Karen was in the living room. Amy tried putting her hand on his shoulder, but it just slid through.

'I promise that it will,' she told him, a smile on her face. 'Believe me, I know what it's like.'

Toby paused and looked at her. Amy's eyes were soft and calming. Somehow, looking at Amy made everything seem quieter. The anxiety that had been building up inside him seemed to melt away like snow. As the worry began to fade away, his eyes focused onto her youthful face.

'Thank you, Amy,' he whispered in a voice much calmer than it had been.

Amy looked into his eyes and nodded.

'That's okay,' she told him. 'You'll have to let me

know how it goes. It's been a while since I've had any decent gossip.'

Toby smiled in agreement, confirming that he would indeed let her know.

'Right,' he said, pulling one of the shirts over his head. 'I need to get going.'

'You can pick that other shirt up first,' Amy told him sternly. 'Come on, you weren't dragged up.'

Toby rolled his eyes and did as he was told.

'Can I go now?' he asked sarcastically.

Amy shook her head.

'Deodorant,' she informed him firmly. 'I can't believe that you missed that one.'

'I was going to put some on!'

'Then go on, do it.'

Toby grabbed a can and sprayed himself.

'Right,' said Amy, looking him up and down. 'Got your money?'

'Yes.'

'Got your phone?'

'Yes.'

'Got your keys?'

'Yes!'

Amy raised her eyebrows. However, they quickly fell back down and she smiled at him. The living room clock chimed twelve, signalling to Toby that he only had half an hour to get to the restaurant.

'I've got to go,' he whispered.

'Go on, tiger,' she told him. 'Have a great time.'

The Olive Branch was located at the end of Lawton's high street. In fact, it was closer to the secondary school than it was to anything else. Just before the school and at the end of the street, sat the restaurant. It was an old building and outside there was a small car park. However, that was empty by the time Toby arrived. As he approached, he noticed the slight form of Lily Roberts waiting for him. She was stood by the door, typing incessantly on her phone. She hadn't noticed him, so he called out to her, alerting her to his presence.

'Toby!' she yelled excitedly, running towards him.

Toby tried his best to contain his nerves and forced a small smile onto his face.

'Hey, Lily,' he said quietly.

Lily pulled him into a hug. It was a nice hug, though a bit awkward. Despite Lily's enthusiasm, it was clear that she was just as nervous as he was.

'Shall we go inside?' he asked.

Lily pulled away from the hug and nodded.

'Yeah, sure,' she said in a friendly voice.

Then, she led him through the door and into the restaurant.

Toby wasn't sure what made a date good. He knew

that he'd know a bad date if he saw it, but he wasn't quite sure what a good date would look like. However, as the two of them sat down at a quaint wooden table and started to look over the laminated lunch menus, he began to think that things were going well between them. After the initial nerves started to fade away, the conversation began to flow and Toby learnt a lot about the girl he'd been sitting in front of all year. She lived in one of the houses in the centre of the village. In fact, Toby realised that he'd passed by her house many times without even realising it. It was funny how things like that happened. Toby learnt that she was an only child and that her dad was a plasterer. Her mum was a hairdresser and they had a dog called Trixie and a couple of goldfish. Lily talked a lot during their date but, when it came Toby's turn to speak, he couldn't think of much to say. He told her about the accident his Mum and Dad had been in and that he was living with his brother and his brother's wife in a house down from the high street. Apart from that, he told her that there wasn't much else in his life of interest. That wasn't strictly true. However, Toby knew that it wouldn't be a good idea to bring up the ghost that lived in his house, especially on a first date.

Once the meal was over, Toby found himself walking back through the high street with Lily by his side. The sun was still out, but its brightness had faded. The wind blew a calm and gentle breeze around them.

'Thanks for walking me home,' Toby said to her.

Lily giggled and looked at him with wide eyes.

'That's okay,' she told him. 'All of my family are home anyway.'

'Ah,' Toby replied, not quite sure what she meant.

As the two of them turned down the road that led to Toby's house, he noticed something brushing against his hand. With a quick glance down at his side, he noticed that Lily was grazing the back of his hand with hers. Toby gulped and took in a deep breath. He grasped her hand firmly in his and the two continued onward.

Finally, they reached the doorstep of Toby's house. Toby could tell that Karen had gone out and that she would more than likely be away from the house for some time. Turning back to Lily, he stared at her and smiled innocently. The two of them stood in awkward silence for a while.

'Hope that you liked lunch!' Toby said loudly in an effort to inject some conversation.

Lily nodded, her head bouncing up and down gleefully as a cute smile grew on her face. The silence continued.

'Kiss her!' a voice inside Toby's head screamed. 'Kiss her, now!'

He knew that the voice was right. Toby knew that he would only get one shot at this. He should have done it a long time ago. God, she was beautiful. Her eyes, her hair, her smile. Everything about her was perfect. So why couldn't he bring himself to do it?

'Could I come in?'

Toby was surprised when the words came out of Lily's mouth. He felt his palms begin to sweat. He didn't know what to do. He hadn't planned for this.

'Say yes, you moron!' the voice inside his head yelled. 'Say yes!'

Toby wasn't sure, but the voice kept on yelling. It rung in his ears, begging him to let Lily in, but Toby had other things to worry about. There was a ghost living in his house. What if Amy distracted him? What if he accidently spoke to her? Lily would think that he'd gone insane. No, she couldn't come in. It was too risky. He would just have to tell her that she couldn't.

3...

2...

1...

'Sure,' he said happily. 'Be my guest!'

Toby slid his key inside the lock. Logic and reason had lost. As the front door swung open, he gestured for Lily to enter, which she did. As Toby closed the door behind them, wild excitement began to fill his body.

'Should I take my shoes off?' Lily asked politely.

Toby looked at her.

'Uh-Huh,' he replied, words failing him. Lily giggled and slid off her shoes.

'I can't believe it!' Toby thought. 'I'm alone with Lily Roberts!'

'Hello?'

The voice came from the hallway. Damn. As Toby stood by the front door, slowly but surely the slight form of Amelia Moore slid into the living room.

Immediately, Toby could tell that Amy knew she wasn't supposed to be there. What was going on was supposed to be a private moment. Most other people would have made themselves scarce at this point, but Amy remained. She had spent the entire day alone and had been forced to deal without romance for over a decade. She was clearly planning on taking advantage of her ghostly nature. Toby knew what she was thinking. Lily couldn't see Amy and that meant that Amy was going to take the piss out of them as much as humanly possible.

'A friend of yours, Toby?' she asked him sarcastically.

A sly smile crept onto her face. Toby focused intently on Lily.

It came as a shock to Toby when he saw Lily leaning into him. Her soft hair brushed against his face as her lips pressed gently against his. Toby could taste the fruity lip balm that she was wearing. It made his mouth taste sugary and sweet. He didn't have much experience with kissing, but Toby knew that, for a first kiss, it was definitely a good one. As Lily pulled her soft lips away from his, he couldn't help feeling sad. The kiss was over. It had been one of the greatest moments of his life.

Toby looked at Lily and smiled. She was so beautiful. He stared into her eyes but something began to distract him in his peripheral vision. That something was Amy, who was leaping jubilantly in the air and ecstatically pumping her fist in celebration.

Toby tried his best to keep a straight face. As much as he wanted to celebrate with Amy, he knew that he couldn't. That would look weird. It was then that Lily leant in for a second kiss.

'I must be dreaming,' Toby thought as her lips got closer to his.

He held his breath and waited. Then he heard it, Amy's voice.

'Go on, my son!' she yelled. 'Go on!'

What Toby did next was stupid. It was a stupid thing done by a stupid person who was just completely and utterly stupid. He knew he had to ignore Amy, that any reaction he gave to his imaginary friend might cause Lily to leave. He knew that and he was determined to ignore whatever jokes she made. However, his determination only stretched so far. After hearing Amy's stupid exclamation, Toby pulled away from Lily and did something that he instantly regretted. He laughed.

It wasn't a little laugh either. Toby wasn't usually one for big laughs and the ones that he usually made were small and restrained. Not this one. The laugh was gigantic, a big hearty roar of unrestrained proportions that leapt out of his mouth. For a moment, it filled his ears. All that he could hear was his ridiculous laugh. Then, the laughing stopped and Toby felt his stomach fall out of him.

'Did I do something wrong?'

Toby felt his heart sink. Lily didn't sound happy. Her voice wasn't bubbly or bouncy anymore. Instead, it sounded hurt and broken, as if the back of her throat were breaking away. In just those five words, Toby heard the sound of Lily's confidence shattering.

'No!' he said quickly, trying to fix the damage he'd caused. 'Of course not! I'm sorry.'

'I thought that I was doing everything right,' she whispered faintly. 'Was it not okay?'

'No, it was perfect!' Toby replied. 'It was amazing!'

'Then why did you laugh at me?'

Lily's voice was different now. The hurt was still there, but there was something else on top of it. Anger. Her lovely brown eyes were red and bloodshot. Toby could see tears welling up around them, stinging and burning against the white. He didn't know what to do. He wanted to speak, to defend himself. It wasn't his fault, it was Amy's! The ghost girl that lived in his house had made him laugh, that was it. Toby knew that wouldn't go down well. He couldn't tell her the truth. His throat was seizing up. He wanted to fix things, but he didn't know how. Lily stared at him, her eyes wide and ferocious. Then, as Toby gazed fearfully at the girl he'd had a crush on for so long, a thought pushed its way into his brain.

"Go on, my son". That was funny.

Toby tried to force the smile down, he really did, but it wasn't enough. As Lily watched, the corners of his lips began to curl upward. He was unable to repress the faint flicker of a smile.

That was enough for Lily. The poor girl wasn't going to be humiliated any longer. Without so much as a look toward Toby, she marched towards the front door. Toby's eyes followed her. He thought that he could hear the quiet sound of crying trailing behind her. He looked at Amy, who had her head tilted down in shame.

'Please, Lily,' he begged, running over to his date and looking straight into her eyes. 'Let me explain.'

'Go on then,' she told him. 'Explain.'

Toby almost told her the truth. He wanted to come clean with Lily. He wanted to tell her everything, about Amy, about Mr Thornhill, about everything. He wanted to stop her crying. Even so, he knew that he couldn't. He couldn't tell her because she would never understand. Instead, he just stood there with his mouth open.

'No,' she said, twisting the doorknob. 'I didn't think that you'd be able to.'

With that, she left.

The living room felt a lot emptier now that she was gone. Somehow, having Lily in the house had made everything seem a little brighter, but that was all gone now.

Toby wanted to cry, he knew that much, but for some reason the tears weren't coming. He couldn't really feel anything. Lily had dragged all of Toby's emotion out of the door with her. She'd left him a hollow empty shell of a person.

Then Toby felt it. It was the fire inside of him. It wasn't a good fire, quite the opposite. It was an awful raging fire that burned at his insides. It was an anger, an anger fiercer and more powerful than Toby had ever known.

Amy.

He turned around and looked at her. Amy's hands were shaking by her sides and she was shuffling her feet awkwardly. She still didn't dare to meet Toby's angry gaze.

'What's wrong with you,' he snarled at her, his teeth clenched tightly together. Amy looked up at him. A portion of her hair fell in front of her face so that only one of her eyes was visible.

'I'm sorry,' she told him, her voice trembling.

Toby wasn't going to settle for that.

'Sorry?' he yelled. His voice was so loud that it made Amy jump. 'You think that you can just say sorry?'

'No,' she replied. 'I feel awful, Toby. I didn't mean for that to happen. I was just trying to have a bit of fun. You know that I don't have much fun being stuck in this house all day…'

'You don't get to do that!' Toby roared. He could see that he was frightening Amy, but he didn't care.

'You can't do that!' he continued. 'You don't get to make me feel guilty! Not after that! Not now, not ever!'

'Toby, please.' Amy whispered feebly.

'You knew this was happening today!' he yelled.

'You knew how much I liked her! You knew everything and you still did it!'

'Toby, I'm sorry…'

'No, you're not! How could you be sorry? You only think about yourself!'

There was silence. Toby knew that something was coming, he could sense it. Amy changed her stance. She wasn't standing hunched anymore. Her one visible eye stared furiously at him.

'Me?' she screamed. 'I only think of myself? How about all that time I spent up in the attic? Huh? Do you think that I liked it up there?'

'No,' Toby replied.

Amy flicked the hair away from her face. Her other eye came into view. Both eyes were red.

'I did that for you, Toby! So that you wouldn't get locked up! Do you know how long I was up there for? Ten years! That's how long! Ten years! Can you even imagine that? It was torture! Every day I wanted to come back down, but I didn't because I never wanted you to get hurt! If you think that makes me selfish, then I don't even know why I did it!'

The silence fell once again. This time it was heavier, like dirt being shovelled on top of a coffin. For a while Toby didn't know what to say. Deep down, he knew that what he'd said was wrong. Amy hadn't meant to make things bad, but it just seemed to be something that happened when Toby was around her. At least, that's how he saw it in that moment. He wondered if he should apologise to her, but the anger was still inside him. He didn't want Amy to get away with this. With his eyes fixed firmly on her, he parted his lips and spoke in a voice that was clear and unflinching. What he said was something that he didn't mean, but that didn't stop him.

'I wish that you'd stayed up there.'

With that awful declaration, Toby strode through Amy's ghostly form and opened his bedroom door, which he promptly slammed shut. Toby had been able to get away from the argument quickly, but not before catching a glance at Amy's heartbroken face as a single tear rolled down her cheek.

19 TRYING TO FIX THINGS

Neither of them spoke for a few days after the incident. It was relatively easy for Toby. He just had to ignore Amy whenever he saw her and instead make conversation with his brother or Karen. However, he later began to understand how much harder it was for his ghostly friend. If he wasn't speaking to Amy, he could just go and talk to someone else. She didn't have that luxury. As the stony silence continued, he was sure that he could see the loneliness she felt etched onto her face. Perhaps he should have apologised. That way, they could have moved on and forgotten the whole thing. Amy would have someone to talk to again if he did that and Toby would have regained a friend.

But anger is a powerful thing, especially when it festers inside the body of a teenager. Toby, despite wanting the silence to end, hadn't gotten over what she'd done. It had irreversibly changed his relationship with Lily. In the week that followed, Lily didn't speak to him once, even though they ran into each other on multiple occasions. She would just look away and hurry past him. Toby guessed that it wasn't just

Amy's fault for making Lily hate him. At the end of the day, he was the one who'd laughed. It was Toby who'd made Lily feel that way.

It seemed to Toby as if the world was crumbling around him. Everything in his life had turned rotten and rancid, leaving him with little to hold onto. Lily hated him, he and Amy weren't speaking, Karen and Daniel were becoming more distant and even Mr Thornhill would be leaving him soon. With the exams approaching rapidly, the old man had taught Toby everything that he could possibly need to know. As a result, there was little need for their tutoring sessions to continue. It was these losses that made Toby feel as though there was nothing left for him in Lawton. That was one of the reasons behind what he did.

It was just after four o'clock when he ran into Mrs Hunter's classroom. Luckily for Toby, she hadn't left yet and was sat at her desk. As Toby darted through the open door, she turned her head slowly towards him.

'Can I help you?' she asked in an impatient voice.

Toby nodded, his eyes focused solidly on her as he presented her with a crisp sheet of paper. Mrs Hunter's eyebrows rose considerably.

'Is that…?'

'An application,' Toby interrupted. 'For Pine Mount. Yes. It's all finished.'

Mrs Hunter rose from her chair. As she made her way towards him, Toby noticed that her face didn't appear as disgruntled as it usually did. This should have made Toby feel relaxed but it only made him more nervous. Then, when she finally reached him, she held out a hand and snatched the application from his grasp. After a cursory read, she looked up from the paper and smiled a yellow-toothed smile.

'Very impressive,' she said.

And with that, she turned away from him and went back to her chair. For a moment, Toby remained standing. However, after a brief glance in his direction, Mrs Hunter waved him away. Toby nodded compliantly. He hurried himself out of the room, looking back only to see her reading his application once again.

After that, a certain amount of space seemed to free up inside of Toby's brain, allowing him to concentrate on something else. Fixing his relationship with Lily.

He found her in the school hall the next day. Lawton Secondary School wasn't big enough to have its own cafeteria, so tables and chairs were set out in the assembly hall during lunchtimes. The school's overpopulation problem was at its most obvious here. Tables were often packed tight with more chairs than they could fit and students from the lower years were relegated to sitting on the floor. Toby didn't usually eat his lunch in the hall. He preferred to stand on his own outside, when the weather permitted. But, today was different. Today he was going to have lunch in the school hall, not only because it was raining outside, but also because he knew the exact table that Lily would be sat at.

The hall wasn't very big and, aside from the tables and chairs, it remained relatively free of furnishings or equipment. This meant that, whenever lunchtime came, tables could be set up in all parts of the room. It was at a table in the centre of the hall where Lily was sat with her friends. Well, friends might have been a bit of a strong word. Of the fifteen people sat at the table, probably only five or six could really be classed as her friends. However, five or six was still a big number compared to Toby, who made up a solid army of one. He expected a lot of opposition to his appearance.

At first, they didn't notice him. In all fairness, the hall was incredibly crowded and Toby tended to be the kind of person who blended into crowds. He debated whether of not to clear his throat and make them aware of his presence, but the hall was too loud and he knew that they wouldn't be able to hear him. Instead, he just stood there, waiting in complete silence until he was noticed. After a while, one of Lily's friends picked up that he was there. The friend was clearly not pleased to see him. After a quick look at Lily, who was sitting on the other side of the table, the friend pointed at Toby to let her know that he was there. Lily stared at him with eyes as cold as stone.

Toby wanted to talk to her but the noise in the hall was too loud. Instead, he beckoned her over to him. That way, they could speak in private. Lily's friend, whose name Toby didn't know, stared at her with wide eyes. It was as if she were asking whether or not she was seriously considering going with him. Lily nodded firmly at her friend and rose from her seat.

Then she faced him, her eyes cold and unfeeling. Toby felt his throat go dry. Suddenly, he became nervous. With another wave of his hand, he beckoned Lily to follow him. With a sharp turn, he made his way through the crowd of students and towards a secluded spot by the bins. Stepping over the legs of a couple of first years, he checked over his shoulder to see if Lily was actually following him. She was.

'I'm sorry for what I did,' he told her as she approached him. Upon hearing this, Lily almost walked away. She probably would have gone if Toby hadn't reached out a hand to stop her. Clearing his throat quietly, he continued.

'Please, listen to me. I didn't mean to do what I did. The thing is, I've never been...'

He struggled to find the words for a moment, but they eventually came to him.

'I've never been in a situation like that before. I was nervous, you know? I want you to know that, because I'd been really looking forward to our date. I'm sorry. I guess that what I'm trying to say is that what I did on Saturday was a mistake. If you'd give me another chance, I promise that I won't let you down. I really like you, Lily.'

Once Toby had finished his speech, a calming sense of relief flooded over him. To an extent, he wouldn't care if Lily gave him another chance or not, because he'd done all that he could. Then again, that wasn't true. He did care and he wanted her to take him back. With bated breath, he waited for Lily to respond.

'I get it,' she told him.

Lily began to look kinder. She wasn't as stiff as she'd been before. Her eyes seemed to have lost their stoniness. They looked softer, more welcoming.

'I was nervous too,' she continued. 'When you did what you did, it hurt. It hurt a lot. I didn't know what I was doing and when I heard you laugh...'

Her voice trailed off before finishing the sentence.

'It just felt like I'd done something wrong,' she finally said after a long pause.

Toby shook his head firmly.

'You didn't,' he told her truthfully. 'It was my fault, not yours.'

Lily seemed to accept that. She didn't say anything in response but from the look on her face, Toby could see that he'd made her feel a little better.

'So, will you give me another chance?' he asked her.

Lily nodded and smiled.

'Yeah,' she told him, 'I will.'

With Lily's forgiveness, Toby felt his outlook on life change from negative to positive. Even though the rain continued to pour heavily onto the pavements, he felt as though the world had gotten a little bit brighter. In fact, he was almost looking forward to sorting things out with Amy. They'd not spoken for so long that it would be a welcome relief to hear her vibrant laughter filling the house again. He did miss her. He missed her voice, her smile, her jokes, but most of all he missed their late night conversations. Perhaps it was youthful optimism that made Toby so sure Amy would forgive him. Then again, maybe it was cockiness. But, as he made his way home that day, he didn't realise that apologising to Amy wasn't going to be as easy as he thought.

As he entered the house, Toby felt a blast of warm air hit him like a ton of bricks. Daniel and Karen never usually left the heating on when they were out. However, it had been cloudy and miserable recently, so it was best to keep it on. That way, they could dry off faster when they got in.

'Hello?' Toby called.

His voice echoed in the empty house. No one was home. That was good. He didn't want Daniel or Karen overhearing the conversation he was about to have.

'Amy?' he called again, this time a little louder.

There was no response.

Sliding off his shoes and picking them up so as not to get dirt on the carpet, Toby made his way across the living room and into the hallway. He had a fairly good idea as to where Amy would be hiding. Toby approached his bedroom door and knocked firmly. He waited for a response but there was none. He twisted the doorknob and entered the room. Once inside, he saw Amy waking from an afternoon nap in her little bed space on the floor. As he watched her come to, he saw that her expression was relatively care-free. Perhaps it was this that gave him false hope.

'Hey, sleepy-head,' he said to her.

He crouched down by Amy's side as she tried to

adjust her vision. However, once she did so, her expression changed. She could see that it was him and her face became much colder.

'Can we talk?' he asked her.

Amy didn't respond, but Toby decided to speak anyway.

'I feel awful about everything that happened,' he told her. 'I know that I shouldn't have said what I did and I just wanted to tell you that none of it was true. I was just upset about what had happened and I didn't know how to handle it, so I took it out on you. It wasn't right and I know that. So, what I'm trying to say is, can we be friends again?'

Amy glared at him. Her eyes were now wide awake.

'You don't get it, Toby.'

'Don't get what?' he asked her in a confused voice.

Amy ground her teeth together.

'Do you have any idea how awful you made me feel? Do you have any idea?'

Toby opened his mouth to answer but Amy cut him off.

'You told me that you wished I'd never left the attic! As if I chose to be found! You found me. I was never going to come down from the attic, but you found me! That wasn't my fault! That's the thing you forget sometimes. I lived up there, in the dark, for ten years because I didn't want to make things worse for you. I stayed up there because I thought that you were my only friend but I was wrong. You don't care about me and you never did.'

Toby didn't know what to say. He was in shock. He'd expected resistance from Amy, but not this much. He wanted to defend himself, to yell back at her, but there were more important things to think about. He didn't want to lose Amy over something like this, so he stayed quiet. Finally, after a long silence, he asked her a question in a weak and powerless voice.

'Do you forgive me?'

Like lightning, Amy jumped to her feet and clenched her pale hands into tight fists. She looked insane, like a maniac, and Toby almost ran out of the room.

'No, I don't!' she screamed at him. 'I don't know if I'll ever forgive you. I never thought that I'd lose you as a friend, but it looks like I might!'

Her yelling was making Toby nervous. He could feel his hands start to shake beside him, his fingers twitching like the legs of a spider. His throat began to close up. It felt as if somebody was strangling him. His steady breathing transformed into heavy gasps for air that he was barely able to conceal from the manic Amy.

'I won't be coming back in here,' she told him. 'I'll go into the back-room, where I'm far away. That way you'll never have to see me again.'

Toby clambered to his feet. He was more worried than ever about losing his only friend. He didn't want to let her go without a fight. But, with both of them at the same level, he could see that Amy was about to snap. Anything could set her off. Toby wanted to talk, to make things better, but he couldn't find the words. He felt incapable, helpless. He felt like he'd lost. Then, Amy marched towards the open door. As she reached the threshold, she stopped. Silently and slowly, she twisted her neck to look back over her shoulder at him. He was the boy who had been her only source of company for such a long time. In a voice that was barely a whisper, she spoke the last words that she would speak that night. As soon as Toby heard them, he knew that the battle was over.

'Goodbye, Toby.'

With that, she was gone.

Toby could have run after her, perhaps he should have, but he knew that there wasn't any way to convince her. Maybe sometime soon everything would get sorted between them but, as he looked around his empty room, he realised that time wouldn't be coming for a long while yet.

That night, Toby lay awake in the darkness, his eyes gazing blindly up at the ceiling. He thought of Amy. Toby wondered if she was having trouble sleeping like he was. It wouldn't be a good night for him, he knew that much, but the worst part came when Daniel got home at three in the morning.

Toby didn't even need to leave his bed to figure out what was going on. Karen and Daniel were prone to fighting, but this was different. The angry yells went on for almost an hour. From the way the shouts were broken with extended gaps of silence, he could tell that some kind of hidden truth was coming out. Everything was revealing itself now. All the secrets were being brought out into the open. Toby almost thought that he could hear specific words being spoken, but they soon disappeared. They just faded into the overall noise of the fight. It was the worst fight that the two of them had ever gotten into, but Toby would have to wait until morning to find out what the outcome had been. Until then, he just lay there, motionless in his bed. He listened as the violent screaming morphed into a broken, unfeeling hum.

Michael Raine

20 BAD NEWS

He should have seen it coming. It had been right in front of his eyes the whole time, yet somehow Toby had been blind. Then again, maybe he just didn't want to believe it. Either way, the truth had come out now and everyone was going to suffer as a result.

Daniel had cheated on Karen. Not just once, but many times. It had been with a woman from his work. She was Daniel's secretary and, after his relationship with Karen had become rocky, she'd provided him with a shoulder to cry on. After that, things had become relatively straightforward. Daniel would go straight from work to the woman's house and would stay there for as long as he could. He would then come home at whatever hour pleased him best and apologise to his wife. He would say that he was sorry and she would tell him not to be as it wasn't his fault that he had to stay late at the office. Karen had believed Daniel's lies for a long time before he was found out. Eventually though, she did find out and that was what had caused the argument. Toby knew all this because Daniel told him over breakfast the next morning. Karen was nowhere to be found.

'She's gone to a hotel,' Daniel told him, his usual positivity gone and replaced with solemnity.

Daniel looked different. His face was sunken and morose and his skin seemed almost grey in the dark living room. Bristly stubble clung to his jawline and even his muscles looked as if they'd lost some of their firmness. It was as if he had deflated.

'What's going to happen?' Toby asked as he ate some of his cereal. It was bland and tasteless. Toby wanted to spit it out, but he didn't.

'Divorce,' Daniel told him.

That was the last word on the matter.

Toby left for school that morning with a dull ache in his heart. His life seemed to be an endless rollercoaster of manic highs and depressive lows, a pattern that he was unable to change. As he trudged down the strangely empty high-street, he noticed a few drops of rain fall onto his skin. He saw them, but he didn't feel them. The only thing he felt was the ache. He didn't blame Karen for doing what she'd done. There was only one person at fault and it certainly wasn't her. If Daniel hadn't done it, the two of them might have been able to work things out. But he had done it and everyone had to pay because of it. Oddly enough, the ending of their marriage wasn't what upset Toby the most. What upset him the most were his thoughts of Amy. As he'd listened to his brother inform him of the family's disintegration, his mind had wandered towards the back-room. There, Amy would have been hiding, listening to the words coming out of Daniel's mouth. She would have known the pain they must have caused Toby. Yet, she'd still not come out. She'd stayed there, silently waiting in the back-room.

KNOCK. KNOCK.

Toby rose from the sofa. He'd been back from school for over two hours and neither Daniel or Karen had come home. Honestly, he didn't know when he'd see either of them again. It could have been in an hour or a day, he really had no idea.

KNOCK. KNOCK.

There it was again. Someone was outside, waiting at the front door. Walking sluggishly towards it, Toby felt a feeling of reluctance rise up inside him. He didn't want to talk to anyone. However, when he finally opened the door, he was pleased to find that a friend had come to visit him.

Mr Thornhill looked older. His slit-like eyes were even smaller than usual and his beard, which had once been full and comforting, was now thin and malnourished. Draped over his back was a thick overcoat with more pockets than anybody could ever possibly need. Perched on top of his head was the woollen hat that Toby had bought him for Christmas. Seeing the old man looking so much older sent a sadness down into Toby's stomach, but it quickly faded.

'Hello, Toby,' the old man said. 'May I come in?'

'Yeah, sure,' Toby replied happily.

The old man stepped over the threshold, his movements stiff and slow. Once he was in, Toby closed the door.

'Where's Amy?' asked Mr Thornhill, who didn't know about what had happened.

Toby looked down at his feet, as if he were in mourning.

'We haven't spoken,' he told the old man. 'We had

an argument, a bad one. So, yeah, we aren't speaking.'

'What was it about?' Mr Thornhill asked.

Toby shook his head.

'I don't want to talk about it,' he told him.

The old man understood instantly and dropped the subject.

'How did it go?'

'How did what go?'

'The exam,' Mr Thornhill explained. 'The Maths exam. It was today, wasn't it?'

Toby made some inarticulate grunting noise and slumped back down into the sofa. Mr Thornhill, sensing bad news, sat down next to him.

'Did it not go well?' he asked.

Toby shook his head and Mr Thornhill sighed.

'How come?' the old man enquired, trying to break down whatever emotional wall Toby was building between them. Toby didn't look at Mr Thornhill. Somehow, it almost seemed rude to look at him after what had happened.

'I couldn't concentrate,' he finally said, mumbling under his breath so as not to make the blow too harsh. 'Too many things going through my mind. I didn't even finish the paper.'

That was when his voice began to crack. It wasn't very noticeable, but it was still there.

'What were you thinking about?'

Mr Thornhill's voice seemed to be coming from very

far away. It was muffled and quiet, as if Toby were hearing it from the other side of a closed window. However, even though the words were far away, he could still hear them and they posed a question that Toby did not want to answer.

'I don't know,' he muttered angrily.

The old man was unconvinced.

'What do you mean?' Mr Thornhill probed, pressing on and trying his best to get Toby to talk.

Toby wasn't budging, at least not anytime soon.

'I meant what I said!' he yelled at the old man, taking Mr Thornhill by surprise. 'I was thinking about stuff. It wasn't anything important, so please drop it!'

The old man stared at him in shock. Toby had never spoken to Mr Thornhill like that.

'What's going on?'

Toby waited a moment before replying.

'Nothing,' he said. 'Nothing.'

What happened next came as a great surprise to Toby. The room, which had already been quite dark, seemed to blacken even further. Toby's eyes even had to strain a bit to see Mr Thornhill in full focus. He could hear the sound of light rain falling from the sky. With his eyes struggling to see, Toby stared at Mr Thornhill intensely. Through the half light, he couldn't quite make out the old man's expression. The pitying look that he'd had only moments ago had faded away, but what had replaced it? Was it anger? Was it fear? Perhaps it was a little bit of both. Either way, when Mr Thornhill spoke his next words, Toby could tell from the tone of his voice that the old man wasn't going to stand for anymore nonsense.

'Tell me,' he said.

The dark room seemed almost to be suffocating Toby. He could feel the hands of the darkness wrapping tightly around his throat. He couldn't see all that well. Was Mr Thornhill still sitting next to him? Yes, yes he was. The world was spinning. The living room wasn't the same living room, but an older one, at least that's how it seemed to Toby. The cream carpet had burned away to show a stained green one beneath it. The pristine white walls had melted, exposing cracked paint below. The sofa was no longer new, but old and ragged. Toby could feel a headache starting. He wasn't fifteen anymore, he was five years old and afraid. He was scared about what was happening to him. He was scared about the new house. He was scared about the monsters in his room. He was scared because his Mum and Dad wouldn't be coming back. They'd died and they were going to stay dead. Toby had no one. There wasn't anyone who loved him or cared about him. He was on his own.

But, that wasn't true. Out of the smoke that clouded his mind, he saw two people walking slowly towards him. They were smiling and holding hands. They looked happy. They were good people who would do anything for Toby and they were very much in love. As the smoke settled and the air became clear, Toby was finally able to see the faces of Daniel and Karen. They looked at him, eyes filled with love, and Toby felt warm. They had saved him and now he knew that he'd never be alone. Then it happened. With a flash of bright light, the bodies of Daniel and Karen snapped into nothingness, leaving only a glimpse of their translucent faces, which had become ugly and full of hate. They were gone and he was alone again. Toby closed his eyes. He could still smell the smoke burning in his nose like a toxic chemical fire. It was stuck there and wouldn't go away. Then, he opened his eyes and saw that he was back in the room with Mr Thornhill. The old man was waiting for him. Toby decided to answer his question. In fact, he told him everything. He didn't leave anything out. Everything that had been rushing around inside of his brain came out and, as Toby began to cry, the old man smiled comfortingly and pulled him into a tight embrace.

It took a while for everything to come out, but when it finally did Toby felt as though a huge weight had been lifted from his shoulders. After getting rid of the sadness that had been building up inside of him, he felt as though his body had been cleansed.

'Are you going to be okay?' asked Mr Thornhill.

Toby, who now felt much better than he had done in days, nodded.

'Yes,' he said firmly. 'I'll be okay.'

'I can stay if you'd like,' Mr Thornhill told him. 'I could wait until your brother gets back.'

Toby shook his head, but smiled all the same.

'No, thank you,' he replied. 'You've done more than enough for me. Thank you.'

Toby walked the old man to the door. Watching as Mr Thornhill rose shakily from the sofa, he was saddened to notice that the old man's movements were stiffer than usual. It seemed as though every step he took was more painful than the last. When they finally reached the door, Toby glanced out of the window. It was partially covered by curtains, but still exposed enough for him to get a glimpse outside. The world looked different to how it had done. The sky, whilst still cloudy and dull, seemed to have perked up a bit. The clouds themselves had also changed since the start of their conversation. They weren't grey anymore; in fact, they were white.

Toby opened the door and breathed in the soft smell of rain on grass. It was a gentle smell and it filled his nostrils quite nicely. Stepping aside to let the old man pass, he watched as Mr Thornhill stepped precariously over the threshold. Once his feet were placed firmly onto the ground, the old man turned to Toby and began to speak.

'I want you to know that, whatever happens with regards to your exam, it will not change how I see you, Toby. I know from our hours of sessions that you are by no means an unintelligent person. If you somehow don't end up with the grade you want, you should know that it is not a reflection on you. You are one of the smartest people I have ever had the pleasure to teach.'

Toby felt a tear swell in the corner of his eye. What Mr Thornhill had said hit him harder than anything he'd ever been told in his life. The old man had been with him through so much. Seeing him standing there for what could be the last time, it made Toby fear that he was going to start crying again.

'Thank you,' he told Mr Thornhill. 'For everything.'

Mr Thornhill, who's own eyes seemed to be filling up themselves, smiled happily.

'If you sort things out with Amy,' he said softly, 'tell her that I said goodbye.'

'I will,' Toby replied.

In what just might have been their last moment together as student and tutor, he stretched out his arms and pulled Mr Thornhill into him. Once their hug was over, Mr Thornhill turned away and walked towards his car. Then, just as he was about to leave, Toby saw something come into the old man's mind. Turning back towards Toby, Mr Thornhill raised an eyebrow and smiled once again.

'Anyway,' the old man grinned. 'Even if your exam didn't go well, there are other things to look forward to. Are you all sorted for the Prom?'

21 SUITS AND DRESSES

The Lawton Secondary School Prom was an event that had been tried and tested by time. An import from America, the prom was a chance for all the final year students to let their hair down in a secure and controlled environment. There was dinner, dancing and all the non-alcoholic drinks that anyone could ever wish for. Despite how boring this would sound to even the squarest of people, the prom was still a big event in Lawton and it was almost an unwritten rule that everyone had to attend. The girls were always the most excited for it. They spent months planning every single detail of their outfits as if they were designing the blueprints for a cruise missile. The boys still cared about the prom too though, just not nearly as much as their female counterparts. They would book their rental tuxedoes months in advance to make sure that they weren't stuck with one of the reject suits. There was always one boy who had to go to prom in a reject suit. It had almost become a sort of tradition and there was no doubt in anyone's mind that such a tuxedo would make an appearance at this year's prom. Everyone was counting on it and Toby was going to make sure that nobody was disappointed.

It was an awful tuxedo. Toby hadn't really been paying attention to the fact that prom was coming and, as a result, he had booked in for a rental suit much too late. The cuffs of it were frayed and, inside of one of the pockets, there was a big red stain that was so disgusting that Toby didn't even want to think about it. Trying it on for the first time in the shop, he noticed that the whole thing was far too tight and that it rubbed against his skin as he walked. The thin seams that held the ancient fabric together creaked with every movement. Also, to make things worse, at least three of the buttons were missing from the jacket, which meant that it didn't actually do up completely. The tuxedo was ugly, it was uncomfortable and it was downright unpleasant to wear, but Daniel wouldn't pay for anything else. His character had changed since Karen had left and it had shocked Toby. The joyful, fun-loving Daniel that he'd grown up with had become cold and cynical. However, more than anything, Daniel had become thrifty.

The majority of people who would be going to the prom were couples. Following the American tradition, it was expected that those in relationships would attend the event together, whilst the single students would go with their friendship groups. This caused a bit of an issue for Toby. He couldn't go with any friends and, unfortunately for him, his relationship with Lily had been cut short.

'It's not because of you,' she'd told him, approaching him one lunchtime.

Toby knew that her statement wasn't true. It was most certainly because of him. The two of them had given it another shot and had even met a couple of times since their reconciliation. However, it wasn't meant to be, at least from Lily's point of view. Toby felt quite the opposite to how she did. He wouldn't have even thought about going to prom without her and had only been excited about it because he'd thought the two of them would be going together. Either way, it didn't matter anymore. Their relationship was over and Toby was back to being single again. Perhaps he should have just forgotten about going to prom. Maybe he should have given up on it and stayed at home, but he knew that he couldn't. He'd booked the tuxedo.

So, as the solitary member in a party of one, Toby sat idly on the edge of his bed and tied the laces on his old black shoes. Hopefully, the event wouldn't be as humiliating as he was expecting. Maybe he'd see a few people that he knew there, that would make things a little less degrading. Toby didn't really have friends, but he did have a few people that he talked to and he hoped that they wouldn't mind him tagging along with them. It sounded pathetic really, when Toby realised what his plan was, but it didn't matter really. His time at school was nearly over and this would be his final chance to enjoy himself. After that, there was only uncertainty and doubt. All of his exams were over, but he still wouldn't know the results for at least another month. His whole future was riding on these exams and it seemed as though results day was creeping ever closer.

Luckily for him, there was at least one bit of good news on that front. Pine Mount had sent him a letter a couple of days previously, enclosed in a white envelope with the college crest printed onto it. Toby had almost been too afraid to open it and had stared at the letter for a good fifteen minutes before working up the courage to do so. When he'd finally mustered the strength to tear it open, a thin piece of paper had slid out onto the floor, falling gently like a leaf caught in a downward wind. Then, with a deep breath, Toby had picked up the letter and begun to read. It hadn't been until he'd got halfway through the third paragraph when he'd finally felt as though he could breathe again. He'd been accepted. There were conditions that had to be met before he could join, but he'd expected that. He just had to get the grades. After getting them, he'd be welcomed into the college with open arms, just not before. This should have helped Toby relax a little but, in fact, it had done the opposite.

As he sat there in his tuxedo, Toby noticed that his bedroom looked brighter than it usually did. He did have the light on, but there was still a great deal of evening sun making its way through the window. He thought it strange for it to be so light at such a late hour. It was nearly seven after all and Lawton wasn't usually the sunniest of places. Still, he wasn't complaining.

Once the laces of his shoes were done up tight, he lowered his feet to the ground and sat in silence. The room was quiet. The only sound that Toby could make out was his breathing. He sighed heavily and surveyed his bedroom. Thinking back to how it had looked when they'd first moved into the house, he noticed that so much had changed. Ten years was a long time but Toby still felt as though everything had grown up all at once, including him. He thought back to what he'd been like when they'd first moved in. He'd been a frightened little kid, scared and uncertain. It was then that he remembered the monsters and where they'd been hiding. There had been one in the long wardrobe at the end of his room. The wardrobe which was still there. There had been one in the hedge too. Toby remembered both of them, the one in the wardrobe and the one in the hedge outside. It had been a long time since he'd last thought of them.

Cough.

The sound came from behind Toby's bedroom door. At first he didn't think anything of it, but then it came again.

Cough.

It was louder the second time and firmer, as though the person making the noise was signalling that they wouldn't do so a third time. Toby knew who it was. He was almost reluctant to open the door. Then again, he didn't want to go to the prom without speaking to her first. Lifting himself off of the bed, he walked apprehensively towards the door. He opened it and stared blankly into the hallway. Amy was there, standing in front of him with her hands behind her back. Toby had made it his mission to keep out of the back-room ever since they'd had their argument. As a result, this was the first time that he'd seen Amy for what felt to him like a very long

287

time. She'd not changed at all, yet somehow he felt that she looked a little different. Her head was tilted down slightly so that she was looking up at him. A few strands of hair had fallen in front of her face. What struck Toby the most about Amy was her expression. Her eyes seemed to convey a feeling of desperation and the tenseness of her body revealed to him a nervousness which she was unable to mask.

'Hey,' Toby said to her quietly.

'Hey.'

Amy's voice was broken. It sounded scratchy, like an old record.

'Can we talk?' she asked him, bringing her hands out from behind her back.

Toby let Amy into the room, closing the door behind them as he did so. He stared at her and saw her neck twist to survey her surroundings. A small smile appeared on her face. Then, as Toby continued to watch her, he noticed that her eyes had been drawn to one of the corners of the room. She was looking at the place where her bed had been. That was when her smile widened. He watched her eyes light up as the memories of all the late nights that they'd spent together began to bubble to the surface of her mind. He felt his eyes begin to well up with tears. He didn't cry of course, it wasn't the right time for that, but the tears were still there.

'I'm sorry,' she whispered, her gaze meeting his.

'No,' he told her, 'I'm sorry. I didn't mean what I said. It wasn't true.'

'I know,' Amy replied.

The two of them stood for a moment in awkward silence.

'So,' she said to him. 'Friends again?'

Toby smiled and nodded firmly.

'Yeah,' he told her. 'Definitely.'

Then, just like that, all the sadness and anger that had festered between the two of them seemed to melt away. With that simple affirmation, the whole awful situation had been put to rest. Toby felt a warm sense of relief fill his body. He had his friend back again.

'You look nice,' Amy told him.

'Thank you,' he replied happily.

He gave her a quick twirl, allowing her to fully take in the entirety of the awful tuxedo. Despite the suit looking so dreadful, Amy still managed to produce a genuine smile.

'Are you going with anyone?' she asked him.

Toby looked down at his feet.

'No,' he told her, shaking his head. 'It didn't work out with Lily. I'm going alone tonight.'

'Ah,' Amy replied.

The silence returned and it was a while before either of them spoke again.

'Well,' Amy continued, trying to brush away the awkwardness, 'at least you get to go to prom. I didn't.'

'Why not?' Toby asked, his head turning to the side quizzically. Amy's expression didn't change and the smile remained on her face

'I wasn't well,' she told him plainly.

'How so?' he asked.

'I got sick a few weeks before it and I didn't get

better until it was over. I was quite bad. That's why I'm so thin. I lost a lot of weight from the illness. That's why I was so skinny when they....'

Amy didn't finish the sentence.

'Anyway,' she said, changing the subject. 'You'll have a great time. Go and have the time of your life and don't let Lily bring you down. You can do better.'

Toby laughed.

'Thanks,' he replied.

'Can I tell you a secret?' Amy asked him, leaning in close so that their faces were only a few inches apart.

'Of course,' he told her.

Amy smiled a wide smile and winked at him.

'I didn't like her anyway,' she laughed.

It was then that Toby heard a sound coming from the living room. It was Daniel calling him.

'Toby! We're waiting for you.'

'Coming!' Toby yelled back at his brother.

He looked at Amy and saw that there was a new expression on her face. It wasn't sadness or nervousness. It was pure pride. It was an expression that made Toby feel a hundred feet tall. It made him strong and caused his lips to curl into a smile once again.

'You'd better go,' Amy told him.

'Yeah,' he replied.

But Toby didn't want to go. He knew that he had to, but he just wanted to stay and look at Amy's proud face. He didn't care about the prom anymore. All that he cared about was Amy. For a few seconds they remained, standing and staring at each other as if the world around them could wait. Then, in a moment of longing, Amy reached out her hand and tried to place it on Toby's shoulder.

It would have been perfect if it had worked, if the hand had touched his shoulder and stayed there, but it wasn't meant to be. Slowly and silently, Amy's pale hand slid through his solid flesh. The two of them laughed it off, neither giving away how sad it made them feel inside. That was when it ended, as Daniel's voice called for Toby once again.

Shutting the door on his ghostly friend so that she could get some undisturbed rest, Toby made his way out of his bedroom and into the hallway. He felt upset at the prospect of having to leave Amy all alone, given that they hadn't spoken in so long. Then again, it was his last night as a secondary school student and he had to enjoy it. As he walked towards the open living room door, he listened to the rhythmic clicking and clacking of the soles of his shoes on the floorboards beneath him. He began to think about what Daniel had said. He'd used the word *we*. There was someone else in the house with them. Who could it be? Mr Thornhill? Toby doubted it. It should have been obvious to him and yet he wasn't able to see it until it was right in front of his face. He walked into the living room and smiled. Standing in front of him was Daniel, dressed in a white polo shirt and fiddling with a camera. By his side there was a woman.

Toby had seen this woman before. It felt like years had passed since he'd last laid eyes on her but it had only really been just over a week. The woman had changed a great deal. She was wearing slim fitting blue jeans and a white shirt that was covered by a blue blazer. The sunglasses which she had previously worn were gone and had been replaced by a pair of thick rimmed spectacles. The woman was no longer dressed like someone trying to impress, but was instead clothed in a way that brought her personality to the forefront. Toby felt a sense of joy expand inside of him. He saw two

metal bangles dangling from the woman's thin wrists, which
swayed gently as she lifted her hands to her face in happiness.
The woman was pleased to see Toby and Toby was pleased to
see her. His gaze moved upwards and he stared in awe at her
hair. It had been dyed a radiant blue. The woman's eyes were
watery, filled with tears that couldn't quite escape, but they
weren't tears of sadness. The woman opened her mouth and
spoke to him in a quiet, yet incredibly proud voice.

'Hey, Toby,' she whispered.

'Hey, Karen,' he said back to her.

Before Toby knew it, he was in the car on his way to
prom. The event was being held in the village hall, which was
bigger than most halls and had more than enough room for the
whole of Toby's school year to fit quite comfortably in it. He
probably could have walked to the hall as it wasn't that far
away, but it had started to rain. Daniel had offered to drive
him down there whilst Karen had stayed at the house. Things
hadn't been too awkward between her and Daniel and the
three of them had actually taken a few good photos together.
However, they still weren't on the best terms. Karen probably
wouldn't hang about for long at the house and Toby was sure
that she would be back at her hotel long before Daniel got
back. She'd get a taxi, probably. As he gazed out of the
windscreen, his back straight and his head up proudly, Toby
tried to distance himself from thoughts like that. The evening
had been great so far and he wasn't going to let bad thoughts
get stuck in his head. The night was young and he was going
to enjoy every second of it. Yet, as Toby engaged in small-talk
with his brother, his mind began to wander. He thought about
Amy. Amy had never been to prom. Toby couldn't imagine
what it must have been like to miss out on something like that,
but Amy had done. That was something that would stick with
a person. Some might say it could even be classed as a regret.
It might even make them stick around when they didn't really
want to. Perhaps that was the case and maybe, just maybe,
something could be done about it.

That was when Toby came up with a plan.

22 THE LAST DANCE

Toby opened the door to his bedroom. He peered through the darkness and stared at her. Amy was fast asleep, curled up in a ball in her corner of the room. Toby had left the light off for her, so that she could get to sleep without any distraction. However, he was reluctant to turn it back on. He was worried that the sudden burst of light would startle Amy and he didn't want that. He didn't want to scare her. Even so, he needed her to wake up.

Toby took a single cautious step into the room. The floorboards beneath the carpet creaked, but only a little. Amy didn't react to the sound. Toby decided to take another step forward. Another creak sounded beneath him. His eyes felt strained. The bedroom was almost completely black and he could only just make out Amy's shadowy form. As he took a third step, he noticed her body twitch a little. He held his breath, not daring to make a sound. He didn't want to frighten Amy; he had to wake her up gently. After a few seconds of silence, he relaxed and took another tentative step forward. That had been very close. It wasn't just Amy that he had to worry about. Daniel was sound asleep and Toby didn't want to wake him either. He didn't want his brother to get in the way of what he had planned. With one final creeping step, Toby made it to Amy's side. He leant in close to her and looked down at her dress. Even in the darkness, he could still make out the red wound in her stomach.

'Amy,' he whispered. 'Wake up.'

Amy didn't stir. It was obvious that she was catching up on some well needed rest, but Toby couldn't let her sleep.

'Wake up,' he said again.

As Toby watched, a soft sound escaped Amy's lips. Soon afterwards, a faint whisper drifted out of her mouth.

'Toby?' she said groggily.

'Yes,' he replied. 'It's me.'

'What's going on?' she asked.

'I need to show you something,' he told her.

Amy was initially reluctant to wake but Toby managed to convinced her. It took a lot of persuasion on his part, but eventually she gave in and unwillingly climbed to her feet. It was a cold night. Toby shivered as he stood next to her. As he led her tentatively across the room, he watched Amy's dress flutter gracefully around her legs. It was as if she had been caught in a sudden wind, though around her the house remained still.

Toby was the first one out the room. Amy was within mere steps of the door when he shook his head at her. She didn't understand, but Toby knew that he had to be the first one out. It would ruin the surprise otherwise. He made Amy wait for almost a minute before letting her come out. He would have kept her there for longer, but she was tired and becoming very irate.

Toby had kept the hallway light off. He'd been afraid that it would wake Daniel up, so the hallway was very dark. When Amy finally emerged from the bedroom, it would have been understandable if she'd had trouble seeing the surprise. However, that wasn't the case. Amy saw it instantly and it confused her. The attic ladder was down and the hatch above their heads had been opened.

'What's going on?' she asked Toby, her voice quiet and unsure.

Toby didn't answer. Instead, he placed both of his hands onto the ladder and began to climb. Then, just like that, he was gone. Toby had disappeared. Amy was left standing in the hallway, looking up at the ceiling with her mouth wide open.

Toby knew that Amy would follow him. As he crouched down by the edge of the hatch, he thought of how well he knew her. He knew for certain that she would climb the ladder. He waited patiently but nothing happened. For a moment, he began to doubt himself. Then, as Toby watched, he saw a black mass begin to rise upwards. It wasn't long before Amy made her way fully through the hatch. She had come back up to the attic.

'What are we doing here?' she asked him.

Toby edged closer to her.

'Aren't you going to turn on the light?' she said to him.

Toby, despite knowing that he couldn't be seen, nodded firmly and stretched his hand upward towards one of the beams.

'What are you doing?' Amy asked him, somehow sensing his movements. 'The light-switch is over here.'

Toby couldn't see Amy that well, but he knew exactly where she was pointing. He felt a smile creep onto his face.

'I don't want that switch,' he told her, his hand resting steadily on the beam above him. 'I want this one.'

With a firm flick, Toby turned on the lights.

It had taken him a while to put them all up, but as soon as Toby saw Amy's reaction, he knew it had all been worthwhile. All around the attic, attached to the wooden beams with brass thumbtacks, were strings of fairy lights. The bulbs, which were tinted red, spread a beautiful glow into every corner, filling the space with a gorgeous light that had never been seen before in the attic. There was an expression of pure joy all over Amy's face. Her eyes were wide, her mouth was open and, as she gazed at the lights, her bruised hands came together so that her fingers were gently touching.

'Toby,' she whispered, her voice soft and overwhelmed by everything.

Toby didn't let her continue.

'You never had a prom.' he said to her, his dress shoes scraping across the floorboards as he edged closer to her. 'I thought that this could be the next best thing. This can be your prom, Amy. I know it isn't much, but it's something.'

Amy stared at him. Her eyes were illuminated by the soft red light. Toby saw that she was tearful. For a moment, he became worried. He was afraid that he'd upset her, but that feeling soon faded. As he watched, the corners of her lips curled upward into a beautiful smile. Toby reached into the pocket of his suit jacket. He grasped his hand around something and pulled it out. Holding it in front of him, he showed it to Amy. It was his phone.

'We'll have to be quiet,' he told her as he began to scroll, 'but I thought that this might set the mood.'

He tapped the screen with his thumb. Music began to pour out of the little device. Amy's face lit up. The soft sound of piano playing filled the attic. With a nod of his head to indicate that she should follow him, Toby made his way across the floorboards and into the middle of the attic. The beams were higher at this point, which meant that Toby could stand fully upright. As he turned his eyes back toward Amy, he found himself unable to speak. She was wearing exactly the same outfit that she'd always worn. However, in that moment she looked more beautiful than Toby had ever seen her. The soft red light fell gently onto her hair and her pale skin shone like the brightest star. As she floated towards him, the bottom of her dress billowing gently against her legs, he thought that she looked perfect. She was radiant.

It was then that they found themselves standing together. Amy, who was slightly shorter than Toby, looked up at him. Her eyes seemed to burn a brilliant scarlet. Both of them smiled at each other nervously. The music continued to play. The air around them felt electric, but something was missing. With a deep breath, Toby gazed into Amy's eyes and reached out a hand towards her. He knew that it might not work but he had to try. The only thing that existed in the world was Amy. He moved his shaking hand towards her and placed it gently onto her shoulder.

Everything was as it should be. As Toby felt his hand touch Amy's cold skin, he knew that everything he'd ever worried about didn't really matter. Nothing mattered except this. As the two of them came into contact, it was as though the entire world had been put right. Toby placed his other hand steadily onto Amy's waist. He felt something cold touch his shoulder. It was Amy's own hand. The two of them were holding each other, ready to dance. As the music hit just the right beat, Toby pulled Amy close to him. Her head rested onto his chest and the two of them began to dance. It was a moment of perfection that could never be bettered. It was the high point of both of their lives.

'It won't happen,' Amy whispered to him, reading his mind with impeccable precision. 'I don't know why, but I know that I won't pass on.'

'That's okay,' he told her.

He really did mean it. It didn't matter if Amy passed on or not. As long as they kept dancing, nothing mattered at all.

For a while they continued, swaying on their feet as the music played. Then, the song came to an end and the dancing stopped. They looked at each other. Moving his hand from Amy's shoulder, Toby placed it in hers. The two of them locked fingers tenderly.

What happened next hadn't been planned. Toby hadn't thought of it when coming up with his idea. However, when it happened it felt as though it had always been intended. It was as if both of their lives had been building up to it. The two of them leaned in towards each other and their eyes began to shut. They didn't see the red glow illuminating their bodies. That wasn't what they were focusing on. Instead they let the moment control them, enveloping them in its grasp as they kissed each other softly on the lips.

But there were no fireworks.

Instead of ecstasy there was only awkwardness. After only a few seconds, their lips parted uncomfortably. The kiss hadn't felt right. It was something that both of them could sense. They knew from the kiss that it wasn't meant to be. As they parted, they knew instantly that both of their minds had drawn the same conclusion. They both managed to force slight smiles in acknowledgement of the fact that had presented itself. They were not meant to be together in that way and that was the unfortunate truth.

Yet, neither of them would let go. They held onto each other, grasping tightly as though clinging for dear life. Neither wanted the moment to end so quickly. Toby pressed the play button on his phone and the two of them danced once again to the music, silently swaying together in the middle of the attic.

23 LOOKING FOR A FRIEND

The next morning was awkward. Not horrendously awkward, but awkward enough for both of them to notice. Perhaps they could have gone on forever without mentioning it, but it felt as though the elephant in the room needed to be addressed. As the two of them sat on the floor of Toby's bedroom in the early hours of the morning, they discussed what had happened. There wasn't any doubt in either of their minds. The kiss had been a mistake. The conversation was awkward but afterwards their friendship seemed to be stronger than ever. In a quiet voice, Amy thanked Toby for what he'd done and affirmed, despite the awkwardness of the kiss, that it had been one of the best nights she'd ever experienced. The two of them rose to their feet and Toby attempted once again to place his hand onto her shoulder. It didn't work. Things were back to the way they were supposed to be.

With the end of prom, Toby's time at school had come to an end. In the weeks that followed, a lot happened in his life. Very soon after that night, Karen moved her stuff out of the house and into her new flat. She'd found one right in the centre of the city. It wasn't very far away, so Toby could still see her whenever he wanted to.

Then came August, the month in which Toby received his exam results.

When the day finally came around, Toby returned home to find Daniel waiting for him. Normally, Toby would have found that strange, given the long hours his brother had used to work. However, nowadays Daniel didn't seem to care much about his job. He still went and did what he had to do, but no more. As a result, it didn't surprise Toby to find his brother sitting perched on the edge of the sofa. In fact, he'd been expecting it.

'Well?' Daniel asked him, standing up. 'What did you get?'

Toby didn't know how to respond. After a brief moment of thought, he decided that it was best not to keep his brother in anticipation. As a result, he just came out with it as plainly as he could.

'I passed everything,' he told Daniel, the corners of his mouth curling upward as he spoke. 'I got all A's and B's. I would have…'

Toby wasn't able to finish his sentence. As soon as the word *passed* had left his mouth, his brother grabbed hold of him and pulled him into a ferocious hug.

'I knew it!' Daniel yelled happily. As he spoke, he tightened his grip around Toby. Daniel's thick arms pushed painfully against Toby's back to the point where he couldn't actually breathe. He wanted to tell Daniel to let go, but his empty lungs couldn't find the strength. Instead, he just spluttered silently until Daniel finally released him.

'What about Maths?' Daniel asked, clapping a thick hand onto Toby's shoulder. Toby, still struggling to get his breath back, took a moment to respond.

'B,' he said, once the power of speech had returned to him. 'Really close to an A.'

Daniel, whose eyes were wide and emotional, pulled Toby into another hug.

'Oh don't worry about that!' he told him. 'You've done brilliantly. You should be incredibly proud, Toby.'

Toby wrapped his arms around his brother's back.

'Thanks, Daniel,' he said. 'I am.'

As the hug came to an end, an uncertain look appeared on Daniel's face.

'So does this mean that you'll be going?' he asked.

'Where?' Toby inquired.

'That boarding school,' Daniel continued. 'The one up north.'

Toby's smile faded slightly. In a quiet voice that sounded both nervous and excited, he replied to his brother.

'Yes.'

For a moment, Daniel looked at him. Toby could tell that his brother didn't know how to respond. After everything that had happened, he could tell that Daniel was worried about letting him go. Daniel hadn't lived alone for a long time and, despite his tough exterior, Toby could tell that he was afraid. Even so, he could see in Daniel's eyes that his brother wasn't going to stand in the way of his dream.

'That's brilliant,' Daniel told him, forcing a smile. 'I am so proud of you.'

Toby felt his smile grow again. He looked into his brother's eyes.

'Thank you,' he said softly.

With that, the two of them slumped onto the sofa. As the mid-afternoon sun lit up the living room, it illuminated everything inside. The big television, the white walls and even the sofa itself. They were all bathed in the light. As Toby looked over them, he saw that thin layers of dust had begun to cover everything. He thought of how the excess had treated Daniel. After all that had happened, all that he had bought, everything had become dusty and unused. The house that they had lived in for so long was now occupied by just the two of them. With a soft sigh, Toby looked at his brother. Daniel wasn't looking at him. Instead, he was staring straight ahead, looking at something that wasn't there.

'So, are you going to do it?' Toby asked him in a quiet voice.

Daniel didn't look at him.

'Am I going to do what we talked about before?' he asked.

Toby nodded and waited for his brother's response. After a while, Daniel spoke in a low voice that barely rose above a whisper.

'Yes,' he told Toby.

'You're going to sell the house?' Toby asked him.

'Yeah.'

The next day, Daniel put the house on the market. Toby understood why he was doing it. With Karen gone and Toby on his way out, there wouldn't be any point in Daniel staying there on his own. It was the perfect time for him to start over and starting over meant moving on. The house had been a great home but circumstances had changed. So, once the house had been put up for sale, all that they could do was wait until somebody wanted to buy it. Until then, there were other things to focus on.

Toby hadn't been able to tell Mr Thornhill about his exam results. The old man, who lived an isolated life, didn't have a mobile phone or a home phone for that matter. As a result, Toby didn't have many ways of contacting him. A few times, he'd walked down to the school in an attempt to catch the old man at work. However, that hadn't come to anything. Whenever Toby had gotten there, he'd been told that Mr Thornhill hadn't been seen by anyone at all. Toby went back to the school three times in search of his former tutor. On the third visit, Mr Hinkley himself came to speak to Toby. The skinny bald-headed teacher looked older than Toby remembered him. Then again, that seemed to be the case with a lot of the teachers.

'Can I help you?' Mr Hinkley had asked, walking out of his office and into the hallway where Toby had been waiting for him.

Toby, who was adamant to get an answer this time, had nodded firmly.

'I wanted to find Mr Thornhill,' he'd replied. 'I haven't seen him in a long time and I want to contact him. I want to let him know that I did well in my exams.'

Mr Hinkley had shot Toby a slimy smile and clasped his hands together.

'Mr Thornhill no longer works for us,' he'd explained maliciously. 'Things weren't working out for him here. We both thought it best for him to accept an offer of retirement. It was an opportunity that he took gladly I can assure you.'

'Is he still living in the village?' Toby had asked impatiently. 'He told me that he lived…'

'Unfortunately not,' Mr Hinkley had said, interrupting him. 'Mr Thornhill no longer lives in Lawton. He is living somewhere else, though I cannot say where. We no longer have any contact with him. I don't know if he ever told you where he lived, but it would be unwise to go there. The house is uninhabited and will remain like that for some time I should imagine.'

'So what can I do?' Toby had asked desperately. 'How can I find Mr Thornhill?'

Mr Hinkley's sickening smile had widened.

'You can't,' he'd told Toby.

With that, he had gone back inside his office and shut the door in Toby's face.

Mr Hinkley's last words stuck with Toby for a while. He wouldn't be able to find Mr Thornhill so there was no point trying. His old teacher had gone away and there was almost zero chance of Toby locating him. Therefore, it was with an attitude of dejection and frustration that Toby decided to drop his search. Instead, he went back to sitting at home with Amy, waiting for September to come. Waiting for the day that he would leave Lawton.

One day, Toby found himself sitting on his bedroom floor, conversing with Amy about nothing really important. There wasn't much to talk about during that period of his life. Despite the warm weather, Toby hadn't really gone out much that summer. Apart from a few days out with Karen and a couple of dinners with Daniel, he hadn't bothered to go anywhere. For the most part, he'd spent his summer inside with Amy.

'So,' Amy asked him. 'Are you going to miss me when you're gone?'

The question took Toby by surprise.

'Of course I will,' he told her. 'I'll miss you a lot. Will you miss me?'

Amy nodded and began twiddling her thumbs. Her question had sent a spark into Toby's mind. It reminded him of something that he'd been wanting to ask.

'Are you nervous?' he asked her.

Amy looked at him.

'Why?' she inquired. 'Am I nervous about you leaving? Is that what you mean?'

'Not just that,' said Toby. 'I mean about us selling the house.'

'Ah,' Amy replied. 'I understand.'

There was a long silence. Toby could tell that Amy was waiting for him to start talking again. He could see that she didn't want to answer the question, but it needed answering.

'Yes,' she finally told him. 'I guess that I am a little nervous. I'll be lonely.'

'Maybe it won't be so bad,' Toby said, trying to comfort her. 'Maybe somebody like me will buy it. Someone who can see ghosts.'

'Yeah,' Amy whispered. 'Maybe.'

There was another long silence. Toby wasn't quite sure of what response he'd hoped for, but it hadn't been the one that he'd received. The question had only succeeded in lowering their moods. He rubbed his temple as he tried to think of a way to make the situation work, but nothing came to him.

'I hope that happens,' he finally said to Amy. 'I just want whoever buys the house to be able to see you.'

'Yeah,' Amy replied, her voice dull and lifeless.

'Toby!'

Daniel's voice was calling him. Toby was surprised. There was something in his brother's tone. Daniel's voice, which was usually low and unexcited nowadays, seemed to sound almost happy.

'Yes?' Toby called back.

For a moment, he waited, listening intently for the reply. What came next puzzled him greatly.

'Come here!' his brother yelled. 'There's somebody who wants to see you!'

Toby and Amy exchanged confused looks. Neither of them knew who it could be. The only person that came to Toby's mind was Karen, but her arrival wouldn't have made Daniel happy. No, it was someone else.

Then it clicked. Toby figured it out. He knew exactly who it was. He was actually surprised that he hadn't realised it sooner. With a wide smile, he looked at Amy and whispered in a quiet yet excited voice.

'Follow me,' he told her.

Toby jumped to his feet. He raced out into the hallway, not even glancing behind him to check if Amy was following. With a crash, he flung the living room door wide open.

Mr Thornhill stood in front of him.

The old man, who was wrapped up in a thick coat despite the warm weather, hadn't come very far into the house. He stood by the front door, his hands in his pockets and his feet placed firmly together. He looked well, which surprised Toby. His face was fuller than the last time he'd seen him and he didn't appear to be slouching as much. The old man looked at Toby and Toby looked back at him. Then, in a beautifully gentle voice, the old man opened his mouth and spoke.

'It's been far too long.' he said.

Without thinking, Toby rushed towards Mr Thornhill and flung his arms around the old man's shoulders. Mr Thornhill was startled for a moment, mainly from the force of the impact, but soon regained his composure. After a moment or two, he grasped Toby's shoulders and pushed him back so that the two of them were face to face.

'I've missed you, sir,' Toby whispered, his eyes beginning to get teary.

'I've missed you too, Toby.'

It was a good few seconds before Toby decided to look away from the old man but when he did, it was too look over his shoulder. In the kitchen behind them, Daniel was making two cups of tea. For a moment, he looked up from the counter-top and smiled happily. Toby smiled back at him, but only briefly. This was because his attention was drawn towards the other person in the room.

Amy looked as happy as Toby did. It had been a long time since Toby had last seen Mr Thornhill, but it had been even longer for her. It had been months since the two of them had last set eyes on each other and, as the only other person in the world who could see her, it was clear from the gentle smile on her face that Amy was feeling very grateful at meeting the old man again.

'Do you want to sit down?' Toby asked Mr Thornhill. The old man nodded and Toby lead him towards the sofa. Leaning back comfortably into the cushions, the two of them turned to each other and smiled. Then, as Toby watched, he saw Mr Thornhill's eyes light up and the old man said something that made everything fall perfectly into place.

'So, I hear that you're looking for someone to buy the house.'

24 SEPTEMBER

By the beginning of September, all of the arrangements had been made. It hadn't taken long for all of the necessary paperwork to be completed and, on the fifteenth day of the month, Mr Thornhill would officially own the house. To an extent, the idea of someone else living there made Toby feel a little upset. It had been his home for so long and the thought of that changing made him uneasy. However, as he knew all too well, things didn't stay the same. Change was just a part of life. It didn't matter whether you accepted it or not. So, until the Fifteenth of September, the house continued to belong to the Burrows family, all two of them. However, Toby wouldn't be staying there for all that time. With his place at Pine Mount confirmed, the beginning of the autumn term was rapidly approaching. A letter had been sent to him to make sure that everything was in order. It had told him what room he would be occupying, who he would be sharing a corridor with and, most importantly, that he had to arrive on site by midday on the Tenth of September. Five days before Mr Thornhill was due to move in.

'Will you cope with that?' Toby had asked Amy during one of their late night talks. 'Will you cope with being alone for five days?'

Amy's response had been to let out a loud snort.

'I've been alone for much longer than that before,' she'd told him. 'I'll be fine.'

So, as the tenth got closer and closer, it became clear exactly how much had to be done. Toby, who'd always prided himself on his organisation skills, found it difficult to make sure that he had everything he would need. It wasn't that he had a lot of stuff, he just wasn't sure what he'd need or how to fit it all into one bag. Not only that but, as Pine Mount was so far away, it meant that Toby would actually have to leave on the Ninth of September and stay in a hotel for a night. That meant that he had even less time in which to get everything sorted. Even with Daniel's help, he still wasn't able to get it all done and, for a few days, it almost felt as if he was never going to get everything organised. It might not have sounded like a big deal, just packing up old stuff, but it was important to Toby. He would be at Pine Mount for a long time and he needed to make sure that he had everything that he wanted with him.

All the stuff that Toby couldn't fit into his bag had to go into cardboard boxes. They were big brown boxes, like the ones they'd had to use when they first moved to Lawton. They couldn't use those ones anymore though; Daniel had found them up in the attic and they'd all gone rotten. Instead, they'd had to buy new ones and it did strike Toby as incredible that his entire life could fit into just one bag and a couple of flimsy boxes. Boxes which would be going to stay with Daniel.

With his relationship with Karen in ruins, there wasn't much call for Daniel to buy a house. There would be far too much spare room with just him in it, even though Toby would be visiting as often as he could. Instead, Daniel had settled on an apartment in the city. It was a nice apartment, from what Toby had seen. It was sleek and modern and had a nice view out onto the river which ran through the city centre. The rent was high, but Daniel had a well-paid job, so that didn't matter much. The extra cost meant that the property also came with a second bedroom where Toby could stay whenever he wasn't at Pine Mount. Toby had only seen a few pictures of it. He thought that it looked okay.

Once all of Toby's stuff had been sorted out, there was nothing left to do but wait. Wait until the Ninth of September. Fortunately, they weren't kept waiting long.

The Ninth of September fell on a Thursday. Students were expected to be at Pine Mount on the Friday and were being given the weekend to settle in before the school year really began. Despite the fact that it would take them over five hours to drive there, Toby and Daniel weren't leaving until around three o'clock in the afternoon as Daniel had to go to work. He'd tried to see if he could leave earlier, but he wasn't allowed. Karen was going to come to the house to say goodbye and Mr Thornhill had promised that he'd be there as well. However, they wouldn't be coming until around three o'clock either. Until then, Toby was home alone, at least as far as anyone else knew. Both he and Amy supposed that it was fitting. It seemed right that he should spend his last day in the house with her. Daniel and Karen could go up and visit him, Amy couldn't.

Toby pulled his phone out of his pocket. It was a quarter to three and nobody was home. He and Amy had spent the day in the living room watching TV, but that had gotten boring around two o'clock so they'd moved back into his bedroom. Now they were just sitting on the floor where they'd spent so many great times together, waiting for the others to arrive. It was boring and both of them were making little huffing noises. They should have been making conversation, but they'd spent all morning doing that and it seemed as though they'd run out of things to say.

As the two of them sat on the soft carpet, Toby

couldn't help but look around. He found his gaze wandering to all of the different parts of his bedroom. As he took it all in, a waft of memories blew into his mind. His bed, which stood in the same place as his old one had, brought back whispers of Amy's voice. They played back in his memory. Thinking of them brought a warm sensation into his chest. Then, with a gentle twist of his neck, he turned towards the window. For some reason, it seemed smaller to Toby. It had been bigger when he'd first moved into the house, he was sure of it, but it wasn't now. Finally, he faced the wardrobe. The wardrobe had always been there, covering the whole wall with its big wooden form. The slits were still there. The slits that he'd gazed through that first night. The ones that he'd seen the monster through. The monster had gone now and so had the one in the hedge. As Toby had grown up, a lot of things had changed. The monsters had vanished a long time ago, but they'd been replaced by a ghost. A ghost that he was proud to call his best friend. Locking the thoughts of monsters away in his mind, Toby turned to Amy. She looked at him with an expression of boredom on her face. As he continued to stare, her expression turned into one of uncertainty. A smile spread across Toby's face, which caused an identical smile to appear on hers.

'Don't forget me,' she begged him.

'I won't,' he told her.

That was when they heard it, the knock at the door. Somebody had arrived and without much time to spare. Daniel would be there soon. As he got to his feet, Toby glanced vaguely around the room. He was looking for his suitcase, but then he remembered that he'd already packed it in Daniel's car. As he ran a hand through his hair, he watched Amy follow his lead and rise to her feet as well. For a moment they stared at each other, neither of them really sure what to say. How could they possibly put their whole relationship into just a few parting words? They couldn't. It would have been impossible but even so, something had to be said.

'So,' Amy began, a nervousness in her voice. 'Will

you come back and visit me?'

'Yes,' he told her.

'Whenever you can?'

'Of course.'

'Promise?'

'Promise.'

The room went silent. Toby looked to his bedroom door and shook his head. He knew he had to leave, but that wasn't what he wanted to do. He wanted to stay with Amy. Still, he knew that he had to go. Silently, he turned back to face her and locked his gaze firmly onto her. Then, he lifted his hand into the air and softly brought it down onto her shoulder.

He should have known that it wouldn't work. It would have been much too perfect if they'd been able to touch, but that was too much to ask for. His hand simply cut through her, not even making a whisper as it did so. They smiled awkwardly in an attempt to hide their disappointment and Toby went into the living room to answer the door.

Karen was the first one to arrive. As he opened the front door, Toby could tell that it was her just from the brightness of her hair. As the rest of her came into view, he saw that she was once again dressed in her blue denim jacket and blue denim jeans.

'Hello,' she said, smiling playfully at him.

Toby found it a little hard to smile back. He wanted to because he was very happy to see Karen again, but his heart didn't seem to be in it. Maybe he'd hoped that Mr Thornhill would come first. That way, he could have had a few more minutes with Amy.

'What's up?' she asked him, her happy face now

concerned.

Toby attempted to perk himself up.

'Nothing!' he said, trying his best to sound happy.

'You sure?'

'Yeah,' Toby told her. 'Just a little nervous.'

That wasn't strictly untrue. He was nervous, but not just because he was moving away. He was nervous about a lot of things, one of them being Amy, but he didn't want to tell Karen that. Even so, his excuse seemed to have placated Karen and it wasn't long before her expression returned to its previous joyful state.

'You'll be okay,' she said reassuringly, stepping over the threshold and pulling him into a tight hug. 'You'll be settled in no time.'

'I hope so,' Toby replied, his voice muffled.

Then, as soon as the words had escaped his mouth, Toby felt Karen pushing him away from her chest and grabbing onto his arms. At first, he thought that he'd done something wrong but, as she spoke, he knew that wasn't the case.

'I'm going to miss you, Toby,' she told him, her eyes watery and on the brink of tears.

Toby smiled and pulled her into another hug.

'I'll miss you too,' he told her.

With Karen still firmly in his grasp, he shut the front door with one hand and turned his head towards the living room. He'd felt her there. He didn't know how, but he had. Amy was standing by the hallway door, looking at him with a smile on her face. It was a proud smile. After smiling back at her, Toby turned to Karen and hugged her tighter. The room was silent.

Then came the sound of footsteps. Toby could hear them through the closed front door. The steps were heavy and slow, but there was a sense of urgency about them. It wasn't long before the footsteps stopped outside of the house. Then there was a knock at the door.

Letting go of Karen, Toby slowly approached the front door. The arrival of this person had surprised him as he hadn't heard any car pull up. Then again, he hadn't really been listening. He could tell who it was instantly. As he opened the door, he was pleased to see the tired form of Mr Thornhill standing in front of him, holding a small blue envelope in his gloved hand.

'Hello, Toby,' the old man said to him.

Toby, who was still a little distracted by what had happened with Karen, took a few seconds to come to his senses.

'Hey, sir,' he finally replied.

Mr Thornhill chuckled and shook his head.

'Do you not think that we've known each other long enough? You can call me by my first name.' he said to Toby, his left eyebrow raised comically.

Toby smiled at the old man.

'Well, what is it?' he asked Mr Thornhill. 'I can't remember. I think I heard it once, a long time ago, but...'

'Charlie,' the old man said, holding out his hand. 'Pleased to meet you.'

Toby grasped the hand tightly and shook it.

'I think that I'll call you sir,' he laughed.

'Hi, Mr Thornhill!' called Karen from inside. Stepping to the side, Toby made enough room at the threshold for her to squeeze beside him. Karen looked Mr Thornhill straight in the eye and waved at him politely. Mr Thornhill, who had only had a few interactions with Karen, seemed to be taken aback by her friendly greeting. However, he waved back all the same.

'Hello, Mrs Burrows,' he said to her. Karen shook her head.

'Please,' she said to him. 'I'm just Karen now. I'm not Mrs Burrows anymore.'

The old man nodded.

'Sorry,' he said. 'Force of habit.'

A moment of silence followed in which nobody really knew what to say. After a while, Mr Thornhill held out the envelope.

'For you, Toby,' he said.

Toby smiled and took the envelope from his hand. He opened it excitedly. Inside of the envelope there was a card, a cream coloured one with an illustration on the front of it. Printed onto the card was a picture of a cartoon ghost, the classic image of a floating sheet with two black eyes and a black mouth. The ghost was smiling, and from its mouth protruded a speech bubble. Inside of the speech bubble there was a joke, an awful joke.

Ghould-Luck

It took Toby a second to get it but, when he finally did, he grinned stupidly and placed a hand over his face.

'Thank you,' he said to Mr Thornhill, chuckling quietly as he spoke.

The old man beamed. Karen looked over Toby's shoulder to see what was so funny. She smiled a little, but not much. Then again, she wasn't in on the joke.

The sound of an engine began to echo in the road. It bounced off the houses around them and landed squarely onto their ear-drums. As the three of them watched Daniel's car turn in towards them, all of their smiles died away.

This was it.

The car turned around and pulled up close to the pavement, so that its nose was facing back out towards the road. Then, with a loud click, the car door opened and Daniel stepped out.

'Right,' he said, his arm resting on the roof of the machine. 'Are you ready to go?'

Toby didn't really know if he was ready. He'd known that this day was coming, but somehow it had come along much sooner than he'd expected. However, even though he was nervous, he still knew that this was what he wanted. With a look at his brother, he nodded resolutely.

As Toby turned to face Karen, he saw tears welling up in her eyes again. Pulling her in for yet another hug, he squeezed her tightly and whispered into her ear.

'I'll miss you, Karen,' he told her.

'I'll miss you too,' she replied.

Stepping out over the threshold and onto the stone porch, Toby found himself surprised by how cold it was. It had been warm all summer, but it wasn't anymore. With his feet on the stone, he found himself side by side with Mr Thornhill. Toby looked at him and saw that the old man was smiling. He looked proud. Even so, Mr Thornhill couldn't hide his sadness and Toby could see the skin under his grey beard turning red, as though he were about to cry.

'Goodbye, sir,' Toby said to him.

He threw his arms around the old man's shoulders. The old man hugged back and, despite his age, there seemed to be a fair bit of strength in his grip. Then, with his mouth next to Mr Thornhill's ear, Toby whispered an instruction to him.

'Look after Amy,' he said.

'I will,' the old man told him.

As the hug came to an end, Toby thought that he saw something move out of the corner of his eye. Mr Thornhill seemed to have waved at someone. The movement had gone unnoticed by both Karen and Daniel, but not by Toby. Even though Karen was blocking his view, he could still tell who Mr Thornhill had been waving at.

'Come on!' Daniel shouted to Toby. 'We've got a long drive.'

Toby sighed. His brother was right. It was time to go.

Turning away from Karen and Mr Thornhill, he stared at the car in front of him. With a deep breath and a clenching of his fists, Toby looked down at the front lawn and placed a foot onto the grass. He could have gone the long way, over the driveway. That would have bought him some time. Still, it was best to get it done quickly. As he walked, he felt the long blades of grass flutter against his jeans. Then, with a single step, he crossed over the edge of the lawn and onto the pavement. Placing a hand onto the car door, he turned his head gently to look over his shoulder at Karen and Mr Thornhill. Both of them were outside now. Karen had moved from her space on the threshold and was standing right next to the old man. This movement on Karen's part had opened up a gap in the doorway. It wasn't very large, but it was enough.

Toby saw her standing there. Her white dress flowed gracefully around her. Her skin, as white as her dress, was still dotted with the purple bruises that she'd always had. They wouldn't ever go away. She'd always have them. Her blonde hair looked cleaner somehow, as if it had been washed by the light of the outside world. Her hair looked different, but her eyes were the same. Glistening pools that looked as beautiful as ever. The two of them stared at each other, not daring to look away. Then, Amy raised her hand. She smiled and waved goodbye to her only friend. Toby waved back at her. It was the only way that they could have said goodbye.

Toby turned towards the car. There he saw his brother, standing with a strong back and a smile on his face. Everyone was smiling today, even Daniel. Toby opened the car door and climbed inside.

It didn't take them long to reach the outskirts of Lawton. As Lawton was mainly comprised of one long road, with a couple of little ones off of it, it wasn't exactly a long journey through it. Toby leant his head against the passenger seat window. As the car bounced along, he felt the side of his skull hitting against the pane of glass. It made the side of his head ache a little, but he didn't care. The inside of the car was warm. His brother, who's eyes were fixed firmly on the road ahead, was staying quiet. There wasn't much to be said. Toby yawned. He could feel himself beginning to doze off and wondered if they would be making any stops along the way. Daniel had said something about stopping somewhere. Where was it he'd said? Was it somewhere in the Midlands? It was. It was somewhere in the Midlands; Toby didn't have a clue where. Still, it would be a long time before they would get there. Toby could sleep until then. As he looked out of the window at the world outside, he saw Lawton in all of its rural glory. It had been his home for over ten years and Toby felt a pang of sadness radiate inside of his chest when he realised that he wouldn't be back for some time. Still, it was there that he'd met some of his best friends and that was something that nobody could take away from him. Toby felt sleep begin to take hold of him. He wanted to sleep, but he didn't want to stop looking, not just yet. Maybe if he closed his eyes for just one second...

Michael Raine

Twenty Years Later...
(or something like that)

THE LAST VISIT

Lawton hadn't changed much since Toby's last visit. Then again, he hadn't expected it to.

As his car drove past the old village sign, it all came into view. The long road which stretched through Lawton's centre was still there and, if Toby squinted his eyes, he could just make out the little side-road that he'd once lived on. Toby had come back to visit many times since he'd been a teenager and Lawton very rarely surprised him. Yes, it hadn't changed much at all since the last time he'd been there and, if he limited his field of vision to just the centre of the village, he could almost imagine that nothing at all had changed since the day that he'd moved out. A day that was two decades in the past now. However, one major thing had changed since he'd left all that time ago.

The developments had come in only a few years after Toby had left. The fields, which had long ago covered every side of Lawton, had been sold off to a company and turned into expensive housing. Big red brick houses, all with their own double driveways and garages, filled the landscape. Only a few little patches of green remained around them. Toby, who was at the wheel of his trusty silver compact, shook his head sadly. Lawton's charm had been drained away a long time ago. Even the sign, which had once been carefully painted, was now covered with spray-paint. The sight made Toby unhappy. Then again, Lawton had been like this for a long time. The last visit which Toby had made to Lawton had been three years ago. He'd been to see his old teacher, Mr Thornhill. The old man had been getting melancholy in his aged state and had needed a visit from somebody. Toby hadn't come back after that, not until now. This visit had also been brought about by Mr Thornhill. The old man had died just three weeks previously.

It hadn't been a painful death, from what Toby had been told. The old man had simply fallen asleep one night and never woken up. It was sad that he should have died in his room all alone. Then again, he hadn't really been alone. It had taken everyone a while to realise that he'd passed away. The body wasn't removed until three days after he'd died. Toby had wanted to be there for the funeral, but it had all been taken care of very quickly by some distant relative of Mr Thornhill. The relative, who Toby had never heard of, didn't seem to care much about what happened to Mr Thornhill. After a quick ceremony, one that had been attended by only a handful of people, the body of Toby's old friend had been cremated, his ashes scattered amongst the reeds of a ceremonial pond owned by the crematorium. That had upset Toby. If he'd known sooner, he would have stopped it. He knew what Mr Thornhill would have wanted in death. The old man had told Toby on his last visit to Lawton.

'Scatter my ashes at Yardley Bay,' Mr Thornhill had told him, placing a wrinkled old hand onto Toby's. Toby, who never liked thinking about mortality, had responded in a croaky voice.

'I will, Charlie,' he'd told him.

That conversation had happened a long time ago and a lot had occurred in the time that had passed.

With a quick glance to his side, Toby saw his wife. Georgia was asleep with her head pressed against the window.

They'd been married a while, almost five years, though they'd been together for much longer. The two of them had met up north, only a couple of years after Toby had finished at Pine Mount. They'd met at university, in fact. She had been studying art and he had been studying psychology. The two of them had hit it off instantly. As Toby watched her, he noticed how her hair fell in front of her face. Not a single feature could be seen. It hid from view her perfect lips and her gorgeous eyes. Toby sighed contentedly and turned back to face the road. The weather outside was cloudy and grey, with a couple of faint raindrops falling onto the ground beneath them. It wasn't great weather, but it could have been worse. Toby thought of how much he loved his sleeping wife. Then, he took a quick glance into the rear-view mirror and smiled.

The little boy behind them was approaching his first birthday. His hair was brown and, even at such a young age, he was already beginning to show signs that he would be inheriting Daniel's sharp jawline. Apart from that, most of his appearance came from Georgia's side of the family. Still, there was one thing that Toby knew couldn't have come from her. It was impossible. It was something that couldn't have happened, that wasn't biologically feasible. As Toby looked at his son, he couldn't help but notice how the little boy's soft and shapeless nose seemed to be developing a strong bridge, one that might even protrude a little more in the future. It reminded him of Karen. Even though she wasn't biologically related to this baby, somehow he'd inherited something from her and that made Toby very happy. He loved his son more than anything in the world. His only child. Little baby Charlie.

As they journeyed further down the worn out road, pot-holes making the car bounce as they went, the developments began to fade into the background. The main high street of Lawton grew ever closer. When they finally arrived into it, Toby let out a long sigh of disappointment.

There had been hardly any investment in the high street over the past few years, but what little there had been had resulted in the creation of one of the strangest roads that Toby had ever seen. On the extremities, at both the near and far ends of the road, most of the shops had been closed. Big graffiti-covered steel shutters had been pulled down over their fronts a long time ago. Then, as they got further into the centre, the chain stores became visible. These places were also worn out and tired looking.

Toby's main reason for coming back to Lawton wasn't to see where Mr Thornhill's ashes had been scattered. He hadn't wanted to go to the crematorium, but Georgia had told him that he'd regret it if he didn't. So, in the end, he had visited. The crematorium wasn't in Lawton. It was in one of the nearby villages, not one that Toby had ever visited. Georgia and Charlie had stayed in the car whilst he had gone to say goodbye. He had walked up to the ceremonial pond, told Mr Thornhill that he was sorry he hadn't visited more, cried a little, and then gone back to the car. That had happened almost and hour ago. They could have gone back to Daniel's flat in the city where they would be spending the night, but Toby didn't want to.

There was somebody he had to see.

Quietly and smoothly, so as not to wake his wife, Toby turned the steering wheel. Slowly but surely, the car began to bend and made its way down the side road. The road where Toby had spent his childhood. It was a road that seemed to be stuck in the past. The pavement hadn't changed and the brown fence that ran alongside it hadn't either. In all honesty, Toby found it a little bit eerie. It was as if he'd stepped back in time. As he drove, the car hit a pothole and bounced, causing Georgia to awake from her sleep.

'What's going on?' she asked him as Charlie began

to cry.

Toby's determined eyes stared straight ahead.

'Potholes,' he told her, his grasp on the steering wheel firm.

Georgia turned around in her seat to comfort their son, telling him that it was all okay and that it would all be over soon, which it would be. Toby had just seen it, poking up from behind the long fence. The roof of the house came into view. He wasn't quite sure how he was supposed to feel, but he drove on.

As they reached the cul-de-sac, Toby turned the car and pulled up alongside the pavement. Whilst Georgia tended to their son's crying, he turned his head to the side and took a look through the car window.

The house was in remarkably good shape, considering how old Mr Thornhill had been when he'd died. The old man hadn't been in the best of health, so he hadn't been able to keep up with many of the repairs. Luckily, a kind neighbour had helped him out on that front. The white walls of the house were well painted, though a bit patchy in places. Even the front door seemed to have been given a fresh coat recently. It shined even in the cloudy weather. The only thing that was in bad shape was the lawn. No one had really bothered with it in the last few years. The grass, which had always been long, was now so to an excessive extent. Still, the house wasn't in bad condition.

'I'm going in,' Toby told his wife.

With only a brief look in his direction, Georgia nodded and went back to soothing their child. Grasping the handle with a sweaty palm, Toby pushed open the car door and climbed outside. He placed the soles of his black boots squarely onto the tarmac. Shutting the door quietly so as not to upset Charlie further, Toby looked towards the house. Now that he was outside, he could see all of it and he was again surprised by how well it had been maintained. The roof was in good shape, despite a couple of missing tiles, and it seemed as though Mr Thornhill had made sure that the house had been well looked after. With a deep breath, Toby walked towards the front door.

As he stepped over the front lawn, Toby felt the long blades of grass flutter against his dress-trousers. Even through the fabric he could feel them, stroking against him. Upon reaching the door, he curled his hand into a fist and raised it as if he were about to knock. Then he remembered that Mr Thornhill wouldn't be inside, so he unfurled it. He took a step off the front porch. Crouching down so that his knees were up by his chest, he placed both hands onto the heavy stone step and pulled it to the side. Mr Thornhill had told him some time ago where he kept the emergency key. Sure enough, there it was. It was a little rusted, but that was to be expected as Mr Thornhill wouldn't have been able to lift such a heavy stone in the last few years of his life. Placing the key between thumb and forefinger, Toby moved the stone back into place. He stepped up onto the porch and placed the key into the lock.

The door opened slowly, creaking as it went. As he stepped over the threshold and into the living room, Toby felt a little surprised at how easy it had been. Closing the door quietly behind him, he crept further into the living room and looked around. Mr Thornhill had lived in the house for twenty years and his influence had most definitely been felt. Old furniture, which he had brought over from his old home many years ago, remained in the same places that they had done for two decades. There was a lot of wood in this room. Wooden tables, wooden sofa frame covered only by two thin cushions, even the television stand was wooden. The décor was quite a change from how it had been when Toby had lived there.

But he hadn't come to reminisce about that. No, he had something else to do.

He tiptoed further into the house. He didn't know why he was making a conscious effort to remain quiet, as the house was completely empty, apart from the person he wanted

to see. Why was he creeping around? He had no desire to
scare his friend or to make sure that he was unheard. He
wanted to have a conversation, so the creeping wasn't really
necessary. Still, he continued to creep all the same.

As he opened the door to the hallway, Toby began to
feel as though he was being watched. He looked over his
shoulder to check that he hadn't missed somebody lurking in
the shadows. There was nobody there. As he turned back to
face the hallway, he found his gaze drawn to the left. There
was the door to his bedroom. The door had been changed over
the years. The old one had grown decrepit and had actually
splintered in a couple of places. It had been replaced with a
different one, one which was now a faded white. Toby felt a
smile forming on his face. Behind that door was the that room
he'd grown up in. The room he'd spent so many years in. It
looked different now, he knew that. Mr Thornhill had
decorated it when he'd moved in, so that it looked more like a
guest bedroom. That way, people could have come and stayed
if they'd wanted. Toby had only been in there a few times. He
could feel his hand reaching for the doorknob.

'No,' he thought to himself.

As he turned to face straight down the hallway, he
saw something that he should have noticed instantly. The
hatch to the attic was open. Arching down from it was the old
steel ladder that Toby had first climbed all those years ago. He
felt the back of his throat go dry. The hatch had been closed
for all of the years that Mr Thornhill had lived there. The old
man had never even attempted to go up to the attic. Why, not
even a month after his passing, was the hatch now open? Toby
walked forward, grasped onto the ladder and began to climb.

As he clambered through the hatch, he realised that
the attic light was turned on. Toby didn't know why it was on,
but it was comforting to know that the light still worked after
all these years. Standing up as best he could in the cramped
attic space, Toby followed his intuition towards a spot that he
knew very well.

Then he saw it, the wooden beam where he'd found her. It looked darker than he remembered. It was as though the shadows that fell onto it had somehow become absorbed into the wood. He knew that she was hiding on the other side.

'Amy?' he whispered.

A pale white foot stepped out from behind the beam. The thin body of Amelia Moore appeared in front of him.

She looked the same as she had the first time he'd met her all those years ago. Her hair was as dirty as it always was. Her pale skin, which lit up the room even more than the light above them, was still dotted with purple bruises. Despite the fact that it had been close to thirty-five years since the day that she'd died, her brilliant eyes still shone as though nothing had happened. As Toby stared at her, he watched her adjust the strap of her dress. Amy looked the same but there was one thing about her that did seem to be different. Despite her eyes being as beautifully bright as ever, there was something hiding behind them. It was a hopelessness, a feeling of despair that Toby picked up on instantly.

'Hello, Toby,' she said to him quietly. 'It's been a very long time.'

'Three years,' he responded, taking a few steps closer to her. 'Three years since my last visit.'

'Well,' she sighed. 'At least you came. I'm sure that Charlie would have been glad of it.'

As Toby remained there, now able to stand fully upright, he watched Amy's judgemental eyes look him up and down.

'You're going grey,' she told him, pointing to his thinning head of hair.

Toby nodded.

'Only in places,' he replied. 'Also, prematurely I might add.'

Amy rolled her eyes.

'How's the wife?' she asked, her voice soaked in passive aggression.

'Good,' Toby told her. 'She's well.'

'Did you ever tell her about me?'

'Yes.'

There was a long stony silence whilst the two of them looked at each other.

'What did she say when you told her?' Amy asked, her voice more concerned than angry.

Toby kept his body very still, not daring to move so much as a muscle.

'She's very open minded,' he replied. 'It didn't cause a problem.'

'Ah,' she mumbled.

The conversation returned to silence.

Toby could feel the smell of damp clogging up his nostrils. He hated this attic; he always had done. The funny thing was that he knew Amy did as well. So why had she come back up there?

'Heard much from Daniel?' Amy asked irritably.

'Yeah,' Toby answered. 'We're staying over his tonight. The three of us.'

'The three of us?'

'Me, Georgia and Charlie, our son.'

Amy looked heartbroken.

'Well,' she replied bitterly. 'It was nice of you to let us know.'

Toby sighed and ran a hand through his hair.

'Mr Thornhill wasn't well,' he said defensively. 'He wouldn't have remembered even if I'd told him.'

'Don't tell me what I already know.'

Amy's voice remained calm, but she was unable to disguise a bitterly hurt tone that rang in Toby's ears. As she spoke, her gaze turned ferocious and her hands curled into fists. Toby bowed his head and looked down at the floor.

'I'm sorry,' he told her.

He knew that wouldn't be enough, that Amy had spent the last three years mentally preparing for this argument. However, he was surprised. As he glanced up at Amy, he saw that her livid expression had gone away. She was still upset, but it was almost as if she couldn't bear to be angry at him. The hopelessness was back in her eyes again.

'You didn't say how Daniel was,' she said in a broken voice.

Toby felt awful. Standing in front of him was his oldest friend and he had let her down.

'Daniel is okay,' he responded. 'He's still with his girlfriend.'

'Are they happy?' Amy asked.

'They seem to be,' he replied. 'They've been together a while now.'

'How about Karen?'

Toby was taken aback by the question. He supposed that it was natural for Amy to ask about Karen after asking about Daniel. Still, he hadn't expected Amy to ask about her.

'Not too bad from what I've heard,' he said quietly. 'She's still in France. Cannes, I think. She loves it down there.'

'You don't speak to her then?' Amy asked.

'Not much,' he said. 'I only really see her at Christmas. Then again, I haven't spoken to Daniel much either."

'How come?' Amy asked, looking confused.

Toby's face remained still, as though made of stone.

'I've been away,' he told her.

Toby had never felt a tenser atmosphere in his life. Amy, who still wasn't sure what Toby was going on about, had her arms folded over her chest and her head cocked to the side in a puzzled manner. Her expression worried Toby, partly because he could see some of her anger coming back, but that didn't matter. She needed to hear what he had to say.

'Where?' she asked.

Toby put a hand up, signalling her to be silent.

'Please,' he said to her, his voice incredibly serious. 'Before I talk, I have to tell you something. I love you, Amy. No matter what happens, I will always be your friend. I promise you.'

Amy looked afraid. Her eyes had widened considerably.

'I love you too, Toby,' she replied. 'What's

happened?'

Toby took a deep breath. This had to work; there wasn't any other option. He had to tell the story right.

'A few years ago I was with Georgia, sorting out some photo albums. I saw an old picture of my mum and dad. It had been a long time since I'd last seen them and I'd almost forgotten that I even had it. But I didn't forget about them. No, I've never forgotten. When I saw it there, lying on the floor, it made me remember something. On the day that I left this house you and I were in my bedroom. You asked me not to forget about you and I promised you that I wouldn't.'

The attic grew darker as Toby talked. The low-lying beams cast thick black shadows all around them. Some of them landed onto Amy's nervous face. She was terrified, worried that Toby was going to reveal some horrible news to her. Yet she still listened.

'That got me thinking,' Toby continued. 'It got me thinking about what it must have been like for you. All those years, stuck up here in the attic. It must have been so lonely and you must have thought that you'd been forgotten. I started to think even more about it. I remembered that time that we went to Yardley Bay and how we'd hoped that you would pass on.'

Amy remained silent.

'Then, something came to me,' Toby continued. 'Yardley Bay hadn't been keeping you here, but something else had. I read all these books about ghost-stories. So many of these ghosts were haunting places because of one strong feeling, like revenge. Something always kept them there and I started to think that maybe you'd been kept here. Kept here because you'd never wanted to be forgotten. You told me of how you got ill before your prom and how you couldn't go. You missed out on one of the pivotal moments of your teenage years. You didn't get better until afterwards. Am I right?'

'Yes,' Amy whispered.

'I thought so,' said Toby. 'You were ill whilst everyone else was enjoying their final days of school. The final days of childhood. That would have made you feel forgotten, right?'

'But what about the dance?' Amy asked.

Toby knew what she was talking about.

'The dance that you and I had? It wasn't going to change anything. You didn't stay here because you missed out on prom. You stayed here because you've been afraid of being forgotten. Inside you must have felt it, but maybe not in a way that you realised.'

'So, what does that mean?' Amy asked nervously.

'It means that you are afraid people will stop caring about you,' Toby told her. 'I was curious about this because Mr Thornhill and I have always cared about you. I didn't know why you'd be feeling this way. I didn't know who you never wanted to forget you. Then, it came to me.'

'I remembered something else,' he continued. 'A memory that we'd spoken about. It was a memory of when you broke the TV. Do you remember? You were upset by what you were watching, I knew that much even as a kid, but I didn't know why. You told me about it when you came out of the attic ten years later.'

'Mum and Dad,' Amy whispered.

'Yes,' Toby confirmed. 'Your Mum and Dad.'

Toby didn't know if he wanted to say anymore. He knew that the impact could be great, but it could also be disappointing. Either way, he had to continue.

'It took me a while to find them,' he told her. 'A long while in fact. I had to do a lot of research but I did find them. I found them in central Italy. They'd moved there a long time ago, so I wasn't sure what sort of a state they'd be in. Still, that didn't matter because I'd found your parents. Two years of solid research had led me to them. I booked the first flight out there. I didn't have an address but I had a town and I knew that if I asked around I would be able to find your Mum and Dad. When I got there, I walked into a bar. There was one man sitting on a stool and the bartender was leaning on a counter top. I went up to them and held up a picture of your Mum and Dad. The man on the stool didn't speak English but I knew that something was wrong when he shook his head. The barman sighed and told me that they'd passed away only a few years before. They'd been living in a flat in the town and had gone peacefully in their sleep. I felt sick. It was like everything had been in vain. I was about to leave, but then I heard the barman say a name. Your name.'

Toby continued breathlessly. As he spoke, he became so wrapped up in his story that it seemed like nothing else mattered.

'He told me about you,' he continued. 'Exactly what you looked like and how you talked and how your parents had spoken about you every single day until they'd died. They'd told the barman everything about you and he wasn't the only one. As soon as the man at the bar heard your name, he nodded and smiled. Then, the bartender went outside and brought a crowd of people back into the bar with him. They were all people who knew your name because of what your parents had told them.'

With one final breath, Toby opened his mouth and finished his story.

'So you'll never be forgotten, Amy. Your parents never forgot you and, because of them, now a whole town knows about you too. They'll tell their children about you, all of them. You'll never be forgotten Amy, not ever.'

The room fell deathly silent. Toby looked at Amy and waited for her response. Even if it didn't work, he would be happy. As long as she said something, he could live with that. Without so much as breathing, Amy stared at Toby and nodded.

'You're right,' she said, and with that she was gone.

She hadn't gone with a fizz or a bang. There hadn't been any fireworks. It had been quick and silent. One moment she was there and the next she wasn't. All that was left was an empty space where she'd once stood.

Toby didn't know how to feel. He guessed that he should be happy. After all, his plan had worked. Amy had passed on to the other side, whatever that may be. That was all she'd wanted, but even so he could feel tears forming in the corners of his eyes. Amelia Moore had finally moved on. With quiet steps that were almost silent, he made his way across the attic and down the ladder. Once he was down in the hallway, he pushed the ladder back up inside and closed the hatch. Then, without looking back, he walked out of the front door, closing it firmly as he did so, and got back into his car. He looked at Georgia, his loving wife and Charlie, who was now sound asleep in the back seat. As he saw his son quietly dreaming behind him, Toby felt a smile rise up on his face. Then, he started the car, turned out of the cul-de-sac and drove out of Lawton for the very last time.

ABOUT THE AUTHOR

Michael Raine is a student who lives in one of the villages just outside of the city of Southampton. He hopes that you enjoyed reading this book.

Printed in Poland
by Amazon Fulfillment
Poland Sp. z o.o., Wrocław